THE GELATIN COAST

DOUG SACRISON

Hi! Hope you
enjoy !

Hi! Hope you
enjoy!

The Gelatin Coast
All rights reserved
Copyright © 2014 by Doug Sacrison
Cover Design: Raquel Segal

To Lindsey Ellis,
whose stupid, pointless, one-page story entitled
"The Horse Who Loved People," beat out my
multi-chapter epic and "earned" her a trip to the
Young Authors conference in second grade
(on a technicality). Had I rightfully won, I may
have rested on my laurels and never written another
word.

1

Near the southern end of the African continent, where the Atlantic Ocean meets the western shore of Namibia, there is a place called the Skeleton Coast. The people of Namibia once called it The Land God Made in Anger, while Portuguese sailors dubbed it The Gates of Hell. Turbulent waters break angrily against the unforgiving Namib Desert, and the coastline is littered with shipwrecks. Dense ocean fogs often cover the area, yet rainfall is sparse. It is exceedingly hot and dry; some may say inhospitable.

Which is what made it odd that one day, following a particularly dreadful storm, a rather large moose appeared on the Skeleton Coast.

The Skeleton Coast is not home to many other living things. One of these being animal experts, and more specifically the kind of animal experts that would know what to do with a large hairy moose. In other parts of the world, animal specialists might be called in to remove whatever wayward animal from where it's not supposed to be and transport it to where it should be. These dilemmas, however, usually involve a snake that has slithered its way into someone's laundry room, and not a shaggy behemoth that has hopped down a few continents. Either way, such animal experts were nowhere to be seen.

Said moose might have gone unnoticed by humans had it not been for a traveling band of prim scientists who had also strayed off their course. Alas, these scientists were not the kind of scientists who might know what to do if one comes across a moose in Africa, but at least they were good enough scientists to recognize that what they saw was, in fact, a moose.

The band of four scientists, two men and two women, along with the two Namibian guides who had already saved their lives three and a half times, had been attempting to study one and a half unique geological features of the Namib Desert. Plans had been far from concrete when they began the overnight journey in the dusty old jeep. Despite the urging of the friendly guides, the scientists refused to solidify these plans. So bouncing around with one carsick scientist (Dr. Anthony Pendergraft), two distressed scientists (Dr. Leslie Aiken and Dr. Leslie Bradford), and one scientist who could read a geological map but not the map of where they were going (Dr. Laura Aingeberry), the jeep had peeled across hills and dunes, eventually coming to rest at the Atlantic Ocean.

"This is definitely not where we are supposed to be," said Dr. Aingeberry, inspecting the map.

"And I'm pretty sure this is not where she is supposed to be, either," said Francis, one of the two friendly guides, as he pointed to the moose strolling on the dunes overlooking the beach. Though he spoke in a language that the scientists did not speak, the meaning was comprehended well.

Only half of Francis's declaration was true, however: the moose was a he.

His he-ness was noticeable by the presence of what appeared to be tree branches coming out of his ears. These branches were, in fact, antlers, which adult male moose often sport.

The four scientists and two guides gaped at the moose, unsure of how to act. The moose plodded along the crest of a small sandy ridge, marching perpendicular to the ocean's edge. His great moose head he kept low to the ground, as if searching for something. He was, of course, and that something was food and/or non-oceanic water. He did not see, or care about, the onlookers.

Dr. Pendergraft suddenly felt better with the attention drawn away from his tummy.

"Well, now," he said through his thick and curvy mustache, "I do say that that creature appears to be a moose."

"Right you are," agreed Dr. Aiken, the only female of the two Leslies.

"Fancy that," said Dr. Bradford, therefore being the male Leslie. "I suppose we should do something about him."

The two guides groaned, knowing they were going to be the ones to have to "do something about him." The joint groan went unnoticed by the oblivious scientists.

"Just what do you suppose we do?" asked Dr. Aingeberry, and by "we," she meant the two guides.

"Well, we could take it with us," said Dr. Pendergraft, through his thick sweaty mustache.

"Take it with us?" replied Dr. Aiken. "Are you daft?"

And daft he was, for within five minutes, it had been decided by four of the six people (the two guides being the minority vote) that the moose should be captured and placed in the back of the jeep, then transported to the village from whence the humans had come.

Their logic, though sketchy, was thus: A moose is a rare thing to come across in Africa, perhaps even more so on the Skeleton Coast. The scientists had no way of contacting anyone with knowledge of what to do in the event of a moose in Africa, so capturing the animal might help shed light on the situation. If left to its own devices, the moose might simply die from all the heat, they thought, and so for the animal's sake, he should be somewhere safer. And perhaps most importantly, though none of them would admit it, the scientists were all exhilarated by the chance to say, "Look what we found!"

So, mustachioed Dr. Pendergraft turned to the two poor guides. "What do you say, old chaps? You think you could wrangle that beast into our jeep?"

The up-until-now friendly guides replied with many naughty words in a language Dr. Pendergraft didn't speak. He took their reply as a stirring "yes." The guides continued to grumble as the jeep coughed to life and drove toward the hairy curiosity.

Both hoped these scientists would tip well.

2

The village was home to many children, including a boy named Earnest. Earnest was no older than ten. He could have been younger than ten, but everyone believed that he was no older. There were no birth certificates in the remote village, so Earnest's actual age was anybody's guess. Everybody's guess was the same: that he was no older than ten.

Earnest was rather thin, likely a consequence of not eating all that much. He was a nice boy, but being nice did not necessarily mean that he was well liked. Though friendly with many other children, Earnest's kindheartedness was not universally reciprocated.

It didn't help that Earnest was an orphan. This was a major selling point in the village's bullying industry.

The name Earnest was not typical for children in the village. He was blessed with the name by the kindly old nuns who had opened a tiny mission a generation ago. The nuns took him in as a baby and named him. They might have given him a name more traditional to the region, but they couldn't pronounce most of them.

Despite the language barrier between the missionaries and the villagers, everyone seemed to get along, so orphans were often brought to the kindly nuns. Eventually the villagers realized they could use the nuns as a sort of babysitting service. So frequently children who were not orphans spent time at the tiny mission, with its two huts and fence of uneven sticks. The nuns were happy to see children, but sometimes fretted about why there were so many orphans in the village.

Their language lessons were decidedly lacking, but still Sister Petunia would often hold Earnest in her lap as she read from an *Encyclopedia Britannica* volume. Though the tomes were old and weathered, Earnest loved the pictures and would inquire about every one. But having only learned the villagers' native tongue, and with Sister Petunia reading in English, nun and child would often look at each other in puzzlement before sinking back into the volumes, as if by ignoring one another they would somehow learn to communicate.

The sections Earnest loved most were always the bits about animals. He loved the photographs and would put his hand on the page so Sister Petunia couldn't flip it. He would lean his head in much further than necessary, so much so that often his eyes would cross as he marveled at some wondrous creature. Sister Petunia would gently attempt to turn the page, but Earnest's steadfast grip postponed any page-turning until every last inch of each photograph was thoroughly examined.

As Earnest aged, he remained on the shorter side. Though far from petite, like the pygmy people he saw in the encyclopedia's "P" volume, Earnest was smaller and thinner than most of the children in the village. Since his head was at a convenient level to be shoved, the older kids often did so. Though Earnest's friends sometimes stuck up for him, Earnest would simply dust himself off and return to whatever he was doing. In the village, there was always plenty of dust to be dusted off.

As time progressed, Earnest's love for animals grew exponentially, though his knowledge of English somehow failed to grow at all. One of the very few English words Earnest cared to learn was "zoo." It turned out to be his favorite word, in any language. Upon learning the word, Earnest abruptly decided that one day he would open a zoo. He went so far as to declare, "I will open a zoo." But since he stated it in his native language, this simply earned him a pat on the head from Sister Petunia, who had only understood the word *zoo*.

How hard could this dream be, thought Earnest, to just put a bunch of animals in one place? He concluded that the only hard part would be catching all the animals.

Perhaps, thought Earnest, *I will be fortunate enough to find lost animals*. Though at times laughed at for his lofty goals, Earnest was not the kind of boy who thought thoughts like, "I'll show them" or "Someday they'll be sorry."

Instead he focused on plans of managing a menagerie.

So what good fortune befell Earnest when one day, as he etched rabbits in the dirt within the shade of a hut, the boy spotted a trail of dust moving toward the village. He squinted against the sun and recognized that the trail of dust was coming from a large jeep. As it twisted closer up the dirt path to the village, Earnest made out the shapes of the foreigners who had been in his village the day before. He knew that the foreigners were either important people, or thought they were, because of the way they carried themselves.

The children of the village ran out to see what the

foreigners were up to, and Earnest followed. Daydreaming of glaciers could wait. Catching up to his peers, most of them shoeless, Earnest tugged at his shorts a little. They were too big for him and every time he ran they dropped a tad. It wasn't a fashion statement; these were the only shorts available to him.

Earnest scooted to the front of the crowd. He noticed that none of the children really knew why they had rushed out to see the jeep, though perhaps subconsciously each child expected to be given a present. Earnest knew better than that, but sensed something alluring about the jeep's reappearance.

As the jeep slowed through the parting gaggle of children, Earnest gasped ecstatically, drawing attention from the jeep to Earnest. The children gave his funny look funny looks, but Earnest's eyes were on the back of the jeep, where, barely fitting under the canvas roofing, was a large furry animal.

As the jeep rattled to a stop, Earnest ran forward to marvel at the beast. The other children were curious, but not nearly as delighted, to see the strange hairy monster. Earnest peppered Francis with questions before the man had even opened his door.

"What is that, Francis? Where did you get it?"

Francis, who had had a long day already, what with getting lost and shoving a moose into a jeep, was in no mood to be peppered.

"I don't know, Earnest. It's their problem."

"Is it dangerous? Can I pet it?" Earnest knew he would try to pet it regardless of the answer.

"I'm not sure, Earnest. Talk to them."

"But I don't know many of their words."

"Draw pictures."

Earnest had already lost interest in his conversation with Francis and climbed in the jeep. He reached over the scientists to touch the moose.

Now, petting a moose is not always the wisest thing to do, but this particular moose was in no shape to disagree. He was very, very tired. And very, very thirsty.

"Do be careful, my boy," said Dr. Pendergraft, chuckling.

"Please don't hurt yourself now," said Dr. Aingeberry, slightly more concerned.

Earnest stopped and smiled, a tactic he used when he didn't know what other people were talking about. But quickly his attention returned to the moose, whose head was out of reach from the driver's seat. As the befuddled scientists exited the jeep, Earnest started to climb into the back seat. But he felt hands around his waist and was lifted out of the jeep by Dr. Bradford.

Earnest didn't struggle, but kept his eyes locked on the moose as they parted.

Dr. Bradford set Earnest on the ground outside the jeep's door.

"Aren't you a curious young fellow? Well, I must tell you that you'll have to be very careful around that moose, because we don't know what sort of temperament he could be in. All right, my small friend?"

Again, Earnest gave a polite smile, which led the scientist to believe his message had sunk in. Dr. Bradford patted him on the head and walked to the rear of the jeep to converse with the other scientists. Earnest followed him and listened to the foreigners' strange conversation.

"Well, it's obvious what must be done," started Dr. Pendergraft, though he himself was unsure what that was.

The four turned to the jeep and put their hands to their respective chins. They all pondered the tired moose, except for Dr. Pendergraft, who was concentrating more on having lunch.

After a pause, Dr. Aiken raised a delighted finger into the air. "We must split up."

"Yes, madam, of course," said Dr. Pendergraft, whose mustache relaxed just a tad when someone else made a decision.

"Two of us will stay here," instructed Dr. Aingeberry, getting the gist of Dr. Aiken's idea.

"...And two of us will head to the closest city, where there will be means of communication, so that we can inform the rest of the world of our discovery!" an excited Dr. Aiken concluded. "Specialists will be contacted and brought back here to inspect the moose."

"Most definitely!" said Dr. Pendergraft and his mustache.

"And the animal should stay here," decided Dr. Aingeberry.

"Brilliant!" said hungry Dr. Pendergraft.

"...Because heaven knows what his health may be like after such a long car trip," added Dr. Bradford, recalling Dr. Pendergraft's upset stomach earlier in the day.

"...And if he stays here, two of us could stay and ask the villagers to help bring him food and water," said Dr. Aiken.

"Of course." Dr. Pendergraft clapped his hands. "Now,

lunch."

So the four scientists marched off. Each patted Earnest on the head as they walked past. Spotting their guide, the four smiled brightly at Francis, indicating that it would be a great help if he would kindly find a place to put the moose while they were busy with lunch. Francis, who had been enjoying a good sit in the shade, breathed deeply as he rose, then walked away.

"Where are you going?" Earnest couldn't understand why people kept walking *away* from the antlered wonder.

"To find a place to put it."

And so the moose was relocated to the village's largest holding pen, which was owned by the village's richest man and usually reserved for goats. This particular pen consisted of sticks and twigs that had been stitched together with rope and twine. The roof was constructed much the same way, but had blankets on top, making the pen one of the shadiest places in the village. The goats were relegated to a different spot to prevent cross-species arguments. No one asked the goats' opinion, but it was generally agreed that an esteemed visitor like the moose should be put up in the town's finest suite.

The moose easily could have broken out, but given the heat and his state of exhaustion, he plopped his giant frame on the dry dirt instead.

For hours, many villagers lined the fence to observe the moose. Eventually the scientists retired to their lodgings. The adults eventually went back to doing grown-up things. The children lingered the longest, watching the strange creature move its head to inquire what they were all looking at. But eventually, even the youngest observers grew bored.

Only Earnest remained on vigil. For him, moose-watching was the pinnacle of human existence. Each time the moose raised his head, Earnest held his breath in anticipation. When very little happened, Earnest felt no disappointment, only gratitude for being allowed to witness such a wondrous display.

"Thank you," he would whisper, after the moose's most minuscule motions.

The scientists brought the poor moose some water in the afternoon, which was by far the smartest decision they had made since discovering him. The moose was quite fond of the water. In fact, the bowl of water was definitely his favorite part of Africa so far. However, given how thirsty he was, it quickly ran out.

So, after the rest of the audience thinned, Earnest drew his attention from the moose's enormous head to his well-being. Picking up the moose's bucket, he politely asked the hairy giant to stay put. Then Earnest sprinted off to find something wet and preferably cool.

Fresh water is not the easiest thing to find in the arid land near the Skeleton Coast, so the sky was darker by the time a somewhat winded Earnest returned to the stall. He placed the bucket of water safely within the moose's reach, then stepped back expectantly, as if he'd just lit a firework. The young man parked his little bottom upon the dusty ground and bobbed his head to catch the glance of the big animal.

Eventually, the moose stared back at him.

It occurred to Earnest that this newcomer lacked a

name. It didn't take long to come up with one. Remembering vividly that Francis and the nutty scientists had referred to the animal as a moose, it was obvious to Earnest that there was only one moniker for this divine creature. With head still tilted and eyes still locked with the moose's, he spoke his new friend's name aloud:

"Mickey."

3

As one might assume, Mickey Moose did not originally hail from the Skeleton Coast. He was born in the pristine wilderness of Alberta. Like most moose, Mickey matured under the matronage of his moose mother. They would stroll through the forest once Mickey learned to walk, which didn't take long given that moose babies are much better at walking than people babies. They ate their favorite foods together, like grass and other types of grass, and often made noises together that are quite normal for a moose, but, coming from a person, could indicate an upset stomach.

At a predestined age, as with most moose, Mickey Moose's mother bid her son farewell, leaving him to fend for himself. Thankfully Mickey was well on his way to becoming big enough for all fending purposes. His antlers grew larger and larger, and sometimes, like other grown moose, he would rub them against an unsuspecting tree.

Mickey lived a reasonably quiet and subdued life for a time, traipsing through the snow in the winter and the grass in the not-winter. His life was much the same as any other moose. Had Mickey been inclined to consider his future, he probably would have imagined living out the rest of his days doing exactly what he had been doing and being content to do so. As it were, Mickey was not inclined to consider his future.

Then one day Mickey did something that few moose

have ever done, to the best of anyone's knowledge: He dug up a dinosaur. (Or rather, a dinosaur's skeleton. Because although it is rare for a moose to dig up fossilized bones, it is probably even rarer for anyone to dig up a live dinosaur.)

Mickey did not set out to become the first moose paleontologist (a profession normally reserved for human beings). His discovery would not have occurred if not for the help of a young man named Trent Browning.

The young Mr. Browning had recently become a husband and, even more recently, a father. His young wife and he had been blessed with a beautiful daughter to whom they gave a ridiculous name that, at the time, sounded cute. To celebrate the birth, Trent had smoked a cigar. This cigar was the first and last he ever smoked, though he had for some time been a tobacco user. But instead of cigars, his weapon of choice had been chewing tobacco.

The young Mrs. Browning, however, did not share this love (nor did Mr. Browning's gums). In fact, she downright hated the gunk. Though the couple eventually married, their engagement was called off twice, with chewing tobacco playing no small part in the first disengagement. The second time, the then-Miss Eiselsen had declared it was the sole culprit.

And so an agreement was reached after their wedding: Trent would completely discontinue his usage of chewing tobacco upon the birth of their first child. This caused the young Mrs. Browning to aim for motherhood ASAP, while the young Mr. Browning felt that the joys of fatherhood could wait. The Mrs. won out, more or less, and their baby was born within a year of their nuptials.

Grumbly Mr. Browning was a man of his word and became an avid gum-chewer.

Thankfully, Trent had other interests, including his love of hiking. Not long after the birth of the ridiculously named child, Trent ventured into the wild for a few days with an old pal named Ethan, who had been an incredible shot-putter in high school. Weary of following a well-marked trail, the two ventured off in a somewhat northeasterly-type direction. Trent chewed his gum the whole way.

Just before they became lost, they happened upon a creek and decided to turn back, retracing their steps. By this time the size of Trent's wad of gum had increased five-fold, as he simply added a new stick each time the flavor ran out. As the pair turned to head back in a southwesterly-type direction, Trent, still a novice gum-chewer, was unable to keep all that gum in his mouth when he used the word "lettuce" in a story he was telling.

Out tumbled the sticky glob, onto the rocks that banked the creek.

The young Mr. Browning looked down at the gum, but, tired of being conscientious, he put a new stick of gum in his mouth instead of picking up his litter. And Ethan and Trent went on their way.

The gum stayed on the rocks until the following morning, when it was stepped on by Mickey's left front hoof as he lumbered down to the stream for a drink. As soon as his foot came down upon it, the gum did what gum does second best and stuck to the underside of the great moose's foot.

Mickey failed to notice at first, but as he drank, he realized something was different about that particular hoof. He pawed about, but the presence remained. After his morning drink, it annoyed him again, as small pebbles and grass stuck to it. Mickey put his foot down, literally. He pawed at the ground ferociously, but to no avail. Mickey's foot remained sticky.

And so the rest of Mickey's day was spent in much the same manner, trekking about, unhappily trying to remove the gum from his hoof. Around midday he stumbled from the forest into a landscape covered in sandstone, where he scraped his foot in one spot.

Scrape, scrape, scrape went Mickey's hoof on the sandstone. He became a moose possessed and lashed out again and again. As this continued, he unintentionally dug a hole. Mickey dragged his foot along in a circular motion and soon the hole became something of a shallow ditch. Slowly but surely, as Mickey strained and twisted his hoof, the creation of the ditch led to the removal of the gum. And there, in this ditch, seeing the light of day for the first time in seventy million years thanks to plate tectonic activity and a moose, was the remarkably intact skeleton of a dinosaur.

Mickey couldn't have cared less.

The moose's hard kicks to the ground had loosened enough sediment that much of the dinosaur was visible. He had, unfortunately, delivered a few swift kicks to the bones themselves and created some cracks, but after that long underground, who was going to notice the difference? There were also little pink, sticky patches all along the surface of the bones.

Douglas Sacrison

Tired from the exertion, Mickey decided he'd earned himself a nice break, and plopped down a few paces away from the excavation. Wrapping his legs underneath him, Mickey breathed heavily as he beheld his handiwork. Quickly disinterested, the moose put his great head down upon the earth and took a nap.

Unbeknownst to him, the moose had stumbled into an area of southern Alberta that frequently turned up dinosaur bones (though rarely uncovered by moose). And so it wasn't surprising that an amateur *human* paleontologist with a faulty compass stumbled upon Mickey sleeping.

Her name was Susie Ebbert, and she had traveled from her home near Minneapolis to search for dinosaur bones. She lacked formal training, but often went digging for bones as a hobby. To many it was an adorable hobby, seeing this grandmotherly woman with curly graying hair, thick glasses, and rosy cheeks root around in the dirt, looking for long-deceased animals.

But Susie Ebbert was something of a criminal. She was known to her friends and neighbors as the petite lady who once in a while reported finding a few dinosaur bones. Little did these friends and neighbors know that Susie found many more bones than she let on. The best bones she sold. As it turns out, some rich people liked to have dinosaur bones in their houses to go with their chandeliers and gaudy modern art.

Many amateur paleontologists feel that the ethical thing to do is report finding dinosaur bones so that scientists can study the fossils. Susie Ebbert was much more concerned with making money. This enterprise earned Susie quite a pretty penny over the years, which went toward an outdoor pool, an uncommon luxury among Minneapolitans, who often endure sub-freezing temperatures in winter.

Usually Susie's dinosaur hunts involved more digging, but when a moose does most of your work for you, you shouldn't complain. She may never have found the spot where Mickey was napping if not for the fact that she had sat on her compass while riding in her minivan, thus breaking it.

Susie traveled with seven immigrants in tow. These men from Latin America had ventured to the United States part of America to find a better life, but decided that maybe if they continued north, life would be even better. When she headed to Alberta and needed able-bodied men, Susie contacted Enrique, their unofficial ringleader, because he spoke the goodest English.

So just north of the border, the seven men met up with Susie Ebbert at a convenience store, piled into her minivan, and did not all safely buckle up.

Upon the minivan's arrival at the site of the napping moose, the napping moose was mostly ignored. However, Susie's eyes went wide when she saw the dinosaur bones.

"Wow," was all Susie breathed. Two of the men took off their cowboy hats in reverence.

After a ninety-second period of awe, Susie Ebbert clapped her hands and looked up. The cowboy hats went back on. Now it was time to get rich.

"Enrique, come with me," Susie ordered. "And tell your men to stay here."

Enrique's friends spoke enough English to know that

they weren't invited on the new excursion, so instead Enrique told a joke in Spanish, simply because it had been on his mind during the car ride, but he had forgotten the punch line. The joke got a mediocre response, then Enrique and Susie were off. Since they had come on similar expeditions before, the six remaining gentlemen covered the fossils with a tarp and sat to eat their packed lunches.

Susie Ebbert and Enrique drove to the nearest town, which was not very near at all. When Susie found a pay phone outside an inconveniently placed convenience store, she rounded up all the quarters in the cup holder, a few from the glove box, and the few on Enrique's person, which he obliged to donate because of the possessed look in Susie's eyes. She also grabbed a slip of paper, which Enrique recognized as an Arby's receipt with some numbers scribbled on the back.

Susie approached the pay phone and began putting in quarter after quarter. Enrique was instructed to stay in the van. He watched Susie drop numerous quarters on the ground in her effort to get them into the phone. Enrique had seen Miss Susie make important calls before, but never quite so frantically and never with so many quarters. He began to think that perhaps Miss Susie had mistaken this pay phone for a slot machine. But eventually she dialed some numbers and started talking.

When a male voice on the other end came on, Susie did her best to tone down her excitement.

"This is Dr. Susie Ebbert," she said (she often lied to people about having a PhD). "I think I've found what you want. A nearly complete skeleton."

The man spoke gruffly. "Where did you find it?"

"I'm here in Alberta," Susie said, thinking better than to tell the story of the sat-upon compass to someone who wouldn't find such things the least bit amusing. "I came across this skeleton in a little glade next to a sleeping moose."

The man's voice gained a sense of urgency. "A moose? A moose, you say?"

Surprised that this fact mattered, Susie replied with a drawn out, "Yes …"

"Now listen closely, Susie." The man ignored her imaginary doctorate. "I want that moose. Yes, I want that dinosaur. But I also want that moose. Alive."

4

On the other end of the telephone conversation was none other than the notorious Mr. Clayton Stern. Mr. Stern was absolutely filthy rich. He was also a rapscallion if there ever was one. And there was one, and it was Mr. Clayton Stern.

However the dickens Mr. Stern had come by his money, he definitely had lots of it. And he was eccentric. Oh, was he ever eccentric, and in all the worst ways. He owned houses on each continent, excluding Antarctica, but only because he had destroyed the house he was building there to collect the insurance. He only dressed in clothes that cost him at least four figures, and that included his underpants. He often spent his money on cars that could float and private planes with full kitchens manned by French chefs or actors playing French chefs. He would sometimes spend his money to the detriment of others, like the time he decided to build a mall on tribal land or the time he bought a professional basketball team and relocated it, simply because he enjoyed watching children cry.

But what Mr. Stern loved to do most with his money was shoot animals.

One thing Mr. Stern did not spend much money on was hunting licenses. It was not his style to adhere to hunting laws. Instead, he paid people off in order to hunt whatever and whenever he liked. The wherever was a different story; he always loved to hunt at his private ranch in South Africa.

And so the devious Mr. Stern, sporter of greasy dark hair and a greasy dark smile, would have exotic animals brought to his ranch for the purpose of shooting them. In the past he brought bears, both brown and black, to his establishment for their execution. At times he would import flamingos. Once or twice he hunted cassowaries on his ranch. He even imported an elephant. Terms like "threatened" or "endangered" meant nothing to Clayton Stern. He operated on terms like "BOOM!" and "KA-BLAM!"

Now, when Clayton learned of the sleepy moose in Canada, he had to have it. Not because it was a beautiful and graceful creature but because he wanted it dead. Of course, Mr. Stern could have imported a moose long ago, but his eccentricity had led him to shoot animals in alphabetical order, starting with alligator. Just the day before, Clayton had shot a poor leopard. With his terrible crusade moving onto the letter M, the fact that a moose popped up next to dinosaur bones seemed serendipitous. It was a good day to be a musk ox.

So Mr. Stern instructed Susie Ebbert to capture and deliver the moose. Excavating a dinosaur was a time-consuming operation, but kidnapping a moose could be done in a matter of hours. Hanging up his fancy golden phone after detailing his plan to the confused Susie, he turned in his expensive leather chair. Diabolically, he interlocked his over-tanned fingers in front of his devilish grin.

It was time to peruse his extensive gun collection.

5

Bright and early the following morning (that is, the morning after Mickey was bestowed with a name), another jeep thundered into the village, its state-of-the-art horn honking recklessly. But most of the villagers were already awake, so if the driver's intention was to awaken everyone, his mission failed.

A handful of villagers waddled over to the jeep as it parked somewhere in the general vicinity of where a town square would have been if the village had one. The children sprinted to the dusty vehicle, in the hopes it contained another moose. Earnest was at the front of this battalion, smiling expectantly. When it became apparent that there was no moose in this particular jeep, disappointment permeated the throngs of young persons. Aside from Earnest.

The man who emerged from the van was rather portly and sported the makings of a reddish mustache and goatee. The reddish was more of an orange, but he felt that putting it that way was demeaning, for he disliked orange. Silver-lined spectacles balanced atop his nose, improving his dreadful vision tenfold. His khaki shorts did not fit him too well, and were a lighter shade than his khaki shirt. Thick socks were pulled almost to his knees, which were quite red, either because they had been out in the sun recently or because they wanted to be more like his goatee.

With difficulty, he grinned at the children, and offered

an unanswered wave to the grown-ups.

The two remaining scientists in the village, Dr. Pendergraft and Dr. Aingeberry (their colleagues having left even brighter and earlier that morning), emerged from their tent, each with a full mug in hand, to see what caused the commotion. Strolling over to the new visitor, they politely waved, praying that this man spoke English.

"Good morning, sir," said Dr. Pendergraft, squinting into the bright morning sun that presaged another insanely hot day.

"Well, good morning to you, too," the man said. He beamed at the scientists, equally delighted to find English-speakers. Then he put out his hand and said, "I'm Yancy Dunblatt, and I'm a moose doctor."

Yancy Dunblatt was not a moose doctor. That was a lie. He was, however, named Yancy Dunblatt, for better or worse. Yancy debated about using an alias, but ultimately decided it would be easier to prove his real name if pressed. And besides, James Bond always used his own name.

When the Southern Louisiana Philharmonic Orchestra needed to replace a trumpet player who departed amidst marital problems, it called upon Yancy Dunblatt. Dunblatt had been lounging around New Orleans for several years, playing his trumpet whenever it appeared profitable. Instead of using his musical talent to open doors (figuratively speaking), he often expected doors to be opened for him, both figuratively and literally, as the usher at the orchestra's concert hall could attest.

Yancy and Clayton Stern met one evening after

Dunblatt's performance at a sold-out concert hall. Sometimes Stern attended performance art events, mostly because other rich people did, and not because he was cultured. The orchestra was quite good, and there was a standing ovation. When the musicians stood to take a bow, Yancy Dunblatt stayed seated and gave a big yawn. This interested Stern.

After the concert, Clayton tracked him down to compliment his performance. Though Yancy could not care less what people thought of his musicianship, he was usually polite to people who appeared rich, in case they were dying to get rid of their money. The two ended up on Bourbon Street, having drinks on a balcony as they lecherously surveyed much-younger women below.

After a while it became clear to Stern that Yancy Dunblatt lacked much in the way of a conscience, so he asked him a unique favor. Clayton Stern felt, in the last few hours, that he did not want to be married to his current wife any longer, so he requested Dunblatt go inform her that she and her husband were getting a divorce. Dunblatt thought it was a marvelous idea, stating the opportunity sounded "fun."

That particular Mrs. Stern was taken aback by her husband's sudden wish to end their marriage, and was denied her request to speak with him personally. Yancy dispassionately said, "Look, lady, I'm just the messenger," then told her not to keep her hopes up about getting anything from the divorce, monetarily or otherwise, since Stern employed an incredible divorce lawyer who denied Clayton's last three wives any more than fifteen dollars.

Amidst diabolical laughter, Dunblatt and Stern drank

well into the night. A sour friendship was christened. Clayton Stern asked Yancy Dunblatt whether he would be willing to do some other nasty favors for him in the future. The portly trumpet player told him as long as he was well-paid, his services were available.

6

In her phone conversation, Susie Ebbert was informed that a vehicle would be sent to take the moose out of their hair. She had been warned that the moose was of great value and required the greatest attention.

Looks of consternation greeted Susie Ebbert's suggestion that her diggers capture the moose. When they didn't hup-two, Susie turned to Enrique for translation, but he just shook his head. So Susie impatiently pointed to the sleeping moose, then put her hands on the sides of her head to indicate antlers. This motion was unneeded because the seven perceptive gentlemen were well aware of whom she spoke.

But because it was more amusing this way, one of the men made a guttural, "I get it now!" sound, which was followed by the same response from his peers, complete with a few slaps to the forehead. Susie sighed, believing she was finally getting through to the men. But as soon as she dropped her hands, the men made displeased and confused sounds, until she reattached her hands to her ears. A smattering of applause followed.

The accidental comedy routine continued for a few minutes as the men feigned a beleaguered comprehension. When the somewhat exasperated Susie Ebbert gave a smile in the hopes that the men would begin the charaded task, the seven began shaking their heads at the request. The somewhat exasperated Susie Ebbert became the fully exasperated Susie Ebbert.

"We don't want to catch that moose, Miss Ebbert," said Enrique.

"Why not?"

"Because he's got those big antlers," replied Enrique. "And big hooves, too. He could beat us all up pretty bad." Enrique made antlers with his hands, though he knew that Susie spoke English.

The little woman groaned. All the while, the large moose continued sleeping.

"Listen," Susie began in her agitated tone, "I'm sure you would get paid quite a bit more if we can capture that moose." She pointed to Mickey, in case there were questions as to which moose she was referring. "All you have to do is prevent the moose from running away. There is supposed to be a truck coming to take it away soon, but we have to keep it here."

Exhausted as he was, Mickey barely moved amid the hubbub. He slowly woke up, though, and from time to time adjusted just a hair. He noticed the people in the glade, but cared little about them. If they were not going to disturb him, he would not disturb them.

But alas, they had every intention of disturbing him, and disturbing him on a grand scale. While Mickey slumbered, the team led by the grandmotherly woman had devised a plan. It wasn't necessarily a good plan, but no one in the party was a particularly experienced moose catcher.

In the minivan there was a large blue tarp. Usually the tarp was designated for protecting exposed fossils from

Mother Nature, but in this instance, along with some bungee cords, it doubled as a moose catching device.

Mickey opened one eye to see numerous men creeping up on him with a large blue thingy held between them. Just as he opened both his eyes, the men lunged forward, amid a few battle cries, but the moose didn't speak Spanish, so he didn't know what they said.

Mickey would have none of this. He very much did not like a tarp on top of him, no matter how lovely a shade of blue it might be. He shook his head and sprang to his hooves. That was enough to deter the would-be captors, none of whom had been in love with the plan in the first place. They retreated toward the minivan.

Mickey eyed them, more confused than anything. But as they were no longer in his personal bubble, the moose saw no use in pursuing them. Instead he shook off the tarp, which only covered one of his antlers and half his back, and the lovely sheet of blue fluttered to the cold ground.

After a bit of cursing from the little woman's mouth, Enrique patted her on the shoulder.

"It's not your fault, Miss Ebbert," he offered. "That's a big moose. The tarp wouldn't have fit anyway."

He was right, but Susie didn't care. "If only we had some sort of tranquilizer."

One of the men sighed and there was a bit of whispered conversation, as if Susie would be able to understand Spanish if it was spoken loud enough.

"What is it, Enrique? What are they saying?"

Enrique sighed. "Well, Miss Ebbert, Carlos has

something that might help."

The aforementioned Carlos had had difficulty sleeping lately, mostly due to a change in his diet (from not-so-healthy to dangerously healthy). Because of this, he had begun using sleeping pills to compensate for all that healthy stuff. But since he had a young child at home and his bathroom cabinet was in a state of disrepair after a windstorm in which the bathroom window was left open, he was forced to carry the pills on his person.

This revelation sparked Susie's interest. A brief brainstorming session developed regarding how to best get a moose to eat sleeping pills. Certain ideas were tossed out instantly.

"What did he say?" asked Susie after another suggestion was quashed by Enrique.

"Jose said maybe we could throw them in his mouth when he yawns," Enrique replied. It was just one of many bad ideas, over half of which involved training local squirrels or birds.

After about ten minutes, Carlos tired of the discussion and walked to the minivan to make himself a sandwich. At this point Carlos again sparked inspiration, by finding a jar of grape jelly inside (though no peanut butter, because Carlos had a peanut allergy). Soon half the group jumped to the same conclusion: They could slip pills into the jelly. Their celebration nearly awoke the moose again.

Mickey eventually woke to see those silly characters tiptoeing away. He cared little about them, especially when he spied a hefty pile of sweet-smelling purple something-or-other not three feet away. Supposing himself a lucky moose, he watched the pile for a full three minutes before deciding to eat it.

Watching the big moose slowly arise and amble over to the jelly, the men made loud whooping calls. Someone cracked open a beer. Mickey looked over, and they fell silent again. After a thorough sniffing, the animal dipped his snout into the goo and began licking it up. Subdued, whispered cheers went up. Another beer was cracked open.

Finding himself to be a big fan of this goop, Mickey ate all the purple, then spent a few minutes licking the ground, before noticing another purple heap nearby. He strolled over and gave it the same treatment he had the first. He walked to a third heap of jelly before feeling he was being overindulgent, and backed himself toward the original napping spot.

The effect was not quite so poetic as the poachers had envisioned. The moose did not immediately succumb to a deep slumber.

Instead, when the truck arrived, its driver saw a groggy moose, staggering about as if it had just finished a marathon.

But the surprise of the truck driver was matched by the surprise of Susie Ebbert and her men, since they did not expect the truck to be large and brown and have the letters UPS written on it.

The irritable driver jumped out with furrowed brow and stared at the moose. "What is he doing?"

"He's all full of jelly," Enrique answered.

The brow did not unfurl. "Clayton Stern sent me."

And so he had. Clayton Stern had people working for him in many, many places. This man was Archie Simenelly. He actually was a UPS driver, and at present was supposed to be delivering packages. But when a call came from Clayton Stern, Simenelly never said no.

Archie met Clayton when the latter was on a hunting trip in Canada, and their joint passion for wild game caused the two to hit it off. Archie's passion was not the same as Clayton's passion, which seemed to revolve around illegality. Archie Simenelly's passion revolved around a harrowing encounter with a gopher that snuck into his house when Archie was merely three, thus causing a lifelong crusade against the animal kingdom. Clayton Stern didn't care why Archie was willing to capture animals for him, so long as he did it.

Simenelly was informed a moose needed to be transported from one spot to another, and Clayton knew the added bonus was that Archie's uncle was a veterinarian, which enabled Archie to steal tranquilizer darts.

Unfortunately, as once in a while happened, Archie lost the tranquilizer darts on the drive because his UPS truck's doors were open. He could not be sure when the three darts had slipped off the front seat, but when the giant brown delivery truck rumbled to a halt near the exposed dinosaur skeleton, Archie wished he'd stored them somewhere safer. This was especially unnerving because the moose was the largest animal Stern had ever sent him after, and the most likely to need a good tranquilizing.

Enrique and company began to pack things up, hoping their day was done. A few started whistling, and Carlos even jumped into the minivan and put on his seat belt.

"You men," Simenelly yelled, "Help me get him into the truck."

A fair number of groans went up, but the men had already sensed their fate. Round three with the moose was sure to be a doozy.

Sometimes Susie Ebbert would play the little-old-lady card to get out of things. This was one of those times. So she sat in the minivan, watching her seven assistants and the UPS driver try to corral the sleepy but fidgety moose.

Susie chewed her jelly and nothing else sandwich slowly as she watched the scene unfold. The men first huddled together, with Simenelly as leader, instructing with plenty of hand motions and pointing. Enrique nodded and pretended to translate. Then the men grabbed the tarp that had not long ago proved so ineffective. Six blokes held a piece of the tarp and began creeping up on the discombobulated moose. Enrique and Simenelly tiptoed behind the tarp-carriers, whispering commands about where to move.

Mickey was bushed, but after eating that jelly he felt like stumbling about the clearing instead of lying down. A couple times he came close to stomping on his dinosaur. But then he would stumble the other way. After shaking his great head a bit and looking toward the minivan, he answered Susie's internal question of whether moose can yawn with a resounding "yes." While his gaping maw was gaping, the men sneaked up a bit further. They held their breath when the head gave a shake and repositioned itself in its pre-yawn alignment. The moose eyed the men suspiciously.

For a long moment Susie watched, jelly sandwich forgotten. As the men and the moose kept still, so did the little woman. Then the antlers began a turn which the hairy body followed, indicating that although the men were viewed as simply an annoyance, he would rather not keep their company.

It was then that Archie Simenelly yelled, "Now!" Not being aware that this was the command to go, the men all jumped. Two men accidentally let go of the tarp. The others recovered after a second and hustled as quick as they could after the retreating moose.

When Mickey heard Simenelly's call, he felt it was his time to bid adieu. So he took off in the opposite direction of the minivan. Unfortunately, sleepiness prevented him from getting too far too fast, so he was unable to outrun five men carrying a lovely blue tarp.

Susie Ebbert again nibbled at her sandwich as a very slow chase unfolded. The men reached out for Mickey with the tarp, but when the moose felt that glossy material on his backside, he gave a quick kick and ambled to his left. He would have darted instead of ambling had he the energy. The men spread out and one fell to the ground, defeated.

Without intending to be sneaky or comical, Mickey walked behind a large tree. From Susie's vantage point it appeared he was trying to hide, but he was just drowsy. The poor moose wanted nothing more than to again lay down and take a much-needed nap, but alas, men were chasing him with something blue. They overtook him as he tried to catch his breath, but he once again eluded them, by masterfully walking to the other side of the tree. The men ran into the trunk and fell in a heap, melodramatically.

Again, Mickey trotted away. As the team dusted themselves off, the moose noticed a nice shady spot up a little embankment. With the men hot on his tail, he crested the rise and moved into the much-cooler cave. Unfortunately for Mickey, this cave was the back of the UPS truck.

The exasperated men heaved their way up the metal ramp and collapsed on the moose, who collapsed with them, and the group of assorted mammals fell in a heap. Simenelly clapped his hands. Enrique blinked his eyes. Susie Ebbert raised her eyebrows. Carlos pet the captive beast.

"You are a good moose," he said.

Three minutes later, Archie Simenelly curtly waved goodbye to the group, which waved back a tad more enthusiastically. With Mickey in the back of the truck, for the most part subdued, Archie would drive straight to the little airstrip Stern instructed him to reach by four o'clock. *I might have to push it*, he thought, *but I should be there in time*.

As the UPS truck bounced away over dirt and gravel, Carlos saw something shiny in its tire tracks. While his comrades were busy waving and calling, "Goodbye, moose," he waltzed over and picked up three tranquilizer darts.

7

It is not often that one opens the glove compartment of one's automobile only to have a bat fly out of it. It does, however, become more likely if the following conditions are met: 1) If the window of said automobile is rolled down; 2) If the glove compartment is open; 3) If the bat were on some sort of errand, for instance a search for food; 4) If the bat was following some large moth that itself flew into the glove compartment; 5) If the bat's insatiable hunger may have caused a certain single-mindedness, resulting in a bit of bumbling around upon entry, enough so that the door to the glove compartment might just swing shut.

It just so happened that each of these conditions were met on that particular morning, and thus when the glove compartment was opened, a small bat did, in fact, fly out of it.

The glove compartment belonged to the vehicle that Yancy Dunblatt had driven into the village, and the vehicle itself belonged to Yancy Dunblatt. And though Yancy Dunblatt was the sole owner of the vehicle and its glove compartment, he was not the only person to approach it that morning. An inquisitive Earnest followed, thinking that this respectable official would be up to something important or interesting. Dunblatt did not like the company, but refrained from pushing or tripping or throwing rocks at the young man, as he did not want to invite suspicion. He noticed the scientists never pushed or tripped or threw rocks at the villagers.

A number of times on the brisk walk, Dunblatt turned to Earnest and feigned politeness as he asked him to leave.

"All right, young man. Run along now. The nice moose doctor has work to do," he said every ten steps or so. Earnest smiled at him, almost leading Dunblatt into believing the message had sunk in, only to have Earnest at his heels on the next stride. Earnest, even if he understood the stranger's funny language, might not have been persuaded.

The pair reached the jeep and Dunblatt unlocked the passenger side door. Earnest stood on his tippy-toes as he peered around the portly bloke's broad backside to see what his front side was up to. He waited patiently just outside the door as the important person entered.

Yancy Dunblatt needed to measure the back end of the jeep. He had underestimated the size of the moose, seeing as he had been using Bullwinkle as a template, and Bullwinkle appeared to be only a few times larger than his squirrel counterpart. He needed to check if the moose would fit, or if he would need to steal the only other vehicle in the village, an old truck used to transport livestock (which was currently out of gas). Dunblatt was almost sure there was a tape measure in his glove compartment. So he leaned forward to open it.

To say that Yancy was surprised by a bat flying straight at his face would be an understatement. He gasped as the confused bat exited the glove compartment. The big man leaned back and pushed at the passenger door before even considering what had just assaulted his face.

Earnest had a different reaction entirely. Also noticing that a tiny creature had flown out of the glove compartment, he too gasped. But his gasp was one of awe and admiration, rather than pure terror. Marveling as the little black thing darted beyond Dunblatt's ear and began circling the vehicle, Earnest realized the large man wanted to get out. Thinking strictly from a scientific standpoint, Earnest saw the possibility of the bat escaping if the jeep's door was ajar. So he slammed it back on Dunblatt.

Yancy gave the little boy an expression that said, "Are you mad?" But Earnest did not return the stare, as his eyes were preoccupied trying to follow the flight path of the circling bat. Yancy tried again, and once more Earnest slammed the door back on him, as if he did not notice the large man trying to exit and simply wanted to stop a draft. On the third attempt Earnest had to put his shoulder into it, while trying to keep his gaze fixed on the scared bat.

Finally the beefy fellow was able to push himself out of the jeep. His hysteria had abated a touch, as he determined the identity of the demonic flying creature and felt the threat was minimal. His greatest concern was being relieved upon. He attempted to give Earnest a furious, curious, disapproving look. But Earnest missed the look, as he was busy closing the door.

Yancy dusted himself off and peered through the dusty glass. He saw the bat make a lightning-fast switchback to rest on the jeep's ceiling. There it sat, panting. But after only a few moments, the tiny flying mammal took off again, heralded by a delighted cry from Earnest.

Unlike his young counterpart, Yancy's interest hastily dissipated. He wanted the bat out of the jeep so he could get his tape measure without being relieved upon. So he opened the driver-side door and backed away, assuming the animal desired nothing more than to fly out of his all-wheel-drive prison. Of course, Earnest would have none of this, and sprinted around the front of the jeep to shut the door again. This time, Earnest turned to Dunblatt and began scolding him.

"You must leave the doors shut so that flying mouse will not get away," he said matter-of-factly. He wagged a finger, too. Of course, Yancy Dunblatt did not speak the language Earnest was speaking. His intent was rather obvious, however. Yancy seethed and opened the door to the backseat. He was not surprised when Earnest quickly heaved it shut. Yancy moved back to the driver-side door and tried to open it once more, this time with an outstretched arm to hold back the boy. Being more agile than the decidedly not-agile Dunblatt, Earnest was able to reach one arm around and shut it again. Dunblatt grabbed his shirt collar. Earnest did not hate much of anything in the entire world, but he hated being held by the shirt collar.

It was Yancy's turn to wag a finger. "Little boy, stop shutting the doors!" Yancy knew he was close to letting his true colors show, something he wanted to avoid while in the village. Earnest furled his brow at Yancy. Their two furled brows faced off, and neither brow would back down.

Dunblatt kept a hand on Earnest's collar and slowly opened the door. He waited to hear the flitting sound of the bat evacuating. Long moments passed, but no sound came. Finally Dunblatt let go of the boy and saw that again the bat had taken refuge on the ceiling and appeared quite content to stay there. Yancy fumed while Earnest beamed.

All this door slamming attracted Francis, who waltzed over from where he'd been having a lovely conversation about the weather (everyone agreed it was hot). Displeased by the ruckus, the guide strode in like a frontier town sheriff. Dunblatt stepped toward him to tattle. Earnest pressed his face against the glass to watch the bat breath.

"What seems to be the problem?" Francis asked in English.

Dunblatt pointed. "That boy is getting in my way. Somehow a bat got into my glove compartment and is now flying about the jeep, and I just want it out." He pointed at Earnest. "*He* keeps shutting the doors."

Francis looked at him curiously. He had never heard of a bat in a glove compartment and assumed the man was lying. Not wanting to mediate the conflict as translator, yet realizing that someone should, Francis sighed.

"Earnest?" Earnest looked away from the glass for just a second to give Francis a friendly wave. "Why won't you let this man open the doors of his jeep?"

Earnest responded without looking away from the bat. "We cannot let this mouse that flies get away, Francis. It is too valuable."

Francis sighed again and turned to Dunblatt. "He wants to keep the bat."

Yancy frowned. "Well, I assumed that much. Tell him to go away."

It eventually came to the two grown men attempting to carry the small boy away. Earnest, legs straight out behind him as he was pulled with considerable force, dug his fingers into the window ledge and held fast, eyes still zeroed in on the bat.

Finally, wheezing from the exertion of tugging, Dunblatt gave in.

"Fine! Tell him he can have the bat, but he needs to get it out of my jeep. Now! I am a busy, important man, and I need to use my vehicle. If he can catch that dreadful thing, he can keep it."

Francis begrudgingly relayed the message. Earnest smiled, then reached out a hand for Yancy to shake. Dunblatt glared at him, then walked away, deciding he would measure the moose with hands until he got his blasted tape measure. Francis started to follow.

"Francis," Earnest called, in the tone of a superior officer, "Fetch me a jar with a lid for catching this thingy."

"Earnest, you can find your own jar."

"Very well." Earnest sprinted to find a jar.

Within two minutes, the excited young researcher was back with a large clay jar. Of course, putting a bat in a jar is not the nicest way to treat a wild animal, but Earnest lacked formal veterinary training. He held his breath, counted to three, swung open the passenger door, and hopped in as fast as he could, slamming the door behind him. He breathed out and saw that the bat had barely stirred.

Earnest attempted to coax the bat into the jar for the next hour or two. Whenever bothered, the bat flew around, searching for an escape route in what looked like some sort of sporadic dance routine. Earnest tried politely whispering nice things to the bat, but it still would not get in the jar. Yet Earnest remained steadfast in his mission.

Finally, with both boy and bat wearing out in the stuffy jeep, the animal came to rest on the steering wheel. The boy just needed to reach over ... slowly ... and prod the thing ... into ... his jar ....

Earnest held his breath as he leaned in. One hand came around behind the bat, while the other hand lifted the jar toward it, as if presenting a gift. He inched his finger along the steering wheel, then tapped the bat, ever so slightly. It moved half an inch. He tapped again. For a split second it looked as though the bat might flutter away again, but it reconsidered and took another two steps toward the jar.

It occurred to the bat that this jar was a lovely shade of black inside, and since the little animal detested all this awful brightness, on the next tap to its backside, after flapping around a smidge, it hopped into the spacious darkness of the jar.

Earnest fell forward, the tapping hand covering the top of the jar as his eyes searched for where the lid might be. As his momentum carried him toward the steering wheel, his leg swung up and collided with the glove compartment's open flap. He jostled it enough that the contents moved around and one of those contents fell out. He looked down to see a tape measure that he didn't care about.

Finding the lid underneath his backside, the boy skillfully finagled the jar to an angle that prevented escape, reached around himself, placed the lid on top, and smiled.

And so Earnest had the second animal for his zoo.

Gingerly placing the jar on the driver's seat, he reached

down to pick up the fallen tape measure. Happy to have caught the bat and slightly appreciative of that cranky man for allowing him to retrieve it, he decided to put the tape measure back, because Earnest was, after all, a nice boy. Lifting it from the floor, he turned to the open glove compartment and gasped.

Aside from a little bat guano, there were a few pieces of paper and instruments that Earnest did not recognize. There was also one that he did: a gun. It was shiny and black and had been jostled about when Earnest kneed the glove compartment's door. The boy did not have much experience around guns, but sensed this meant no good. A familiar furrow creased his brow.

In the long, proud tradition of humans jumping to conclusions, Earnest decided the gun must be intended for shooting Mickey. Appalled by this thought, Earnest decided he must act. Leaving the glove compartment open, he took his jar and exited the jeep, unaware the bat had crawled back out.

Only while lounging in the shade did it occur to Yancy Dunblatt that there was a gun in the glove compartment that the boy might find.

This thought did not concern him greatly, however, because he failed to believe the young man was bright enough to cause any trouble beyond a car door being shoved in his face. Regardless, he got up off his haunches when the gun came to mind.

The fake moose doctor made the jaunt toward his jeep, walking with the spryness of a sofa. Once there he saw that the boy had finally left. He peered through the window to see if the bat or any other wild animals were carousing inside. With the coast clear, Yancy opened the door and reached into the glove compartment. He saw his square tape measure and grabbed it, then saw his handgun. *Good,* he thought. *That little brat didn't find you.* He realized there was also a bit of bat guano inside. This caused him to swear a few times. Along with being a dastardly person, Yancy Dunblatt was also a lazy one. So he did not clean out the bat's mess, in part because he had no cleaning supplies on hand. Thinking he might return with a shirt he would steal to clean up the animal business, Yancy made off. He locked the jeep, but once again left the glove compartment wide open.

Earnest, jar in hand, walked to the moose pen for a bit of thinking. Presuming the gun was intended for shooting poor Mickey, Earnest determined they must escape together.

The gun was not intended for shooting the moose, however. Rather, it was intended for shooting anyone who got in the way.

8

The tiny airstrip, little more than a clearing amidst tall trees, was usually reserved for rescue aircraft and private planes. As Archie Simenelly's UPS truck arrived, the moose-courier hoped to see a large cargo plane with a crew of big, strong men to transport the animal from his vehicle to theirs.

Unfortunately for Archie, instead of a large cargo plane he saw a sleek, state-of-the-art private jet. Outside of it stood a pretty flight attendant with lovely light brown curls.

"You've got to be kidding me," he said aloud. Simenelly cringed, realizing this was what Clayton Stern had sent him.

When Clayton Stern's luxurious jet touched down on the quiet little airstrip in Alberta, there were but two passengers: Richard and Monica Roenick, a wealthy and newly Floridian couple. The pair sat in two of the plane's luxurious seats, of which there were few, thus making the whole compartment quite spacious and regal. The only uncomfortable seats were in the cockpit.

The Roenicks were longtime friends with Stern, if one could say that Stern had any real friends, seeing as how he just used them to gain something. But they hardly seemed to mind; Richard and Monica were quite drunk.

So they were unsure if their eyes were deceiving them

when a giant moose tried to board the plane. However, the girth of his antlers barred entry. With the Roenicks' annoying drunken chatter about the problems with public schools forgotten, the couple heard grunts and groans coming from behind the giant head, which had turned to look at them. Monica blinked and Richard rubbed his eyes, then they switched blinking and rubbing duties. But a moose was still looking at them.

They rose to investigate. The kind, curly-haired flight attendant, looking more than a tad stressed, smiled at them.

"Please return to your seats," she said. And the drunk couple obeyed and buckled up tightly.

The grunting and groaning emanated from Archie Simenelly and the pilot and co-pilot duo. They were on the last step of the little staircase, trying to push Mickey through the plane's door. Perhaps because he was all tuckered out from a long day, or perhaps because the sleeping pills were still working, or perhaps because he was too disoriented to put up a fight, the task of relocating Mickey from the UPS truck to the private jet was comparatively simple, when compared to the tarp incident. It just took a lot of prodding. But getting him *into* the private jet was another story. Moose were not made for air travel, and planes were not made with moose in mind.

As they pushed the moose's hindquarters, the three men were straining to tell the flight attendant to adjust the big furry noggin so it would fit. She was not keen on this venture. But once the two pilots and one UPS driver hardened their tone, she grabbed onto the base of the antlers and twisted with a firm but gentle hand. The moose seemed even less keen on this venture than she was. He snorted and glared at her. Flight attendant training kicked in and she smiled back.

It was not so much any human effort as the attitude of the moose that finally got him through the door. Because as he cocked his head as if to say, "Excuse me! What do you think you're doing?" the antlers turned just enough and, coupled with the steady pressure being applied to his rump, caused him to lurch into the passenger cabin. The moose pushers fell in an exhausted but accomplished heap. Mickey's displeasure at having his antlers tugged was quickly replaced by his curiosity about the new surroundings, which was quickly replaced by a desire to eat, seeing as how he was a wild animal.

The flight attendant tried to direct him forward a bit but had no delusions of having him put on a seat belt for takeoff.

She was a pleasant young woman named Candy. She usually had a lovely demeanor, but if one looked into her eyes, one might glimpse something sour beneath the sweetness of her name. Though not necessarily depressed, Candy wished she was doing something else. Anything else.

Having become a flight attendant with a successful commercial airline, Candy loved the idea of employment in a flying office. And with a name like Candy, it seemed fitting to be the smiling face to which travelers would answer questions like "More coffee?" Although she did not intend to spend her entire adult life at the same job, it fit her quite nicely for a while.

But Candy was simply searching for a job and not a career. She began to think it was time to move on, and her friends and coworkers urged her to find what made her happy. Unfortunately, one day while enjoying a cup of coffee in Cairo's airport, she met a certain Clayton Stern. He came off as polite and charming at first, and having never met him, Candy was unaware that he was neither.

Whether or not Clayton was drawn to her romantically was unclear, but she had no interest in him (whew!), partially because he was old enough to be her father. At the time, Clayton was married to two separate women who were unaware of each other. This tidbit he concealed from Candy. But when she made it obvious she was not interested in him despite his offer to pay for her coffee and scone, he switched gears. Stern offered her work as a flight attendant on his private jet (or private jets). This was in part because Clayton Stern felt it was important to keep pretty ladies around. The villainous rich man wrote down the astronomical wage he was willing to pay her. Candy became quite excited and said, "You can't be serious," a number of times throughout the rest of the conversation, each time using inflections and stresses in different places ("You *can't* be serious;" "You can't be *SER*-ious;" "*You* can't *be* serious," etc). Stern made it blatantly clear that he was.

Candy truly wanted to say no, despite all the money, because she felt that the flight attendant stage of her life was wrapping up, but at the same time she felt it might be a terrible idea to turn down a means for paying to go back to school (and then some). So after being given one of Clayton Stern's many phone numbers (the one which he did not answer with an agitated shout), Candy smiled and said she would let him know soon.

Within four days her life was completely upended. At first all seemed well. Being a handsomely paid flight attendant on a few luxurious private planes was not so bad. But it wasn't long before she was truly ready to call it quits with flying. And it was only a few days after that when she began to see Clayton Stern's true colors. Candy was not especially fond of them.

And now there was a moose on the plane. As the young flight attendant slunk behind the animal to close and secure the door, she told herself this would be her last flight. But it wasn't the first time she planned on walking up to Mr. Stern to tell him she was quitting.

With the plane rumbling to life, Candy briefly closed her eyes to focus. She put on a smile as she turned to address the passengers.

"Ladies and gentlemen, thank you for flying with us today," Candy began. "Please listen as I give you a quick rundown of safety procedures on this flight."

Mickey half-heartedly listened to the speech.

Moments later the plane began its departure, and every human eye in the passenger compartment watched to see how the moose would react.

As it turned out, Mickey was not especially keen on flying. However, without a great deal of room to show his frustration, he mostly made grumbly moose noises each time the plane did anything. His great furry legs had a bit of trouble keeping their balance, and a couple times during takeoff it appeared as though the moose might topple over.

But then he would regain his balance, due to the confined space, which made toppling difficult.

Soon the plane was high above Alberta and headed for Africa, a long flight indeed, but one made shorter by the speed at which Clayton Stern's expensive jet could travel. In the end, the Roenicks never asked any questions about the moose. Candy would tiptoe around him to deliver wine and spirits to them, but they never inquired about his presence, and coincidentally Mickey never asked about them. Candy wondered if they, too, were used to Stern's eccentric ways, or if they were too full of booze to be sure of what they were seeing.

The vast Atlantic Ocean had occupied most of the view for quite some time when Candy decided to scour the plane for something Mickey might eat. She put a loaf of fancy French bread in front of him, which he slowly nibbled over a twenty-minute period. She also tried some other things, like yogurt, red bell peppers, some mashed potatoes, and a tin can (to research how similar a moose was to a goat). Candy also presented him with a bowl of water, much like she would a dog. She liked animals, and though this particular one was quite an inconvenience, she enjoyed his company more than the company of the Roenicks. Her kindness seemed to be appreciated, just a little. As he calmed gradually over the course of the flight, Candy wondered what it was that Clayton Stern wanted with this moose.

Hours and numerous glasses of wine later, the plane neared its first stop. Mickey was startled when the captain announced that the plane would be landing in Namibia soon. Candy petted him on the head. Mickey was not entirely displeased with this. Of course the Roenicks put up a stink, demanding Candy explain this unexpected landing. Candy calmly informed them that the Namibian stop was planned, and that she had brought it up to them numerous times. The Roenicks both got huffy.

Always one to be full of crap, Clayton Stern had instructed the pilot to make a quick stop just south of Namibia's border with Angola so they could pick up a bucketful of water from the Cunene River. Stern had read somewhere that the river's silt content made its fish taste better, so he was going to experiment by allowing his dinner to swim around in this special water before being broiled. The pilots were also told that should the Roenicks disembark the plane they were to be left behind (Clayton Stern did not even like his friends).

Candy ran through her normal landing routine, but it did nothing to quell the Roenicks' fussiness. Mr. Roenick kept removing his seat belt, insisting that he knew what he was doing (whatever that meant), and Mrs. Roenick kept taking her tray-table out of its upright and locked position. Mickey, on the other hand, behaved better than both of them. He made some strange noises and a few stomps, but altogether refrained from showing extreme duress.

Once the jet reached a complete stop, the lead pilot hustled out to get the allegedly enchanted water, and the Roenicks demanded the moose's immediate removal from the aircraft.

"Our layover is a very short one," Candy replied, but knew their displeasure was somewhat justified: like any normal moose might do, Mickey had felt the need to relieve himself a few times during the flight. Candy could do little about it, because she was unable to get around him. The Roenicks said they just could not stand Mickey's stench.

Candy gave up and prodded the moose to the exit door. It was just as well, she concluded, since she was really sick of those dreadful people anyway.

Stepping down the little ladder into the African heat, Mickey clumsily followed Candy. She prayed he would not bolt, as she had no leash for him. The pair stood next to the plane for a few moments as they collected their bearings. Then Mickey began vainly searching the ground for food. He took a few cautious steps toward the nearby river.

Candy noticed that the pilot was not alone. Large bucket in hand, he seemed to be having a jovial conversation with a couple of young men on the south bank of the Cunene. Behind the men were two trucks, and some other men and women pushing a small boat into the muddy water. Most were wearing shorts and t-shirts. The lot did not look like locals.

Then one of these two gents spotted Candy and her moose companion. He poked his mate and pointed, and the two got all worked up into a tizzy. Soon their cohorts were similarly tizzied. This tizzy would have mystified Candy had Mickey not been standing by her side. However, she wondered why the group was not snapping pictures instead. The two gents looked at the pilot, who shrugged before giving an explanation Candy couldn't hear.

The mysterious group formed a whispery huddle. The pilot shrugged some more.

After a few moments, Candy saw a decision had been

made. The pilot shrugged even more. Three men from the group approached Candy, and the first spoke to her as he scrutinized Mickey.

"We're taking the moose with us," he said.

Candy foresaw trouble from these guys, but not a moosenapping. "You're what?"

The man, who introduced himself sternly as Eduardo Dawkins, tried to clear up the picture for the befuddled flight attendant. These people were part of an environmental group called ABABAHAB, which was an acronym for something, but none of them knew quite what. The group comprised one team that was going downriver to meet up with a different team to try to stop a large oil tanker coming east from Brazil. Something about its emissions and the chances of an oil spill had gotten under their skin.

Dawkins said his group's intention was to help animals whenever they were in need, even if it was slightly inconvenient due to scheduling conflicts. The ABABAHAB team had concluded that Mickey was being transported as part of the illegal pet trade. When Dawkins pressed, Candy admitted she had no idea why the devil she was escorting a moose across the globe, first class. She explained that Clayton Stern was known to be an eccentric person at times.

Candy fussed a bit, knowing she would be in a fair amount of trouble for losing a moose, but Eduardo Dawkins was civil, aware that the nice flight attendant was just a pawn in some bad guy's scheme. Feeling outmatched, Candy begrudgingly negotiated Mickey's transfer.

"Thank you, madam," Eduardo said. "Don't worry. This is best for him."

Candy nodded. She hoped allowing the moose to be kidnapped might be her ticket out of her stupid job. But she was going to miss her new pal.

A couple of the ABABAHAB crew hustled over with some rope and made a leash around Mickey's left antler. The moose made characteristic snorting noises, but was then presented with part of a sprout and carrot sandwich and opted to follow. Candy watched with crossed arms as the great moose lumbered over to the ABABAHAB trucks.

It seemed the ABABAHAB men and women were unsure what to do now that they had possession of the moose. Candy grew sick of watching them debate and climbed back aboard the shiny jet.

"Where's the moose?" asked Mr. Roenick when she entered the cabin and took a seat.

"Oh, he was kidnapped," she responded.

"Oh," said the Roenicks, perhaps guiltily.

9

With wind whipping through his fur and whistling around his antlers, Mickey stood stoically in the back of the dinghy. Next to him sat a young man named Trevor Holman, whose smooth touch on the handle of the outboard motor steered the craft down the Cunene River. His four ABABAHAB colleagues bunched up front in an effort to offset Mickey's weight. The small boat was not meant to hold five people, let alone five people and a moose, so they rode dangerously low in the water.

The auburn-haired, fake-expensive-sunglasses-wearing Trevor was a twenty-year-old Californian. After high school, he bounced around from job to job until feeling called to ABABAHAB by its image-conscious website. After a good deal of time wondering when he might see some "action," here he was, driving a small boat to harass some of the world's most nefarious polluters.

At present, Trevor fancied Kara, who was leaning out over the front of the boat, but he also fancied Lenore, who was sitting right next to Kara. They were American and French, respectively, and had dark brown and dirty blond hair, respectively. The young ladies sat next to Eduardo Dawkins, the man acting as the small team's leader, but only because the group did not technically have a leader. Eduardo, sporting neatly trimmed facial hair ironically designed to make him look rugged, was sitting next to Shoe (at least that was how everyone had been pronouncing his name), a lanky European fellow with an odd, indistinguishable accent.

Trevor guided the boat with the coolness of a seasoned ABABAHAB vet. Truth be told, it was the first ABABAHAB adventure for Trevor, as it was for the rest of the party. Though Trevor had been with the organization for some time, it took a while for the group's leaders to trust him, or the others, to do anything. And perhaps that withholding of trust was rightly placed, since the team had decided that the best thing to do with a giant moose was to take it with them in a small boat.

Their combined smarts deduced that maybe their boss, Ashley Fogelbrower, would know what to do with Mickey. The master plan involved meeting up with other ABABAHAB boats and taking over the oil tanker (though the prevailing opinion was that this seemed an unreasonable goal). So the moose should have plenty of room to run around on the ship's deck before Fogelbrower would likely hatch an idea that entailed ABABAHAB being publicly praised for returning a kidnapped animal to its natural habitat. Or something like that.

The boat reached the Atlantic Ocean in short time. The boat's timing could not have been worse, however, as the sky quickly darkened. Unwittingly the passengers headed into the worst storm the Skeleton Coast had seen all year.

Mickey realized that he liked boat rides even less than plane rides.

10

Benito Martinez met his future wife, Maria, in a coastal fishing village in Nova Scotia. Both being native Puerto Ricans, they were quite curious about what the other was doing in such a remote place, so far from home.

The answer was simple: crab. Benito and Maria both lived and breathed for crab meat. Equally strange events had led them to the Nova Scotian coast and the renowned but apathetically named Jeff's Crab Restaurant. After living on the east coast of the United States for many years, word of the legendary establishment had reached their ears and crab-ravenous stomachs. The fact that two Puerto Ricans entered his restaurant on the same day, let alone the same month, also seemed strange to Jeff. He nonetheless delivered the crab, which was as delectable as rumored. Dining at separate tables soon turned into an impromptu date, and a relationship began. A straitlaced restaurant-goer who didn't believe in fate witnessed the meeting and went home to rethink his life.

Luckily or unluckily for Benito, Maria mentioned during their second date, long after Benito had fallen hopelessly in love with her, that she hated sports. She was, in fact, the most staunchly anti-sports person that anyone in her life had ever met. This revelation, though grating for Benito to hear, led him to a vital conclusion: he would have to keep his profession secret from Maria.

Unbeknownst to his new sweetheart, Benito Martinez was an All-Star third baseman for the Baltimore Orioles. His crisp fielding and tremendous power at the plate had led him to prominence, while his great stature had led to the agonizingly generic nickname "Big Ben." Benito realized that the nearly impossible task of keeping his career from his wife was possible because, as fate would have it, Maria hated the media just as much as she hated sports. Despite being an intelligent and articulate woman, Maria avoided newspapers, computers, television, and radio.

Benito recognized his good fortune and realized that the final step was to come up with a cover for his real profession. He knew that he must pick a field in which he had some basic knowledge, since it would be hard to pull the wool over Maria's eyes, bright as she was. So he told her he was a crabber.

Benito orchestrated an elaborate plan to keep his secret from Maria. The travel associated with playing baseball all over the U.S. (and one city in Canada) actually aided his story, as he claimed to be constantly out at sea, harvesting grumpy little crustaceans.

Benito knew *someday* he should tell Maria the truth, but he was a procrastinator. He was also aware she might eventually find out, but hoped it would be long after he retired from the sport.

When (yet again) the Baltimore Orioles did not make the playoffs, Benito Martinez began discussing the possibility of a vacation with his wife. He had oodles of money to blow and felt a vacation was a great way to blow it. They decided that, given their love of the sea (or at least its bounty) they should go on a cruise. At first Maria was skeptical that Benito, who spent so many months at sea each year, would want to go right back out there for his vacation, but oh well. January somethingth was picked as an adequate departure date, and Benito called to make reservations. When asked if he was *that* Benito Martinez, he replied by saying he most certainly was not.

With an elaborate note left for the house-sitter regarding the hiding patterns of their fluffy white cat, Ugeth, Benito and Maria Martinez hustled out the door of their modest (to hide his salary) house to the awaiting taxi. His fake mustache was glued upon his face.

Benito insisted on wearing a fake mustache when they traveled. He had "good" reason, of course, but for his well-being it was imperative that Maria not learn that reason. Should someone recognize him, Benito's marriage would be in doubt. But explaining why he wore a fake mustache was a real trick. Coming up with a way to pull the wool over such a smart woman's eyes took an excruciatingly long time. He had considered saying that his upper lip was very susceptible to sunburn. He had considered saying that he was continually considering growing a mustache and wanted to see how it might look. He had considered saying that it was a family tradition. He had considered saying he was a spy. But, again, Maria was not a woman who was easily fooled. Keener fans sometimes saw through the fake mustache, but not often. He would change his voice, or duck behind potted plants, or pretend he didn't speak English, or throw small objects in the hopes of diverting his fans' attention. Maria at first ridiculed him for this behavior, then came to believe her spouse suffered from some sort of social anxiety disorder. Benito latched onto this idea, and told her he had worn a fake mustache in public since the age of five. When Maria asked why he had not been wearing a fake mustache when they met in Nova Scotia, Benito responded that he was not afraid of Nova Scotians.

Of course, one might wonder why Benito Martinez did not simply *grow* a mustache in the offseason. Trouble was, he was baby-faced and could not grow a mustache if his life depended on it.

The couple slid into the back seat as the cab driver returned from setting their bags in the trunk.

"So the airport, correct?" the driver said to the mirror.

The couple both gave affirmative grumbles.

"Where are you off to?"

After a pause, Benito mumbled something unintelligible.

"What's that?" inquired the driver.

"Miami," Maria said. "You'll have to excuse my mumbly husband."

"Miami. What takes you there?"

"Our cruise leaves from there."

"Oh, no kidding!" And the driver launched into a story of his sister and her family contracting the stomach flu on a cruise. Benito and Maria stared out their respective windows. The driver either failed to notice the couple's hostility toward one another or chose to ignore it. Probably he chose to ignore it. Long accustomed to driving characters who wanted to be left alone, the driver kept talking.

"So what do you do?" he asked.

After a pause, Maria jabbed Benito.

"I crab," said he unhappily. Quizzically, the driver glanced back. "I am a crabber. I catch them."

"I love crab!"

"I did … once," Maria lied. She very much still loved crab, but also loved passive-aggressiveness. Benito peered her way. Maria pretended not to notice.

The driver chuckled, non-adorably. "You work at sea but are going on a cruise?"

Although they had jointly agreed upon the cruise idea, Maria turned on Benito.

"That's what I said!" she exclaimed, leaning forward. "He wanted to go!" And with this, she flung her toned arm with its rigid, accusatory pointer finger in Benito's direction. Unaware that he had turned toward her, the errant finger landed directly in Benito's eye, very jabby-like.

Benito erupted in a squeal, causing the driver to swerve across the yellow line for a moment. The hulking athlete clutched his eye. Maria regretted her action, but did not apologize.

"Oops."

Through his literally blinding pain, Benito saw an opportunity. Despite the fact that the couple was running behind schedule and any delay could result in a missed flight, Benito informed the driver they had to make a detour.

Numerous hours and crossed arms later, the Martinezes arrived at a large Miami dock, complete with a cruise ship roped to it (an airplane, and not the taxi, had taken them most of the way). They stared up at the gargantuan boat, trying to convince themselves they were in a collective good mood. With arguments over the definition of the word "needless" behind them, a weathered old man wearing the same uniform as some of the less-weathered cruise ship workers asked Benito a nervy question.

"Why are you wearing an eye patch?"

"Because I am missing an eye," he replied haughtily. The salty old sailor gave a wry smile and a bit of a cackle as he walked away to retrieve someone else's luggage. Maria smacked Benito's arm for lying to the man, then approached the steps leading up to the deck. The mustachioed, eye-patched Benito followed, holding firmly to the handrail because of his significantly reduced vision.

11

And so, under cover of the blackest of evenings, Earnest and Mickey the Moose escaped the village. The boy tied a little cord around Mickey's antler, and strangely, the irritable moose followed. The unlikely pair trudged as quietly as one can trudge into the deserted hills beyond the village. Temperatures near the Skeleton Coast regularly get colder at night, so Earnest was not especially comfortable. Mickey, however, was nearly in ecstasy after the harrowing daytime in the unbearable heat.

It was not until the pair had reached the first sandy hill that Earnest glanced back at his village and recognized his life was about to change drastically. He had been outside the village only a couple times in his life, and never with a moose. Without electricity, the village was rather dark, but a starry evening produced enough light to make out the huts. Earnest looked up at the stars and pondered how far he would have to walk before the village was just a dot, like a star.

"Well, Mickey," Earnest began, "It is now just you and me. We will get you to safety where no one will be shooting at you. Then maybe I will make a zoo, and everyone will come and look at you and love you very much. I'm sure we will both be happy at my zoo."

The moose did not argue. With a smile, Earnest patted his great head and stared into his great eyes, then gently tugged the cord and led him further away from the village.

The pair walked well into the night. Eventually Mickey stopped for a restroom break, though not a long one because he was still not properly hydrated. When Earnest first heard the noise he became frightened. But when he recognized the source, he felt like he should partake in the festivities as well.

"My bladder is full like yours, my friend," said Earnest. Then he turned his back to the moose, in case the creature would otherwise be offended. Earnest whistled a tune as he piddled, but it was not a song Mickey recognized, unsurprisingly, in part because the tune was being written on the spot. Soon, the boy decided to add words.

"Oh, my friend is a moose, hurrah, hurrah,
and I am a friend to mooses.
We are going away to not get shot,
because you won't be allowed to shoot mooses at my zoo."

The song did not rhyme in English nor in Earnest's language, but that didn't seem to faze him. The rest of the evening Earnest whistled the tune and sang that lone verse. Mickey never joined in.

Eventually Earnest, who had deemed himself team leader, decided they were a safe distance from the portly orange-haired man. Time to sleep for the night. For the first time in days, Mickey he was slightly comfortable, given the cool nighttime temperatures of the region. So he would rather have eaten. But given that his companion seemed to be settling down with his leash, the moose hesitantly followed suit. Earnest had been carrying a blanket he now placed over his friend's back and smoothed out.

"Tomorrow we will find something," Earnest said unconvincingly. He was a fierce optimist, but if pressed might have admitted he was unsure of their destination. The boy chose not to let this unsettling thought ruin his time with Mickey, though. After patting the sand, Earnest laid his head to rest. Mickey stomped around for a few more minutes before also settling down. Earnest saw how the moose placed his head across his legs and tried to mimic the posture. It did not suit him.

"That does not seem comfortable, Mickey," Earnest said. "Perhaps you should sleep like me." With eyes tightly closed, the boy lay on his side, huddled in a half-fetal position, and smiled wide to show just how comfortable he was. After a few minutes of readjusting, though, Earnest realized that he was not very comfortable. Lying in his shorts and t-shirt, he was cold. After hemming and hawing, the boy got back up and walked over to the moose.

"I am very sorry, my friend, but would you mind if I take back this blanket?" Earnest was embarrassed to ask. When his request met with silence, the boy gingerly removed the blanket and tiptoed back to his spot. Lying down again, he felt much better.

"Thank you, Mickey," Earnest whispered as he closed his eyes. The great moose slept cozily, dreaming he was back home standing in a large puddle.

12

Some ideas are better than others. But sometimes, if you have enough money, even your bad ideas can become reality.

Case in point: one Fillmore R. Puggleston, a self-made European rich guy who made his fortune on snail traps (those thingies you put in your garden so snails will quit eating your plants). Puggleston had lived the second half of his life comfortably in the U.S., collecting money from snail-trap sales and investing in new projects to make him more money still. Among the most recent of these financial endeavors was his newfound dream (which he convinced himself was a lifelong dream) to own a line of cruise ships.

Here his bad idea comes in. Putting together money from other wealthy friends and from who knows where else, Fillmore opted to get his cruise line up and running before it was really ready.

Fillmore R. Puggleston decided that he would have one ship in his fleet. The others would come with time, he said. Rather than waiting until the whole operation was top-notch, he would spend money on the production of the first boat and its voyages, with the other boats to come after a boatload of money was made from the first venture. Now snail traps and other people's money can only get you so far. So Puggleston knew he would have to cut corners, but decided that the corner-cutting should not be done in the shipbuilding stage. He wanted the ship to be spectacular; the jewel of the sea.

The realists on his team said the corner-cutting would really need to happen during the shipbuilding stage. They made the ship much smaller than Fillmore originally wanted. He still got to have most of the fanciness that he sought; it was just that the ship was about half the size of the one in his blueprints. Puggleston's elaborate plans for voyages were going to demand more cutbacks. After going through paperwork in search of savings, Fillmore decided things like security could be skimmed down. Why would you need much in the way of security if you were way out in the ocean?

The cruise ship was called the *Queen Ivan*, but not because she had personally named it. In fact, there had never been a Queen Ivan (to the best of researchers' knowledge) who could have named it. Despite being owned by a company that sounded Scandinavian, the person who named the boat had never lived in a country with any queen, living or dead. There was a good deal of debate amongst passengers as to which monarch this moniker referenced. The truth was that the ship was simply named the *Queen Ivan* because the man who named it thought it sounded fancy. Crew members were taught that the official response to theories regarding the ship's name was to smile and agree.

Smiling and agreeing was the official response to a great number of things. Young shipmates learned this during their training. The staff was mostly picked by having the hiring officer count the number of pleases and thank-yous used in an interview. Not everyone who worked on the *Queen Ivan* was unnervingly polite, but they all could be when it mattered.

There was one exception. A salty old seaman by the name of Riggins was employed as a concierge. No one knew his first name (or if he had one), and no one quite knew why he was given a job on the ship. First of all, it didn't seem like the kind of job he would want. Secondly, he scared all the passengers.

Riggins was somewhere between an especially grizzled fifty and a rather mobile ninety. The stories he told did little to clear that up. They detailed the adventurous life he had led, from boyhood as a pickpocket to some vague wartime fighting to years and years upon the sea as everything from an Arctic tug boat captain to a research assistant tailing giant squid. Riggins, a small hulk with incredibly weathered skin and one eye that seemed to protrude farther than the other, would wait until a few shipmates were behind him in a narrow corridor, then turn to launch into some fantastic tale that usually ended with a dear friend's demise and his own narrow escape from the icy clutches of death.

Though he hardly noticed nor cared, most of his shipmates dismissed his stories as made up and avoided him as best they could. They watched for telltale signs a story was about to start and suddenly would find some errand to do. However, two of Riggins's coworkers did the opposite, hanging on his every word and often giving up on the errands they were supposed to be doing.

The first was a pretty young blonde woman named Melinda. Although she was taking some time to explore the world, she would soon be off to college after an illustrious high school career. She was the president of the German

Club, co-chair of the prom committee, and vice president of the Underwater Hockey Club, among a great many other honors. Her friendliness was the stuff of legend.

The second was a young man named Toby, who was none of those things. He was rather mousy, with scruffy hair, and he probably would have sported a scruffy beard had he been able to grow one. He was only on a cruise ship because he was "taking some time off from high school," as he put it. His laziness was the stuff of legend. Toby loved to play the board game *Clue*, and that was about the extent of his interests. Until he met Melinda.

When he first spotted her, Toby assumed he must be in love, though it might've been the rocking of the boat. Only one year his senior, she infatuated him from the get-go, what with her beautiful white-and-green-striped polo shirt and sparkling white tennis shoes. It didn't matter that he wore the exact same uniform each day on the boat; her green stripes were greener than a thousand emeralds and her white tennis shoes sparkled brighter than the sun, in a lovely, non-blinding way.

Now Toby had, of course, not told Melinda about his feelings for her or her clean laundry. But day by day he inched closer to actually talking to her. One day Toby noticed that the salty old sailor, whose every word he hung onto as if he were a prophet, had another fan in Melinda. His conversation piece appeared like a shining light cascading from Riggins' head amid the call of an angelic choir (it was the first and last time anyone thought of Riggins in this way).

So Toby listened to the man whose only love was the sea, and watched as his hand gestures emphasized how out of place he seemed in a green-and-white-striped polo shirt and sparkling white tennis shoes. And Toby would look around to see if Melinda might sense that a yarn was being spun and come running. Sometimes she did, and the two would listen to Riggins tell of how he fought off rabid sea turtles in a hurricane or performed the marriage of a duke and a cabin boy who turned out to be a beautiful lady. Melinda and Toby were enraptured by the tales, until the clipboard-toting cruise director walked by and broke things up. The director, who was half Riggins's age (whatever that may be), always looked at the old sailor with an expression that said, "Who hired you?"

The *Queen Ivan* was bound for Cape Town, South Africa. Fillmore R. Puggleston wanted to corner the market on persons wishing to cruise from America to Africa, a market that he viewed as so far insufficiently tapped.

The itinerary called for two days in Cape Town before sailing back to Miami. It seemed simple enough, but crossing an entire ocean was a daunting task. If anyone was up for it, though, it was the *Queen Ivan* (so said Fillmore R. Puggleston).

She (the ship) was shaped like many ships. There was a finished wooden deck, with lots of space for suntanning. Around the middle of the deck rose a big tower, which housed the control room for piloting the boat. Near the back end (the bow?) was a helicopter landing pad (for emergencies), and between it and the tower was a pool, so that passengers wanting to take a dip didn't have to jump overboard. Surrounding the deck was a railing, so that passengers didn't fall overboard even if they weren't trying to take a dip. Below deck were the living quarters, which were on numerous levels and circled the outside of the ship. In the middle was the lavish main hall, which had places to eat and sit and act like you were on a cruise. A large domed skylight provided much of the main hall's lighting (during the day, of course). Point is, the *Queen Ivan* was quite lovely.

The crew and passengers were not always quite so lovely.

13

Yancy Dunblatt was unhappy when he realized the moose was gone, and used more than a few naughty words. Usually you don't lose objects as large as a moose, unless you forget to set the hand brake on an old car when you park it on a steep hill.

It was early in the morning when Yancy recognized Mickey was gone, so he thought he could at least get a quick start on the search. Also working in his favor, he believed, was the fact that the village lay among quite a bit of sand, leading to his assumption that it would be easy to find the escapee's tracks. He also theorized the moose had not escaped on his own volition, but had an accomplice. Yancy could not be certain who the culprit was, but noticed a certain lack of hovering being done by that little boy whose name might have been Herman or Furnace or something. Dunblatt cursed him, but then smiled devilishly, hoping he was the thief so that he could teach the boy a lesson.

If it is that kid, Dunblatt thought as he walked toward his jeep, *this shouldn't be much of a problem.* Assuming the boy was stupid because he was young, Yancy thought his search should be over in a matter of minutes. Perhaps he would be back with a moose in tow before any villagers woke up.

Reaching his jeep, Dunblatt threw open the door and climbed in. He adjusted his bulky self a bit to get the groove back in his seat after that stupid kid had messed it up the day before. He chose not to put on his seat belt (tsk). Then he put the key into the ignition and turned it.

Nothing happened. He tried again, but still nothing happened. Dunblatt cursed the vehicle and smacked the steering wheel before making another attempt. When once more nothing happened, he decided to investigate under the hood. Before exiting the jeep, however, he looked over to the passenger side and noticed something. He hoped the problem was not that stupid, but feared that it was.

The glove compartment gaped open. It appeared that the little light inside had been on for nearly a day. And it had run the jeep's battery down, killing the power. Dunblatt took a deep breath. Then the jeep started swaying to the rhythm of his hissy fit.

14

Luxury cruise ships do not ordinarily have stowaways, but the *Queen Ivan* was no ordinary ship.

The stowaway was a man in his mid-thirties named Jamie Brewster. He was something of a departure from the stereotypical stowaway. Rather than a poor, young orphan searching for a new life, Jamie Brewster had had a successful career as a helicopter pilot for a television news station in Savannah, Georgia. He did not sneak on board the ship in tattered rags. He snuck in a pair of comfortable jeans and an Old Navy sweater.

Late at night, on the eve of its departure, Jamie had followed the guidelines found in cartoons when people or anthropomorphic animals sneak onto ships. It had taken a little work to sneak past a men he assumed might be guards of some kind, but Jamie found that if he told himself he was being sneaky it helped. Attempting to climb the massive ropes mooring the *Queen Ivan* to the pier presented a more difficult problem. If any person looked his way, he was sure to be spotted, even though his Old Navy sweater was a dark green. Then there was the added trouble of whether anyone was on deck. He scratched his chin as he pondered how to get up there.

Then it occurred to him to attempt the other method of sneaking on a ship seen in cartoons: to hide in some crate that was going to be loaded on board. This would be ridiculously uncomfortable, he knew, but he saw no other way. Besides the rope, which he was quickly ruling out.

Jamie looked about for some sort of crate to be smuggled in. He realized that the images in his mind mostly came from ships that might have been used by Christopher Columbus, what with giant sails and large wooden barrels full of flour or beer. Of these, he espied none. There were a few large metal boxes and plastic coolers a stone's throw away from him. It looked like they were supposed to be on the ship, but as a result of someone's laziness, weren't.

After being ever so patient to ensure no one was watching, Jamie found himself inside one of the large coolers. It was more comfortable than he guessed it would be, and wasn't cold because there was no ice in it. He couldn't find a mechanism to lock it from the inside, which wasn't surprising, since he was likely the first person to climb inside it. He just hoped no one checked its contents.

After quite a bit of time spent worrying, then a period spent quietly humming all the songs he knew about sailing, Jamie fell asleep.

It wasn't as though Jamie Brewster made a habit of sneaking aboard cruise ships. In truth, this marked the first time he chose this particular means of travel. But he felt there was just cause in this instance.

Just days prior, Jamie had been ruminating about how much he enjoyed his job. Each day he would report to work, drink his two cups of coffee, and wait for a story to fly over. After loading up a cameraman and whichever pretty news anchor was available, he would fly off into the greater Savannah skyline. Jamie was an accomplished and mostly trusted pilot, though he often had to be talked out of doing aerial tricks to impress the pretty news anchors.

Usually Jamie was put on traffic duty, in which he would fly about finding bad traffic for the camera-person to shoot and the anchor to tout as a sign of the apocalypse. The cameraman who usually rode with Jamie was a bearded man named Tom. The accompanying anchorwoman was Janet Ford, who both men got along with better than the prima donna former traffic anchor Brad Rutzell. Janet was constantly applying powder to her nose, but not as much as Rutzell used to. When the camera wasn't rolling she liked to bet on things. This was preferable to Rutzell's constant criticism of Jamie and Tom. Thankfully Rutzell had moved on to a news station in Missouri after a salary dispute.

The day that changed Jamie Brewster's fate started like any other, the only recognizable difference being that he drank three cups of coffee that morning. After flying over a neighborhood to film an unexplained car fire, he reported back to headquarters for some lunch. Little did he know that while his mouth was full of a chicken salad sandwich, a high-speed car chase was unfolding not far from where he sat. When his boss burst into the staff lunch room, Jamie put down his newspaper (Jamie always got his news from the paper).

"Brewster!" yelled the thickly mustachioed news producer. "High speed chase headed toward Broughten Street! Get on it!"

Jamie got up, eyes wide, mouth still full of chicken salad. He snatched his lucky faded red baseball cap off the table and met Tom in the hallway. They gave each other a forceful high-five. Three minutes later the two men and Janet were in the navy blue helicopter with **CHANNEL 7** painted on its sides, delightedly headed for the kind of scoop that would be shown in promos for years to come.

Without looking up from her compact mirror, Janet spoke into her headset. "Twenty bucks says it's Madeline again." Madeline was Madeline Truesdale, the area's lovable repeat offender, who every so often would get herself into a high-speed chase in or near Savannah after robbing a gas station, and whose latest jail sentence ended prematurely only a few days prior due to good behavior.

Tom disagreed. "I don't think Madeline would get herself into trouble again this soon."

"So does that mean you'll bet me twenty bucks?" Janet asked, still powdering her nose.

"Nah, I don't want to bet."

"Come on, you chicken," Janet pressed.

Tom sighed. Janet started fixing her mascara. "What do you think, Jamie?"

Jamie casually guided the helicopter southward, then saw that the sun might cause him grief and readjusted the red cap on his head, which created a need to readjust his headset. "I will bet ten dollars the car is red. That is all."

Janet considered. "I think it's blue."

Tom gave his two cents. "I bet it's silver."

"Okay. Deal," concluded Janet, moving to her other eyelash.

"What if it isn't one of those colors?" Jamie asked.

"Oh, it will be," replied the confident Janet.

The car was black, of course, and soon the helicopter crew was able to find the chase, well in progress. The luxurious four-door automobile was speeding around recklessly, dodging other cars by mere inches, altogether following very few traffic laws. It appeared to the three aboard the helicopter that the driver was either very late for an appointment or was dabbling in something that the police would not like. They all agreed it was probably the latter, so no bets were placed.

It was a lovely, sunny afternoon and the job of flying a television news helicopter was proving to be all Jamie had wished for. Janet reported the unfolding events as Tom pointed his camera at the black car and the pursuing police cruisers. Every once in a while Jamie would do a quick 360-degree turn and then speed back up to the car, just to keep things fresh, but otherwise the chase continued down the highway with lots of sirens and honking and a couple minor fender-benders.

"Oh, hey," said Jamie, "We're getting close to my mom's house." This was true, as Mrs. Brewster, a large woman who always wore a smile as if she would be naked without it, resided in a modest but comfortable house not far from the interstate. Tom and Janet were only marginally interested in this tidbit.

Eventually the highway was closed off and a spike strip was put down so that the black car's tires would be mortally wounded. The black car had no choice but to go over the spike strip, and the helicopter crew instinctively winced at the pain caused to the vehicle, which seemed to scream, "Ooo! Ow! Ow! Ow! Ooo! Ow! Ow!" as it veered to its right and off the road. Within moments the vehicle's four occupants were out of the car and running toward the neighborhood beside the highway.

Unfortunately for the Savannah Police Department, a rookie on the squad nicknamed Slow-Mo failed to hear his chief's instructions quite right, and the spike strip was placed about a hundred yards short of where it was supposed to be. So when the fugitives evacuated the black car and dashed away, the poor police officers were not immediately able to apprehend them.

"Foot chase!" yelled Jamie, voice amplified in the headsets, deafening Tom and Janet. Jamie kept the helicopter over the scene and the six collective eyes of the helicopter crew witnessed the police capture two of the four bad guys. The other two, it appeared, would take a bit more cunning to catch.

So much cunning, in fact, that the search continued well past lunchtime. The criminals had escaped into a neighborhood full of trees and shrubs, so the two remaining fugitives were blessed with plenty of places to duck behind and crawl into, thus trying to spot them from the air proved difficult.

"Oh look," Jamie said. "We're back by my mom's house again."

"Which house is it?" asked Janet, glad to have something else to look for.

"It's that kind of gray-greenish one over there," Jamie said.

"There's more than one of those," Tom pointed out, peering over Janet's head.

"It's that one," Jamie said, pointing.

"Oh, that one," concluded Janet, looking at the wrong greenish-gray house.

"Ah," said Tom, as if a museum worker had just

corrected some piece of information for him. Jamie noticed that their faces were cocked about forty degrees off.

Jamie sighed. "No, it's that one," he said, pointing again. Janet looked puzzled.

"Well, I don't know which one you're talking about," Tom admitted. Jamie noticed the window was fogging up from the three faces pressing against it, like small, uncouth children at the zoo.

The helicopter pilot decided to open the window.

Suddenly Janet's long blond hair was flapping everywhere, like an outraged octopus. This was followed by paperwork that seemingly came out of nowhere performing some sort of anarchic dance routine around the cabin. Tom jumped back. Janet attempted to close the window but was unable to see with all that hair flapping around her face. Jamie decided he should probably shut the window so that they would not lose any of the dancing paper.

But as Jamie leaned slightly to his left, the winds from outside the aircraft snatched his lucky red baseball cap, which had been placed precariously atop his head after readjusting his headset. Instinctively, Jamie threw out a hand hoping to catch it, but alas, the winds had claimed it and were unwilling to negotiate. It swirled then tumbled toward the pavement. Jamie speedily shut the window.

Tom sat back up as Janet ran her fingers through her long, lovely hair with great urgency (it was all there). Before either of them could criticize Jamie for his questionable decision, the pilot spoke.

"My hat fell out." He paused. "I'm going to go get it."

"I don't think that's wise..." Tom said.

"Jamie, I'll buy you a new hat," Janet chimed in, in a tone of voice the pilot wouldn't have liked had he been paying attention to her.

"You guys don't understand. That hat means a lot to me." And so it was decided, since Jamie had control of the helicopter. Tom tried to protest once more.

"Jamie, I really don't think this is possible, let alone..."

The pilot interrupted. "Don't worry about it. I'll land in my mom's backyard. It's big enough. Then you guys will know which house is hers." His smile was not reciprocated by the cameraman nor reporter, who wished they had just pretended to see his mother's house.

Jamie Brewster was friendly enough, but he was a bit of a showoff at times. One of these times was now. He was going to try to park a helicopter in someone's backyard amidst a residential area that had too many trees to find fugitives, let alone park a helicopter. Sometimes rescue pilots had to land in a smallish space to retrieve the sick and injured, but Jamie had no experience flying rescue helicopters.

Tom made the sign of the cross as the helicopter descended. It banked to the left before Jamie quickly swung the tail around. A little too quickly for Janet's liking, who pitched forward a bit.

"Sorry, Janet," Jamie responded, chiding himself for his careless move. His intention was to impress the flight crew, not to give them reason to throw up. He concentrated a little harder, flying the helicopter back toward the right, inching it ever closer to the ground. The tops of the trees popped up suddenly in the passengers' line of sight, worrying Tom and Janet a tad more. Jamie began humming, which Janet hoped was a sign he was "in the zone," as he sometimes mentioned, instead of a sign that he had stopped paying attention. With a little movement of his hips, Jamie rotated the helicopter a smidge more, then held steady and eased it into the soft, unmowed grass of his mother's backyard.

Janet and Tom sighed in relief. Jamie gave a little fist pump, subtle enough for no one to notice.

"See," he said. "That was easy! I could have done it with my eyes closed." Jamie removed his headset. "I'll just run over and get my hat. I saw where it fell. I think it's still in the street." To quell their protests, he grinned and grabbed a walkie-talkie from the cockpit.

"It will take like two seconds," he said into it to prove communication was still available. Then Jamie hopped out of the aircraft, leaving the engine running. He immediately turned the walkie-talkie off so he wouldn't be annoyed by his coworkers' impatient nagging.

His two second estimate was a bit low, but a few moments seemed feasible. Jamie hustled across the grass in his comfortably-fitting jeans and tennis shoes, leaping effortlessly over his mother's flowerbed and into the quiet suburban thoroughfare. Thankfully no cars were coming, as he would not have heard them over the sound of the helicopter's revolving blades. He thought he saw something red halfway underneath a green Ford Taurus a stone's throw away. Rather than throw a stone to test the estimated distance, Jamie walked toward it. He squatted to take a look, and lo and behold, his lucky baseball cap was lying underneath, like a frightened animal hiding from a frightening animal. Jamie smiled and picked it up. He slapped it on his knee to dust it off, then popped the hat back on his head snugly.

The satisfied helicopter pilot thought that he might as well say hello to his mother. So, leaping the flowerbed once more, he returned to his starting point. He briskly strode around to her sliding glass door in the back. When he spotted his mother, she had a broom in her hands and an agitated look upon her face. It appeared she was about to go outside to try to shoo the helicopter away, but upon seeing her son she clapped her hands and slid the door open for him.

"Jamie! What are you doing parking a helicopter in my backyard?" It was a fair question. She seemed confused but also delighted to see her dear son, who should visit his mother more often.

Jamie casually pointed over his shoulder and shouted over the sound of the aircraft. "We were in the area." Mrs. Brewster felt this answer sufficed.

"Well, come on in! Come on in!" she shouted back, beckoning with a large but gentle hand, which was connected to the rest of her large but gentle self.

"I can't, mama," Jamie said. "We've got to go again. I just thought I'd say hi."

Mrs. Brewster put her hands on her hips and gave a melodramatic frown. "You can't just come here and say hello and leave again. Come on in. Let's have some sweet tea."

"Mama, I really need to go. I only stopped so you wouldn't worry that there was a helicopter in your backyard."

"You gonna tell me my fancy news helicopter pilot son don't love me?"

Jamie sighed. It wasn't that he didn't want sweet tea, but that he finally felt like he should be responsible. "No, mama. I love you..."

Mrs. Brewster smiled and threw her arms wide. "Then good. We'll have some sweet tea."

She turned and walked into her house. Jamie followed, deciding that having a quick drink with his mother could do no harm. He looked back and indicated "just a second" to the remaining occupants of the helicopter then shut the sliding glass door behind himself.

The house got quite a bit of natural light, which complemented the brightly painted walls and seemed to soften the near-deafening sound of helicopter blades. Jamie followed his mother down the hallway, glancing at the pictures of himself growing up. He had not grown up in this particular house, but had done most of his growing in Madison, Wisconsin. His mother had grown up in Savannah, however, and decided to move back later in life. Jamie eventually followed her when he found an ad which read ***News station in dire need of helicopter pilot***. He loved his mother very much, so he felt it would be an honor to fulfill this dire need.

Mrs. Brewster pulled out a chair for her son at the little table in the kitchen. She walked past the table as her son gingerly lowered his tush onto the wooden seat. Most of the chairs in her house were a little hard, so instead of sitting on a slant, Jamie pulled his wallet from his back pocket and placed it on the table. Knowing his mother's admiration for good manners, he also removed his lucky hat and set it next to the wallet.

"I made a fresh batch this morning," Jamie's mother beamed without turning around. Jamie tapped his knee in anticipation and nodded. His mother's sweet tea always seemed like the best tea in the world, despite being made from a packet. Nonetheless, Mrs. Brewster always put tender loving care into things like mixing Kool-Aid and cooking Top Ramen. She carried the heavy pitcher to the table along with two glasses. Jamie rose for just a second to glance through the window above the kitchen sink. Content to see the helicopter still there, he sat back down.

And so mother and son had their tea. A lovely way to spend an afternoon. The sweet tea seemed sweet enough to make a traditional bitter-tea drinker spit it out, which was just the way both liked it.

"This is really good, mama," Jamie said after an especially satisfying gulp.

"Oh, I don't know. Maybe it could have a little more sugar." Mrs. Brewster was always so modest when it came to her impeccable hosting. "Here, have some more," she said, pouring more tea into Jamie's glass even though it was far from empty. "We might as well finish this pitcher."

"I really can't stay long," Jamie responded. "I've got work to do."

"This son of mine," Mrs. Brewster said with a roll of her eyes. "Always working. He'll work himself to death, this one." It was hardly true, but was the kind of statement Mrs. Brewster became more and more likely to use as she aged.

"Well, we've got to get back in the air. There's still a couple of criminals running around here."

"What? In my neighborhood?" Mrs. Brewster did not actually sound too concerned. Jamie detailed his eventful day and soon lost sight of the fact that he was supposed to be flying his helicopter instead of chit-chatting with his mother, no matter how delightful her company might be.

So the confab continued until somewhere in the midst of his story about the strange things his boss brought for lunch, it suddenly occurred to Jamie that the near-deafening sound of helicopter blades was becoming less near-deafening. His eyes went wide a second before he leaped out of his chair. His mother failed to notice the difference in volume, so she puzzled as her son sprinted away.

Jamie's eyes stayed wide as he rushed to the sliding glass door. He could not stop repeating, "oh no oh no oh no oh no" in his head, even as he slid the glass door open with as much force he could muster. Stepping outside the house, he looked up to see the very same helicopter he had been captaining steadily rise from the ground, unmistakably not being captained by him any longer. It followed the same path it had when he landed it, as if the helicopter had gotten sick of waiting for him and decided to retreat the way it had come. Even when his mother and her hips came swaying out to his side, Jamie could not close his gaping mouth.

Peering up at the escaping vehicle, Jamie noticed that the new pilot appeared to be a man with black hair and what might have been a thin mustache. Seated next to him was another man with black hair and what was even more likely a thin mustache. Then, heads peeping out the window from behind the front seat, Jamie could make out the fretting faces of Janet and Tom.

"Uh-oh," was all Jamie's mouth could produce in his poor attempt at extrapolation. Whatever was going on did not look good.

"Oh my," his mother said, wiping her hands on her apron.

All of Jamie's neck-craning was interrupted by his first clear thought in what seemed like eons. He reached into his pocket and extracted the walkie-talkie. He delicately turned it on, afraid of what might ensue. Swallowing hard, he pressed the button.

"Hellllll-lo?" he said, in the drawn-out, unassuming way an elderly grocer might answer the telephone. The response was not so calm.

After a few moments of incoherent screeching, Janet calmed enough to yell, "Jamie! What are you doing? Where have you been? We've been trying to talk to you!"

Jamie tried to see if remaining calm, or rather playing dumb, would help while he watched the helicopter hover straight above his mother's backyard. "Okay. Well, I'm here now. What's up?"

Jamie's nonchalance did not rub off on Janet. *"What's up? What's up?"* Janet asked mockingly. "We are! While our pilot is still on the ground!"

"True enough." Jamie tried to politely chuckle at Janet's pun.

"Now listen closely, you moron..." (it would be a while before Janet would feel bad for calling Jamie a moron), "Tom and I have been kidnapped." She paused. "I think."

Jamie winced. He'd been holding out hope that things weren't as bad as they seemed. Perhaps Janet or Tom had skimmed the owner's manual and were headed back without their superfluous pilot.

"Okay."

"Far from it, Jamie. Now apparently our captors are from Mongolia, and are part of some secret society that couldn't be that secret if they're telling us about it."

"I see."

"Apparently Tom and I are going with them."

"No, don't," Jamie offered.

"We weren't given much of a choice! When they saw that you had abandoned us here, they decided that a news crew could prove useful in the near future."

"Oh no. You're hostages," Jamie sounded concerned, finally.

"No! They want us to cover some news story they are going to be a part of." She paused, perhaps for dramatic effect. "It involves lost treasure, apparently. I don't know, Jamie!"

"*Treasure?*" asked the helicopter pilot, repeating the operative word for dramatic effect. He thought to himself, *My, this is turning into a strange day*.

Then Jamie heard some static and was only able to make out one thing amongst the crackle. "...shipwreck," said Janet between fuzzy noise.

"What was that?" Jamie tried.

There was a pause, as Janet was apparently having the same trouble. "Huh?" she asked.

"Where are they taking you?" Jamie asked.

"Hang on," replied Janet. There was a pause. Jamie could hear the newswoman leaning over her seat and asking her captors where they were headed. "Somewhere called the Skeleton Coast."

"The what? Where is that?" Jamie asked. He had never heard of the Gelatin Coast.

"I don't know! Find out and do something, you jerk!"

Jamie was about to reply to this last comment when a new noise presented itself. It was a very loud knock on the house's front door, coupled with a repetitive ringing of the doorbell.

"I'm coming. I'm coming," muttered Mrs. Brewster. Jamie felt a premonition that this was not a neighbor asking to borrow sugar. He ducked back inside the house and turned off the walkie-talkie. Holding his breath, he tried to listen to the conversation on the other end of the house.

When Mrs. Brewster opened the door, she was greeted by two sweaty policemen.

"Good afternoon, ma'am. Were you aware that a helicopter just took off from your backyard?"

"Of course I was aware, officer," replied Jamie's mother with an equal or greater amount of curtness. "What do you take me for?" As the officer began to reply, Mrs. Brewster muttered to herself rather loudly. "A helicopter lands in my back yard and this guy thinks I don't notice it. My word..."

The younger officer looked at his partner, then raised his voice a little. "Ma'am, did you happen to see what was going on with that helicopter and why it was in your backyard?"

Meanwhile, her son had tiptoed over to a living room window. He was a bit concerned to see two police cars alongside the house and a third pulling up behind them.

Jamie observed the policemen and policewomen conversing. The helicopter's landing and subsequent takeoff had caused the search party to come running, and driving, over. Jamie was unsure of what his next move should be. The cops were on his side, he told himself, but he had just allowed a very expensive vehicle be stolen by the men they were after, along with a reasonably expensive news team. He bit his nails and listened some more.

"You tell me," Mrs. Brewster offered, perhaps just to stall.

"Well, we are trying to figure that out," the young sweaty officer said. "But if you were unaware, we were in hot pursuit of a couple of fugitives in this neighborhood."

"It's looks like it's been hot," Mrs. Brewster said, pointing to the perspiration on his uniform. To even things out she did the same to his partner.

"Ma'am, I'm not going to beat around the bush..."

"Good."

"One of your neighbors watched the helicopter land and called the police because he thinks that one of the fugitives entered your house." Jamie gulped.

"What? Which neighbor?" Mrs. Brewster craned her neck outside her door. "If it's that Randy Brown again, I swear..."

"Ma'am, are you saying that you are not aware of any criminal running into your house?"

Mrs. Brewster changed her tone of voice. "I'll tell you what, if there was a fugitive that ran in my house, he sure *must have run out the back door by now*. After maybe *taking some hard candies with him*." Jamie heard his mother's very blatant hint. She had never possessed the gift of subtlety.

Jamie did not want to be falsely imprisoned as one of the fugitives, and even if he was able to convincingly explain the truth, he concluded he might still rot in a jail cell for some sort of "helicopter negligence." Wondering if it was the right course of action to run from the police, he felt the worst course of action would probably be to sit in the living room and continue to bite his nails. He tiptoed back toward the sliding glass door, stopping first to reach into the candy dish on the coffee table.

"Ma'am, I'm going to say this in simple terms: We have reason to believe you are currently harboring a fugitive. Are you?"

Jamie felt scared and guilty for what he had gotten his mother into, or what she was getting herself into, as he heard her start some kind of rant. "You know, you live on a quiet street for how long, and you pay all your taxes, and then one day..." Jamie cautiously slid the door open and stepped into the backyard. He wondered if he was a terrible son.

"Good luck, Mom," he whispered. Then realized that he should be wishing himself the same. Over near where he had landed his aircraft, three officers were busy looking at the ground and searching the grass for evidence. Jamie gasped, then slapped a hand across his own mouth to silence this gasp. The officers were looking the other way, so Jamie inched his way along the wall of the house. Holding his breath, hands splayed out to either side of him, he tried his best to blend into the wall, which was painted a grayer green than his Old Navy sweater.

One policewoman stood up from where she was inspecting a patch of grass, and it appeared she might turn toward the house. Jamie squatted, then hurled a rock as hard as he could toward the opposite end of the yard. The impact produced a rustling in a patch of bushes. This was enough to get all three officers to turn their attention to the noise. Jamie took the opportunity to run as quietly as he could toward the street, which involved some exaggerated raising of the knees. Once there, he ducked behind one of the unoccupied cop cars and looked back. None of the cops were looking his way so he sprinted across the street into that Randy Brown's yard. He ascended the short fence, darted through the back yard, over another fence, through the adjoining backyard, tiptoed through some bushes, and was in another street. The new fugitive began nonchalantly walking down the road. He politely smiled at a woman who was watering her plants.

As his breath slowed to a reasonable rhythm, Jamie pondered his next move. He finally considered turning the walkie-talkie back on. Unfortunately the helicopter was already out of range, so all he received was static that sounded very annoyed with him. At this point, he also realized that his wallet was not with him. He recollected taking it out and putting it on his mother's kitchen table, next to his baseball cap. And there was no going back for it now. They would ID him and track him down.

Jamie saw a fire hydrant and sat upon it to pout. He was in a real fix. His sitting lasted only moments, though, as he resolved to make a plan rather than waste time sitting on a fire hydrant that might soon be swarmed by police officers.

It came out a bit like this: Jamie hopped a few more fences until he reached the highway. He decided to stick out his thumb in the hopes of being picked up by some kind strangers, or some kind of strangers. After only ten minutes or so, his efforts were rewarded and he climbed into a large van owned by a friendly couple from New Zealand on their way to Miami.

The two Kiwis were chatty as could be, and Jamie did not want to be rude to his saviors, so he listened and chatted back when they allowed him to get a word in. The discussion was therapeutic for Jamie, and he sometimes forgot his predicament. Thankfully the couple had quite a few maps. He felt that it was his mission to find a shipwreck on the so-called "Gelatin Coast." Regrettably, no map had any mention of this "Gelatin Coast." He did, however, find one short write-up in one of their travel books about a place called the "Skeleton Coast." Jamie hoped they were one and the same, or at least near each other, but fretted when he read the short blurb about it.

Africa. He would need to get to Africa.

After several hours, they arrived in Miami. The friendly Kiwis asked Jamie where he would like to be left, and he quickly blurted out that the coast would be best, thinking it was closest to Africa.

His brief time spent in Miami was a bit of a blur. He had no money. He was probably on some sort of government watch list. He tried to consider his options. He sat on the bench for over two hours before noticing a brochure on the ground a few yards away.

It had a cruise ship on it.

Excitement turned to concern, then to determination, and with some asking around somehow Jamie figured out that, miraculously and perhaps ridiculously, there was a ship departing the next day for Cape Town, South Africa. According to his fuzzy calculations, this Skeleton Coast deal was sort of on the way. Knowing that he could not pay for a cruise ticket, Jamie felt that his only option for saving the lives of Janet and Tom was to sneak aboard that ship. Could also be fun.

The irony was that a cargo ship was leaving for Capetown even earlier the next day, and it was scheduled to reach land two days prior to the cruise ship, but Jamie never heard anything about it.

The stowaway pilot was rudely awoken early in the morning when the cooler began to rise from the ground, much like a helicopter taking off. A crane was transporting the box to the deck. It rose straight up, with a soft swinging motion. Jamie took a few moments to recollect where he was, as he usually did not spend the night crammed in a refrigerator. Then he started screaming.

Though he knew a cooler would not be the most comfortable or luxurious accommodations for travel, Jamie had failed to fully grasp just how terrible it might be. The rough treatment of the box made him feel like he was on an inflatable alligator in a squall. He was tossed and jostled about inside the small compartment, but with little room to be tossed and jostled, he continually hit his head against the hard plastic. It did not take long for Jamie to feel nauseous. The nausea inserted periodic lulls into what would have otherwise been continuous screaming.

It occurred to Jamie in those dreadful moments what he had learned from cartoons was a hideous fallacy. He should be softly laughing to himself as his brilliant plan unfolded, before sneaking out of the box at nightfall, no worse for the wear. Instead, Jamie acknowledged this was the most agonizing process he had ever been through and wondered if the refrigerator had accidentally been jettisoned into space. Among his constant bleating were a few wishes for a quick death.

Luckily for him, the moving cranes and loud voices drowned out his yelping, as did the music from a half dozen sets of earphones owned by the workmen. After what seemed like an eternity, but only about ninety seconds, the refrigerator came to rest firmly on the ship's deck. As his hands clutched for his heart, Jamie noticed that somehow, someway, he had refrained from throwing up on himself.

15

Sand. All there was was sand. Hills upon hills of sand. Some of the hills turned into mountains. Mountains made of sand. And rocks. Here and there, nestled among all the sand, were rocks. Big, rough, heavy rocks. Sand and rocks. As far as the eye could see.

Even optimistic Earnest could admit that things looked grim.

"Well, Mickey," he said, "I hope you like sand."

Then the pair trudged on through it.

16

Clayton Stern's house in South Africa was a fortress. He had the money to build one, so he figured why not. It towered above the grasslands of his extensive ranch. The doors were made of stainless steel, the windows all had bulletproof shades, and everything in the house was computerized and operated by remote control. It was enormous, which seemed rather unnecessary, given that Clayton Stern thought he lived alone. He did not live alone, however, seeing that his personal assistant lived with him. But in Clayton Stern's eyes, an assistant didn't count.

Stern's lackey at present was named Isiah Burtlyre. He was originally Stern's lawyer, but Stern had, over time, been able to convert his lawyer into an assistant without Burtlyre really noticing. That way, Stern thought he could kill two birds with one stone. And given the amount of trouble he often got himself into with environmental organizations, it seemed wise to keep a lawyer around at all times.

Burtlyre was walking from one of the two laundry rooms with a large basket of Stern's darks, balancing a stack of thick folders on top. The lawyer/maid was dressed in a tailored suit, and his $1200 dress shoes click-clacked on the wooden floorboards he had polished the day before. He passed the huge, curved elephant tusks and the displeased crocodile head mounted on the wall, which indicated he was on the right path (had he passed the stuffed grizzly bear and the hanging albatross it would have been an indicator that he was not). Burtlyre made a few more turns and came to the large double doors of Stern's second-largest office. Balancing the laundry precariously on one knee, Isiah reached through the dangerously ridiculous doorknob made of elk antlers and entered.

As customary, Clayton Stern was yelling into the telephone on his desk.

"Well I don't live in Panama, so I don't see why I need to obey Panama's laws!" he shouted. Although his logic was flawed, he was also lying, since he owned a sizable house in Panama. Stern slammed the phone down dramatically.

"What is with these people, Cubby?" he asked Burtlyre, shaking his head. Stern had started giving his lawyer colorful nicknames, none of which stuck and none of which pertained to anything.

"I have no idea, Mr. Stern," Burtlyre conceded. He indicated the laundry. "I finished your darks. Did you want them with you or in your bedroom?"

"On the roof. I want them extra bright. Did you starch the shirts?"

"No, Mr. Stern. Not yet."

"Well get on that," Stern snapped, because it was the only way he talked.

"All right." Burtlyre walked to the enormous metallic desk to present his employer with the thick stack of papers atop the laundry, again balancing the basket on his knee. "Here."

Stern looked confused and agitated. "What's this?"

"This is the file folder on Canadian bylaws concerning extradition and extortion. And also the Drummond consultation file and the Murphy comments ... you asked for."

"Oh." Clayton eyed the paperwork. "That goes in the fire."

"Yes, Mr. Stern."

Stern turned to look out his floor-length window across the plains. After he retrieved a pair of gigantic binoculars from a bronze tray table by the window, his deceitful eyes scanned the horizon.

Burtlyre was departing with the cumbersome bundle when he about-faced.

"And your lunch should be ready in about an hour. I'm going to make French onion soup."

Using his head to prop the door open as he pivoted around it, Isiah froze when his boss yelled.

"Wait! I see those lemmings again, Blue!"

The lawyer/maid turned back toward the window. The binoculars remained pressed against Stern's cruel but lovely eyes.

"Mr. Stern, I thought you were on to the letter 'M,'" Burtlyre pointed out, well aware of Clayton's alphabetical vendetta on the animal kingdom. And since it had only been a couple of days since shooting the poor leopard, he assumed that "L" was taken care of.

"I'm still on the letter 'L' until that moose is on my property," this story's villain said. "Besides, I can bend my own rules."

Burtlyre sighed, but not because he was unaccustomed to his employer's eccentricity. Rather, Isiah Burtlyre was a baby when it came to heat.

Again without peeling his eyes away from the binoculars, Stern spoke. "Hold off on your fancy French onion soup. We're going to go hunt lemmings, Ace."

Lemmings don't really live in Africa. Their home is usually in much colder regions (like whatchamacallits, with the antlers...). But this group of unlucky lemmings had been delivered about a month ago. Thankfully for them, they had so far been able to escape their captor, but their luck turned when they'd meandered back to his property.

The noble lemming is a small mammal that scurries about ever so quickly. It would take a fair amount of skill to shoot such an animal. Clayton Stern wanted a challenge.

Ten minutes after they were spotted, an open-air, overly armed jeep bounced across the open expanses of grassland that made up the northeast corner of Clayton Stern's property. Both men were still wearing their tailored suits; Burtlyre in his "chocolate" ensemble and Stern in shiny silver, which was now reflecting painfully into their eyes. A fine layer of dust covered them as the jeep crossed the dry land. Clayton didn't seem to worry about wrecking a suit; he could always afford a new one.

Both men sat in the back seat. Neither of the men was driving the jeep. But both men were aware that letting a jeep drive on its own would be an unneeded risk. So the job of driving fell to Clarence, Stern's personal driver. Clarence didn't say much. In fact, he didn't really do much either. He usually just drove, chain-smoked, and wore big sunglasses. Burtlyre was not especially fond of Clarence, since while the lawyer/maid slaved away in the house with both paperwork and housework, the driver usually just sat outside or in the garage, wearing his sunglasses, smoking his cigarettes.

Stern surveyed his land with a different pair of big binoculars, searching for telltale signs of the lemmings he had spotted. Spotting none, he put down the binoculars and lifted the colossal and cumbersome rifle resting in his lap. Peering through the scope, he fired wildly toward nothing at all. The rifle's recoil caused the butt end to slam into Burtlyre's shoulder. The lawyer/maid fell most of the way out of the jeep, which lacked doors despite having six top-of-the-line cup holders. If he had been wearing his seat belt, perhaps he would have fared better, but alas ...

Clarence looked in his rearview mirror and saw that Burtlyre was hanging most of the way out of the jeep, but did not slow down, because Clayton had not told him to. The only thing that kept Burtlyre from tumbling completely out of the vehicle was catching his foot on a heavy metal box under the driver's seat. The box was full of ammunition, needless to say. Stern leaned over and pulled Burtlyre back into the jeep by his expensive leather belt.

"Maybe I should move to the front," said the lawyer/maid.

"Nonsense," said the lemming hunter. "Just watch where you put your shoulder."

And with that Stern again raised the gun and peered through the scope, while Burtlyre massaged his sore shoulder and leaned as far away as possible.

Suddenly Clayton saw movement in the distance that could only be described as scurrying. He stood up and pointed for Clarence to veer to the right. One-handed and nonchalantly (the way he did most things), Clarence steered in the direction of the finger-pointing.

But as the jeep slowed to sneak up on the lemmings, Clayton Stern's cellular telephone went off. The ring was loud and dreadful, as it often is with lovers of extravagance. The tune carried across the plains, and might have been the cause of the lemmings' sudden departure in the opposite direction. Stern handed the large gun over to Burtlyre without any warning or concern about safety. The lawyer/maid took it apprehensively as Stern reached into his silvery pocket and extracted his telephone.

"Hello?" he yelled into it.

After a pause, he yelled louder, "What?" then motioned for Clarence to stop. Clayton stepped out into the swirling dust and furrowed his brow as he listened. Soon he said some very naughty words, the gist of which was, "I am very mad about all of this and I want you to fix this problem right away." Then he threw the phone on the ground.

"Rocketman!" he called to Burtlyre.

"Yes?" asked his lackey, gingerly placing the gun on the seat and stepping out of the jeep.

"Pick that up."

Burtlyre did so with his non-injured arm. He handed it back to Stern, who angrily stared off into nothing, and then slapped the phone away for Burtlyre to once again retrieve from the dirt.

"Come on. We've got to go," said the cranky hunter. "I've got some people to yell at."

17

Hans Heissel always, always, always buttoned the top button of his shirts. Usually these shirts were either light blue or slightly darker blue with plenty of buttons (for buttoning), but always, always, always the top button was firmly buttoned in place. This buttoning was often done in front of a mirror. Just to make sure he got that top button.

Hans Heissel was born right when expected, the only child of a wealthy couple in a wealthy district of a wealthy town in Switzerland. His childhood was a pleasant one, filled with visits from affectionate grandparents and the companionship of a loving puppy. He was doted upon with all the luxuries a wealthy family may throw at their only child. The weather in Switzerland fit him well, as did the German language, and so he grew into a content, if rather straitlaced, young man.

Hans became a distinguished violinist by the age of nine. His performances drew crowds, and even tourists hiking through the Swiss Alps would stop by for a listen. After every performance, however, Hans would sternly watch the audience applaud before reporting that he was flat on this or that note. People thought he was being cute. He was not.

Hans also developed equally applaudable skills at table tennis, though slightly later in life. This surprised some, since he seemed a less-than-athletic teenager. His gawkiness worked to his advantage, however, as many opponents underestimated this self-serious young gentleman with his top button buttoned. During his teenage years, Hans' parents brought him to numerous junior championships throughout Europe. He excelled at many of these, including a tournament in Prague that he won despite being in a great deal of pain incurred from tragically tripping into a vending machine.

But most importantly, Hans Heissel was a math genius. This was apparent when, by age four, Hans volunteered to do his parents' taxes. Thinking this was adorable, they allowed him to check their math. He found three errors. Hans flew through more and more advanced math courses in his schools, and then was sent to numerous new schools. He seemed unfazed by all the hoopla surrounding him. Hans simply solved the math problems put in front of him. At the age of thirteen, Hans was taken to a university campus to solve a very difficult and very long math problem. He conquered it quicker than anyone expected but felt the ensuing celebration was unnecessary and trite. To Hans, it was a duty.

Unfortunately for Hans, his math skills were light-years ahead of his social skills. Yet he was completely oblivious to this. Often he would walk into a jovial conversation and ask someone to repeat a joke they just told, then solemnly say, "Hmmmm," and break down its merits, making everyone lose their appetite for comedy. He liked receiving birthday presents but did a poor job of showing his appreciation, with comments like, "Thank you, parents. Is the news on yet?" He sometimes reminded people when they were not invited to a certain party. Hans was rarely hated, but he confused a great many people.

Whizzing through college, Hans dealt almost exclusively with math courses and avoided classes that sounded challenging, like social studies. He continued buttoning his top button. He gained some collegiate friends, but even these seemingly like-minded and math-loving types were sometimes baffled by his social ineptitude. Womankind was rather enigmatic for Hans, and he for womankind. Once in a great while he would consider asking a young lady from a math class to dance with him or stroll in the moonlight, but he would quickly reconsider, seeing as such things seemed frivolous when there were still unsolved math problems plaguing humanity.

After college, Hans Heissel turned his attention to getting a job. Some mathematically inclined persons decide to teach. But Hans had no hope of becoming a math teacher since he lacked the tools to deal with students (though some math teachers lack these tools but give it a whirl anyway). Besides, Hans Heissel held little interest in teaching others how to do math problems that he already mastered. It was much more interesting to continue solving math problems that gave other people fits.

So Hans searched for jobs that involved high-level math. He inquired about code-breaking work with the Swiss military, but as the Swiss military was not really into activities that could be viewed as anything more than neutral, Hans found little need for someone like him. He considered attempting to get a job with another country's military, but reconsidered when he began to wonder if a drill sergeant would constantly be yelling at him to show his work.

There were some jobs involving sitting around with scientists in big tunnels underground doing math problems to figure out if particles would collide just right. Personally, Hans wasn't keen on working with things that tiny, which he worried could easily be misplaced.

Another option was to work with computers. Hans was approached with numerous computer-related jobs, all of which he turned down because he hated working with computers. Things like the arrow keys annoyed him, because sometimes his palm would accidentally cause the screen to change and he would spend several moments assessing what had gone wrong.

Eventually, under pressure from family members, potential employers, and his former professors, Hans Heissel chose a job as an analyst. He wasn't even sure what the job entailed, except probably analyzing of some sort, hopefully the math sort. It turned out the job entailed sitting and waiting for men in suits to get frustrated with their own math skills, so they would find Hans sitting in his shirt and tie and present him with a set of math problems and an ultimatum. Sometimes the men did not even wait until they got frustrated, but came to Hans first so they could take an early lunch. Basically, a giddy Hans Heissel would arrive at work five to six minutes early and sit in his office chair, tapping his fingers, until a stack of papers was plopped on his desk or a woman or man poked her or his head into Hans's door to throw out some numbers in need of crunching. He either didn't notice or didn't care that his co-workers were taking advantage of him so they could avoid thinking hard. Hans just enjoyed doing math problems all the live-long day. It was seemingly the ideal job for him.

Then one day Hans Heissel decided to become a pirate instead. It was far from premeditated. He didn't hate his job or argue with his parents. He simply decided that he would be a pirate.

And so, armed with not much more than a few nice pens and a top-of-the-line calculator, Hans set about on his new career path. The first step seemed rather self-explanatory: He would commandeer his parents' yacht. This did not take much work, as Hans simply went down to the lake where the boat was docked and climbed aboard. The friendly old Italian man who always worked at the marina even gave him a wide toothless smile and a wave. Hans did not wave back.

The problematic scenario facing Hans was that Switzerland does not touch any ocean to speak of and as most people know, none of the best pirates are lake pirates. So Hans set about moving the yacht from the lake to an ocean. He would have to ask his parents for help in this endeavor.

When his mother and father were informed, very matter-of-factly, of his decision to commandeer their vessel, they seemed unsure about his new career path. Of course, Mr and Mrs. Heissel were the kind of parents who were always supportive of their grown son, no matter what the circumstances may be, so they agreed to help Hans Heissel (Jr.) transport the yacht into salt water.

Hans rode in the front seat of the rental truck that towed the yacht from Switzerland toward the Gulf of Genoa in Italy, an adequate place to start his enterprise. Halfway through the drive it occurred to Hans Heissel that if he were a good pirate, he'd have told the man at gunpoint to drive him to the ocean for free, but since his parents were paying for this venture, the new buccaneer let it slide.

While the truck driver was negotiating the yacht into the water, Hans Heissel did two important things. First he bought a newspaper. This did not seem all that monumental at the time, but newspapers were being sold within sight of the dock and Hans had some change in his pocket.

A moment later a young Italian boy approached Hans Heissel. The boy was rather dirty, wearing some beat-up old clothes that looked like they were in the wrong century. He had a bit of mud smeared on his face (though he had himself smeared on the mud to look more impoverished). It seemed reasonable to surmise that the boy was an orphan of some sort, so it came as no shock when he stretched out his palm and politely asked Hans Heissel for some money.

Never one to beat around the bush, Hans looked hard at the boy and asked, "Are you an orphan?" Generally this is not the politest way to address someone.

The boy sighed and made his eyes well up with tears. "Yes, sir, I am. A poor, dejected orphan." In actuality the boy was used to the hand life had dealt him, so the emotional response was an act. Hans Heissel did not necessarily see through the act, but did not pay attention to emotions very often.

"Do you want a job?" Hans asked in a steely and straightforward manner.

The boy scratched his head. "Well ... what is it?"

Hans pointed to his yacht, which was being slowly backed into the water. "I am a pirate. Would you like to join my crew?"

The boy was confused about the joke. But he was a young boy in search of adventure. "Yes, sir. Very much."

"Good. You are my very first shipmate. You will be a deckhand. I am Hans Heissel." He paused. "Your captain." He paused again and then presented his hand. The boy shook it.

"I am Ronaldinho," the boy said. This was not completely true, but he had adopted the name a while ago because he had no parents to stop him. "Thank you, Captain."

Hans Heissel looked at his own palm. "You will need to start washing your hands more often."

A few minutes later, the pair emerged from a shop with loaves of bread under their arms. Ronaldinho had brought up the idea of buying some food before their journey, and his new captain had seen it as a fair decision. Suddenly a thought occurred to Hans, but he could not see a hat shop. He frowned angrily. Every good pirate captain needed a hat. Bringing this concern up to Ronaldinho, his one and only crew member posed an idea.

With the yacht now resting alongside the dock of the marina, the truck driver and the men on the dock looked up in wonder. Some laughed. Now approaching them was Hans Heissel, wearing a massive, triangular newspaper hat. Next to him walked a very dirty little boy, frantically licking an ice cream cone (actually gelato, his reward for the brilliant idea of making a newspaper hat). Hans looked resolute, as if the hat were a badge, unaware that the laughter was aimed at him.

The yacht was soon cast off and departing the marina. Captain Hans Heissel, adorned with cumbersome newspaper hat that constantly needing adjusting, stood at the large wheel. With a sense of adventure swelling through him, his fingers reached to the collar of his shirt and undid the top button.

Then he called Ronaldinho to his side.

"For your resourcefulness in finding a hat, I hereby promote you from deckhand to first mate."

Ronaldinho let out an excited whoop.

"This ship probably needs a new name, too," Hans noticed, concluding (correctly) that the name *Peaceful Sunrise* was not likely to instill fear in people's hearts. Recollecting the most dreaded, unfair math teacher he ever had, Helga Dillenburg, the new captain rechristened the ship as the *Helga II*.

Wanting to get things going quickly, Hans Heissel spotted another yacht moored at the outer edge of the marina, populated by some elderly persons. Hans drove the *Helga II* over and parked alongside them. He and Ronaldinho scurried on board the other yacht and demanded whatever money and jewels they carried with them. The elderly persons seemed amused by their shenanigans and cackled. Coincidentally, the owner of the yacht was a Swiss man who once worked with Hans Heissel, Sr.

"Say, aren't you Hans Heissel's kid?" the gentleman asked.

"I might be, old man."

The boat's owner began telling tales of his days working with the pirate captain's father, then commented on how strange it was they should happen across each other.

"You know, the last time I saw this young man he was probably in a stroller..." All of the elderly people were so amused by this fact that they laughed and started asking Hans all sorts of questions, only some of which he answered. After a few minutes Hans Heissel again pestered the elderly people about taking their money and jewels. Eventually this tired joke became annoying, and they started to tell him so. Many of them moved to a different part of the yacht. The boat's owner, assuming that Hans was having financial troubles, finally extracted his wallet and unhappily handed him some bills. Hans demanded more, and the man begrudgingly complied, since he could afford it. Neither of the pirates thanked the man as they left.

Though now in a foul mood, the man yelled after Hans, "Tell your father I said hello."

And so Hans Heissel was even more so officially a pirate (more or less). With Ronaldinho by his side, he drove the *Helga II* out into the Ligurian Sea, leaving good-for-nothing dry land behind them. Of course, it became apparent quickly that Hans Heissel was susceptible to sea-sickness. So the very next boat they came across, they completely cleaned out of Dramamine.

Hans Heissel needed a crew. One dirt-covered nine-year-old boy was a good start, but Hans was aware that in order to run a successful operation, that number needed to multiply a bit. Every good pirate captain needed a band of ugly, quarrelsome men as crew. Dividing the sums of numerous large numbers by what he called the "scallywag constant," Hans deduced that his best bet would be to start his search on the island of Corsica. So the captain and his young first mate set sail (actually they used a large inboard motor) for the isle to their south.

Upon reaching their destination, the pair found a quiet cove and moored the *Helga II* to a mostly-sunken houseboat. The pair took the *Helga II*'s life raft to shore and hid it in a group of trees. Hans did not want to pay marina fees, on account of being a pirate.

Thankfully for the captain and first mate, not far from shore was a road with a scenic view that led into the nearby town. Armed only with math skills and a gigantic newspaper hat, Hans Heissel opted against trying to commandeer a motor vehicle, instead deciding to walk.

As the sun made a flashy departure to brighten another part of the globe, the pirates reached the town. Hans's instincts drove him toward what was considered the "bar district," which was impressive given his general unfamiliarity with bars. Approaching a street that had four pubs close to one another, the captain stood scratching his chin as he deliberated which seemed sleaziest, until a car honked at him to get out of the street. Hans and Ronaldinho just entered the nearest one.

What a wise decision. The establishment was packed with gruff, muscular, somewhat hairy non-gentlemen, each with a mug in hand the size of Ronaldinho's head. Hans Heissel beamed with excitement. The bar patrons did not. They did not take kindly to men with newspaper hats.

Hans saw that a good portion of the men all wore the same royal blue and yellow uniform. If they were already uniformed, these men were halfway to being a crew. He also noticed that many of the uniformed men were bruised and bandaged. One had crutches. Hans inquired with the bartender.

It turned out that the uniformed group was a professional rugby team (though not a very good one, the bartender noted). Actually, the men were technically a *former* professional rugby team (which made them worse, added the bartender), since the team had recently been disbanded. In fact, right after their game that afternoon. Apparently the team's owner had gone bankrupt when his family decided to cut him off and the team was the first thing to go. Seeing that the team was not what one would call a top-tier organization (being a second-rate team in a third-rate league that few people paid attention to), league officials decided losing this particular team would be a good cost-cutting measure. And so, the flabbergasted members of the rugby squad now sat licking their wounds (one of them literally) in a bar in a town on Corsica, unsure of how they would get home.

When he learned that the team was called the Pirates, Hans was sold.

So Captain Hans Heissel gave a detailed presentation on the unique opportunity he was offering. It took a little bit of coaxing, but whether they had little hope of resurrecting their rugby careers, or were enchanted by the idea of life on the high seas, they collectively agreed to his proposition. On second thought, it was probably because they were really liquored up.

Once they shook hands to accept the offer, the former rugby team changed their collective opinion of Hans Heissel's hat.

Walking back along the scenic stretch of road to the *Helga II*, the captain got to know the new recruits. The men came from all across the globe, it turned out. There was Jacques, the tough bearded Frenchman who had served as the team's captain, along with Wiley, an especially tall man from Tanzania; Roderick and Marshall, the fraternal twins from New Zealand who insisted that they looked alike; and Christof, who appeared in every regard to be a Viking. There was also Warren, Paul, Jaomir, Kurtis, Zangley, Mort, Sweety, Coastal Abe, Fingers, and a man they referred to as The Moocher, among others. Hans only picked up a few of the names. One of the most grateful men presented Hans and Ronaldinho with some extra jerseys. Hans appreciated it for the sake of regularity.

And so Captain Hans Heissel Jr. had a crew. He did not demote Ronaldinho, though.

Off the pirates went, to plunder and even pillage a little. The first order of business was to get some clothes and food for the new crew members, some of whom awoke less sure of their decision than they had been the night before. Acquiring these things proved simpler than it should have been when they happened upon three yachts that were until recently occupied by a group of young people (but owned by their parents) who vacated the boats to play on the beach. Confiscating the yachts' entire wardrobe proved a manageable task. To be decent, the pirates left a bathing suit or two for the young ladies.

It did not take long before the *Helga II*'s cramped quarters led to grumbling from the crew, who passed the message along to the first mate. Ronaldinho approached his oblivious captain.

"We don't all fit so good anymore," the young boy said.

"Very well," replied Captain Hans Heissel.

And so the crew found another group of over-privileged, under-dressed young co-eds frolicking on a beach, and stole their boat without being noticed. Within a couple of weeks, Hans Heissel owned a fleet, small though it may be.

It was soon decided that patrolling the shores of Corsica was only adventurous to a point, so the pirates set out on the high seas. By this time the members of the rugby team were wearing their uniforms less and less in favor of the posh commandeered clothing. However, Hans Heissel continued to wear his royal blue and yellow jersey each day. Over the top of his long-sleeved button-up shirt. Ronaldinho also chose to wear his jersey, even though it was extra large so he was swimming in it.

The soon-to-be-terror of the yet-to-be-dreaded pirate Captain Hans Heissel Jr. had begun in earnest.

18

Every Saturday and Sunday night was karaoke night aboard the *Queen Ivan*, in the dance hall that was rarely danced in, a big room with finished wooden floors and those folding chairs with leather cushions. The dance hall also had mirrors on most of the walls, leading to the nickname "Hall of Mirrors." The room had a few especially stubby chandeliers because the ceiling was low. One crew member, millimeters short of seven feet tall, was thus forbidden from entering the Hall of Mirrors. He entered once, and very nearly needed stitches.

One Sunday evening, mostly middle-aged tourists in typical touristy garb filled the Hall of Mirrors. They pretended that they just stumbled upon karaoke unawares, but might as well stay for a drink to watch someone else make a fool of him/herself. In reality, none of the clientèle were very good at acting, so it was rather obvious they were all there to sing a favorite Elton John song or number from *Grease*.

The DJ aboard the *Queen Ivan* was the youngest crew member, a home-schooled lad of fifteen, who was something of a cowboy, having grown up on a ranch in southern Colorado. He had the unusual bullet point on his resume of experience garnered under the tutelage of a mother who was the premier church disc jockey in four mostly rural counties, emceeing any church functions that specifically called for dancing. So, like mother, like son.

Toby wandered into the Hall of Mirrors when he was cleaning something or was bored. On this evening, unfortunately, it was the former, as the bartender had overestimated his vodka-bottle-juggling abilities. So Toby was beckoned. He begrudgingly cleaned up, since it was his job, but wished the bartender understood that trying to show off to customers carried with it more consequences than when Toby tried to show off his ability to juggle dustpans for passing seagulls.

He entered the Hall of Mirrors with broom and dustpan under one arm and mop and bucket pushed with the other. His expression soured further when he was greeted by the fourth-rate vocals of a graying man in loafers and polo shirt coughing up a certain arrangement of every other word from "Radar Love." Toby could immediately discern where the man's wife and relatives/friends were seated from their loud cackling. The young man walked toward the bar and easily scoped out where the many-proof mess was. Pushing the mop and bucket against the wall, he opted to first sweep up the glass.

When what to his wondering eyes should appear but Melinda. She was seated on a stool by the bar with zero drinks in front of her. Despite it being a bar, minors among the crew often sat to keep the bartenders company, citing international-waters twaddle. Her blonde hair fell back behind her ears and cascaded down her magnificently laundered polo shirt. One of her legs was crossed in front of the other, and her hands were clasped in front of a well-toned knee, which was connected to a foot that was kicking to the bass line of "Radar Love." She was smiling merrily and seemed to think that the graying man and his loafers put on quite a show.

Toby turned and looked at the singer, and it suddenly occurred to him that this was the greatest karaoke performance he had ever witnessed. Certainly this man could get some sort of record deal once they hit land. Toby let a delighted grin smear across his face and laughed an "I'm not laughing *at* you, I'm laughing *with* you" laugh. The woman who was nearly in tears at the loud table even looked over and saw Toby give her a thumbs-up. Caught up in the exuberance, Toby bucked trends and, placing the broom against an unoccupied bar stool, approached Melinda.

That smile of hers didn't waver as he neared, nor did her marble-sculpture pose. She gazed over and presented such a warm countenance that had Toby been made of weaker-bonded elements, he certainly would have melted. It appeared that she was more than happy to see a familiar face.

"Hey!" Toby began, almost pinching himself for being too enthusiastic.

His enthusiasm was matched, though, or multiplied by 2.6, and with sincerity. "Hi, Toby!"

She remembers my name, thought Toby ecstatically. Well, let's go, feet. That's enough for one night.

But he was able to keep this thought in check, and instead spoke with resolve. "This guy sure is great, isn't he?"

"Yeah. He's a riot."

"I really like this song." Toby nearly winced, wishing he could retract that statement. He felt he had just killed any chance of impressing the girl of his dreams.

"Me, too!" responded Melinda.

A pause singed the air between them, which Melinda didn't notice as she watched the man with the microphone. The pause felt like a tide change to Toby.

"Neat," he chirped.

Mercifully the song ended. Melinda and Toby clapped and cheered. The singer acknowledged them with a wave and returned the microphone to the young, self-serious DJ. Toby nearly panicked as he sensed Melinda was about to say she needed to get going. Instead, she turned toward him.

"Have a seat, Toby."

The mousy young man did as he was told. Had she told him to find the captain and stab him with a fork, he may well have done so.

"So what's new?" Melinda casually asked, lightly leaning on the bar, as if leaning toward the drink she didn't have.

Toby told himself to remain even-keeled.

"Not much. They just sent me down here to clean up the mess the bartender made."

"I'm right here and you aren't speaking that softly," pointed out the gaunt-faced bartender.

Toby was alarmed, but as the bartender grumbled while he wiped a tumbler, Melinda chuckled. So the young man relaxed a little, once again.

"What about you?" Toby inquired.

Melinda sighed. "I just had some time on my hands, and I like coming down here on karaoke night. It's always fun to watch people."

"Right," Toby smiled. That was all he could muster.

"So what do you think of that Riggins guy?" she asked with genuine interest.

Toby told the truth, since he thought that's what she wanted to hear. "I think he's great! I honestly didn't know how I would entertain myself aboard this ship. He's really helped in that department."

Melinda chuckled. It was a cute little chuckle. Toby couldn't help but love the sound of it.

"Yeah, he's one of the most interesting people I've met in long time," she said. "Did you hear his story about having to use himself as a propeller to get back to Argentina from the Falkland Islands?"

Toby smiled and looked at the floor. "Yeah. That was a good one."

"I wonder how often any of it is true," wondered Melinda. This hadn't occurred to Toby. He had an exceptional record of taking people at their word.

"I don't know" was the best he came up with.

"Well, I would think that at least bits and pieces must be based in fact," Melinda thought out loud, "but I think some elements of his tales are too outlandish to believe, of course." She chuckled again.

Toby missed his cue to reciprocate the laugh. He was staring at the floor, suddenly a tad disappointed that all of those stories might not be gospel truth. But looking up to see Melinda's expression, quickly added a chuckle of his own.

He shook his head and shrugged. "I guess we may never know."

Melinda nodded. When she looked toward the dance floor, Toby's frown resurfaced. Melinda's attention had been piqued when she noticed the DJ's eyes were scouring the room.

The young cowboy spoke into his microphone. "So, we are out of singers for the evening, if no one else wants to come up and give this here thing a try."

"Did you hear that?" Melinda said as she turned back to Toby.

"What?"

"Apparently they're all out of karaoke-ers." Melinda was adorable when she made up words.

"That's too bad."

"I guess this crowd isn't the outgoing type," she said as she surveyed the sparse gathering.

"Mmmm," mmmed Toby, as he too looked around.

"Hey! We could go up there!" exclaimed Melinda.

Toby gulped. *It had been a trick! That's what she was trying to get at all along!* Being in front of crowds, however sparse or intoxicated they may be, was not his idea of fun.

"Oh, naw, that's okay," he said.

"Oh come on! It'll be fun!" Melinda looked as though she really thought this was true.

"I'm really not the singing type."

"Please? I don't want to go up alone." Though warm and outgoing, Melinda lacked the show business gene. She only sang in front of a crowd on a couple of church youth group trips, and only when she was around friends, laughing hysterically.

She looked at him with eyes that he could not say no to, hard as he might try.

"Well, okay."

Melinda looked angelically astonished. "Great! Thank

you! Now what should we sing?"

"We could sing another Golden Earring song," suggested Toby, but immediately thought, *No, idiot! Nobody knows any other Golden Earring songs!*

But he was saved, as Melinda presumed it was a joke. She didn't even know what Golden Earring was, though she concluded it must be the band that did "Radar Love" when it was not being performed by the graying man in loafers.

"What about something from *Grease*?" asked Melinda.

"Well, what about something else. Like..." Toby tried frantically to wrap his head around any song that wasn't from that movie, but now all he could think about was the fact that he accidentally knew all the words to "Summer Lovin'," "Grease Lightning," and "You're the One that I Want." He cursed himself. "Like..."

"Ooh!" Melinda started. "What about 'Don't Go Breaking my Heart'?"

Toby did not want to sing that, or anything. But from the look in her eyes, he could sense her mind was already made up. So he would do it, though he worried that it was too soon in their relationship to be pleading with one another to refrain from breaking each other's respective hearts.

Melinda trotted off to report to the young cowboy DJ. *Oh, how she trots,* thought Toby. A moment later she was back, sitting at the bar and smiling at him. He ascertained how pensive he must look when Melinda patted him on the shoulder and said in the most twinkling tone, "This'll be fun!"

And in less than ten seconds, the DJ, with labored

enthusiasm, announced, "Let's get Melinda and Toby up here!" Melinda's face brightened, though Toby could tell she was also nervous.

"Wow! That didn't take long!" she said as she hopped off her bar stool. Toby shuffled his feet along as if being led to the gallows. Melinda was not so forward as to escort him by the hand. At the DJ's command center, the young cowboy was fidgeting around for a second microphone, found it, and handed it to Toby, seeing as Melinda had already commandeered the one on the microphone stand. Toby walked up to Melinda's side and pretended to copy her smile. As the intro to the song began, Toby asked the obvious question.

"So do you want to be Elton John or Kiki Dee?"

Melinda did not know who Kiki Dee was. "Um … I'll be Elton John."

"Okay," Toby responded.

The song began, and Melinda botched the very first line, which shouldn't have been that hard since it was the title of the song. Toby smiled (again) and Melinda giggled at herself, though none of the people in the audience did. On the next line, Toby's part went smoother, though unemotionally, and he didn't even need to read the words from the little TV. He figured that probably lots of people think Elton John's part is easier because they know who Elton John is, but really Kiki Dee's portion was the simpler of the two because it was mostly the response to Sir Elton's bullet points. Oh well.

Melinda eventually realized she might not know as many of the words as she assumed and began reading straight from the screen, looking up at Toby only at the chorus. Toby didn't need to look at the screen. He had a chance to watch Melinda. *Oh, how she could sing!* She squinted a little at the words here and there because her contacts weren't in, but she could carry a tune well enough after playing the flute for six years. At each chorus, when she looked up at him, chortling at the mistakes she made, Toby would look away again, too shy to sing directly to her. He would turn to the crowd and pretend, for her sake, that he was having a good time.

As the last chorus began, Toby worked up the courage to face her. He found a spot directly above her head and stared at it. This seemed a little odd to Melinda, who wondered if he, too, had contacts that weren't in. As the song faded to its conclusion, Toby chanced a quick glimpse down her forehead and into her green eyes. It made her smile. It made him hiccup.

Though the performance would have procured a dismissal from even the most lenient of reality show judges, there was a polite round of applause. One man, who had not been paying attention, whistled loudly. Melinda smiled gratefully and Toby smiled hesitantly.

He devotedly followed her from the stage to the bar. They picked two new seats since two women and a man had somehow taken their spot while they were singing, despite the bar being mostly empty. As crew members, they were not allowed to argue over seats.

"That was fun!" Melinda exclaimed. Toby inspected her face and thought, *Oh, she's serious!*

"I guess it wasn't so bad," he conceded, whether he believed it or not.

Melinda pointed as two and then three people walked

toward the DJ. "I think we started a trend. Or restarted one, I guess."

Toby sighed, which is what he sometimes did when he didn't know what to say. Melinda added, "Well, thanks for doing that."

"Oh, yeah. It was no problem. And I guess it was kind of fun." Still feeling awkward and searching for something to say, Toby impulsively knocked on the bar instead.

"Yeah," Melinda said. It appeared she was just about to say something else, hopefully something lovely, when the gaunt-faced bartender walked over, looking displeased.

"What's this?" he asked, looking at Toby. He mockingly knocked on the bar, imitating Toby's rap. "What's this?" he asked again in quick succession.

"I … er …" went Toby's mouth.

"Do you need something? Is this how you beckon your servant?" He knocked on the bar again. "What *is* this?" One more knock.

"No. I …was just trying to explain something to her," Toby pointed at Melinda and immediately regretted it, since it looked like he was blaming her.

"Well, if you don't *need* anything, there is still a mess to clean up," the gaunt face said as it walked away. Melinda giggled once the bartender was out of earshot. She covered her mouth to not offend Toby.

"I'm sorry. Really," she said.

Toby's attitude brightened to see her amused by the encounter. And although he loved to be around her, he realized he was thus far very bad at it, so should be thankful for the bartender's excuse to quit while he was ahead.

"No, it's okay. But I guess I should probably go clean up that mess."

"Well it was fun seeing you. And thanks." And after a pause, "We should try that again sometime."

Toby smiled. "Yeah. Or something."

As he about-faced, Toby recognized two things. Firstly, he realized that "Twilight Zone" might also be a Golden Earring song, and not late-career Steve Miller Band as he had thought. Secondly, he recognized how lucky he was to have spent that much time with the woman of his dreams. He walked away, heart all aflutter.

19

Most pirates do not use advanced mathematical techniques for better pirating. Most pirates do not chart the course of currents and storm patterns with complicated equations. Most pirates do not use algorithms to accurately predict where the best pirating can be accomplished, or how to get the best gas mileage for their boat.

But Hans Heissel Jr. was not most pirates. Despite his new line of work, he had not forgotten his roots. And it did him well to have had that past life.

So each day, the captain of the *Helga II* and the corresponding fleet sequestered himself in his quarters with numerous maps and pads of paper and made copious amounts of calculations. His brow stayed furrowed for hours at a time while he worked out the best course of action for his small armada. His trusty calculator was at his side, but never needed.

Since Hans Heissel Jr. never liked to work where he slept, he first set up his "office" in the back (stern?) of the yacht. It included a swivel chair they had pillaged early on and four sheets of drywall made into a cubicle. There was no roof to it. Hans Heissel had not calculated how often gasoline fumes would waft into his cubicle, so after a few days his work station was relocated to a cozy spot a few paces back from the yacht's steering wheel. This way he could also shout commands to any crew member at the helm (though he rarely did, given his concentration on all that math stuff).

Of all the countless calculations Captain Hans Heissel Jr. made, perhaps the most valuable were those calculations that helped elude capture. When one ambushes a yacht, and then another, and then another, and then a sailboat, and then a few commercial fishing boats, and then so on, the authorities will probably take notice. As they did with the case of Captain Hans Heissel. But unlike most other pirates, Hans did not rely on hiding out or running to stay away from the authorities. Instead he calculated the probabilities of what law enforcement officials would be where and when they would be there. Hans took into account his fleet's previous locations and activities, so that with each new pirating destination his calculations would become longer and longer. It was just as well with Hans, who enjoyed the math as much as another person might enjoy petting a fluffy cat, or if one is allergic to cats, then something equally therapeutic. So whenever the lawmen and law-women believed they were one step ahead of Hans Heissel, Hans Heissel was actually two to three steps ahead of them.

A typical pirate attack would go as such:

The unfortunate boaters would be minding their own business, having the most pleasant of days. They might even be saying to each other, "Honey, isn't this just the most pleasant of days?" as they lounged on the deck, sunbathing, or fishing, or drinking champagne, or whatever their hearts' desire might be.

Just then, they would see another yacht on the horizon.

And make nothing of it. Until that yacht casually chugged right up to them. A man wearing a button-up shirt would be standing near the railing, smiling, and address them like so:

"Good (morning/afternoon/evening)!" to which the curious boaters would usually respond to with "Good" and the appropriate "(morning/afternoon/evening)."

A young boy with dark hair would then step up beside him on the railing, looking adorably forlorn. Behind the pair would be a group of smiling men, appearing quite gentlemanly. The first gent would once again speak.

"I am truly sorry to bother you on this beautiful day, but it seems my extended family and I are nearing the end of our supply of fuel, as some sort of dangerous fish seems to have punctured our fuel tank. We were about to radio for help when we noticed that our radio was smashed in a freak ladder-carrying accident. Would it be at all possible for someone to come aboard and seek help with your radio?" Or some variation on this template.

It was not the most creative or simple plan (but Hans Heissel's forte was math, not play-writing). In some cases the boaters might need a bit of coaxing (often involving the young man starting to cry), but eventually even the hardest nuts to crack took pity on the men with the broken radio.

At this point the man in charge would turn and pick a couple of the strapping, smiling gentlemen to board the boat beside them. After roping the boats together, the two men would oblige, but would be grumbling with each other. The man in charge would chide them; "Zachary! Conrad! Stop fighting!" The men would lower the volume of their grumbles as they stepped onto the adjacent yacht. At least one of the happy boaters would escort them to the radio. Upon reaching the contraption, the two men would start their argument back up again. The confused boater would act oblivious or politely try to defuse the situation. Too late!

As the altercation escalated, one of the men would push the other into the radio. The fallen man would clutch his eye with one hand and feel for the radio's receiver with his other. Then he would take a terrible tumble, carrying the receiver with him. Upon ripping it out of its socket, his partner would run to tattle on him, leaving the boater in a state of shock. With the pushee lying on the deck with a dead receiver in hand, the pusher would alert his boat about the accident that just occurred.

As the confused boaters turned their attention to the man's shouts, they would be surprised to find that the gentlemen on the other yacht had become decidedly ungentlemanly. Those gentlemen pulled a fearful arsenal of weaponry and pointed it menacingly at the now not-so-happy boaters. Unlike the crew, who suddenly seemed to be multiplying from below decks, the man in charge would wear a rather smug but awkward grin, and with dramatic flair, would extract from a nook or cranny not a gun, but a very large and cumbersome newspaper hat.

"Ladies and gentleman," he would call in a contented voice that hinted at social ineptitude. "I am Captain Hans Heissel Jr. I apologize in advance for all the trouble we are going to cause you." He did not sound malicious, but he also didn't sound all that sincere. "We will now rob you blind."

So with their trusty captain's unorthodox approach to buccaneering, the pirates enjoyed a growing number of successes. Through skillful computations (done alone in the captain's quarters), the crew enjoyed the spoils of robbing from the rich and giving to themselves.

Sometimes the pirates would mess up, and the authorities would be notified before plundering ensued. Though he might chide his crew for the misstep, in actuality Hans Heissel reveled in the chance to further his dangerous game of cat and mouse with the sea's nebulously aforementioned "authorities."

They would sometimes make port so they could spend their money better, but Hans rarely took shore leave. He felt it was his duty to love being at sea (despite his constant need of Dramamine). The crewmen found themselves rolling their eyes more and more often as their captain referred to the sea as his "mistress."

A handful of the ambushed took the offer that Captain Hans Heissel presented each of his victims: a spot aboard his crew if they pledged him their loyalty. Here and there a bored rich kid or man having a mid-life crisis signed up, seeing it as the best example of opportunity knocking.

Of course, the added pirates led to crowded boats, and the realization that more boats were needed in the fleet. So a few more yachts were commandeered, including one from which the owners, a retired couple, decided to join the pirates' ranks rather than lose their vessel. Hans begrudgingly agreed that if everyone eventually got sick of pirating, the couple could have the yacht back.

And the fleet ventured farther and farther. At times even Hans Heissel was unsure of their location, and only a floating Hong Kong newspaper or breaching narwhal would lend any indication. It was a pirate's life for Hans Heissel Jr., who finally felt like he had found his life's calling, even though anyone else would have said, "No, your calling is math."

20

Among the stranger hiring decisions aboard the *Queen Ivan* was that of a young pastry chef named Leonid Cupabascim. He was a rather bright young man, though somewhat lacking in experience in the field of pastry-making. But Cupabascim more than made up for it with enthusiasm and a willingness to listen.

Originally the pastry chef position was to be filled by a woman named Maudeen Caruthers, but when her prize-winning goldfish died suddenly, she gave up the position and entered a period of mourning. Though twenty-five years her junior, Cupabascim was the obvious choice, mainly because he was the only applicant and the ship was departing in a matter of hours.

Leonid (or Leo to his friends, but never to his family) was the son of parents who had immigrated to the United States from separate parts of Asia long before his birth. Working on fast, noisy cars was a hobby of his and had once been semi-profitable, before he turned his attention to pastries. Another passion was basketball, which he loved to play, and once loved to watch, until a certain Clayton Stern moved the team Leonid grew up loving. A degree in biochemistry was well under way when Leonid opted for cooking school instead. The Cupabascims were not especially pleased to hear this news, having wanted their son to become a doctor or scientist. Perhaps if their son had been getting better grades at his college he would not have orchestrated a change in career plans.

So not long after graduating from his cooking school, word of an opening as pastry chef aboard a luxurious cruise liner found his ears by way of a longshoreman friend of his. "Aw snap!" said young Cupabascim. "That'd be awesome." And being the godsend the cruise line's hiring manager was looking for, but assumed would not be found on such short notice, Leonid was hired before meeting anyone aboard the ship.

Late one night, Toby found himself out strolling the deck of the *Queen Ivan*. The evening was chilly, as it seemed many evenings were in the middle of the Atlantic Ocean. Toby had long since misplaced his company-issued fleece pullover, so he was draped in a thick blanket he had pulled out of a hamper. Wrapping it about him, he could imagine himself as a sailor aboard some ship hundreds of years ago, off to find buried treasure or perhaps to simply transport fish or flour or coffee beans or something. He wondered if sailors of yore would have pulled blankets from the hamper. But no matter how hard he tried to imagine himself swinging from the crow's nest or firing the cannons, his romantic notions of shipboard adventure kept returning to him as cabin boy, continually swabbing the deck.

Toby had had trouble sleeping, which was why he found himself awake in the middle of the night. Something in a pastry baked by that Leonid character did not agree with him, and he felt that fresh air would do him good. The deck was quite still, as most of the passengers were snuggled in their beds or at one of the ship's bars. Toby walked to the port side (or was it the starboard?) and watched the calm blackness of the sea lazily roll over as the ship cut through it. Straight ahead the moon in the cloudless sky reflected off the water just as it did on page three of the *Queen Ivan's* brochure. Toby felt comforted by the tranquility of the night, but wondered if his stomach would ever feel better.

His thoughts once again wandered to Melinda. Propping his elbow on the railing, he sighed with his cheek in his hand and stared into nothingness endearingly. He knew it would never work between them. She was from an upper-middle-class family, and would be going off to college sometime soon, while he had not yet worked out what to do once the *Queen Ivan* returned to Miami (including finding a way home from the dock). She was beautiful and smart, while he took blankets out of hampers. And she was a whole year older than him! That age difference could probably never be reconciled. *Oh, Melinda*, thought Toby, *If only...*

Sighing again, he pushed off the railing and walked over to the other side of the ship (so, starboard maybe? Or...) to see what thoughts could be had there. The scenery was quite similar, minus the presence of the moon, which remained on the other side (port...?). Was there a way to let Melinda know how he felt? All his ideas revolved around passing notes or gossiping with her friends. And since he could not recollect Melinda having any close friends aboard, it seemed this was not a valid option.

It was as Toby was leaning over the railing, entertaining these thoughts about love notes and box socials and whatnot, that he noticed movement on a lower level of the ship. The mousy young man squinted into the darkness at something moving about near the back (aft?) end of the ship, about twenty feet below him. He peered as hard as he could peer. He gasped. *Melinda!*

No, it was a fishing pole. He was glad he had not called out loud. But then he pondered just what a fishing pole was doing extended over the side of the *Queen Ivan*. As he watched, the pole bobbed just a hair, and its line trailed out behind the boat. For the most part the scene appeared completely peaceful, almost ordinary, as if there was nothing odd about a fishing pole hanging over the side of a luxurious cruise liner in the middle of the Atlantic Ocean.

Toby spent little time contemplating protocol. He moved a few steps closer to where the pole was, keeping enough distance that he would not frighten it away. He yearned to see the pole succeed in its purpose, most likely by catching a big one. He tried telling himself this was a stupid hope and that he was trying to solve a mystery, but when the pole bent he gasped with excitement. A fish! Perhaps. Whoever was holding the pole pulled it back and began reeling in speedily. After a lengthy battle with the mighty creature of the deep, the line was finally reeled in enough for a sizable fish to pop out of the water. Toby gave a little clap. He could not tell if the pole's owner heard this outburst or not, but either way the line, pole, and displeased fish were all quickly yanked back into whatever door, window, or porthole they had come through (well, the displeased fish wasn't going *back* through) .

The whole incident was strange, of course, but Toby chose not to investigate further, since it was only getting later and he couldn't really see what rule of conduct was being violated by the mysterious fisherman or fisherlady anyhow. He looked out at the wide ocean once again, and seeing that it was back to its standard calm, retreated toward his sleeping quarters, thinking of ways to metaphorically link his love for Melinda with the recently witnessed fishing expedition.

21

It was late one other night and Toby was returning some laundry to its home when he noticed a trail of water on the floor in one of the hallways. Not usually one to do much detective work, Toby might have left the curious trail to its own devices had he not considered this was one more obstacle he could get in trouble for. He could hear the cruise director saying, after a passenger slipped and threatened to sue, "You saw a puddle and you didn't do anything about it?" So Toby thought he would explore further (instead of just cleaning it up).

Strangely, the trail led to a door meant for staff only, because it opened to a room that was all pipes and important machine parts that Toby had no business being in. What business a trail of water could have in there was beyond him. Yet he opened the unlocked door and entered.

The inside of the room was large and rather dark and full of tubes and gears that went through walls and must have been connected to other tubes and gears found elsewhere on the ship. Toby could admit to himself that it was a little scary, especially walking around alone. A flashlight would have proved useful at this juncture, but overhead was a soft light that at least illuminated enough for Toby to see where he was stepping. Deeper into the room the young man went, walking quietly and cautiously, as if he were in a horror movie and was about to be stabbed. But Toby felt that the more time he wasted here, the less time he would spend doing some menial task.

The trail of water was thin in places, and was nice big puddles in others, so he continued alongside it, attempting not to slip and break his hip (since this was now a very real fear of his, seeing as how he heard numerous passengers worry about such an event). Toby theorized what the trail could lead to, but his ideas were either too boring or too far-fetched, so he stopped theorizing.

Three feet short of the back wall, near a point where tubes and gears and whatnot went through to the neighboring room, Toby found himself looking up at a large cylinder. It was iron-colored and not that exciting. But it was dripping. Onto his white-and-green-striped polo shirt. He peered upward for a few minutes trying to discern where exactly the drip was manifesting itself, but in the dim light he had little success. He shrugged and decided that the tiny drip had somehow made a puddle, which some crew member had somehow traipsed back into the passenger cabin. It was not a very exciting conclusion, but Toby didn't care that much. He would just tell a more senior coworker and call it good.

He almost made it the whole length of the room, side stepping puddles and watching where he put his head, when he heard a sneeze. It chilled him to the bone, and he felt himself break out in a cold sweat, though only on one shoulder. Realizing that his cold sweat was simply the water that had dripped on him, he gulped hard and once again began tiptoeing toward the back of the room. Though it was probably only a worker of some sort fixing some small mechanical trouble, Toby stayed alert.

He ducked into a nook in the back corner of the room that was semi-protected from view by a set of large pipes, then noticed a few pieces of torn cardboard, dull enough in color to easily go unnoticed, patching up some of the spaces between piping. Toby was confused. Hearing another sneeze, he jumped a little, then calmed himself and inched toward the enclosure. As he went around to the one exposed side, he saw wrapping paper creating a makeshift door into the hideout. Unsure and uninterested in protocol, Toby peered through a shoe box-sized gap in the cardboard pieces.

Inside the little fortress, Toby saw assorted odds and ends, some silverware, and a fishing pole. Also a man wrapped in a towel. The man whistled a tune and appeared to be in good spirits. Until he glanced over and saw Toby's head.

The man screamed. Partly because he was wearing nothing but a towel. Toby screamed back, then turned to flee, but upon getting confused by the pipes running all along his head, turned completely around to face the little enclosure again. He looked for the exit, before a hand came through the wrapping paper and pulled him into the makeshift den, accompanied by soft shushing noises.

"Shh. It's okay, it's okay," said a reassuring voice behind him, before the hand let go. Toby turned to see the man in the towel giving a very forced grin as he used one hand to secure the drying implement around his waist. "Okay, hi," he continued, holding out his other hand. "I'm Jamie."

Toby was very confused. But this Jamie character seemed harmless, so with a puzzled look, the mousy young man offered his hand for the shaking. The two hands performed their ritual and released. Jamie kept smiling as he asked in a cordial voice, "And who would you happen to be?"

"I'm Toby," Toby said.

"Toby! Great! Awesome, Toby! It's great to meet you!" Jamie replied, maybe a bit too energetically.

"Hi," Toby said, hesitantly.

"Hey, you want to have a seat?" Jamie pointed to one of the two upturned plastic crates inside his tiny fortress. Toby didn't see why he shouldn't, so he obliged. Jamie exhaled with relief and then looked around for something with which to entertain his guest.

Toby decided quickly that this man in nothing but a towel posed no threat. He might have been a little too quick to jump to this conclusion, and it fleetingly occurred to him that his high level of trust might someday get him into trouble, but at the moment the mousy-haired boy was too curious about Jamie to be concerned with his own safety. Curiosity had a real ebb and flow with Toby.

Jamie Brewster was rather shocked when the young man took a seat. He was expecting some reply along the lines of, "Let me go! Help! Help! Help!" or "Please, sir, I don't want to die!" or at best "You've got two minutes to explain yourself before I go alert the captain." Instead he now had a teenager seated in his hiding spot, seemingly unconcerned about finding a stowaway. Jamie thought he should do everything to keep this Toby character happy. He glanced about and fiddled with his hands as he searched the small enclosure. Then he saw something that might help, atop a pile of clothes.

"Cookie? Does Toby want a cookie?" He held out the red package to Toby and regretted his wording. Just as he realized he should have eaten first to prove they were not poisoned, the boy grabbed one. Jamie took one himself. He bit into it and grinned. "Mm! These are good cookies."

"Thanks," said Toby, after a moment's pause. The two continued eating their cookies, nodding slowly at nothing in the quiet awkwardness. Jamie offered another cookie and Toby accepted.

"So what are you doing down here?" Toby asked, effectively dropping the bomb Jamie was hoping might be deflected with enough cookies. Jamie had two simple choices: either tell the truth or lie. It was a dilemma he had pondered numerous times already during the *Queen Ivan's* voyage, but he somehow kept putting off creating a good excuse to use if discovered.

"What am I doing down here?" Jamie repeated, then more reflectively re-repeated.

"Yup," Toby said through a mouthful of cookie in his regular nonchalant tone.

Jamie turned his back to his visitor and searched the small fort. He did not know what he was searching for, but hoped something would jump out at him to aid his decision. He thought he might flip a coin to see whether to explain the real circumstances or make some up, but since he had left his wallet at his mother's house, he possessed no coinage. So he flipped a cookie.

Okay, heads you tell the truth, tails you make up a lie. With this thought, the toweled stowaway flipped one of the cookies. It broke in half when it hit the ground, but the larger portion had the underside up. *All right, you lie.*

"Well, it's a long story, Toby," Jamie said as he sat down upon the other crate.

As his story unfolded, a strange thing happened: Jamie accidentally told the truth. Maybe deep down he yearned to update someone about what had been going on in his life in the last few days. He really meant to lie, and it hadn't seemed like such a tall order, given the fact that any lie would probably be more plausible than his real story.

When he finished, he looked at Toby, sure that the boy would be disappointed at being lied to. Instead, Toby's expression showed he was impressed.

"Wow," the young man said, nodding his head. "You've had a busy week."

"I'll say," Jamie agreed.

"So you're after treasure..."

Jamie bit his lip. "Yeah, I guess so."

"On the Gelatin Coast..." Toby continued.

"Yup," replied Jamie. "Except I don't know too much about the treasure. But when I find it, I figure it will probably help me get my coworkers back."

"I would think so," said Toby. "My understanding is that treasure could probably fix some other problems, too."

"That would be great," Jamie said, cautiously. He started to wonder if Toby's point was that he needed some bribing to keep quiet about discovering a stowaway. But the teen switched topics.

"How is it no one else has found you yet?" he asked Jamie.

Jamie shrugged. "I really don't know. I had been kind

of wondering that myself." The truth was that the man who was supposed to be checking the pipes was very lazy and better at lying than Jamie.

Toby sighed. Jamie froze to see what the sigh signified.

"And I'm going to put all this stuff I borrowed back," Jamie pointed to the fishing pole. "I swear."

Toby didn't seem to hear him. "Well, Jamie, I wish you luck upon your way." The teen put out a hand to shake. "I better go because I'm supposed to be moving laundry around or something. And I don't want to get yelled at again."

Jamie shook his hand guardedly. He smiled meekly as he made an important request. "Um … so, I guess it would be really great if … you didn't mention that I'm down here. To anyone."

It appeared to Jamie that a light bulb when off in Toby's head. "Oh man, I hadn't even thought about that," the boy said, then straightened. "Yeah, no problem."

Jamie wanted a bit more assurance. "Really?"

Toby shrugged. "Yeah, really. I won't say anything. It's no problem," he responded as if he had been asked to pick up a loaf of the cheapest white bread while he was at the grocery store.

Jamie did not know what to think of this new acquaintance, but felt better. "Thanks," he said.

Toby waved and made his way back to the hallway. He was delighted to have met a stowaway and would have desperately loved to have shown him off to Melinda, but figured that he better not. He found the laundry bin again and whistled as he pushed it in a generally northern direction.

22

They had shaved Janet's head. Her captors had shaved all of Janet's beautiful golden locks, leaving the anchorwoman bald.

Other than that, however, Janet had few complaints about her treatment.

As she sat gnawing on an apricot, the newswoman contemplated her last few days. They had been bizarre, sure, but bizarre could mean good news for a reporter.

Though sitting in a helicopter in a suburban backyard during a police chase had been strange enough, things only got stranger once Jamie entered his mother's house. Janet became livid, and Tom had been none too pleased either. But the two sat in the helicopter with their arms crossed, crossly awaiting Jamie's return so they could berate him. Janet kept tapping her foot, and after a few too many minutes she contemplated physically extracting her pilot from the house.

When a figure appeared at the cockpit's door, Janet began ranting before realizing that the person was not Jamie.

"What is wrong with you, Brewster! You are the single most...!" Janet gasped.

He was an Asian man with a long, flowing mustache and thinning, wispy longish hair. The man looked at her and then at Tom, then gracefully hopped into the driver's seat. Instinctively Janet looked to the other door for an exit, but it, too, was being entered. By another Asian man. With another long, flowing mustache. He might have been a little heftier than his partner. Now it was Tom's turn to gasp. Once comfortably seated in the copter with belts buckled, the two men put on two radio headsets that were lying around. They began speaking in a language neither Janet nor Tom understood.

Janet and Tom were unnerved. And stuck. There would be no way to push past either of the men to escape. They remained silent, holding their breath as they awaited further developments. The men kept talking, using their hands to illustrate whatever stance each was taking. There was a bit of pointing, and a little bickering, which can often be distinguished by non-native speakers.

Then the man in the passenger seat turned around. He forced a smile, then attempted to offer an explanation in heavily accented English.

"Good afternoon," he began.

"Good afternoon," replied Janet.

The man nodded. His partner flipped some switches on the helicopter's controls and fiddled around with all the knobs and gauges that you would expect one might fiddle with before takeoff.

"Um ... could we get out, please?" asked Tom.

The man in the passenger seat said this would not be allowed, and a moment later Janet and Tom could feel the helicopter disengaging from the ground. At this point the news team was briefed.

There was something about digging up treasure, and something about a place called the Gelatin Coast. This was all the information Jamie Brewster would receive, but there was a good deal more.

It turned out that the man talking was named Koke and the gentleman orchestrating the aircraft's ascent was named Kipchak. The two men belonged to an organization which they claimed was quite secretive, but after Janet's fateful radio conversation with Jamie, her journalistic pushiness uncovered that their outfit was actually trying to be quite the opposite.

Their organization produced "traditional" medicines derived from animal body parts. This was apparently a sizable trade in certain regions of Asia, and their group, called the Abominable Snowman Dragons (or rather, the Associates of Mr. Abominable Snowman Dragons, in a somewhat poor translation that made them sound like a magical law firm), was looking to become a major power in this trade. The Associates were attempting to turn the trafficking of animals, especially endangered species, into a marketable enterprise.

And that's where Janet and Tom came in. Koke and Kipchak, along with their now-arrested brethren who lost the foot race with police, had been in Savannah, Georgia trying to steal a certain pangolin (an intriguing animal worth giving a look) from the city's zoo. It was not a crime that was usually attempted. Due to the confusion they caused, the men were able to extend the hunt for them into a high-speed chase and the eventual stealing of a helicopter. As luck would have it (for the Abominable Snowman Dragons and not Jamie Brewster), Kipchak had served in the Mongolian military and learned to fly helicopters in his younger days. When the four fugitives split up, Kipchak and Koke had stayed together. Kipchak never really thought he would actually come across an unmanned helicopter just itching for the taking, but there it was sitting in someone's backyard.

Happening upon a news crew was more good luck for the Mongolians. Both Kipchak and Koke had the same thought in mind. At first, Janet believed that she and Tom were going to be high-profile hostages, a prospect that sounded mostly unappealing, but might garner a good deal of publicity if she was not executed. She went on to assume, when Koke told her they had use for the news team, that the men intended to make some sort of terrorist video, in which Koke and Kipchak would demand millions as the camera dramatically panned past the bound and malnourished Janet and Tom.

Her assumption was incorrect. Janet and Tom were to be used in a television commercial for the Associates of Mr. Abominable Snowman Dragons. While in the United States, the men tried to see if there was interest enough to expand their organization's operation there. And what better way to appeal to a wider audience than through a commercial? The Mongolians thought it was an excellent idea, one which their leader would be delighted with. They had yet to consider how the commercial might be seen, or who exactly would be watching it. Koke and Kipchak thought only of the production.

Janet and Tom did not have much say in the matter, but their captors tried, with their thick accents, to make the idea sound like a golden opportunity. They kept mentioning Hollywood, and how this commercial would make Janet and Tom "big shots." Janet and Tom were unconvinced.

The helicopter flew unimpeded to the waters east of Savannah, since witnesses believed it to be an unassuming news helicopter. Had Jamie Brewster contacted authorities about the mix-up, things may have been different. But seeing as how Jamie thought he had suddenly become America's most wanted fugitive, no one stopped the helicopter. Kipchak and Koke turned the radio off. Corresponding radio controllers assumed a mechanical glitch.

Kipchak deftly maneuvered the aircraft onto a dark and aged barge-like ship that was sitting in the harbor. Janet and Tom remained uninformed until after the ten-point landing that the boat was manned by semi-criminals who had been paid off to transport the Mongolians to Africa.

The news team was rushed into the ship's bowels, as Kipchak and Koke feared them being seen. The captors tried hard to act more like guides than captors, smiling to indicate that Janet and Tom were doing a good job of following them. Occasionally Koke or Kipchak would point to something interesting as if they were in a museum, in the hopes of making their guests feel more at ease. Eventually the path led to a room that Koke and Kipchak seemed somewhat apprehensive about entering. When they winced and opened the door, Janet and Tom could see why.

A section of the boat had been turned into an ocean-bound zoo. Separated spaces were transformed into animal cages, most of them occupied. Here was a peacock, there was a badger, and over yonder was a porcupine. In other cages were a hefty pig, an ocelot, an orangutan, a koala, a Komodo dragon, a gazelle, and a three-toed sloth. None looked all that keen on being there.

Koke and Kipchak smiled as they showed off their wares. The news team was not unimpressed, but both were concerned for the well being of the captive critters. It looked like the animals were at least being fed, but their cubicles made the analogy of death-row inmates an easy one to draw. Out of the corner of her eye, Janet was almost sure the orangutan was rapping a tin cup along the bars of his cage.

Paying little heed to the reactions of Janet and Tom, the smugglers led on through a metal door to a staircase. Janet did not look back for fear of seeing the animals plead with her. As the small group ascended the stairs, Janet and Tom saw their captors had led them into some sort of command center. Numerous men were seated around the table, some smoking. The room was dimly lit, until Koke turned on a bank of lights, awakening a couple of sleepers in yellow and orange rain slickers.

What Janet and Tom were not expecting was to recognize any of these men. But they did.

Aside from two more Mongolians who greeted Koke and Kipchak, the rest of the men were American. Of the five guys who were obviously a crabbing boat crew, Janet recognized four, and knew three of their names. It took her no time at all to identify them from reality television. The men were the stars of a program that followed the strenuous life aboard their crabbing boat.

Or at least they had been, until the show was canceled about nine months prior.

The huskiest man, Captain Orvelly, a gruff but lovable

leader on the show, acknowledged them.

"Hello and how do you do," the gruff man said gruffly, then immediately turned to address Koke and Kipchak. "What did you just do?" he asked, speckling the question with a few oaths.

It became apparent to Janet and Tom that kidnapping had not been part of whatever contract the Mongolians had struck with the crabbing crew. Koke and Kipchak gave some nonchalant shrugs, failing to see what "the big deal" was. After some non-heated arguing between the two sides, Janet and Tom were invited to take a seat at the table. Fred, who Janet remembered as the misfit of the crew, constantly being chided by his surlier shipmates on the show, was ordered to get them some food. He returned shortly, pushing his glasses back up his nose, with the biggest bag of pretzels Tom had ever seen. As they were fed, Koke, Kipchak, Captain Orvelly, and Fred tried to catch them up.

"We needed a boat to transport our animals around," offered Kipchak.

"And we came cheap," reported Captain Orvelly, rather displeased with himself.

"After years of trying to catch wild animals," Koke said, "our organization realized the easiness of just taking animals from zoos." Janet and Tom could not see the easiness of this endeavor, assuming that zoos are well-guarded. This assumption was mostly correct. It became apparent from the Mongolians' narration that their organization was not necessarily adept at stealing animals from zoos. Rather, there had been safety in numbers: apparently sixteen men had made the trek to kidnap animals in America, with Koke, Kipchak, and the other two at the table the only members not in jail.

When the subject reached how the reality television crabbers had become involved, Captain Orvelly became tired of the conversation and got up to leave, along with a couple of the other crabbers.

"You see," Fred began, "we were never very good at crabbing. We got a show because we apparently were more entertaining than most other crabbers and because we came cheap." He pushed some curly black hair out of his face, leaving a smudge of some goo you'd find on a crabbing vessel. "So when our show got canceled, we needed another means of employment, because scouring the ocean for crab just wasn't working out that well.

"So when these guys came looking for a boat to drive some animals around in," Fred continued, "Captain Orvelly jumped at the chance. Then most of the crew grumbled like they always do." Fred adjusted his glasses again and sniffled. He had not been the hunkiest guy on the television show. "Now here we are. Transporting all those animals around while everyone assumes we're out crabbing."

"Oh," said Janet. She tried never to let news surprise her, but this time it had.

Eventually Janet and Tom realized they had been updated as much as they were going to be. The Mongolians grinned at them and repeated the word "Hollywood." Fred was put in charge of showing them to their makeshift quarters, which he quickly straightened up. Since Fred seemed to be the nicest member of the crew, Janet tried to take advantage of this.

"Fred," she said, "what exactly are we doing?"

"I'm not completely sure," he replied. "You'll have to ask someone more in the know." He shrugged and pushed his glasses back up his nose. "I guess we are going to some place in Africa called the Gelatin Coast, though. Or something like that. The Mongolians have some business there. I guess we get paid for all of this, somehow. Probably through the treasure they've been mentioning. I don't know. This is pretty new to us."

As soon as he left, all four Mongolians arrived, all smiles.

"We hope you are both very comfortable," Koke told them, ignoring the fact that their quarters resembled a damp broom closet, though damper.

"Thank you," replied Tom, hesitant to make trouble with their captors.

"Oh," smiled Kipchak politely, turning to Janet, "and we need to shave your head."

23

The Johnson-Katsopolis wedding was set to take place aboard the *Queen Ivan* three days before its arrival in Capetown. Both Delilah Johnson and Joey Katsopolis came from wealthy families, and said families decided to put quite a bit of this wealth into their luxurious destination wedding. The company that operated the *Queen Ivan* thought it was a lovely idea, as long as they could take plenty of pictures to put in brochures. The whole concept for the wedding went a little overboard (excuse the choice of words), so some of the more traditional family members condemned it as being too nontraditional. Namely, many of the Katsopolises (along with the Samponsopopolises— Joey's mother's side) felt that the wedding should be in the church that thirty-something years before held the Katsopolis-Samponsopopolis wedding. Of course, part of Delilah and Joey's rationale was that being married on a boat might help to keep the number of traditionalist relatives to a minimum.

Still, plenty of family members decided to come on the wedding cruise, which of course was not a wedding cruise for the rest of the passengers. The couple's honeymoon was to occur in Cape Town, which would offer the wedding guests something to do while the newlyweds went off on their own. None of the guests had ever been to Cape Town.

Although Toby was often called upon to clean up messes aboard the *Queen Ivan*, they were usually messes others had created. But when, through a strange mustache and beguiling eye patch, he discerned the face of All-Star third baseman Benito Martinez, Toby dropped the porcelain plate he was holding. It shattered on the floor amid shattering noises. It took Toby a good two and a half seconds to even notice. As he watched the celebrity trying to inch away, Toby stepped over the jagged pieces and walked toward the famous baseball player with a twinkle in his eye and a dumb grin on his face.

Many people, like Benito, were standing in line for the buffet. Many of them witnessed the mousy young man drop a plate and then abandon the mess. Plenty of witnesses turned up their noses at this display of neglect, yet others watched in curiosity as the boy moved toward the back of the line. He seemed to be approaching a tall gentleman who wanted nothing to do with him without making it look like he wanted nothing to do with him. The man tried to look unconcerned by inspecting fruit on the buffet table as he moved backward. Eventually the man left the buffet line altogether with nothing but half a piece of cantaloupe on his plate.

Benito pretended to inspect the fire alarm, then noticed out of the corner of his eye that the boy was still in pursuit. Cursing, Benito exited into the hallway and stepped into an alcove leading to a locked door, plate still in hand. Seconds later the boy found him trying to hide. There was still a stupid smile on the young man's face and he seemed oblivious to the fact that Benito was trying to avoid him.

"Oh my gosh," Toby started. "It is so ... um, much

honorful to make meet you..." For half a second Benito hoped maybe he had mistaken him for someone else. "...Mr. Martinez." Nope.

With that, Toby put out a hand. This was apparently a very big moment in the boy's life, Benito thought. He looked at the outstretched hand. "I'm Toby ... sir."

Still recoiling, Benito presented his hand. Toby flushed and took it. "Wow."

"It's nice to meet you, Toby," Benito told him. This was not true.

"What happened to your eye?" Toby finally asked.

Benito did not know what to say. "Nothing."

"Oh, wow," Toby replied. "Neat." So the two stood there looking at each other, each anticipating the other's move. Benito was not saying that he needed to leave, which the cabin boy took as an invitation for discourse. In Benito's brain this disguise had been foolproof, yet now he was cornered and essentially at the whim of this energetic fan. If this boy blabbed, he was a dead man.

"I like your mustache," Toby offered. This was not completely true, since Toby thought the mustache looked fake and rather stupid. However, he knew enough about the world to know that you are supposed to shower celebrities with compliments if you run into one.

"Thank you," Benito replied. Another pause followed as the guys sized each other up.

"Wow," Toby repeated. "I can't believe Benito Martinez is on board this ship!"

His voice was a little too loud for Benito's liking. The elder man put a muscular finger to the younger's lips. Toby was taken aback a bit, but tried to keep smiling because he did not really care that one of his favorite baseball players was weird, so long as they were hanging out.

"Yes. About that..." Benito began in a subdued voice. Toby cocked his head to listen. "You see, *you* know that I am on board this ship, and *I* know that I am on board this ship, but I'm not so sure everyone else needs to know that I am on this ship."

Toby nodded and Benito continued. "You see, I am here with my lovely wife, and we feel that if too many people were aware that I am here, it might compromise the enjoyability of our vacation."

"Right..."

Benito now spoke in a whisper, so Toby leaned in a bit. "So that is why I have chosen to wear this disguise. To conceal my identity."

"I see..." Toby looked deep in thought.

"Obviously I could not pull the wool over your eyes, though, Tony." Benito said this to make the young man feel like they were pals. It did not aid his cause to call the boy Tony, though.

Toby's lip twitched. "It ... it's Toby." He was scared to correct such a talented baseball player, for fear Benito would say it was Tony now.

Benito made a warm, apologetic motion with his thick, athletic arms. "Toby! Of course it is Toby. I'm so sorry."

"It's okay, Mr. Martinez. And I can keep your secret."

Benito placed a mammoth hand on Toby's shoulder. "Thank you, young man. You will help everyone to have a better vacation. We don't need people running around saying, 'O look, there's Benito Martinez! We should go heckle him and his wife.'"

"Because of your late-season drop off?" Toby asked, referring to the fact that in August and September of the past season, Benito's offensive production had fallen off the table, leading to numerous headlines with questions of how big Big Ben really was.

"Actually, I just meant heckling in general," replied Benito, biting his tongue instead of arguing that he had suffered from a pinched nerve and heroically played through pain.

Toby wanted to run and tell everyone aboard the ship that he had personally discovered Benito Martinez, as if the ballplayer was some sort of buried treasure. But the man's wish for peace was starting to settle in. In Toby's mind, nothing could be better than being recognized everywhere you went, smiling and signing autographs, having people laud you with compliments that weren't necessarily warranted. But if Benito Martinez—who had so far come across as quite pleasant—wanted to be left alone, then Toby would oblige him.

"So, Toby," Benito said, wiping a minuscule bead of sweat from his sizable brow, "can I count on you to keep this our little secret?"

"Sure, Mr. Martinez. But, um..." Toby looked at his feet. "Could I possibly get an autograph?"

Benito beamed at the mousy young man. "An autograph? Of course! That's no problem!" Was Toby blackmailing him? The young man was a good actor if that was the case, and Benito currently had no leverage. He could spare a signature for his own well being.

"Great. Thanks. Um..." Toby looked around for something to autograph. Seeing no better option, he turned around. "I guess … could you get my collar?"

"Well, I don't have a pen on me right now, Toby." Benito was scared this would suddenly cause his confidant to turn on him and return to the buffet line with full disclosure. Instead the boy just looked disappointed.

"Oh. That's okay."

"But I'll get you an autograph later."

Toby brightened. "That sounds great."

"Yes. I will get a pen, and I'm sure we will run into each other again. Then maybe I could sign something other than your collar."

Toby could not think of anything better to sign than his collar, but the commitment of a future autograph was good enough for the time being. "All right, sir. I'll find something really good."

Benito was feeling almost completely relieved. "Wonderful. Just remember, don't tell anyone I'm on this ship. This secret is between you and me."

"Got it."

Smiling, Benito raised his plate and moved back toward the banquet hall. "Okay. Bye Toby."

Toby smiled back and headed down the hall in the opposite direction, whispering, "Bye Mr. Martinez. It was a pleasure to meet you."

"Oh, the pleasure was all mine," Benito blurted out, feeling slightly bad because the statement was not entirely true. Then he ducked back into the buffet line and hunched his shoulders.

Toby continued down the hallway until remembering the plate he smashed. He was too excited to clean at the moment, though. He decided to spend fifteen minutes pretending to look for a broom before going back.

(Of course, numerous other passengers had recognized Benito Martinez through his flimsy disguise, but had the wherewithal to say nothing.)

24

Jamie Brewster felt like throwing up again. He had not thrown up the last time he had felt like throwing up, and once again he did not throw up, but he definitely felt like throwing up.

He was bobbing about in a life raft amid choppier water than he had ever seen, including water on television. The waves tossed him upward then threw him back down, as if the sky wanted to get a good look at him but quickly changed its mind in disgust. This mind-changing continued in a vicious cycle, moving Jamie this way and that as he worked hard to refrain from falling out. The continuous wailing noise he made attracted a handful of inquisitive seabirds.

The previous night Jamie "borrowed" a life raft (along with some sheets, in case he got cold) from the *Queen Ivan* to make his escape. The next portion of his brilliant half-plan was to reach dry land. From there he would hunt down his co-workers on the Gelatin Coast, after hopefully finding the treasure that might gain him leverage. He gleaned enough information to calculate what night the *Queen Ivan* would be closest to the coast. In the few days since he met Toby, he had coaxed the young man into helping, though all Toby was willing to do was release the winch that lowered the boat. And persuading him to do that much was no easy task—Toby kept his eyes closed and convinced himself he was releasing the winch by accident.

Now Jamie regretted this plan, because he was convinced the sea was going to kill him.

The truth was Jamie was very lucky, and this was among the calmer mornings to enjoy in the waters along the Skeleton Coast. The choppiness should have come as no surprise, as many a sailor shipwrecked along the shore could attest. In fact, Jamie was so lucky that despite his useless attempts to steer the boat, he quite by accident caught a current heading toward land. The thick fog deterred him from noticing that the shore was slowly becoming an attainable goal. Intermittently the beach would make itself visible, but Jamie was too busy keeping his eyes closed.

He was nearing the point at which he would resign himself to a horrible death at sea when the waters around him suddenly calmed. Sitting up straighter, Jamie slowly opened one eye. Through a tiny crack in the fog's veneer he spotted some sand and a few rocks. Still of the mind that he was nearing his doom, Jamie assumed it was a mirage. He squinted, still keeping his other eye closed, and soon the vision disappeared behind more fog.

"Ha!" he exclaimed aloud, standing up in the boat— something you should avoid in boats. "I knew it!" Sometimes, people seem to be more concerned with being right than with their own well-being, and for a moment this was the case with Jamie Brewster. Then he wailed again.

Suddenly, a nice big wave came crashing forward. Like a giant hand indicating that paper beats rock, water cascaded into the craft, trying to claim the boat and its captain for the sea. Yet, with Jamie now lying nearly flat against the bottom and holding on for dear life, the lifeboat was pitched toward the shore.

Suddenly the boat was on something hard. After considering it unlikely that he would ever experience that other third of the planet again, Jamie felt as though there was ground underneath him. It did not seem possible to the newly christened pessimist, but upon opening one eye again, he pushed himself off the bottom of the boat and peered over the side. It was sand.

Jamie could not contain his elation. "Yip-ee!" he exclaimed, poking at the damp sand as if he were dialing someone's telephone number. Then another large wave came crashing in, and Jamie found himself well beyond damp. He jumped up. Enough fun, he thought and pulled the boat away from the sea's icy tendrils, up the soft slope. Jamie was not sure where he was headed, since he was walking backward and the fog around him remained quite dense. So he took a seat.

Jamie chided himself for not coming up with a plan during the ship's transatlantic voyage. *Oh well*, he thought. *I'll just have to start walking and try to find something or someone helpful.* Then it occurred to Jamie that he was all alone, so he repeated this thought out loud. Yelling was fun. Next he sang a Christmas song, which elicited no response beyond the crashing of waves.

Standing back up, Jamie decided that he would begin by moving the boat to a safer spot in case he needed it in the future. He dearly hoped he would not. Tugging the boat some more, Jamie assumed that somewhere in the fog would be some sort of embankment or cave along a cliff to hide his ship. With no one around to hear him, he grunted aloud like a tennis player every time he gave the boat a pull. Further and further he and the dead weight went. "Heave! Ho!" Jamie called.

After some minutes of this monotonous dragging, Jamie's back ran into something hard. Hoping it was a cliff wall, along which he might find an opening to stash the boat, Jamie reached back with one hand. Instead of rock, though, he felt metal. Surprised, he turned around.

Sitting there in the sand, shrouded in fog, was a helicopter. Jamie's jaw dropped. And it was not just any helicopter. **CHANNEL** 7 was painted brightly in yellow on the navy blue door panel. Standing in disbelief, Jamie put his hands on his hips. Then he circled the aircraft to make sure his eyes were not playing tricks on him. To make sure it, too, was not a mirage, he dragged both hands along its body, much in the style of a kindergartener finger painting. Reaching the driver's side, he inspected carefully, and found the familiar scratch where the rival news team from Channel 5 had keyed his helicopter.

"Oh, my goodness," he whispered.

Cautiously opening the door, he was relieved to find no skeletons, but also dismayed that Tom and Janet were still missing. There was a pile of food in the back seat, which was not inside the last time he flew in it. This puzzled him, but simply finding the helicopter had taken most of the surprise out of him. He even realized that the keys were still in the ignition.

"Well," he said, addressing the aircraft, "you won't be able to explain this mystery to me, and I still have to find Janet and Tom." The addressee made no reply. Turning to address the boat, Jamie said, "Thank you. I hope you are still here if I come back." The boat, too, stayed silent.

Jamie backed up and stared at the helicopter. *His* helicopter (well, Channel 7's). He shook his head again.

"How....?"

After a few more moments of inspections, having no other definite conclusion about what prudent thing to do next, Jamie climbed in the cockpit.

25

Hans Heissel was not a big fan of guns. Upon becoming a pirate, Hans realized he lacked real interest in killing anyone. Murder simply failed to spike his curiosity. Also Hans Heissel wanted to avoid gunfire because he had read too many reports of accidents involving guns, so he had little to no faith in avoiding such accidents himself. Here and there the story of someone shooting himself in the foot or shooting himself while using a gun to remove a hubcap would find its way to Hans. Such cautionary tales stuck with him.

Still, Hans understood that as a pirate, the need to inspire fear in one's victims was imperative. So, after one sticky situation during an assault on a houseboat that housed a curmudgeonly man with a revolver hid next to his emergency flare, it was decided that perhaps firearms could prove valuable. (Hans and crew were eventually able to subdue the man after throwing a fair amount of garbage onto his houseboat until he ran out of bullets.) Hans also warmed to the idea when he recognized his fascination with spinning and twirling guns around as fast as he could.

Procuring a supply of firearms was a bit of a trick, but a trick Hans Heissel was up for. Unfortunately, there are many guns going to and fro on the world's oceans. He actually did the world a favor by intercepting a large supply of guns headed for a secretive and nasty organization that was planning to use the guns for evildoing. For better or worse, however, this supply of guns was separate from the nasty organization's supply of ammunition. This did not faze Hans Heissel. The pirate captain decided bullets were unnecessary, since scare tactics should be enough, and it would lessen the chances of his crew accidentally shooting themselves in the foot.

Each crewman was equipped with an unloaded gun. They were then instructed to wave them about sporadically when the time was right in a sort of non-rhythmic intimidation display, which came to look like some sort of strange animal mating dance. But even mating dances can be quite frightening if they involve guns.

The boat that Captain Hans Heissel and crew were currently pirating about in was a ferry from Chicago. The means in which the sailors had commandeered a passenger vessel from a city that was nowhere near an ocean was anyone's guess, and not even Hans Heissel was certain how it came to be in their possession. Nevertheless, it was their flagship at the moment, but definitely not their only ship. There had been a good deal of argument about whether or not to install a cannon on board the ferry (now being called *The Haunted House*, because Hans thought this sounded scary). Hans was unsure, given the low success rate of installing cannons on the yachts in his fleet.

The ferry's amenities were not so comfy as some of the other boats they now owned, but it was definitely spacious. Instead of having numerous rooms for separate tasks such as sleeping, there were a few very large common rooms shared amongst the crew. The ferry's size was a fun escape from their routine luxury yachts because they could play tag on board, but since the pirates had gone soft with their indulgent new lifestyle, the ferry was just not comfortable enough for many of them. Hans Heissel pondered whether there was something that would be the best of both worlds ...

26

As the Skeleton Coast quite often finds itself completely enveloped in dense fog, Earnest and Mickey were quickly becoming completely enveloped. This worried Earnest at first, as fog this thick never entered his village. But the boy felt that if Mickey was being courageous about the strange, pervasive whiteness, then he should not show weakness in front of his new friend. Mickey was not really being courageous; courageous was not usually the right word to describe him.

The thick, salty fog kind of stunk, in Earnest's opinion.

"Mickey, I'm not sure what I think about this fallen cloud," Earnest told his companion. If anything, Mickey was having a slightly better time than he was before the fog rolled in. The moisture was a slight, if teasing, reminder of home.

It occurred to Earnest that he could not be sure where they were headed if he could not see anything. Of course, he had never really known exactly where they were going. Running away with the big, furry animal was more a desperation move than a calculated strategy. Earnest had assumed that the two would find something and he'd be able to state, "Ah, Mickey, here we are."

What had appeared to be morning trudged on toward later morning, though in the heavy fog time had almost gotten lost itself. Not that time mattered much to a moose and a young boy who had never owned a watch. As the morning continued its leisurely passage, mostly unnoticed because of its lack of a foghorn, Earnest realized he was becoming hungrier. Mickey had long since realized the same. Although Earnest was not counting his footsteps, he would sometimes guess, and notice that every hundred of his estimated steps he would be a little more inclined toward eating.

"Oh, how I wish I had something for eating," Earnest thought out loud. Mickey thought the same thing, though in less words. For whatever reason, the moose continued to follow the boy, perhaps because it seemed he might know where food was. He was also the nicest person Mickey had met since leaving home, though this factor did not matter quite as much to a moose.

Earnest put his head down and resolutely kept his slow pace, gently tugging on the rope attached to Mickey's antler. Mickey also put his head down, though he was searching desperately for lunch. A rare look of consternation crept across Earnest's face, which he was aware of and wished gone. On and on they marched.

The fog also seemed to dampen any sounds trying to creep in. Few sounds could be heard anyway, but the change in pitch and volume made things that much more spooky, and not the fun kind of spooky. Once in a while they heard the call belonging to a shorebird of some kind, but the call would be muffled, as if the bird was battling a cold. March, march, march they went through the near silence.

Then a new sound presented itself from some faraway spot. With its increase in volume came Earnest's increase in interest. As it came closer it appeared to have a sort of thrumming quality to it, Earnest thought, like someone punishing a bongo drum. Mickey, of course, paid it no heed at first because he had never met food that loud. Earnest decided to call a halt to discern what the noise could be. At this point it was loud enough that even Mickey was a tad curious, mostly as to whether he should run away and how far his tired legs might get him.

When the thrumming got close, Earnest concluded it was in the sky somewhere. He gazed up, brow furrowed, hand shielding his eyes, waiting to see if the noise would show itself. Louder and louder the sound roared. Mickey decided he was not that curious and tugged a little at his leash. Earnest tugged back with equal force. They were staying put to get some questions answered.

"I will know you," Earnest said, though at this point he could not hear himself over the sound of the approaching thingy.

Suddenly it appeared. Not because the fog broke apart, but because it was close enough to break through the fog, right above the boy and the moose. Subsequently, Earnest's curiosity was marginally satisfied as he turned his attention to not being smooshed.

It was a helicopter, though Earnest had never seen one before and therefore did not know this. Mickey had seen one before but did not care. The two hustled to the closest dune, which they could not see so much as hope for. Earnest could not help but continually look back. The great, dark, noisy thing from the sky was making a strange circle above itself that seemed to be constantly moving. There were a couple big legs underneath it, somewhat resembling skis (of which Earnest also had no knowledge).

Soon the helicopter made its landing. A rough one, to say the least. The right side touched down first, buckled forward a little, then lifted again before both skis came down at the same time. The back end pressed into the sand before the front. Since the sand was very uneven, it hobbled about like an elderly dog trying to sit down, nearly tipping the helicopter's tail into the sand. With some grating noises and fidgeting, the front plunked down, too, and the helicopter appeared to rest.

Earnest looked back again to see that the air machine was now comfortably seated in the sand. The boy watched intently as the circle above the contraption slowed down, until he could make out that it was made up of some sort of large knives. The knives did not seem too intimidating, though, so Earnest became all the more intrigued. He took a few steps toward the helicopter. At this point he could see that there was a person inside. Less cautiously than perhaps he should have been, Earnest walked toward the aircraft, leading the less enthusiastic moose along with him.

Jamie Brewster looked up to see a strange young boy walking toward the helicopter, and behind the boy was ... *was that a moose*? Indeed it was, he recognized, after rubbing his eyes, slapping his cheek, and looking again. His supposition that finding his own helicopter would be the strangest discovery of the day was already being challenged.

Jamie had decided to try to fly the helicopter once he found it, thinking that a) it was his (well, Channel 7's) and therefore his right; b) that the view from the sky would be better suited for searching for coworkers and treasure than the view from the ground (if some of the fog cleared); and c) he would be much more comfortable in his familiar cockpit than wandering a deserted coastline in jeans. Sure, it had also occurred to him that it could have been abandoned because it no longer worked, or that someone had laid a trap, but he still thought the pros outweighed the cons. So, after a thorough check of the engine systems, and a good look at the blades and even some of the wiring, Jamie concluded it was safe to fly. So up he went.

Unfortunately, he had failed to notice that the helicopter was nearly out of gas. He was well on his way south when he finally made this frightening realization. He wondered for a moment if that was the reason the aircraft was abandoned, but then set his mind to the more pressing matter of avoiding an untimely end. Somehow, Jamie was able to keep a reasonably cool head about him (perhaps because it was not the first time he had run a helicopter out of gas). He knew that if he could land before the engine stalled, he would be fine. Well, at least as fine as he was before finding the helicopter.

Without meaning to, he whistled the love theme from *Titanic* as his eyes scoured the land for a place to plop down. There was so much fog he had trouble seeing much. He did not want to accidentally descend upon an outcropping of rock, since it could mean his demise. Nor did he want to descend upon a rhinoceros, since it could mean both his demise and the demise of a rhinoceros. So, willing the helicopter to stay airborne, he noticed what appeared to be a level patch of sand where the fog parted. He whistled an octave higher and lowered the helicopter to the ground just as the last drop of fuel was burned (or so he imagined).

On reasonably flat ground again Jamie took a deep sigh of relief as the helicopter's engine coughed and died. Happy to have avoided perishing in flames, Jamie was also burdened with the fact that his one hope was now out of fuel. Only then did he spot the little boy and his moose slowly approaching him. Though Jamie wondered about their motives, he considered signs of life as a step in the right direction. Still emotionally drained, Jamie pushed open his door and stepped out onto the sand, which swirled up into his nose due to the helicopter's still-rotating blades. Slowly the blades got lazier and lazier until it was safe for Jamie to take his face out of his sweater.

When the man pulled his face back out of his shirt, Earnest was pleased to see a person with whom he shared a similar skin color. He thought that maybe this man spoke his language, so he hustled up to him through the churning sand, loosening the grip on Mickey's leash.

"Hello, sir. Hello."

The man blinked and blinked and used his arms to swat around his face. Earnest wondered if this was perhaps a greeting or comedy routine the man was doing to impress him. He smiled at the man and nodded his head a little.

"Hello, sir. I am Earnest," he tried again.

Gaining some composure, the man tried to smile through the cloud. "Hi there, guy," the man said in some funny language Earnest did not understand. It might have been that language the scientists and moose-shooter had used, but Earnest did not know and did not care.

Darn it, thought the boy, before shrugging and saying, "Oh well."

Jamie could finally see somewhat straight and watched as the boy shrugged at him. He couldn't tell if this meant he'd lost interest or not. Jamie had not really heard what the boy said at first, so he offered his hand for shaking.

"Hi, I'm Jamie."

The boy took the hand and inspected it. He approved and handed it back to Jamie. Jamie looked at it, too, now curious himself. It seemed fine.

"You don't speak English, do you?"

The boy smiled at him.

"I guess not." Jamie looked off into the distance. "This is going to be tough."

Earnest was not sure what to make of the man from the sky. He did not appear as cranky or old as the other strangers he recently met. He looked back up at the man's face and inspected it. The man appeared puzzled for a second, then offered an uncomfortable, forced smile. Earnest was not used to these types of smiles, but thought that from the looks of it the man was harmless. And maybe he could help get Mickey to safety. He smiled back, sincerely.

Jamie was unsure what to do about his new acquaintance. The boy didn't necessarily look like a con artist, but Jamie couldn't be sure. Of course, a foggy desert was a terrible place for a con artist to find victims, so that was a point in his favor. Maybe this boy could throw him some tidbit, even though it might require a bit of deciphering. And he wondered why this character had a moose for a pet. But after thinking he was completely and utterly alone, it was nice to have company.

Jamie offered his name again. "I'm Jamie," he said deliberately, pointing to his chest.

Though the boy might have been naïve about certain cultural differences, introductions were not beyond him. He pointed toward the gentleman and said in a thick accent, "Eym Shay-mee."

Jamie smiled, impressed at his professorial skills, but tried again for complete comprehension.

"Pretty good, dude. Let's try once more." Pointing more deliberately to himself, he said, "Jamie."

The boy tried again, copying the finger-pointing in a more dramatic fashion, "Shay-mee."

Jamie beamed at him. "Yeah! Close enough!" The boy smiled back. "How about you?"

Earnest kept smiling up at the man, curious what interesting thing he would do next. Shay-mee was quite nice to introduce himself like that. He said a few more unintelligible words, but Earnest just kept smiling. Then Shay-mee pointed at Earnest, who nodded at him. The man's hand movements slowed down, as if this would somehow help the boy understand his request.

Pointing to himself, he slowly said, "Ja-mie…" Then pointing to Earnest he made some rolling gestures, like dance moves. Unsure what he was blabbering on about,

Earnest eventually got a little bored and decided he would share his own name.

"Earnest," he said, pointing to himself. The man clapped his hands, delighted to hear this.

"Earnest," Shay-mee said back to him. Happy to see he had made this man happy, Earnest mimicked his delight. Then he turned to the moose standing a few yards behind him and said, "Mickey." Shay-mee pointed and repeated the name as a question. When Earnest nodded and said, "Mickey" once more, the man laughed and clapped his hands again. He seemed to be very amused at Mickey's name. Earnest felt this confirmed that he was good at naming things.

Mickey watched the pair as they smiled and laughed. He did not really care. Mickey just wanted something to eat. He soon lost interest in the humans, until the man pulled something out of the helicopter. Mickey failed to care what it was until Earnest approached him with an outstretched hand full of it. Sniffing, Mickey recognized that the hand was holding food. Earnest set the loaf in front of him. Mickey turned his full attention to eating it.

It occurred to Jamie that perhaps the mysterious food in the cockpit was poisoned, but he doubted it and also was hungry, which outweighed other concerns. The boy and his moose also appeared hungry, so sitting down for a picnic in the fog seemed the sensible thing to do. Jamie found some granola bars, some bags of cereal, a few boxes of crackers, a few loaves of bread, and a few gallons of water. His detective work dictated the food could not have been there long if the bread was still in working order. He also found some rope, which he believed might come in handy.

Jamie continued to ponder what a boy and a moose were doing walking through a desert, but had little hope of finding answers, given the three-way language barrier. He assumed Earnest was just as curious about why he had landed a helicopter right in front of him.

Earnest did not really care why Shay-mee had landed a helicopter right in front of him. What he did care about was what they would do next. He thought he would simply follow this nice fellow until they found whatever it was they were looking for. Unless he was headed back to the village, Earnest concluded. That place was no longer safe for a moose.

So the trio sat and had their picnic for a little while before Jamie realized he should definitely save most of the food for the trek ahead. After diligently searching the cockpit for useful and/or edible things, he packed everything up in the soaking wet sheets he had "borrowed" from the ship. Throwing the bundle over his shoulder, he looked at his bare footed new friend.

"Well, Earnest, it was a pleasure."

Earnest smiled at him.

"I am going to start walking, okay? And I'm just going to see if you follow me. How's that sound?" After no reply, Jamie subtly saluted the young man and began stepping away from the defunct helicopter, taking slow strides through the sand.

Earnest hopped up from his cross-legged position and grabbed Mickey's leash. Mickey wanted something else to eat, but it appeared that the food might be leaving with Jamie, so he arose.

"Hey!" Earnest began, hustling after him. "Shay-mee, don't you want to take your flying machine with you?"

Not understanding him, Jamie assumed the boy was asking him to wait up. He felt some relief. "Okay, let's go." Then he stopped short. "You know, if you hadn't wanted to come, I would have given you guys half of this food. Seriously. I swear."

Earnest repeated himself, only louder, and with some emphatic pointing to the helicopter.

"Oh, that," Jamie countered. "It doesn't work anymore." He showed Earnest a thumbs-down sign and made a whoopee-cushion noise with his tongue.

Earnest got the message that Jamie did not want to take the vehicle with him, though whether or not he was sick of it, Earnest was unsure. Either way, he followed the pilot.

Jamie stopped and put the bundle down. "Good. I'm glad you guys are coming, because I didn't really want to carry this," he said, then started to place the bundle on Mickey's back with some of the ropes. Mickey did not appreciate this, but refrained from kicking the man who helped him find food. With the lopsided bundle attached to Mickey's back, Jamie patted the moose hesitantly. He was much more cautious than Earnest seemed to be. Mickey just looked at him.

"All right, let's go," said Jamie. Earnest nodded, assuming correctly what had come out of his mouth. After they took two steps, however, Mickey shook himself to remove the burdensome pack. This dampened Jamie's mood, who tried twice more to attach the bundle to the moose and twice more was rejected. Finally, heaving the load onto his own back, Jamie set out once more, leading the newly formed unlikely team of helicopter pilot, boy, and moose on their trek south. Their destination was anyone's guess.

27

Maria Martinez became a fan of tanning on the *Queen Ivan's* deck. She would put on a pair of raindrop-shaped sunglasses from the 1950s she discovered at a yard sale, don her non-revealing bathing suit which looked as though it, too, came from the 1950s, and sit in a reclined lawn chair for hours on end. She would always hold one of those large, silly reflector things at her neck and always brought a book for some reason. Since she needed two hands to hold her reflector-thingy, the book would remain unopened on a little table next to her. Benito never accompanied her, but few male passengers spent their time in lawn chairs with big reflector-thingies on their faces.

While she lounged on the sun deck, Maria built a rapport with some of the crew members. Most were incredibly friendly, often graciously thanking Maria for handing them empty glasses, as if they had been presented with fine jewelry for their birthdays. Their insincerity annoyed Maria, though it appeared she alone was annoyed.

Which was part of the reason she liked Toby. The mousy young man was friendly enough but did not seem to feel the need to worship each guest like some deity who required appeasing or sacrifice. He was a little timid, but not overly so, and Maria felt he probably acted that way around teachers and grocery store clerks, and was not just putting on a show for the ship's clientèle. And when she had first asked for his name and thanked him for taking her empty glass, the young man seemed surprised. Since then he had opened up a bit when he ran into her, telling her about his high school and complaining about his coworkers. He had even alluded to having a crush on a fellow crew member, which amused Maria to no end. So now, when Toby came walking over with a huge smile on his face, Maria assumed he had decided to divulge more details about the lucky young lady.

"Hi, Mrs. Martinez!" Toby began, handing her a small white towel she had not asked for.

"Hello, Toby. What's up?"

Toby looked to his left and looked to his right. Noting that the coast was clear, he glanced down at Maria and spoke in a loud whisper. "I didn't know you were *that* Mrs. Martinez." Then he gave her a conspicuous wink.

Maria smiled back but gave him a quizzical look. "I don't think I follow you, Toby."

Toby chuckled. "It's okay, Mrs. Martinez. I *know*."

"And what is it you know, Toby?"

"That you're *THAT* Mrs. Martinez." He gave her another wink, twice as conspicuous as the first.

Maria put down her great big reflector thingy. She was a little frustrated that she did not know what Toby knew. "Really, Toby. I'm not sure what you are talking about."

Toby scratched his head a little. "Aren't you married to Benito Martinez?"

"Yes..."

Toby thought. Maybe she was just being coy. And since he was not really searching for an autograph from a famous baseball player's wife (though he was sure it was a very nice signature), he thought he would leave the woman alone if privacy was what she desired.

"It's okay. Sorry." Toby reached for her empty glass. But Maria was curious.

"No, really, Toby. What were you talking about?"

"Well, aren't you … Benito Martinez's wife?"

"Yes, I am."

Toby was aware that there probably was, somewhere in the world, another Benito Martinez. "The same Benito Martinez that is on this boat?"

"Of course…"

Toby sighed. "The same Benito Martinez that plays third base for the Baltimore Orioles?"

"What does that mean?"

The boy paused. "Baseball."

"Oh, no. My husband does not play *baseball*." She said the word in the kind of way that a baseball fan would take offense to. "He is a crabber."

Maria seemed sincere, so Toby was confused. It showed on his face. He thought a second longer, then sighed and smiled. "It's okay, Mrs. Martinez. I *know*. But don't worry. I promised I wouldn't tell anyone."

"Tell anyone what?"

"Exactly."

"Toby, please tell me what you are talking about." Maria now removed her ancient sunglasses and sat up, swinging her legs over the side of the chair.

Toby appeared a bit concerned, but then looked around once more before speaking. "I talked to Benito. Mr. Martinez. I saw through his eye patch and mustache. He said he would sign an autograph for me. But I had to promise I wouldn't tell anyone. And I haven't. And I'm not going to."

Maria was concerned. Something was very wrong. Her first reaction was that that something had to do with Toby. She reached up and touched his forehead.

"Toby, I think you have cabin fever."

"Huh?"

"Sometimes it happens to people on boats, I've read. If you're out at sea for a really long time, you can get it from being cooped up all day and all night."

"I … well, maybe. But I still think I'm getting your husband's autograph. Because look what I just traded some sucker for this morning."

Toby reached into his pocket and extracted a baseball card. He handed it delicately to Maria. It had a very clear picture of Benito in a baseball uniform swinging a baseball bat at a baseball. Maria blinked a number of times. Ever so slightly her hand began to shake. Slowly her grip tightened.

Toby tried to be polite. "Um, just be careful with the edges," he said, though he had been the one to shove the collectible in his pocket. He failed to notice Maria turn red, assuming it was the sun.

"Thank you, Toby," Maria said through a concrete smile, handing the card back.

"Oh, no problem, Mrs. Martinez." He placed the card back in his pocket. "You must be very proud of your husband."

"Oh, you have no idea," Maria seethed, not knowing what that comment actually meant.

Toby gave a polite smile at her odd reply, then hustled away, convinced that the woman suffered from cabin fever.

28

Well, it really should come as no surprise, but the crabbing boat transporting the Mongolians and their captive, but well-treated, news team ran aground on the Skeleton Coast. Who knows what some of these people were thinking when they were trying to successfully park a boat there, but it's nearly impossible to do so. It was foggy, as it often is on the Skeleton Coast, which was part of the problem. Also part of the problem was the unfamiliarity of the spot. Blame could also be attributed to the Mongolians' poor directions. Maybe the crabbing crew should have known better than to try approaching this unfamiliar and terribly dangerous coast. Or maybe it should have come as no surprise that this particular crew, who were used to making entertaining television, should attempt such a stunt. Goodness me.

The ragtag band of Jamie, Earnest, and Mickey trudged on southward. It was hot. And sandy. And no one was really having a very good time. But on they walked, for lack of anything better to do.

Earnest kept assuming that Jamie knew where they were going because he was a grown-up. Jamie kept assuming that Earnest knew where they were going because he was a local. Mickey did no assuming, but hoped they might stop to eat soon. It was somewhat Ouija board-esque.

The trio had moved in a somewhat southwestern-type direction after they first departed the downed helicopter. Eventually they again reached the coast. The coast is often a nice reference point if you are traveling. It is also useful to keep traveling along it if you are looking for something on the coast, as this party was. So once Jamie, Earnest, and Mickey hit the coast, they hugged it closely as they marched along its shores. But hugging a coast is not as comfortable as hugging a teddy bear.

29

While throngs of people were frantically scurrying about to get every last detail in order for the big wedding later in the day, Delilah Johnson and Joey Katsopolis were goofing off.

The soon-to-be-married couple had sneaked away from the wedding hubbub, despite the fact that their mothers were going bonkers. Ironically ignoring one tradition, which dictated not seeing each other until the actual wedding, the two conspirators had escaped to fulfill another tradition: accumulating something old, something new, something borrowed, and something blue. Though unsure what magic these things would conjure when grouped together, Delilah and Joey felt it would be a bit of fun escapism from all the brouhaha, even if it meant a huge inconvenience for the rest of the wedding party.

Pulling Joey's hand along behind her, the mischievous Delilah peered through the hallways of the *Queen Ivan*. So far their search had been fruitful. From Grandpa Katsopolis they had acquired something old: a box of stale Ritz crackers. From Delilah's stinky cousin's room they had acquired something new: some dark bacteria from his sink that was definitely not there at the beginning of the cruise. From a middle-aged woman near the pool they acquired something blue: a tear-jerking Nicholas Sparks novel she recently finished (with a blue cover).

But something borrowed still eluded the couple. Which

was why they were sneaking about the boat. In hushed tones the pair had decided they would kick start their marriage with some good old-fashioned larceny. Of course that is not what they were calling it; they told themselves they were simply going to take something and return it after the wedding. Hence the "borrowed" portion. Thinking that it was all cute and romantic, they giggled as they crept along.

Grinning like a slice of cantaloupe, Delilah stopped and turned to Joey. "Are you sure this is a good idea?" she whispered.

"No!" Joey whispered back, feigning distaste for the situation. "And it was your idea!"

"Oh yeah!" Delilah said, pretending to suddenly remember this fact. She tugged her fiance a bit harder and continued her search.

Coming across a large portrait of a different cruise ship on the wall of this cruise ship, the couple stopped and considered.

"What about that?" asked the bride-to-be.

"It's really big," replied Joey. "And it's probably nailed to the wall."

Delilah nodded and they moved further down the hallway. Moments later they came across a fancy end table that seemed to be in the way of passersby. Atop the table was a plant in a nice vase. Joey pointed at it.

"What about this?" he asked in his hushed tone.

"No, I don't have a green thumb and would kill it before we put it back." Delilah continued tugging her betrothed along. If they had looked closer they might have noticed that the plant was fake.

Suddenly an elderly couple emerged from one of the hallway's many doors. Joey and Delilah froze and held their breath. They gave a pair of polite waves and did a very bad job of looking natural. The elderly persons waved back, then walked away wondering why the young couple looked like they were being held at knife point.

Delilah and Joey continued along the opulent hallway. Creeping around a corner, they saw another portrait of a ship on the wall up ahead of them.

"That looks like it might be smaller than the other one," Joey whispered, before remembering his own words about pictures being nailed to walls. Delilah scrunched her face up, unimpressed. A door to their left indicated a men's restroom. Joey was running out of ideas.

"I could go see if there is anything in there," he said. "Maybe just some paper towels." But they both felt that paper towels were nowhere near as exciting as the elusive something they had set out to nab. Delilah shook her head and tugged him along a bit further.

Then, up ahead, on the wall to their left, Delilah saw what they hadn't known they were looking for. Her face lit up, and she pointed. Joey followed the direction of her finger and nodded.

"That's a good idea," he said. She smiled at him as the two, giddy as all get-out, crept forward to steal the fire extinguisher.

30

The *Queen Ivan* had a sizable and lavish gym, so well maintained that the odor of people sweating all over everything was nonexistent. The area contained aerobic bicycles, stair climbers, treadmills, large colorful inflated balls, stacks and stacks of dumbbells, a closet full of yoga mats, garbage can-sized containers full of fluffy white towels, cages for lifting free weights, machines for lifting non-free weights, and most importantly, no fewer than twenty televisions.

One of the gym's most frequent frequenters was one Benito Martinez. Although he hid his baseball playing from his better half, he did not hide his rigorous training regimen. On any given day, odds were good that you'd peer through the spotless glass of the gym's doors and see Benito Martinez exercising (except you wouldn't know it was Benito Martinez because of his ingenious disguise).

On this particular day, the gym was abandoned save for Benito, which was just the way he liked it. No one to give him a glance that screamed, *You look familiar...* Now there were only the mirrors and the reflection of this strange, mustachioed, eye-patched character watching him. Benito was tempted to remove the now-bothersome articles, yet he knew that at any second someone might breeze through the door to see his naked and famous face.

The next moment, as Benito stretched a medicine ball toward the ceiling, someone did come through the door, but it could hardly be considered breezing. More like storming. Maria came storming through the gym's glass door. There was hellfire in her eyes.

Benito was scared. He dropped the heavy ball. With a dull thud the ball clumped to the floor, getting part of Benito's big toe in the process. He hopped up in pain as his attention turned from his wife's devil eyes to his new injury. He clutched his foot and turned a circle. Maria's death stare followed him, her hands in hardened fists at her sides. Completing his circle, Benito once again faced the angry shadow of the woman he married.

"You deserved that," she breathed.

A fragile elderly couple, chuckling as they slid along in their big, floppy sandals, had their sliding interrupted by the eruption of Benito Martinez limping from the ship's gym. Hot on his tail was his lovely wife, Maria, shouting at him in Spanish. The elderly couple did not speak Spanish. It was just as well, because they would have been offended or confused by the ensuing discussion.

"You lied to me, you liar!" Maria redundantly shouted.

"What are you talking about, dear?" Benito asked, only half-turning back as he ran.

Rounding a bend in the hallway, Maria lunged and narrowly missed. "You play baseball!"

"What? What is baseball?" Benito asked, sounding as stupid as the dirt he regularly played on.

Nearly within striking distance, Maria shrieked, "Don't play stupid with me, Benito!" as she tried to kick him. "I saw your baseball card!"

And with that Benito knew his goose was cooked. The

former All-Star had been hoping his haystack of lies could be improved by shoveling more lies onto it. If she had seen his baseball card, then the sham was up. He considered that pleading might be the only way to stay alive as he hustled past an ornate hallway table that seemed to be there just to get in people's way.

Turning and opening his un-patched eye, he saw his wife pick up a vase from the table to throw at him, which made him reconsider the safety of pleading. At least until he had an adequate lead.

Toby was pushing a cart full of clean towels from the *Queen Ivan's* laundry room to the numerous towel drop zones. So full was his cart that he could barely see over the top. Toby simply hoped no one was in his way. He had been chastised for running into affluent ship passengers with laundry baskets and food trolleys a number of times since the voyage had begun and was not looking forward to another chastising. Yet, Toby was unwilling to make two trips with the towels.

The overcrowded towel bin pushed through a set of doors, taking him onto the outside concourse (a shortcut he had been told not to use), where he noticed a terrible chase ensuing. Maria Martinez was bearing down upon the terrified and hobbling Benito Martinez, still in mustache and eye patch. Toby tried to back himself through the door, but it was too late. Benito had spotted him, and his one unpatched eye fixed on him imploringly. Toby assumed that the other eye was looking at him in the same manner, just under the eye patch.

"Toby! Why did you tell her?"

"I didn't do it!" Toby yelled, again following instinct, before he had any idea what Benito was talking about. "Ididn'tdoitIdon'tknow!"

"Leave him out of this!" screeched Maria, pointing a finger like an evil sorceress. Benito ducked behind the bin of towels as Toby did the same. Unsure what else to do, Toby thought seeking cover would be wise. Benito reached up and grabbed a handful of towels as they appeared to be the most accessible means of defense.

"What did I do?" Toby asked Benito frantically.

"You said you wouldn't tell anybody about our secret!" Benito yelled in a whisper, though whispering, however loudly, seemed asinine at this point. Maria approached the towels and grabbed the bin in the hopes of knocking it over to apprehend the accused.

"I didn't!" Toby defended himself. Benito groaned as he pulled the bin back toward them.

"You told her!" he pointed out.

"She's your wife! You didn't say I wasn't allowed to tell her!" Toby argued.

"I said anybody!"

In the struggle, a couple of towels became casualties, being lifted into the wind. Swirling upward and over the deck's railings, the towels waved good-bye on their way out to sea. Though rarely the ship's most dedicated worker, Toby took pride in getting towels to their destination. He gasped.

"My towels!" cried the young man, lunging after the fallen troops. It was too late, though. Maria got her opportunity when Toby gave up the little bit of cover he was providing Benito. She charged through a pile of fallen towels toward her husband, nearly knocking Toby overboard in the process (training sessions had made clear that passengers were always right, so yelling at a passenger for almost killing him was out of the question). Benito scrambled up to retreat further. But with her deft maneuvering, Maria grabbed his ankle. Benito screamed.

Toby, peeling himself from the ship's miracle-working rail, turned and stumbled two steps over to the fighters.

"Mrs. Martinez, please! You'll scare the rich people!" he pleaded.

Maria, trying to reach through towels to get two hands on her husband's ankle, did not turn to the young man. "I'm sorry, Toby. But please stay out of this."

Unsure what to do, Toby placed a hand delicately on Maria's shoulder, and gave her a polite pat. "I would, Mrs. Martinez, but I'm supposed to help with conflict resolution, so my boss doesn't yell at me again." Toby knew he'd be blamed for any problems that occurred within his general vicinity.

Benito scooted away on his hindquarters and was able to wiggle out of his sneaker. Her grip faltering, Maria was left with only a shoe. Instinctively, Benito gave a gleeful chuckle at his momentary victory. He wished he were not so susceptible to instinct. With his wife still struggling through fallen laundry, Benito took the opportunity to arise and run. Now hobbling with his injured foot no longer shoed, Maria saw he would be easily caught.

Toby jumped as Maria exploded upward. "Mrs. Martinez, please stop! There's no fighting on the ship!" He joined the chase across the ship's deck. "What's so wrong that we can't fix?"

"He lied to me!" shouted Maria, wishing she could just ignore Toby, but knowing full well that he was such a nice young man that his questions deserved answers.

"Everybody lies sometimes!" shouted Toby, losing ground. He quickly realized it was not the most thoughtful response.

A number of passengers had become curious about the antics unfolding before them. Though it went unsaid, it was widely agreed that the scene was, at the very least, entertaining.

Tripping through deck chairs, Benito saw a door that he felt could help. He rushed for it, but stubbed his injured toe on a rainbow-colored chair that he should have easily noticed. Its inhabitant, a sleeping woman who was not nearly so red when the *Queen Ivan* had left Miami, sat up quickly, hoping for an apology that did not come. Instead she was greeted with Maria and then Toby, who took a terrible tumble on top of her, but rolled off and apologized enough for four people.

Benito reached the door and threw it open, and as happens during most chases, ran into a chef carrying a large cake. The cake was a lovely shade of pink. Where the chef was going with the cake was immaterial. Said cake flew into the air and landed atop the chef's head, as if it had read the wacky-chase-instruction manual. Benito failed to notice. The athlete turned to shut the door, pushing with all his might as his wife reached the other side and began pushing the opposite direction.

Once Toby regained his feet, he met Maria at the door.

"Toby! Help me push this door open!" she exclaimed.

The flustered young man winced. "I don't think I

should, Mrs. Martinez. Maybe we can work this all out. Quietly."

Maria kept pushing. "It's too late for that."

On the other side, Benito wondered how much longer he could hold the door.

Riggins was watching the horizon with his good eye. A large yacht appeared. Followed by another. And still another, though it might have been a ferry or a tugboat. The weathered old sailor sniffed the air without adjusting his gaze or even blinking his eye, which desperately wanted a blink, which the tempered Riggins was denying.

Numerous harmless-looking yachts.

Trouble was a-brewing.

Captain Hans Heissel Jr. was whistling something grandiose. Something from a movie he had seen long ago, perhaps. At the bow of the *Helga II*, his gaze never wavered from the prize on the horizon. No one troubled him. Until First Mate Ronaldinho went ahead and troubled him.

"Captain..." began the boy.

"Tut tut," Hans said, waving for his most trusted adviser to be quiet and enjoy the moment. "This will be our greatest triumph, First Mate Ronaldinho."

"Yes, sir," said the boy, and joined his captain in staring at the cruise ship in front of them.

"Think of what fun we will have aboard that ship. Everyone will have a finely furnished room and plenty of movies to watch, probably. I can't even imagine what wonders might be aboard a cruise ship. A nice pool, fluffy bathrobes, buffet tables, those travel-sized bars of soap..."

Ronaldinho, sometimes a clearer thinker than Hans Heissel, turned to him. "We are taking the ship, Captain?"

"Oh, yes, First Mate Ronaldinho. Simply robbing them blind won't be enough. That ship is ours." Strictly speaking, it was not, of course, but Hans Heissel had come to the conclusion that he ran the ocean now.

It occurred to Ronaldinho that not everyone was on the same page. He departed to update the pirate men and women, leaving his captain to stare at the cruise ship they were rapidly approaching.

"We were meant for each other," he told the *Queen Ivan*. Hans Heissel was not yet a master of words.

Melinda, fresh from brushing her teeth and hair, found Riggins at the ship's railing, seemingly staring at nothing. This came as no surprise, but she inquired anyway.

"Hi, Riggins. What are you looking at?" She squinted in the direction of his stare but failed to see anything all that exciting.

"By the twitching of my toes, from that direction something icky blows."

Melinda was used to his cryptic blabber, though not so much to his rhyming. She turned to him and cautiously asked, "What do you mean by 'icky'?"

Riggins did not turn his gaze from the horizon. "Oh, you'll see."

Melinda shrugged and turned back toward the water. "Okay," she said, noticing a few boats in the general direction of Riggins's stare.

Douglas Sacrison

Some details of the Johnson-Katsopolis wedding had changed since the *Queen Ivan* first set sail. One thing that became negotiable was the time the wedding would begin (partially due to the fluctuating food order that was stressing out pastry chef Leonid Cupabascim). Delilah and her mother felt that if things needed to be pushed up or pushed back, it was no big deal to simply inform the guests that plans had changed because they were all on one boat. They had not considered that many of Joey's elderly relatives were enormous fans of structure and tradition. So when, two days prior to the wedding, guests were informed that the time had changed, there was a bit of an uproar from some of Joey's relations (much of the fuss was voiced about in Greek, though, so Delilah's feelings were spared).

The upshot was that on the day of the wedding, Joey's grandparents, great-aunts, and great-uncles were befuddled about the whole affair. Someone should have written details down for them. Since that had not occurred, the relatives opted to get dressed as if the wedding were at seven in the morning, then wait around until someone came to fetch them.

Amassed in Joey's paternal grandparents' suite, all spiffy-looking, they awaited orders and reminisced about the old days in the old country. Some spirits were enjoyed, despite the time of day.

Then, notwithstanding some hearing loss amongst the group, a familiar sound was heard. Some general shushing quelled one uncle's story and all present leaned forward to pinpoint the noise.

Crash! A pause. Crash! Another pause. Then another

Crash!

Without saying so, each person in the room (save for Uncle Leo, whose hearing was shot) recognized that sound. The sweet sound of plates being smashed against the ground, with much gusto. Plate-smashing is a long-standing tradition at Greek weddings (though one that usually occurs after the ceremony, a fact this group discounted).

"We're missing the wedding!" exclaimed Grandma Katsopolis. So out the door they went, some quicker than others. They rushed as fast as their geriatric limbs could take them. From their quarters, to the deck, to a wide door, down a hallway, around a corner (they were unaware this was the long way), and bursting through the doors, they entered the banquet hall.

They were surprised to find no wedding at all. The noise, however, they had been correct about. Numerous plates were being smashed, with much gusto (though angry, not joyful, gusto). With an already sizable and intrigued (or horrified) crowd gathered around, a furious woman was picking up fine porcelain plate after fine porcelain plate, and then throwing them in the direction of a mustachioed, eye-patched man who was crawling across the floor.

The elderly wedding guests were relieved that the ceremony had not started without them.

At 9:51 a.m. (whatever time zone the ship was in), the *Queen Ivan's* small security force was notified of a domestic dispute unfolding in the ship's banquet hall. Surprised by the news but eager to do something, the security officers hopped up and headed toward the alleged skirmish to investigate.

Benito Martinez questioned his decision to move the chase into the banquet hall. He had acknowledged that food may be thrown at him, perhaps, but not heavy, fine porcelain plates. Maybe if his toe didn't hurt so much he would have been thinking clearer.

Toby was still in tow, wincing every time a plate smashed against the floor. The mess, he knew, would be his to clean up.

"But Mrs. Martinez, your husband is a *great* baseball player!" Toby shouted.

"Toby! Stop!" yelled Benito from his spot on the floor. "You're not helping!"

At this point, Maria launched into a speech about how Benito had deceived her and was a terrible husband, but since your narrator's Spanish is subpar, we will suffice to say that it was heart-rending. Toby also did not speak much Spanish, but was able to discern a certain amount of dissatisfaction, especially as the speech was accentuated with another smashed plate.

"Please, Maria!" tried Benito, taking a different angle, "Those plates are expensive!" And then a deserved smash.

As the aged wedding guests stepped further into the long room to better investigate the scene, the *Queen Ivan's* small security force made their way through the door. They, too, were surprised at Maria's choice of plate-throwing, especially given the readily accessible food. And they knew they needed to stop the enraged woman before there was nothing left on the ship to eat from.

Seeing that "the professionals" had arrived and his chances of getting an autograph today were slim to none, Toby decided it was okay to skip out on the rest of the situation. Slowly inching away from the security guys, he got one last glimpse of Maria cocking a plate above her head. Then he was back out in the fresh air.

"Whew!" he said, glad to have turned over jurisdiction to someone else. Completely disregarding the towels, he walked along the deck railing, peering out to sea. What a calm day, he thought, moving further from the unpleasant noises emanating from the banquet hall.

Toby clutched his heart when he saw his beloved Melinda. She looked so sparklingly clean he assumed she must have been polished recently, like the statue of a Greek goddess to whom she deserved comparison. Next to her stood the ever-gnarled Riggins, whom Toby did not find quite so attractive, but nonetheless interesting. He decided to approach the pair.

When he strode up to the old man and young woman, he noticed they were both staring at something on the horizon. He shot a cursory glance that way to show that he and Melinda had some of the same interests, but being terribly unobservant, saw nothing. Then he chose to speak.

"Hi, guys," he said, before worrying that Melinda was someone who gets fussy about being referred to as a guy.

Melinda turned and smiled. "Hi, Toby."

"What are you looking for?" Toby asked, turning back to the horizon.

"Riggins saw some boats out there, coming this way."

Toby squinted and saw the small grouping of yachts aimed at the *Queen Ivan.* He wondered how the salty old sailor had better vision than him. Maybe he was just more observant.

"Oh. Neat," Toby stammered.

Riggins finally acknowledged the younger man's presence. "Neat," he scoffed. "Ha!"

Toby's befuddlement elicited a response from Melinda. "Riggins made some comment about them posing a danger …" she said, offering an adorable shrug. Toby shrugged back, which made Melinda smile. They turned back to the sea. Toby kind of wished the boats would disappear, so that he and Melinda could stare at a blank horizon, perhaps while holding hands. But he could settle for this. What lovely boats they were.

In contrast to the seemingly peaceful view from the ship's deck, the scene in the banquet hall had reached a boiling point. The security guys were trying to figure out how to best disarm Maria. They were given pause because of all the Spanish that Maria was speaking, and wondered if they should say something in English or try to recall their collective one year of high school Spanish. Just before an attempt to overpower the perpetrator, things took a turn for the worse.

"I'm sorry, Maria!" begged Benito Martinez, hiding beneath a table. "I never wanted to hurt you!" he shouted.

"How could you marry someone and lie to her so … completely?" Maria demanded, coming around the edge of a table to line up a clear shot.

Cornered, Benito Martinez knew he only had one chance. Mustering the most sincere facial expression he could, Benito spoke.

"I lied because I love you."

Maria looked deeply into his wet, beseeching eyes before she responded.

"That's the dumbest thing I've ever heard in my life."

With that, Maria raised another plate above her head and threw it toward Benito. The plate smashed on the hardwood floor, but a large chunk flew up and struck her husband's temple. Benito was knocked out cold.

For the first time since Toby showed her the baseball card, Maria Martinez felt a modicum of remorse. Not for the plate-throwing, just for hitting her target.

"Oops," she said as the security guys strode over.

The ocean became incredibly calm, as if it too was paying close attention to what was about to unfold, when the *Helga II* came astride the *Queen Ivan*. The ship stopped to accommodate the visitors. The *Queen Ivan* dwarfed the yacht, but the yacht did not seem to mind. At its bow was the somewhat-dread pirate Captain Hans Heissel Jr., calculator in hand. He tried his best to hide a wry smile.

At this point, news of the incoming fleet had caused numerous extra persons to join Melinda, Toby, and the smirking Riggins at the ship's railing. Pushing his way to the front of the pile was the cruise director, a bespectacled, balding man, always with a clipboard in hand. The senior staff members, never having been approached by a small fleet of yachts, had put him in charge of investigating. It was generally assumed that the boats were lost and asking for directions.

The cruise director stared down at Hans Heissel. Hans

called up. "Ahoy!"

"Ahoy," the cruise director replied. "Do you speak English?"

"Well enough," Hans Heissel replied in his intriguing Swiss accent.

"What can we help you with?" asked the cruise director, with an air of displeasure, since an encounter with yachts was not listed on his clipboard.

"Funny you should ask," the pirate captain said. "We have been caught in a terrible storm and been thrown quite off track." Immediately a fair bit of money changed hands at the railing.

Somewhat relieved but still hoping to get rid of the fleet, the cruise director pointed in the direction the sun was hanging out. "Ah. Well that way is east."

A normal person might have chuckled at this dismissal, but the socially inept Hans Heissel accepted it because he likely would have said the same thing. His response was locked and loaded.

"Yes, of course, but more importantly, during the terrible storm most of our restrooms suffered great damage. Many of us having been holding it for quite some time now," Hans said, trying unsuccessfully to sound piteous. "We beseech thee for permission to use your maps and bathrooms."

The cruise director turned and used his walkie-talkie to update the ship's senior command on what was transpiring. So eager to offer the ship's services to the distressed fleet, the most senior crew members radioed back to send sincere condolences and invite the pirates on board the ship (of course, they did not know they were pirates).

The cruise director turned back and gave an insincere smile. "Our bathrooms are your bathrooms."

Hans Heissel smiled back, quite sincerely.

Quietly, Riggins stepped away from the railing to return to his quarters.

So, with the ship's whole small security force tending to a plate-throwing incident and a senior staff who really dropped the ball when it came to precautions, the *Queen Ivan* was invaded by pirates.

They ascended an extended ladder one by one, with innocence in their eyes and piracy in their hearts. Though many thought it would look best to carry knives between their teeth as they climbed, their commander had instilled in them a need for secrecy. Among them was a single Taser, procured during some Christmastime plundering. It was strapped to the leg of Jacques, the rugby team captain.

With that insincere smile still adorning his face, the cruise director led Jacques, Kurtis, Mort, Fingers, and a handful of other pirates toward the nearest bathroom. In no time the cruise director had been Tased, tied up, and hidden in a closet next to the bathroom. Next, the pirates emptied their pockets of the newspapers they were carrying and quickly started a small fire in one of the stalls. Though it was not part of the plan, the pirates went ahead and used the bathroom (though it would have been wise to do that before they lit it on fire).

Upon rushing back out and hearing that the majority of the security detail was attending to an incident in the banquet hall, the pirates had a good laugh at the fact that the fire, meant as a diversion, proved unnecessary. A barricade made of overturned tables and life rings tied around door handles was rigged at each entrance to the banquet hall, trapping all the people who migrated there to witness the marital dispute. This was accomplished without causing much of a stir because the ship's crew was preoccupied by more pirates climbing the ladder and acting out a strong desire to use the bathroom. With no cruise director to be found, the young crew members were pointing to different bathrooms, always with a smile. One more bathroom fire was lit before Kurtis had the chance to inform his comrades that the security team was already indisposed. The people in the banquet hall failed to notice that they were at this point trapped, so intrigued were they by the aftermath of Maria's tirade.

Next on the list of things to do was find the bridge of the ship to overtake the vessel's senior staff. It would have been easier to find if the pirates hadn't Tased the cruise director so prematurely. Since the pirates were still not presumed to be anything but stranded sailors, they were able to ask other staff members how to reach the captain. After politely asking each question, they would of course Tase each poor staff person and tie them up.

There was some discontent among the few passengers that were paying attention to the pirates' actions, but they were too chicken to do anything. So it was back to sunbathing.

Eventually the pirates found their way to the bridge, where they met up with the ship's captain, a somewhat boring fellow who consequently had not made it into this story until now. There by the master controls they shook hands with some nicely dressed men who were apparently important on the ship. Then they Tased them. (This was really much easier than it should have been). They did not Tase the boring captain, however. They told him to put his hands up. Then the pirates had a blast destroying the ship's radio.

"Wha … what are you doing?" he asked, more surprised than he should have been after letting strangers run around his ship unsupervised.

Jacques, the big bearded Frenchman, informed him, "We will let our captain inform you."

Meekly, the ship's captain replied, "Okay."

After telling him to pretend to be calm, the pirates led him back out onto the deck and over to where Hans Heissel eagerly awaited their conversation. The Swiss-born former mathematician grinned up at the captain, who gave a timid nod back.

"Hello, Captain," Hans Heissel said.

"Hi … there," was the reply.

"I am Captain Hans Heissel," the pirate leader told him. "I would like to have a word with you."

"Oh sure," the boring captain said. "Whatever you would like."

The steady stream of pirates climbing the ladder was halted for a moment as the timid, boring man was helped onto the ropes and began his descent onto the hull of the *Helga II*. Hans Heissel might have extended a hand to help him or to shake if he were not so poor at social interactions. Hans was rather giddy about what was going on, though, and it showed. He stepped up as the cruise ship captain steadied his feet. Hans whispered in his ear.

"I am a pirate, as are all these guys. And all those guys up there. We are commandeering your beautiful ship."

The boring captain had been afraid of that. He whispered back in Hans' ear, "Oh no, you wouldn't want to do that." The plea was horrible.

"No, I'm very sure that I do," Hans whispered, though the whispering served no real purpose. To show that his life was not in danger (just his boat's), he put a comforting hand on the small of the other man's back, which just made matters worse for the poor guy.

And Hans Heissel was true to his word. With the steady trickle now arming themselves before climbing aboard, the *Queen Ivan* was thoroughly swimming with pirates at this point. As more men from the other yachts hopped on board the ship, the passengers and crew of the *Queen Ivan* were rounded up. They did as they were told because of all the gun-waving, since none of them were aware of the lack of bullets (even if they had been, no one really wants to get smacked with a gun). The pirates started with the people on the deck, who finally stopped their suntanning when they were poked by said guns.

These scantily clad persons were herded to the *Queen Ivan's* lifeboats. Much pleading and fretting was had, along with a bit of grumbling. Next the pirates went through and knocked on cabin doors to scoop out the remaining passengers. These people, most of them wearing more than the sunbathers, were escorted up to the deck and into lifeboats, too. The people unwittingly trapped in the banquet hall were hauled out, displeased by the scene into which they stepped. The security guys slapped their foreheads as they were tied together. Even the cruise director was retrieved from the closet. Hans instructed the buccaneers to load boats with passengers first. Thus the ship's staff were mostly tied to the railing or individually lashed to a deck chair as they watched in horror. There was so much confusion that the process was reasonably efficient.

Scared, frustrated, and accepting her fate as diplomat amid the hubbub, Melinda decided she would address the pirate captain. In the subdued panic, it became clear that none of the inept senior staff members would be any help. So the skills learned on her high school's debate team would be put to the test. Donning a brave face, Melinda stood up as tall as someone tied to a deckchair could.

"I want to talk to your captain," she proclaimed. Some passengers were frightened by her action, while others thought it laudable and planned to say so on the ship's comment cards.

The pirates were somewhat surprised, assuming that of all the people who were likely to put up a stink it would be a slightly older, tall, strapping male. But these are the kinds of preconceived notions one would expect from a group of burly pirates, so whatever. The armed brigands looked at each other, shrugged, and decided the request might as well be granted.

Melinda was led to the bow, where Captain Hans Heissel Jr., newly christened commander of the *Queen Ivan*, stood looking out to sea, hands behind his back and newspaper hat atop his noggin.

"Um, Captain," Melinda said.

Hans turned to her and smiled. "I am that, yes. The much-feared and worry-provoking Captain Hans Heissel."

"Okay," she replied. Melinda swallowed hard before she spoke again. "I must politely request, on behalf of the crew of the *Queen Ivan*, that you please leave the ship in peace now."

"Why would I do that?" Hans asked, but not in the smug, sarcastic tone you'd expect from a bad guy. He was genuinely curious.

Melinda was unsure of her best approach. "Because we are simply a peaceful cruise ship full of innocent passengers. And staff. This attack is unwarranted."

Hans Heissel was confused. "The people on this ship all have a bunch of money, don't they?"

Melinda was leery. "Yes..."

"Then this attack is very non-unwarranted." He nodded stoically.

Melinda frowned. She was finding the man less intimidating than she had guessed, but more befuddling.

"Captain, for your own sake, I recommend you leave because the navy will be here soon and it will be your neck that is in danger." Melinda was almost surprised that the comment leapt from her mouth, especially since necks in danger had not yet been addressed. The pirates behind her looked at each other, impressed.

"No. This will not happen," Hans told her, then turned back toward the sea.

"Well, why not?" Melinda asked.

"The ship's radio does not work anymore," replied Hans, turning back toward her, and continuing the turn until he faced the waters once more.

"Well, what are you going to do with us, then?"

Hans's circular rotation again stopped when he was facing her. He gave a convoluted expression that suggested he had yet to think about this. "We pirates will leave all you non-pirates on yonder coast," he said, waving an arm in the direction of the African continent, which was right over there. "And then we will drive off in your boat. It will work out well for us."

"Please, Captain," she responded. "Have mercy on us and just take wallets and passports and then leave us alone."

"Thank you," Hans said, snapping his fingers. "I had forgotten about that." He sighed and wrinkled his nose for no apparent reason, in the fashion that a socially inept person might do something for no apparent reason. "I am marginally apologetic for this inconvenience, but I have made my decision to take this ship and I am sticking with it." In truth, Hans was not even marginally apologetic. The fact that he was really ruining everyone's day had no effect on him.

Hans Heissel turned so that he was again gazing out at the vast ocean. With a wave of his hand, he commanded the attending pirates. "Take her away, boys."

Melinda tried to protest, but Hans was not listening. She took a modicum of solace in the fact that it appeared no one would be killed. At least not yet.

The awkwardly smug Hans Heissel surveyed the ocean, his wet playground, and the land growing larger just to the east. A breeze nearly caught his newspaper hat, but his quick reaction snatched it and returned it to its proper place.

"Ah! Not even you, wind, are a match for the dreaded and unapologetic Captain Hans Heissel!"

31

The last phone call had decided things. Placing the super-fancy cellular telephone that resembled a spaceship back in his multi-hundred dollar pocket, Clayton Stern decided that he had only one option. He would go to the Skeleton Coast and settle things himself.

"Tiddle-pumpkins," he said to Isaiah Burtlyre, "Pack my things."

32

Jamie Brewster was left unaware that two gentlemen with whom he shared a common destination had gotten themselves into quite an adventure not long before his arrival on the Skeleton Coast.

(Obviously before Jamie found it) Koke and Kipchak were flying about in the very same Channel 7 helicopter that had been getting people in so much trouble lately. Upon reaching the coast, Koke, Kipchak, and their cohorts had set about furthering their business. It was decided they would use the organization's new toy to scope out their next target, which had seemed a slightly more daunting task before the hijacking of a helicopter.

So, with the crew members of the crabbing boat sifting through the wreckage of their vessel, the other two Mongolian smugglers dawdling around trying to stay out of the clean up effort, and the news team plotting the possibility of escape versus staying put to cover a good story, Koke and Kipchak left everyone behind to fly away. The trek was meant as a day trip, so the aircraft had been filled with rations. And also hay.

Oh, what sand! The dunes were quite lovely from the air, when you weren't walking along them, and their shadows played across each other like the shadows that might play across a beach volleyball court, only much larger. The flight was lengthy, and though picturesque, its purpose was unsuccessful. Koke and Kipchak scoured the ground, but for all the thoroughness of the inspection, they did not see any black rhinoceroses.

This should not have come as a big surprise, seeing as how the black rhinoceros is a rare creature to spot on the best of days. Though it can sometimes be found in the land just east of the Skeleton Coast, it is not an animal that allows itself to be seen too often. In fact, Kipchak and Koke did not spot many creatures at all, what with the landscape being significantly less popular among animals than, say, the tropical rainforest. They had also hoped to see the elephants that are sometimes spotted carousing about the interior dunes. But it was concluded that an elephant might be too large to fit on board their ship (of course, a black rhinoceros was, too, but they had not considered this).

After quite a bit of time aloft, Kipchak came to recognize that the helicopter was running out of fuel and that they needed to land. He guided them back toward the coast, as they continued scoping the ground for their quarry, sometimes mistaking big rocks for rhinoceroses. But Kipchak, a skilled pilot from his military days, put the helicopter down with relative ease.

Being rough-and-tumble types, Kipchak and Koke opted to continue their quest for the elusive black rhinoceros. Kipchak felt the helicopter was safe until their return, when there would be at least enough gas to get them back to the crabbing vessel. So strapping their tranquilizer guns over their shoulders and grabbing the hay bale, meant for luring a rhino, the two trekked east, into the unforgiving dunes.

It was a pretty dumb idea. They found a nice spot atop

a dune and waited with binoculars and guns at the ready, hoping to tranquilize a rhinoceros until they fetched the former crabbers to come help transport it back to the ship. Or, if need be, they could just extinguish its life and take the important parts for their medicines (the trouble being their boss' desire to have live animals).

Thankfully for the black rhinoceroses, Kipchak and Koke failed miserably. For hours and hours they sat patiently, but eventually got bored and hungry. So as twilight set in, they opted to return to the helicopter for dinner. They lugged the hay bale with them, wishing they hadn't. The sky became darker and darker, as it does in most places in the world as night approaches, and fog rolled in.

Soon Koke and Kipchak found themselves where they thought the helicopter should be. Yet it was not. So they wandered through the fog all willy-nilly. The hay bale was deemed an acceptable loss, and the two men dropped it (they would come across it twice more). It was a rough night for the men, but probably well deserved for their desire to kill a black rhinoceros, and seemingly every other endangered species. A couple hours before sunrise, Koke and Kipchak found themselves back on the coast, where their boat sat in a heap. It was decided that the helicopter, too, was an acceptable loss, especially given its lack of gas. So the two poachers marched up to the crabbers' vessel.

When asked what had happened to the helicopter, Kipchak and Koke said it had been attacked by a black rhinoceros.

33

What with the moose fiasco and her sketchy boss and having to deal with the supremely fussy Roenicks, Candy the flight attendant decided she had had enough of her current job. (Mostly it was the Roenicks, with the moose being a distant second). And this time she had really had it, unlike those other times when she had had it. But whether she had really had it then or had only truly had it now, she had also had it with saying she had had it, and thus this was really the point at which she had had it, whatever *it* might be.

Being a polite and honest young woman, Candy felt it was only right to travel to his home and inform Clayton Stern of her resignation in person. She was not looking forward to the encounter, but felt that her boss, though somewhat creepy, deserved that much. He did not, of course, deserve that much, but Candy was unaware of how vile Clayton Stern truly was.

So Candy had the pilot fly her to Clayton Stern's fortress in South Africa. She let herself in, as always. Entering his second-largest office, she did not find Stern, but did accidentally find a pile of interesting paperwork and a map of a region familiar to her. Surprised, she decided to use Clayton's phone without permission.

34

At high tide, the motley crew of Earnest, Jamie, and Mickey trudged their way through the brutally dry dunes of the Skeleton Coast. Progress was slow at best.

Jamie's running shoes filled with sand and thus seemed to weigh twice as much as when he purchased them. Here and there he would stop and say, "Hold on," which Earnest would get excited about, thinking his new friend was having an epiphany. Each time Earnest would be slightly disappointed when Jamie took his shoes off, one at a time, to dump out the sand. With each dumping, more sand was reluctant to depart, and thus more sand accumulated in Jamie's shoes.

Earnest, on the other hand, seemed to be just fine with his choice of footwear, since by not wearing shoes he avoided sand accumulation. Few people in his village troubled with shoes. Because of this practice, Earnest's feet were quite tough. At one point, Jamie, frustrated with his shoes, pointed out how Earnest's feet were like baseball mitts. Earnest was unsure what a "baseball mitt" was, but smiled and showed off his soles when Jamie pointed at them.

Mickey, however, had the best walking equipment, as his feet were essentially shoes. Of course, moose feet were not meant for walking through sand, so he had a bit of trouble finding steady footing here and there.

But though a solid place to step was hard to find, he

made another discovery that he liked even more. While Jamie and Earnest looked out to sea, in hopes of spotting who knows what, Mickey glanced to the other side of the dune and saw something that was considered food to certain mammals (and a bed to others). A hay bale sat in the sand, ripe for the taking. Mickey ambled toward it.

Earnest and Jamie were surprised at the presence of the hay bale, out here amongst no farms whatsoever. There was no hay baler, nor any farmers, nor cows. Just one large hay bale.

Though Jamie and Earnest ate no hay, they were glad to see it as well, because it meant their poor moose friend would not starve. It also meant they would not have to give him rations of "people food." In no time Earnest's curiosity drifted from the hay bale, but Jamie's quizzical expression didn't waver as he watched the moose devour the yellow grass.

After a period, Mickey eased up on the hay. The bale was noticeably smaller at this point. Earnest sat atop it, looking down as Mickey's great head nibbled where his feet dangled. Earnest giggled each time the moose's lips came close to his toes. Jamie, sitting on the dune and marveling at all the places sand had infiltrated his person, was amused at Earnest's little game. Mickey could not have cared less, but hoped the toes would not get in his way. Moose can get irritable quickly.

"Be careful, Earnest," Jamie advised, though he wondered if his little friend's feet were so tough that a couple toes bitten off it wouldn't ruin his day.

Jamie hoped maybe Mickey would be more agreeable to allowing the hay to be tied to his body than the other stuff. It took some time and patience and all of Jamie's vague memory of knots learned in six months of Boy Scouts, but he was able to attach the hay bale to Mickey's back.

"It's for your own good, you know," Jamie told him, looking straight into the large moose eyes.

On they trekked, trekking up dunes and trekking down dunes. Trekking through rocky places and not-so-rocky places. In time, the sun dropped below the horizon, as if off to take a nice dip in the Atlantic Ocean.

They spent the night on top of a dune, not far from the beach. Mickey, who had here and there plopped down along the journey because he felt it was bedtime, was quite willing to turn in when his human counterparts found the resting spot. He was not quite so pleased with Earnest's decision to use him as a pillow, and made some noises to indicate his displeasure. Jamie used a variety of hand motions before Earnest got the message that the moose did not like the idea. Jamie and Earnest ended up trying to sleep on the sheet that had contained the team's provisions. It was not the most pleasant sleeping arrangement for any of them. Soon Jamie realized that the roaring waves blitzing the coastline were going to keep him up all night. A while later he also realized that he was going to be very very cold, because even though Africa can be very very hot, it could get very very cold at night along the Skeleton Coast. Jamie longed for the confines of his old hiding spot on the *Queen Ivan*.

As perhaps mentioned earlier, the Skeleton Coast is littered with the skeletal remains of ships that met their demise. So it should come as no surprise that in the morning, at low tide, Mickey, Earnest, and Jamie came across such a wreck. It did, however (come as a surprise, that is), seeing as how the three travelers were not blessed with an expansive knowledge of the Skeleton Coast.

Mickey was unimpressed. Earnest, however, was delighted, because he saw that Jamie was overjoyed. His eyes lit up as if he saw what Santa brought him, and once again not thinking things through, he hustled toward the metallic mess. Recalling Janet's words, "You moron!" but also "treasure" and "shipwreck," Jamie was sure this was the thing for which he had been searching. It was not as good as finding Janet and Tom, but perhaps this shipwreck's treasure would lead to their rescue. Earnest was intrigued by Jamie's behavior, as it seemed very ungrown-uppy. He shrugged at Mickey, who did not reciprocate, but seemed to share the sentiment. With Earnest gently tugging the leash, the boy/moose combo hustled behind the former news team helicopter pilot.

"Shay-mee! Wait!" called Earnest. Jamie did not answer, as his feet were already slapping the wet sand. A big stupid grin painted his face, and though he had no idea what the shipwreck was hiding, Jamie was convinced it would only increase the width of his big stupid grin.

He reached the boat and speedily inspected it. Most of the ship was atop the sand, cocked at a strange angle. It seemed to be made of rust and looked like it had been sitting in the spot for many years. And though dilapidated and foreboding, it was mostly intact. Jamie took a big gulp as he stepped through a large hole in the ship's hull.

Thankfully there were also holes in the deck that provided some light for Jamie to see. Not so thankfully, he failed to see anything of merit. Thankfully he also saw nothing that could be construed as dangerous, unless of course you count the rusty and jagged metal that was just itching to cave in. But at least there were no armed men or crocodiles (armed or otherwise). Jamie scratched his head and decided to look around further.

A minute later Earnest's face arrived and poked through the same hole in the hull. Mickey was not apt to explore, nor was he small enough to fit through the hole.

"Shay-mee?" Earnest asked.

"I'm not seeing anything, Earnest," Jamie told him without turning around. "It would help if I at least knew what I was looking for."

Brows furrowed, the two searched for a few minutes. There were some wooden objects that might have once been something but were now just soggy. None of these appeared to be treasure. There were some metal boxes that were tossed on their side and covered in sea salt and rust, which did not contain much more than sand. There was something that resembled a desk and there were a few frayed wires coming out of some place. Who knew what this boat was in its heyday.

Earnest decided to move one of the metal boxes to mimic Jamie and was enthralled to find a number of tiny crabs partying. They panicked upon their discovery, and scrambled around this way and that, some pinching the air to demonstrate their ferocity. Earnest cried out in his happiness at finding these silly little warriors.

"Oh-oh! What are you?" he exclaimed. "You are wonderful and funny at the same time!" He beckoned his friend. "Shay-mee, look! Look what I have discovered, Shay-mee!" Earnest hoped that whatever Jamie was looking for, these little creatures were either that thing or something even better.

Jamie walked over and looked down. Earnest grinned up at him and was surprised that his quizzical expression did not morph into celebration.

"Those are good-looking crabs," Jamie told him unenthusiastically, patting Earnest on the back. Earnest picked a few up and lifted them toward Jamie's face.

"These are fantastic! Are they what you have been looking for?"

Jamie backed away from the tiny snapping invertebrates.

"Those are really great, Earnest. But they aren't exactly what I'm looking for." Of course, neither of them realized that a question had been posed and answered in separate languages.

Jamie straightened and surveyed the ship's interior once more. He concluded this wreck definitely did not hold the treasure he was seeking, which should have come as no surprise because, as mentioned at least twice at this point, the Skeleton Coast is full of shipwrecks.

"Well, Earnest, let's head out."Jamie pointed to his head then to the hole in the hull. Earnest was confused by this signing, and more confused when Jamie mimicked a bunny hopping away, leaving him to wonder if the man had gone crazy in the ship's cabin. But soon the boy decided it was time to leave and did so. He gazed down at the little crabs, who had, by now, all tried to make burrows in the wet sand to hide from their young inquisitor.

"I will leave you now," Earnest told them, "so I hope you can go on without me." Then, although unsure how he would manage to carry them around, the boy decided that a few crabs would be excellent for his zoo.

Mickey was about twenty yards down the beach at this point, seeing no reason to stand around the rusty structure. Earnest hustled after him, crying his name and being careful not to crush the little crabs. He rushed past Jamie, who was looking exasperated, having had his hopes dashed so recently. But as his young friend reached his moose friend, Jamie recognized something in the distance. His eyes lit up once more. There, a good mile away but there nonetheless, was another shipwreck. He picked up the bundle and slung it over his shoulder. Maybe Jamie Brewster would find this treasure yet.

Earnest caught up to Mickey, who looked over but kept moving down the beach. The young man moved the five crabs to one hand as he put the other hand on the moose's furry side for support while he caught his breath.

"Mickey," said Earnest, "you left us!" But he could not stay mad at his zoo's biggest star. "I'm sure you had your reasons and they were not personal."

Jamie caught up with the rest of his party a few minutes later, smiling at Earnest. "Well, guys, I don't know about you, but I have faith that we'll find this treasure yet."

Earnest was happy to see his friend back in working order. "I don't know what you said, but maybe we can look at that boat," he said, pointing to the derelict ship he had noticed long before Jamie.

The crabs were put into one of the empty water jugs, along with some sand and sea-water. Nobody thought about feeding them.

35

Despite all his love of numbers and counting and whatnot, the Great Hans Heissel (as he recommended he be addressed at this point) had not taken the time to count all his little pirates. He had not made a list of names, nor even made tic marks on a piece of scratch paper. So as his forces had grown, he'd done no more than make some good estimates (he was, needless to say, very good at estimating). This meant that at any given point, Hans was not surprised to see an extra few pirates along for the ride.

When Fingers, Warren, and Jaomir found a large, muscular, mustachioed gentleman wearing an eye patch and sporting a large scar on his face, they assumed he must be a pirate. And in most instances, finding such a person among pirates would be a fair assumption to make. In this instance they had actually found a professional baseball player.

Benito Martinez was a bit dazed and confused as he regained consciousness and gathered his wits. What he could piece together was that he'd been struck on the head with a plate thrown by his wife and now a different group of people, a more menacing group, was aboard the ship in place of those who had been when he last closed his eyes. He considered that it might be a dream, but could not recall ever having a dream where he had such a headache. So he sat in the same heap in which he'd collapsed and surveyed the ships' new crew, until Fingers, Warren, and

Jaomir approached him.

"Hey you," Warren said as Fingers poked Benito with a large wooden spoon he had found on the floor. With this poke, Benito began to get his bearings.

"Come on," Warren continued. "The captain said we could set up a plank." He paused. "To make people walk on."

Benito looked from one face to the next as if he were an inquisitive puppy.

"Quit napping and come on. It's going to be great," Fingers informed Benito.

"And the captain won't be happy if he sees that you are just napping all day," added Jaomir.

Benito's brain wasn't in any mood for thinking after absorbing the force of the plate. Instead Benito followed the advice of his body, which chose to follow the pirates' advice. Warren and Jaomir cheered to see their compatriot excited about the plank as Fingers gave one more poke with the spoon.

Benito squinted at the sun as he stepped out onto the deck. The three men he was following multiplied as news of the plank spread. As he walked, his senses begrudgingly returned to him. As they did, his brain told him to continue playing along.

"They think you are a pirate!" he whispered to himself, though it would have been wiser to say this inside his head. He observed many gruff-looking men and a handful of gruff-looking women hustling about the ship's deck, rearranging the chairs to their liking. Many were headed in the same direction as Benito. When he came close to the ship's railing he saw that a concert-like atmosphere had erupted due to the new plank. (Surprisingly, where one would expect pirates to act like the crowd for some godawful Swedish metal band, they instead stood in rigid anticipation, more like the well-behaved, middle-aged crowd at a Sting concert.)

Jacques, long removed from his days as a sensible rugby team captain, balanced himself precariously on the ship's rail and put the finishing touches on some second-rate hammering. A hearty cheer went up from the amassed pirates. Benito felt it wise to join in. He also felt some sweat accumulate on his brow, and though the day was hot enough, it was probably due to the stress of finding oneself among a group of dangerous outlaws. Benito only half paid attention as a volunteer was picked from the crowd to give the plank a test run. And he cared considerably less than most of the disappointed pirates when, after a loud crack, the volunteer tumbled into the ocean.

While most of the buccaneers placed bets on whether the volunteer, a featherweight, would be devoured by sharks, Benito found the opportunity to dismiss himself.

"Oh boy, am I in trouble," he whispered out loud, again almost blowing his cover.

36

The crabs were grouchy. This was nothing new, as they were crabs, after all. Earnest, however, was not skilled at reading crabbiness.

By this point, it was not solely the crabs who were in a sour mood. Jamie was frustrated that no treasure nor coworkers had been discovered. Mickey was pretty sick of walking through the sand and would often have a seat, frustrating Jamie even further. Only Earnest retained his high spirits, since the farther he walked, the bigger his adventure.

"Shay-mee, did you see that small creature with a knife on its tail?" Earnest asked after seeing a scorpion. "Shay-mee, what sort of animals do you think are across the water?" he inquired, pointing out to sea. "Shay-mee, how many grains of sand do you think are on this beach?" he asked when he ran out of semi-relevant questions.

Earnest knew full well that it was unlikely these questions were registering with Jamie, but he still wished to engage him as best he could. Jamie, at first happy to have the young man's company, could have done without all the chitchat after the discovery of the shipwreck devoid of treasure. The empty boat had impressed upon him just how difficult the task ahead was, and the next empty boat and the next empty boat after that had just reinforced this notion. Jamie kept telling himself not to show any displeasure to Earnest. At present, the boy was the only friend he had. Aside from the moose, who was wearing on his patience with all of his sitting down.

Night fell at some point. The whole party was tired and hungry, though Earnest had gone to bed hungry before, so it annoyed him less. A part of Jamie wanted to press on, but it was overpowered by the part that wanted to shut down.

The moon softly illuminated the trio as they settled in for the evening atop a nice rounded dune. Mickey had been ready to call it a night for a good five hours, so plopped down like a building being imploded to make room for condos. Earnest followed the others' lead, nestling up against Mickey, who might have been less fond of the nestling if he weren't so tired. Jamie was borderline pouty, sitting down with crossed arms. He hmpfed as he glared down the moonlit coast.

Earnest, though unskilled in crab psychology and—arguably up until that moment, also regular old human psychology—saw his friend was unhappy and hoped he could cheer him up. The boy stepped into Jamie's line of sight and made a funny face (though it was not all *that* funny), as if the helicopter pilot were a crying toddler who might be appeased by this low brow humor. Jamie was confused. But when he deduced from Earnest's protruding tongue and ear-tugging that he was not attempting communication in the local custom but rather attempting to improve the man's spirits, Jamie smiled. It was a tired but honest smile, and Earnest clapped when he saw it.

"Thank you, Earnest," said Jamie. "But don't leave your face like that or it might stick." In his youth Jamie's mother had delivered this advice and forgotten to come clean once

Jamie grew up.

"I am sorry if I scared you, Shay-mee," Earnest apologized, though it was apparent there was no permanent damage.

"I wish I knew what you were saying, Earnest," Jamie told him.

In the morning, Jamie awoke thinking about how nice the sun felt on his body. Then he remembered where he was and felt much less nice. The situation had not improved during the night, except that now everything was brighter. Peering down the shoreline, Jamie's mood mimicked the sunlight and brightened slightly when he saw another derelict ship half a mile away. He may have been more excited had he not already been disappointed by a number of treasure-less and coworker-less shipwrecks. Nonetheless, he thought it would be a good place to start the day's hunt.

Hearing his friend's stirrings, Earnest arose smiling, tried to hide a yawn, and patted Mickey on his moose tummy.

"Arise, Mickey," the boy said to the tummy and the rest of the moose. "We need to follow Shay-mee," because Jamie had quietly gone to investigate the nearby shipwreck without waking his comrades. While many might appreciate being allowed to sleep a little longer, Earnest was offended.

Unsuccessfully tugging Mickey, Earnest hustled to catch up. "Shay-mee! Shay-mee, wait!"

Jamie sighed when he heard Earnest's displeasure. But displeasure did not sound quite the same in Earnest's language as it did in English. So when the boy caught up and said, "Shay-mee! You left us behind! We want to come, too! Can't you see how much Mickey wants to come?"

"A shipwreck," Jamie said, pointing and shrugging.

"You cannot just leave us like that, Shay-mee," Earnest continued, wagging a finger. "We have to stick together if we are going to do things, and stuff," he added, because he did not know the ultimate goal of their hike.

Jamie combated with, "I'm glad you enjoyed the few extra minutes of sleep, Earnest, but you could have slept longer. You didn't have to jump up and follow me. I would have come back for you after I discovered there was nothing on that shipwreck."

"No, Shay-mee. No, no, no!" Earnest's frustration was waning.

"Anyway," Jamie said, "There's another ship over there. I was going to check it for this elusive treasure." He pointed toward the new shipwreck.

Earnest gasped delightedly when he saw the dilapidated ship. "Another dead boat! What are we waiting for, Shay-mee? There could be more strange little animals! Or anything!"

Rebooted with positive energy, Earnest lead the way, with Mickey trudging along beside him because a shipwreck meant some shade.

A while later, the three reached their quarry. Earnest found a large gash from when the ship had encountered a sizable rock. He scrambled inside. Jamie followed with less enthusiasm. Mickey kept watch outside (well, he plopped down in the shade).

The wreck was once a respectable-sized barge, with the

large ship's cargo hold being the portion the two humans entered. The ship was tilted on its side, and another gash from another rock allowed a fair bit of sunlight to wash in. Jamie observed this boat's demise had been a bit more recent than the other wrecks because it contained less gunk. Still, he was not particularly optimistic about finding any treasure.

"Well, here we are, Earnest," he said. "One more stupid boat that is devoid of the riches we're looking for." *Riches* was not a word Jamie was used to saying.

Earnest, however, was elated. He climbed through the wreckage, hoping to find some sort of intriguing creature or its cousins. Jamie followed, muttering to himself about riches. They passed some secured boxes and crates, and some unsecured crates and boxes, not thinking much of them. Earnest was making a beeline for the back of the ship, throwing caution to the wind as he made his way over dangerous edges and structures that looked ready to cave in at any moment. Jamie might have warned him of the peril had he any parental instincts. Instead, the helicopter pilot was becoming preoccupied with the boxed cargo. A shred of hope hinted that maybe it was treasure inside the cases. Earnest was becoming preoccupied himself, as he had discovered a deceased sea star near the back of the cargo hold.

"Shay-mee! Shay-mee, look! A living hubcap of some sort!" he called.

But Jamie was not allowing Earnest's preoccupation to overpower his own preoccupation, as he found a large wooden crate that was broken open. Jamie saw that inside the broken crate were numerous cardboard boxes, mostly soaking wet. He gripped the first box and pulled it to him, closing his eyes and wishing as hard as he could that there would be sparkling bars of gold, big rubies, and mysterious bejeweled crowns inside. Pulling the cardboard flaps wide, he dared to open his eyes.

It was kitchenware. A box full of spatulas. He opened another cardboard container. A box full of pots. Another was a box full of pans. Rolling pins. Colanders. A whole bunch of kitchenware. No riches. Dejected, and scolding himself for getting his hopes up, Jamie let out a big sigh as he stood over the box of spatulas.

Earnest ran over and pushed the deceased sea star into his face.

"Look at this crazy thing!" he said.

Jamie did not want a deceased sea star in his face. "Neat, Earnest," he said, gently pushing it away. Then he vented, or perhaps had a revelation. "You know, I don't know what exactly I was hoping to do once we found a literal boatload of treasure, but I think I thought it was really going to help out."

Earnest smiled, assuming Jamie was spouting facts about the sea star. The helicopter pilot sighed again and let his head drop. Without really meaning to, his gaze meandered through the box of spatulas. His brow furrowed as he cocked his head, trying to see if he was imagining things. But alas, as he extracted one of the spatulas for closer examination, he realized he was not.

There, on a red rubber patch on the black plastic handle, was the company's logo, which spelled out, in extra-fancy writing, the word *Treasure*.

37

"Think, Benito! Think!" Benito Martinez was whispering to himself. Stuck on board a newly re-christened pirate ship and mistaken for a pirate, Benito knew he was in danger. But his more immediate problem was that he was very hungry from his long day. So his first order of business was to eat.

It was mildly thrilling to walk into the large kitchen, which had been off-limits when Benito was a mere passenger. As a pirate, nothing was off-limits. Glancing around, he considered there might be other perks to being a pirate. Realizing this was not the train of thought he should be following, he slapped himself. Forgetting his new scar, he screamed a little when his open palm touched his face.

Immediately, a figure popped up from the other side of the long kitchen, causing Benito to scream again. But the figure looked scared, too, so Big Ben cautiously walked over. He felt relieved to see a chef hat instead of a pirate hat.

"Please don't kill me," said Leonid Cupabascim. He'd had to make that request a number of times that day.

Benito looked around, then spoke in a hushed tone. "I wasn't going to."

"Oh thank God," Leonid said, sliding back into the seated position he'd been in when Benito entered. His right arm remained raised. Benito noticed that the young chef was handcuffed to a waist-level metal railing that ran through most of the kitchen. The railing had been meant for the cooks to have something to grab onto in choppy waters. The pirates apparently found another use for it.

Leonid looked up. "If you want me to make something, please pick something pretty simple."

Benito was confused. "What?"

The dejected cook jiggled his right arm. "You guys only left me with one arm to cook with."

"No, no!" Benito said, grinning at Leonid. "I'm not one of them."

The chef was puzzled. Benito decided the situation called for full disclosure, and that requests for autographs were not as bad as being killed by pirates. He flipped up his eye patch.

"I'm Benito Martinez!" he whispered. Leonid's expression did not change. He was more of a basketball fan (at least until the despicable Clayton Stern bought and moved his favorite team; now he only watched college basketball). He was not so good with professional baseball players.

Benito pushed further. "I was a passenger!" Still the puzzled face. "I was in disguise!"

"You were a passenger disguised as a pirate?" asked Leonid.

"No, not as a pirate."

"Then why do you have an eye patch?"

"Some people who aren't pirates wear eye patches."

"None that I've met."

"Well, either way, I'm Benito Martinez." He was still waiting for this to register.

Finally Leonid remembered seeing this man in the dining hall pre-pirate attack. "Okay, I think I remember you..."

"Good!" Benito said, expecting the next comment would regard an autograph.

"So they left you here, too?" Leonid asked.

"Yes! They think I'm a pirate!"

"Well, I can see why. You're wearing an eye patch."

"I know."

The two felt slightly better, knowing they were not completely alone on the hijacked vessel.

"When they were rounding up all the passengers, their captain realized it would be nice to have someone to cook for them," Leonid vented. "He came down and threatened me, but he isn't very good at threats. His guys dug up some handcuffs from security and did this to make sure I didn't go anywhere. They didn't consider that I might need two hands to cook." He softly banged the back of his head on the oven he was leaning against. "And I'm right-handed."

Benito nodded and sat beside the chef.

"Well, we sure are in a pickle," he said, hoping that the baseball reference might jog Leonid's memory regarding celebrities sitting next to him.

"Yeah, man. I guess so," replied Leonid.

Soon the two men got into standard questions like *What should we do?* and *How do we get out of this?* Much head-scratching ensued, until they generally agreed that the passengers should probably be saved, leading to, *...But how?*

As the brainstorming session progressed, both brainstormers were frightened by the sudden emergence of a crotchety old sailor, who mysteriously emerged from the walk-in refrigerator with frosting on his face.

38

The Great Hans Heissel had done one nice thing for the passengers of the *Queen Ivan* (though not on purpose). He had calculated when the mighty waves of the Skeleton Coast were (relatively) calm before sending the overcrowded lifeboats to shore. So the passengers all somehow made land, though sixty percent of them had thrown up on the ride.

They clambered up the beach, some crying, some swearing, some silent, some still intoxicated from their morning cocktails, some finally realizing the pirate attack was not a prank, and a couple still not realizing this. The former passengers and the former crew marched their way up the wet sand, leaving the boats where they landed. Most people did not get the opportunity to change clothes before they were herded into lifeboats, so there were some decidedly bad clothing options for the Skeleton Coast; mostly bathrobes or casual-yet-still-somehow-semi-formal wear. Some of the passengers who needed assistance on this short hike were aided by some of the crew, who still felt an obligation because they continued to wear their green-and-white striped polo shirts. Other crew members no longer felt this responsibility, and were therefore not tipped.

No one was in a very good mood. The bright side was that it was a nice day out (though it would soon become unreasonably hot).

The group regrouped at the bottom of the closest dunes, which were far enough away from the water that it appeared the tide never reached them. The dunes did not provide much in the way of shade, but it felt like maybe later in the day they would (they did not). By this time, one might think that the senior crew members would have taken charge, maybe even accepted some responsibility, and begun explaining to the passengers the emergency plan. Instead, they all looked at each other, hoping that someone else would do something. The passengers huddled together with their families and/or drinking partners, consoling one another as best they could.

Soon passengers started wanting answers, though. The least of which was why a man, a boy, and a moose were moving down the coast in their direction.

Melinda walked around the sandy refugee camp, trying hard to think straight, since it appeared that no other crew members were. As she paced, she looked for opportunities to aid any passengers in need of attention, particularly young children and the elderly. Following her like a loyal puppy was Toby, who was more concerned about finding a granola bar or something. Being the hardest-working crew member, Melinda sweated in her polo shirt, but he failed to believe it. He was amazed at how powerful and assertive she appeared, and all without breaking a sweat. Her example failed to rub off on Toby, who was lucky enough to find a middle-aged woman who had a couple of granola bars in her purse.

Melinda eventually became aware that Toby was walking behind her, and assumed he shared her desire to help out.

"I can't *believe* these guys," she whispered, nodding toward the senior crew members, who were sitting in a small group, discussing what the ship's manual said about similar catastrophes.

"Yeah, me neither," agreed Toby, though he thought she was indicating the Johnson-Katsopolis wedding party, who were standing around in their Sunday best.

"We're going to have to do something soon if nobody else does," Melinda said.

The two kept walking through the throngs of accidental beach goers, with Toby listening to Melinda and trying to figure out how to impress her. He patted a child or two on their heads in an effort to look compassionate. One of the more exasperated passengers beseechingly grabbed Toby's arm and asked, "Are we going to die?" Not knowing the answer, Toby simply shrugged. As he caught up to Melinda, the question helped him become aware of how dire their straits were. Toby recognized he might not make it out of the bizarre situation. And more importantly, he thought, Melinda might not, either. The idea made him want to find another granola bar.

Although their two trains of thought were different trains headed in different directions at different speeds, they happened to arrive at the same thought at almost the same moment.

"Hey," said Melinda, triggering Toby to finish with, "Where's Riggins?"

Their eyes swept the crowd. Both worried whether the old codger had lasted through the events of the past few hours.

Searching high and low for Riggins, Toby noticed from afar another familiar face and became slightly fanatical because maybe this familiar face could help. Though now the familiar face was accompanied by a young boy and a moose.

39

When Jamie Brewster first spotted the newly settled colony of castaways, he strongly considered turning around and going back the way he'd come. With proverbial egg on his face given the whole *Treasure* debacle, he did not care why hundreds of affluent people were milling about on Namibia's oddly named Gelatin Coast.

A few things made him reconsider leaving: first, Earnest seemed elated to see members of his own species, even if it wasn't his favorite species in the world. (Even Mickey appeared pleased at the prospect of joining other people, perhaps because they might be more useful than the two jokers who had dragged him through a desert.) Secondly, Jamie heard the voice of reason speaking up, because any human contact was better than marching further through a barren wasteland.

So Jamie, Earnest, and Mickey approached the throngs of people who had all come unprepared for an impromptu camping trip. Many looked up, while many others simply did not care about a moose and his friends since they already had enough problems. The heat was beginning to get to people, so some assumed they were seeing a rather peculiar mirage.

When Jamie noticed Toby had broken from the crowd and was approaching him with a girl in tow, he could not help but grumble under his breath. He liked Toby, but some people are just not the kind of people you want to see when you are in a bad mood.

Toby's mood was much improved. For no good reason, Toby thought that maybe Jamie could help fix their predicament. And if that was the case, Toby could dazzle Melinda by being the one person who knew this savior. The day was shaping up to be a potentially good one for the mousy young man, if he blocked out all the wailing and crying of the passengers.

Melinda was confused when Toby grasped her hand in a manner uncharacteristic of what she knew about him thus far. He seemed determined and confident, for once, despite the fact that his grip was still so flimsy she wondered how he was able to operate silverware. His newfound confidence sparked her curiosity and bled into her through their connected hands, like a leaky battery.

"What are we doing, Toby?" Melinda asked as they passed sweaty onlookers, despite being pretty sure they were going over to the guys with the moose.

"I know that guy," Toby answered, without looking back.

They passed some of the useless clustered senior crew members, who knew people would be demanding blood momentarily. Toby made exemplary eye contact with the captain and cruise director, puffed out his chest, and pointed toward the moose and his cohorts.

"There!" he exclaimed. "That guy's name is Jamie, and maybe he can help us." After taking another breath he added, "He's pretty important."

So Jamie made a sighing, whimpering, harrumph noise as he saw the group of people approaching him multiply. Conversely, Earnest's excitement was multiplied by the number of approachers, while Mickey's level of excitement was divided by one.

"Look, Shay-mee!" Earnest said, with only his delighted tone decipherable for the pilot. "Some people to help us!" The boy waved and assumed Jamie was on the same page.

Jamie, Earnest, and Mickey were on high ground, so as Toby led everyone up the small rise, it was understandable why the new arrivals were held in such high regard. Jamie tried to smile.

"Hi, Jamie!" Toby sounded like a fifteen-year-old trying to sneak into a nightclub.

"Hey..." Jamie drew a blank. "...Toby."

"We were attacked by pirates and stranded here," the boy stated.

Oh for goodness sake, thought Jamie, *You people don't do me any good*. But instead, he looked aghast. "I'm so sorry, you guys. That's terrible."

Earnest by now had gasped delightedly numerous times and was swiveling his head at the conversation like it was a tennis match.

"You speak their silly language, Shay-mee! Good for you!" the boy told his friend, patting him on the back.

Toby was now in love with this sense of importance, so he turned to the rest of the group. "Jamie here is a professional treasure hunter." The young man was bad with details. "So maybe we could negotiate with him to send for help or something."

Jamie saw the situation was worse than he thought.

"Whoa, whoa, whoa," he whoa-ed, putting his hands up. "What?"

Toby gave an uncharacteristic wry smile. "One

moment," he told the crew. The mousy young man turned to Jamie, but first gave a polite nod to Earnest, who happily returned the gesture.

Toby made his offer. "I was thinking Jamie, if you would be so merciful, you could use some of your treasure to contact and buy these people to safety, since, I can absolutely assure you, they can pay you back. And then some."

Toby turned and gave Melinda a thumbs-up. Turning back, the miserable look on Jamie's face puzzled him, especially given the gigantic smile on Earnest's face.

"Toby," Jamie spit out, "I didn't find any treasure. There *is* no treasure." And to drive the last nail into the coffin, he added, "I'm as stuck as you guys are. *We* are just as stuck."

"Hmmm. But what about your coworkers?"

"I don't know," he muttered. "I have no idea. I haven't made any progress since I last talked to you." His shoulders sank.

Toby sized up the moose and considered that it didn't count as progress. Looking from Jamie to Melinda, and seeing her worry, and worrying that he had let her down, Toby gave up, too.

Jamie put a hand on Toby's shoulder, because it seemed the proper thing to do, and took a step forward. Clearing his throat, he addressed the senior crew members.

"I'm sorry. But I'm not any more help than anyone else you've got down there. Arguably, I'm considerably less help. I'm just lost and in trouble, too."

A collective sigh stirred up a little sand, but no one noticed.

"But, wait," said an unnamed crew member. "Why do

you have a moose with you?"

"I don't know," Jamie sighed.

40

On the desolate shores of the Skeleton Coast, the day quickly became a mess. Naturally, and deservedly, many of the passengers turned their frustration toward the *Queen Ivan's* crew. The captain and the cruise director and some other senior crew members naturally got the brunt of this displeasure, though the trickle-down blame pointed a finger at anyone in a green-and-white striped polo shirt. The castaways broke into factions, and even splinter groups, but generally all the dispossessed people agreed that their own specific complaints were the most important. These factions designated representatives, whose resumes had some sort of leadership qualities or who had lived in an arid climate at some point. These representatives mostly just yelled at crew members in a louder voice.

After much open-palmed calming motions from the cruise director, all this hullabaloo led to the decision that all the faction leaders and crew members would converge for a large meeting.

The meeting was, arguably, worse punishment than being stranded by pirates. Oftentimes, having a meeting to discuss things sounds like such a spectacular plan to some people. It is only during the meeting, while they are half-listening to somebody talk about who-knows-what, that they realize nothing is going to be accomplished.

Also, there were no doughnuts.

Nonetheless, a meeting was called and, for appearances, was held atop the most regal-looking dune. On the agenda were such hot button issues as where to get food, how to find or make shelter, how to call for help, and what time it was. But the biggest problem, it turned out, which fought its way to the forefront of negotiations, was what to do about the Johnson-Katsopolis wedding. The wedding was supposed to have happened at eleven o'clock (a time that had since passed in several time zones) in the stunning banquet hall of the *Queen Ivan* (a ship which had since been commandeered).

Noticeably absent from this official squabbling match was the moose and his cohorts. So while the shouting escalated atop the dune, Mickey, Jamie, Earnest, Toby, and Melinda were having their own gathering. None of them had the gall to refer to it as a meeting.

While they sat in a semi-circle, Toby was picking up rocks and throwing them at nothing. It was kind of therapeutic, but it failed to take his mind off his failure to win the heart of Melinda. It was also sinking in further that he was probably going to die on the desolate Gelatin Coast with all the ship's passengers who disapproved of his hiring. What a day!

Earnest saw Toby's new occupation and deemed it more stimulating than all the chatter, so he picked up some rocks and began emulating Toby's dispassionate tossing of them. He even made faces like Toby was, in an effort to better his aim.

Melinda, Jamie, and Mickey refrained from rock-throwing, though Jamie kind of wanted to join in. Mickey lay on his side, again tuckered out from walking in the heat and cranky with these humans who weren't feeding him. Melinda and Jamie racked their brains for a way to improve their lot. As they talked, Toby half-listened.

"I just don't understand why kitchenware would be important to kidnappers," Jamie said, after giving a lackluster run-through of his story, with many episodes out of order.

"I don't know, either," Melinda offered.

"And I'm surprised that moose is still alive," he continued.

"Right," Melinda said, eager to change the subject. "Now I think the first thing we need to focus on is how to call for help. Those jerks at their special meeting are probably thinking about making tents out of nothing, but I think it would be much wiser to get moving." Melinda rarely referred to people as jerks; she was much nicer than that. But circumstances afforded her the slip. "Now, Earnest here, is his home or village nearby? And are there phones or anything?"

Earnest looked up from his rock-throwing and waved at the young lady.

"I have no idea," responded Jamie. "His situation makes even less sense than yours." Jamie shrugged. "I just found him wandering around with the moose."

Melinda took a deep breath. "Great."

Toby looked up. "I'm sorry," he said to her.

She turned to him. "For what?"

Toby shrugged guiltily. "I don't know. I'm just sorry about all of this."

After saying it, Toby worried that the fair Melinda would chastise him for weakness.

"It's okay, Toby. It's not your fault."

"Well, maybe not the pirates, completely. But I shouldn't have gotten your hopes up about this guy." He tried and failed to inconspicuously indicate Jamie.

"Right," Jamie agreed.

"No offense," Toby told him.

Jamie sighed. "It's fine. I don't know why I got into this mess, anyway. I'm no treasure hunter. I should have just gone ahead and gone to jail in the hopes that Janet and Tom didn't end up dead."

"Yeah, probably," Toby agreed, throwing another rock.

"Well, I think it's good you wanted to save them," Melinda chimed in, changing Toby's mind again. "Even if the plan wasn't all that ... thought out."

"Thank you," said Jamie.

"Now, anyway, we're all here now, and maybe there is a way to call the authorities if we can get to Earnest's village."

"Maybe," agreed Jamie. "But I don't know where it is. Maybe he didn't come from a village."

"Then where would he have come from?" Toby asked before passing a nice rock to Earnest to replenish his arsenal.

"I don't know," Jamie shrugged. "With that moose, maybe he came from a zoo."

Upon hearing the word *zoo*, Earnest hopped up. "Zoo?" he asked exuberantly. "Did you say zoo? Is there a zoo nearby or did you come from a zoo?"

Of course, with no one speaking his language, the only word that could be understood was that three-letter z-word.

"Zoo?" Jamie repeated, excitement growing in his voice.

"Zoo? Could we go to a zoo?" Earnest now bounced around the small group as if he were imitating popcorn.

"Yes, a zoo?" Melinda asked, hoping that she had just found a glimmer of hope.

"A zoo!" exclaimed Earnest. Then pointing to Mickey, said, "Yes, we could go there, and maybe Mickey would be safe and like living at this zoo."

At this point, all parties, excluding Mickey, were overjoyed about each others' joy. Of course, none was aware of the egregious misunderstanding, as Melinda, Jamie, and Toby drew the conclusion that Earnest was emphatically pointing to the moose to say, *Yes, we have just come from a zoo. And we should all go there together.* Toby was even sure he could translate, *And there is a phone there for you to call the navy.*

"I guess it's entirely possible that there is some animal preserve nearby," Melinda concluded.

"Yeah, maybe Earnest owns it," joked Jamie, to no response.

"Well, great, then!" said Melinda, making strong eye contact with Jamie and Toby, the way teachers tell you to make eye contact. "We'll go to this zoo and try to contact the authorities! Let's go alone so we don't run the risk of those guys on the dune wasting two days deliberating over the issue."

"Right," agreed Jamie.

"Right," agreed Toby.

"Zoo," sang Earnest, as he continued to bound around the little circle, lightly playing the tambourine and/or keyboard on everyone's head.

41

For Maria Martinez, it had been a long day. It had been a long day for all the passengers of the *Queen Ivan*, but especially for Maria Martinez, who was even more upset about her new marital problems than she was about the whole pirate business. Also, she recently discovered that Benito had been left behind. He was unaccounted for, which probably meant that his unconscious body was just left lying around. Perhaps the pirates had killed him by now.

Maria Martinez was wishing she were not Maria Martinez. As in, she wished she was still Maria Consuelos, her name before getting married. Or at the very least she wished she was Maria Martinez, but married to a much nicer Mr. Martinez. She could have been concerning herself with the fact that she and hundreds of others were currently stranded on a beach, with no shade. But Maria just needed time to herself. So she had left all the other passengers behind and gone for a walk. Being cross, she kept her arms crossed, which made her walk funny. But off she went. With so many other people to worry about, few castaways noticed one cranky woman wandering away from the group.

"Look at me! I'm Benito Martinez, and I *loooove* lying to my wife!" she muttered to herself. "I do that sport where you hit the thing, but only to torment my poor wife, who does nothing but love me and care about *good* things, like things that aren't sports." Maria stopped and uncrossed her arms momentarily. "And I get knocked out when one little plate hits my head!"

As she walked she kicked the dune. Though often categorized as a nature-lover, Maria really wished this stupid sand was paved. She decided she would just crest the hill and have a seat on the other side to collect herself, away from the hundreds of other stranded passengers. Reaching the top and giving it a boot, she descended and took a seat.

However, her therapeutic sit-down was over before it started, for as she made herself as comfortable as a grump could hope to be, she noticed, not so far away, a crummy-looking boat. Or, rather, an old shipwreck. Though an odd distraction, this did not immediately improve Maria Martinez's mood. She thought she might go inspect it anyway.

42

The grand meeting atop the regal dune had not been a complete failure. After a forceful push from the delegation led by Delilah's irate father, it was decided by nightfall that the Johnson-Katsopolis nuptials would take place the following morning. Despite protests, it was felt that a wedding on a beach would be almost as ideal as a wedding aboard a luxurious cruise ship, even if it had to be *this* beach. All the guests and the priest were in one spot, was the argument, so they might as well get it over with. Some were quite upset by the attention being paid to the wedding, but were appeased when it was decreed that all the stranded passengers were now invited to the service (the crew, however, was not).

Meanwhile, the group containing no invitees (two crew members, two nomads, and a moose), unless they were someone's plus-one (which had barely been addressed in the wedding discussions), sat making their plans for the journey to the imaginary zoo. They ate a little of the little bit of food left from Jamie and Earnest and Mickey's trek. Although Melinda had argued momentarily that the food should be distributed to the passengers, Jamie argued that their small group was the one undertaking the journey, and thus would need the extra nourishment. Toby pretended to agree with Melinda, though he was hungry enough to consider joining Mickey in eating the remaining hay for dessert. Post-snack, the motivated trio of Jamie,

Melinda, and Toby drew some schematics in the dirt and dumped the sand out of their shoes as they prepared to depart.

Without looking at him, Melinda politely inquired of Toby, "Sorry, could I... can...?" And she indicated needing his shoulder to balance on while she dumped the sand out of her other shoe.

Toby froze for a moment before his cracking voice replied, "Sure!"

Melinda smiled a thank-you and put her delicate hand on Toby's shoulder, then focused on her footwear. The young man felt a wave of happiness splash through him, from his shoulder to his toes where it rebounded and shot back toward his hairline, though this might have been the abusive heat.

Thankfully, she failed to see Toby blush bright red and gaze longingly at her brightly shining blonde hair. Jamie noticed, however, and had to stop himself from making an immature *'Whoooooo!'* noise like sitcom audiences make when characters get all smoochy. In a knee-jerk reaction, he turned to Earnest so they could lock eyes to wordlessly say, *'Look! He likes her!'* But when Jamie turned he noticed that little Earnest had tuckered himself out from all his dancing, and was now curled up against his moose friend, fast asleep. Mickey must have been worn out from watching the zoo dance, and had also passed on to dreamland.

It was, after all, getting late, so going to bed (even without a bed) did not seem unreasonable. When Melinda finished fidgeting with her shoe and released her grip on Toby's shoulder, the young man finally breathed again. As

Melinda opened her mouth, Jamie playfully put his finger to his lips.

"Look, you guys," he whispered, motioning over his shoulder. "Earnest fell asleep."

Melinda and Toby both sponged up the heartwarming sight. And although they had quite the daunting mission ahead, none of them wanted to wake him (also they were frightened of displeasing the big moose).

"Okay, we could let him sleep for a while," Melinda whispered after a bit of discussion, "But nighttime will be the coolest time to travel, I would think."

"Right," agreed Toby.

"So we'll wake him up in a few hours and have him point us in the direction of this zoo."

"Great," said Jamie. "Then we'll all be slightly rested and ready to go."

"We could sleep in shifts," chimed in Toby, proud to contribute.

"Okay, sure," said Melinda, causing Toby to secretly pump his fist in celebration. Again, Jamie caught it, but said nothing.

And although he was dead tired and hated the idea, Toby added, "I'll take the first shift."

"Thanks, Toby," Melinda said, and after a little more inconsequential discussion, she and Jamie had brushed around some sand and laid down upon it for their naps.

Toby fell asleep before either one of them.

43

And of course, it was suddenly morning. *Whoops*, thought Toby, the failed night watchman. He awoke moments after Jamie had, who had awoken moments after Melinda had, who had awoken a good half hour after Earnest had. Mickey and Earnest were nowhere to be seen.

Part of the reason they were nowhere to be seen was that once again, a heavy fog had enveloped a good chunk of the Skeleton Coast. So when Jamie, Melinda, and Toby all sat up and peered around, they failed to see much beyond their little campsite.

"What...? How...?" stuttered the groggy Melinda, rubbing her eyes.

Toby raised his hand as if in a classroom. "I think I fell asleep."

Rather than saying, *Well, so much for walking through the night*, as a person who always states the obvious might, Jamie pointed out, "Well, at least we weren't eaten by lions in the night." Then he scratched his head and shook some sand off. Toby pointed at him to agree that this was a good point.

"Where's the little guy?" Melinda asked, a pang of worry in her soft voice.

"Also the big one," Jamie noticed, referencing the moose.

The fog was so thick that the trio wasn't even sure if the hundreds of passengers were still nearby. They hopped up to look around for Earnest and Mickey, and were thankful that the boy and moose had graciously left a trail of footprints in the sand. Following said trail, the helicopter pilot and young cruise-shippers headed into the thick mist.

"Earnest!" Jamie called into the fog as they trudged along.

Melinda, following his lead, called, "Earnest, honey, where are you?"

Wanting to aid her angelic voice, Toby simply yelled, "Honey! Come back!" before questioning his choice of words.

The tracks remained visible as the minutes passed, and though the three-person search party was not completely sure which direction they were heading, there was a gradual slope, and the noise made by what sounded like waves became greater, leading them to believe they were nearing the water again. Melinda was concerned for her new little friend who had drummed on her head. If only there wasn't so much stupid fog, she reassured herself, they would probably be able to see Earnest. And his moose.

After what seemed like a long time to Melinda but only a short time to Jamie, and a medium time to Toby, they heard a noise that sounded like a moose sneezing, and they supposed it must be Mickey. Whether the noise was actually a sneeze or some moose sound, they would never be sure, but regardless they quickened their pace.

Of course, with dramatic flair, the fog began to lift slowly, and within a few moments, Earnest came into view. He was hustling away from them, once again in hot pursuit of his big, hairy, antlered companion. They could see he was not far from the haughty morning surf, and headed into it at an angle, allowing the fingertips of cold seawater to clamber over his small toes.

"Hang on, Earnest!" Jamie called, "Wait up!"

The boy finally noticed his pursuers. He stopped momentarily to wave, then about-faced and hustled after the moose again. Mickey passed out of sight of Jamie, et al, as a wave of fog enveloped him once more. The three hurried up to see if he was headed toward the zoo of legend.

Then, with three times as much dramatic flair as the previous lifting of the fog, the fog lifted. All the haze about them dissipated to reveal the moose, now standing still, but rising upward, as if ascending to the heavens.

Directly behind him, and coming as a surprise to everyone, was the *Queen Ivan*.

The scene flabbergasted all present, including Earnest. Slowly, surely, Mickey rose. He was stoically standing aboard a lifeboat, which he had climbed into of his own accord. From the beach, the team could see that the moose was not alone aboard this rather sturdy lifeboat. Accompanying him upwards was a bearded man whose complexion could currently be described as a sort of olive green. For the most part this man seemed oblivious to the moose towering over him, preoccupied as he leaned over the side of the boat. It appeared to everyone below that the man was quite sick.

Mickey did not seem to mind nor worry about contracting this stomach virus. In fact, it had been the bearded man's expelled tummy contents which had attracted the big moose to the lifeboat, since, after all, Mickey was still an animal and sometimes animals do gross and impolite things, like go sniffing at throw-up. Thankfully Mickey had decided that sniffing was enough, but before getting a chance to exit the lifeboat, the men aboard the ship had begun hoisting it back up. At first jumpy about the new development, Mickey quickly opted to just go with the flow.

While his counterparts stood in awe of the grounded ship and the ascending moose, Earnest got over his flabbergastedness quickly. Having never encountered a cruise ship before barely fazed Earnest; he was focused on the safety of his friend.

"What is this thing?" he asked, turning to Jamie.

Jamie kept looking upward.

"We must get Mickey back," Earnest concluded. "I don't think I like this stupid thing that is taking Mickey."

Failing to discern Earnest's criticism of the cruise ship, Jamie, Melinda, and Toby wondered what it could possibly be doing there. Melinda quit wondering first.

"Hey!" she yelled. "Hey up there!"

Melinda felt direct contact was the only way to solve the mystery. This course of action could have been deemed unwise, as it was by Jamie and Toby, who sprang up at the sound of her voice and pulled her into the shadow of the *Queen Ivan*, out of sight from anyone on deck. Melinda was taken aback by the sudden dragging.

Jamie's tone was surprisingly polite. "What are you doing?"

"There's no way to get on board that ship without their help," she stated.

"Oh," Jamie said.

Toby was embarrassed that he had taken Jamie's side in pulling Melinda out of sight, so he blamed his instincts.

"Still," Jamie continued, "I feel like we should discuss our plan before rushing into anything."

"Yeah, I'd love to have a snack before we raid a pirate ship," admitted Toby.

Melinda, an understanding person, understood the argument that she should share her plans before yelling at pirates. But given what she knew of Toby's personality and Jamie's questionable decision-making skills, she felt a need to take on a leadership role.

"I didn't say we were going to raid a pirate ship," Melinda whispered. "But I really feel like we're going to need to make contact with them."

In all of this chitchat, the trio failed to notice that while Earnest had jumped with them into the shadow of the ship, he soon moved back into the now-glaring sun. The lifeboat was being lowered back over the side. Earnest had every intention of climbing in it.

When it reached him, the young man saw that the sick green man was still in it, now accompanied by a blond gentleman whose skin had turned pale rather than green, but who looked equally out of sorts. Mickey, however, was gone. Earnest politely nodded at the two men. They returned the gesture, before leaning over the sides of the boat to throw up some more. Earnest stepped around the mess they were making and entered the craft. He took a seat and crossed his arms as the men went about their business.

Noticing all of this, Jamie, Melinda, and Toby made frantic gestures encouraging Earnest to disembark. This rudimentary sign language was easy for Earnest to understand, but he respectfully refused. He had to save that moose. Jamie, feeling a responsibility to protect his little friend, realized he would need to go extract the boy about the same time that Melinda decided she should aid young persons making rash decisions. Toby tagged along.

Then, with sensational timing, the lifeboat rose once more. The three hurried to catch the departing public transport. Jamie and Melinda both hustled over to grab Earnest and haul him out, but Toby misunderstood their intentions and hopped in the lifeboat. He offered a polite nod to the sick occupants (who returned the gesture), before realizing that his friends had different plans.

"Wait … what?" he asked, standing up in the little boat (something you should never do!).

"Toby, what are you doing?" Melinda asked frantically, as the boat inched up further. Jamie was trying to motion for Earnest to come down, but the boy was resolute about staying in the lifeboat, arms crossed.

"I … I thought we were…" Toby stammered. Feeling the movement, he sat back down. He looked at Earnest, who shrugged sympathetically.

"No! We're…"

Toby did not let Melinda finish. "Okay, I'm getting out." He swung his legs out. The lifeboat was now about eye level for a tall person standing on the ground.

It was Jamie who made a split-second decision. "No. We're getting in."

"I thought…" confused Toby began. But already Jamie

had started doing a pullup and was trying to simultaneously motion for Melinda to do the same. She gave the helicopter pilot an "I hope you're right" look, then jumped to grab the boat's side. Toby immediately hopped up to aid her. The rocking motion caused both of the sick occupants to once more lean over the side and groan.

Though maybe she didn't need the help, Melinda appreciated that stony-faced Toby was trying. He gripped her hand and tugged her in. She noticed that his grip was better than the last time they shook hands. His regularly loose grip might have caused a Humpty-Dumpty effect.

On the other side of the lifeboat, Jamie was having a terrible time, as no one on board was secretly in love with him. Earnest, however, offered joyful encouragement in place of physical help.

"Oh, Shay-mee! You have decided to come, too!" cried the boy. He beamed and gave Jamie a pat on the head.

Up and up the lifeboat went, past multiple levels of passenger decks. With Melinda safely in the boat, Toby took some labored breaths from his uncharacteristic physical exertion. He saw that she had performed the monumental feat of somehow avoiding perspiration, save for a single bead of sweat on her forehead. It was the cutest bead of sweat he had ever seen. Unfortunately, she wiped it away, though it incidentally benefited her hairstyle. Melinda looked at Toby, and he thought they shared a moment, but really the batting of her eyelashes was due to her contact being out of place.

"Thanks," she said.

Things were only getting worse for Jamie, whose grip was becoming less dependable as his hands sweated more and more. Earnest was proving no help and neither were the ill men.

"Shay-mee, climb in," Earnest told him. "Why aren't you climbing in?"

Jamie was assuming that Earnest had found some new bug or was trying to describe the throw-up on the lifeboat's floor. The poor dangling helicopter pilot (who considered himself athletic but had never been able to do more than four pullups or run a mile and a half under twelve minutes) was about to call for help from Melinda and Toby when the lifeboat reached sight of the deck.

What they saw was downright harrowing.

Scattered across the deck were the most terribly wretched-looking pirates. Not wretched-looking because they were no good at pirating, but because most of them looked dreadfully ill. Some lay sprawled out across the deck. Others were leaning over the rails, anticipating more throwing up. Still others were lying in uncomfortable positions across the deck chairs, bodies half on and half off. *So it wasn't just the two in the boat*, the newcomers all thought. *Everybody here is sick*.

Except Mickey. He was doing just fine. He was standing on the deck, looking royal.

The least sick pirate, who was running the winch that raised the boat, noticed the extra people.

"Hey!" he said, but little else, because he, too, was sick enough.

"Hi," said Jamie after recognizing that the element of surprise was out of the question. "Um, could you help me..." and to clarify, he continued, "...stop dangling."

The young pirate sized up the situation. "Yes, but after that I think you're all our prisoners."

Jamie paused. "Fair."

"Okay, let me go check." The young pirate hustled off, leaving Jamie to continue dangling.

Earnest was emphatically waving at Mickey, who evoked less of a response from the pirates than a moose boarding a cruise ship deserves. But the pirates were mostly all feeling icky, so only a few made a lackluster attempt to capture him. These few remained sitting as they did this.

Melinda's mind was going a mile a minute. She was afraid of being a prisoner aboard a pirate ship, but was trying to rack her brain for a way out of their quandary. Toby was afraid, too, but was also considering whether he would accept an offer to join the pirate crew. Jamie was mostly uncomfortable, left hanging over the side of a cruise ship as he was.

Moments later the young pirate reappeared. "Cap'n says to let you down, and you're our captives and stuff and he wants to talk to you."

"We accept," Toby stated, standing up in the boat again.

More moments later, Jamie, Melinda, Toby, and Earnest were led by a few grumbling pirates into the ship's banquet hall, where more pirates lay on the floor groaning. The large room had been transformed into a makeshift palace chamber of sorts, with Captain Hans Heissel seated on a foldable deck chair wrapped in streamers meant for the wedding, atop a glass coffee table atop three mattresses precariously on top of a plastic table, surrounded by half the potted plants found aboard the ship. This setup had been among the first orders Hans Heissel had given upon commandeering the *Queen Ivan.* Earlier, he had been basking on his throne. Now he was folded over in his seat and groaning, newspaper hat askew.

Spotting visitors, he quit grousing and sat up. "Oh, thank goodness! You're here!"

Jamie, Melinda, and Toby were all baffled by his exclamation.

Melinda spoke first. "Sir, what happened here?"

Hans Heissel threw his head back and yelled toward the ceiling. "Oh, it was awful! We couldn't stop ourselves! At all, for a while there!"

Bewildered glances were traded between Jamie and Melinda, and even Toby to a certain extent. Earnest wondered why this man was wearing a strange hat, and kind of wanted one.

"What are you talking about?" Melinda asked.

Hans Heissel sat up a little. "The cake! It's the cake that got us."

Jamie was certain that the captain had gone mad. "What did the cake do to you?" he asked.

"Can't you see the massacre?" Hans replied. His arm lazily made a sweeping arc to indicate the fallen crew members.

"A cake made you all sick?" Melinda asked.

"Not just any cake," Hans Heissel responded, shaking his head. "The most foul cake the world has ever seen."

This information still left many questions in the captives' minds.

Melinda wrinkled her brow. "Cakes usually aren't supposed to have that effect..."

Toby took a determined step forward. "We will join your crew, Captain," he stated firmly. While Melinda and Jamie had been focused on solving the new mystery, Toby had devised this heroic way to save his compatriots' lives, which might just impress the girl next to him.

It did not. Believing the poppycock about the diabolical cake to be the strangest thing she would hear that day, Melinda found it hard to fathom this new outburst.

"What?" she spat, turning to Toby. Jamie put his head in his hands.

"I ... I'm saving us," Toby whispered, hoping that she simply missed the connection.

"Are you crazy ... er than him?" Melinda angrily whispered back, pointing to Hans. Toby was pretty sure that he had really blown his chances with her this time.

"Fine, yeah, whatever," Hans Heissel replied. "That's great. Back to me, though." He clapped his hands twice to regain their attention. "Anyway, all our tummies are miserable."

"But, sir," Jamie began, "how did the ship run aground?"

"Oh that," Hans Heissel said. "Well after all those passengers were banished, we finally remembered that we should put out the fire that we started in the bathroom as a distraction."

"That was a good idea," Toby said.

"Thank you, crewman," Hans replied. "But we thought it shouldn't be a very big fire, being that we only started a small fire."

"Right..." said Jamie.

"Sometimes fires grow," Toby explained.

"Correct," Hans agreed. "Correct. But when we tried to put it out, we found that the closest fire extinguisher was missing. Then we found that the next closest fire extinguisher was missing, also. And when I say 'we' I mean my crew. Not me. I was basking in the opulence of my new ship. So then we tried to find the missing fire extinguishers, to no avail, and when I was informed of the problem, I gave the order that all other activities should stop until the fire extinguishers were located."

Jamie sensed that Hans Heissel had been eagerly awaiting the opportunity to spin this yarn.

"But alas, at this point many of my men had made an incredible discovery, and much attention was drawn to it." He paused for effect and eyed his listeners.

"What was it?" Melinda asked.

"An enormous wedding cake. Many times more enormous than any I have ever seen. And since my men were very hungry, it was decided that this would be the perfect celebratory feast." He threw his head back again. "Oh, we were so careless back then! If only we had seen the errors of our youth before it was too late."

"Wait, you and your crew stopped trying to put out the fire so you could eat this wedding cake?" Melinda clarified.

"It looked so good!" Hans Heissel wailed. "And also, not quite. I tried to give out my order, but the men were already eating the cake. By the time everyone realized the importance of making that fire be out, they were all full of cake, and the effects had started to take place. The throwings-up and all."

"Right," said Jamie.

"Why did the cake make you all so sick?" Melinda asked.

"How should I know?" Hans wailed. "Some of my men say 'it be karma' because we stole this ship and whatnot. But I, being a man of numbers, feel that it couldn't be that simple."

"And the one cake really made you *all* sick?" Melinda pressed.

"It was a big cake!" Hans extended his arms to illustrate. "The biggest I've ever seen, remember?" Then he slunk back into his chair and rubbed his stomach.

Three sick, salty men entered the hall, followed by Mickey. They were leading the big moose by an orange floatation ring on a rope. Mickey may have minded the ring around his right antler if not for the smell of food inside. Captain Hans Heissel did not seem as surprised at seeing a moose as he should have been.

"Captain," said Christof the pirate, who was followed by Kurtis the pirate and Victor the pirate, "we found this big animal on deck."

Earnest was happy to see Mickey, and hustled over to pet him. Though not one to show much affection, Mickey liked this smaller person slightly more than the men with the leash.

"Very well," said Hans Heissel from the side of his throne. "I will keep him as a pet."

"No!" Jamie blurted out, making him wonder if he had grown more attached to the moose than he was willing to admit.

"Yes," Hans replied impassively. "Bring him here."

The three pirates, rubbing their stomachs and quietly moaning, walked Mickey toward Hans Heissel's throne. Earnest walked with him. The captain did not seem to mind the boy. Hans's attention was drawn to his new hoofed possession. He watched the beast nuzzle into an untouched bowl of grapes next to the throne. Finally the captain turned back to his guests.

"Anywho, we crashed the ship because we were all getting sick and running around looking for fire extinguishers and whatnot. We finally found some extinguishers on the other side of the ship from the fire, but by then we were fully not paying attention to where the ship was going." He paused. "We got the fire out, then," he reported, almost apologetically.

Jamie, Melinda, and Toby all nodded their heads. Earnest handed a grape to Mickey.

Captain Hans Heissel straightened, unsuccessfully. "So here is what I need from you."

Jamie and Melinda were somewhat surprised.

"I want you to make mine and all our stomachs feel better," Hans continued. Before there was a response, he elaborated. "You are by far the healthiest people aboard this ship. I want you to scour my boat and heal us."

"Well, we don't know what is wrong with you," Melinda stated accurately.

"Enough! Just go figure something out. Find tummy medicine! And quickly. Kurtis and Christof and the other pirate, you may stay here and wallow with me."

The three pirates laid down to do so. Jamie looked at Melinda, and the two felt it was time to go. They turned toward the door and pulled Toby with them.

"It is a good thing that you decided to join my crew," Hans said. "Otherwise we probably would have made you walk the plank. And it would have hurt more since we have run aground."

"Very good point," Jamie said, smiling.

"Do well, new crew." Hans waved with one hand and used the other to rub his mid-section. "Please don't change your minds and try to escape because we will most likely kill you."

Jamie, Toby, and Melinda all nodded. Realizing they were down a member of their party, Jamie motioned for Earnest to follow them, and got no response.

"Earnest, let's go," Jamie called. Earnest simply waved at him.

"He shall stay with the animal until further notices," Hans Heissel stated.

The three oldest members of the former party of four exited. Earnest looked up briefly. "Goodbye Shay-mee and the other two friends!" he called before turning his attention back to Mickey and the rapidly disappearing grapes.

Outside the banquet hall, Jamie thought hard, while Melinda turned to Toby.

"I'm sorry, Toby," she said.

Being as the apology was unexpected, the mousy young man became worried. "For what?"

"I thought you were just being rash when you told him we would join his crew. I guess you had things more figured out than I did. You probably saved our lives."

"Oh, right. That. It's fine," said Toby. He beamed as she looked away, and congratulated himself on a job well done, thinking his work was done for the day. And it may have been, had he not noticed that one pirate was waltzing about the deck quite un-sick. The more he squinted, the more this particular buccaneer looked familiar.

"Well, should we see if there is like, a Pepto-Bismol locker somewhere aboard?" Jamie asked.

"I think we need to find a way to call for help," Melinda replied.

"Well maybe, but should we instead fix the tummies first?"

Toby spoke up. "You guys, come with me."

With his partners in tow, the young man walked tall toward his discovery.

His discovery, noticing that someone had discovered him, hunched over, pretending his stomach was upset as well. Recognizing that his discoverers were not bad guys, his eye lit up, and he motioned for them to follow. Hustling around a corner, Toby met up with the scarred, mustachioed, eye-patched faker.

"Mr. Martinez!" Toby yelled, before being shushed. As Jamie and Melinda came up behind him, he inquired of Benito, "What are you doing here?"

"They think I'm a pirate!" the hulking baseball player whispered loudly.

There was a pause. Toby asked, "Why?" just as Melinda said, "You're not?"

"No," Benito Martinez said, sighing. "I'm Benito Martinez."

Melinda, solely a tennis fan, wondered if this should matter.

Jamie, however, squinted. "Really?"

"Yes, I swear."

Jamie could not resist saying, "Prove it. I'll throw you a ball and you drop it," referencing Benito's recent defensive gaffes. Jamie stifled his laughter, remembering the immediate problem, what with the pirate ship and whatnot. "Sorry."

Benito knew that despite present company's opinion of his defense, these people were the best he had to work with. "I'm glad you're all here. We need your help."

"Who is 'we'?" asked Melinda.

"And what's going on here?" asked Jamie.

"I'll tell you," Benito said, and wasted precious time divulging his story.

So it turned out the cake fiasco was the handiwork of Benito and his cohort Leonid Cupabascim. They had been racking their brains in the ship's kitchen when that strange elderly man exited the walk-in refrigerator with frosting on his face. The cranky old soul said nary a word. This sparked Leonid to recall that stored safely (up until then) in the walk-in refrigerator was the mammoth wedding cake intended for the Johnson-Katsopolis nuptials.

Brainstorming fast, the two men devised a devious plan, which they felt was justified given the deviousness of the ship's takeover. Since this salty old pirate proved that pirates must love cake, they thought it wise to poison the cake, thus incapacitating the *Queen Ivan's* raiders when they ate it. Soon they realized that the ship was not carrying much in the way of poisons. That's when the conversation expanded to things you just should not eat, and realizing that the passengers had left all their personal effects behind, it was decided that the cake would be decorated with toothpaste.

Of course, with Leonid handcuffed to the kitchen as he was, Benito was sent on a recon mission to raid each cabin and fill a garbage bag with as much toothpaste as he could recover. As discreetly as possible, Benito Martinez slipped from room to room accumulating the goods, fibbing along the way to inquisitive pirates about his desire to find some Tylenol. Arriving back at the refrigerator, the pair absolutely covered the grand cake with toothpaste. They applied several layers to be safe. And ignored the curious, smoky smell, emanating from elsewhere in the kitchen.

Stepping back to marvel at their handiwork, it occurred to Benito and Leonid that this plan was far stupider than they originally believed. But just as they went back to the drawing board, a small battalion of hungry pirates entered the kitchen and espied the culinary mountain. Giddy as schoolboys from a bygone era in which schoolboys were allegedly so giddy, the pirates celebrated their find. Soon word spread to the rest of the crew and (somehow) the cake was transported by fourteen men, through an enormous freight elevator, and on to the deck for all to share. It was quite thoughtful of them. Assuming at this point the pirates would discover the cake tasted disgusting, Benito and Leonid rubbed their respective brows and wondered why they were such blockheads.

But, somehow, their plan went off without a hitch. The pirates demolished the cake like it was incriminating evidence that needed to disappear. The cake became a symbol of their victory. There was much joviality, such as there often is with cake-eating, but seemingly even more so. The pirates, apparently not having sweets for so long, had agreed that the cake tasted somewhat funny, but were too concerned with eating it to deal with such trivial things.

So the buccaneers filled themselves with cake, and the outcome was roughly as expected. Toothpaste is one of those annoying things that is just not designed for human consumption, and their bodies reacted accordingly.

"Isn't that something dogs do?" Melinda inquired, unsure if she was impressed or not.

"Perhaps," Benito replied. "But sometimes even dogs know better."

Though Benito's tale about the poisonous cake was arguably captivating, Jamie found his mind wandering elsewhere during the yarn-spinning. The pirates were ill, enough said, thought Jamie. So off he went to explore the ship. His time spent aboard the *Queen Ivan* had almost exclusively been spent hiding, save for the fishing ventures, so he wanted to familiarize himself with the boat, in case he needed that knowledge in the near future. Without being noticed because of the entrancing story, Jamie hustled off, hoping to return before its conclusion.

When the helicopter pilot made his way across the deck, he looked through the large panes of the glass dome in the center of the ship that created a skylight for the large interior main hall. Though Jamie knew he was pressed for time, he stopped to climb past the **DANGER!** signs and onto the dome. He admired this part of the ship, since it seemed like the opposite of hiding in the dark.

Peering in, he gazed upon the ship's open area, an enormous room he had never dared enter. What caught his eye was at the far end of the hall. He spotted a group of ten pirates amassing around the large fountain. Squinting, Jamie was amused by what he saw, if his supposition was correct.

And it was. Fillmore R. Puggleston, the owner of the *Queen Ivan*, did not drink alcohol. He never had and never intended to do so in the future. But he believed that passengers aboard his cruise ship might like to. Never having to measure out his own drink proportions and therefore unaware of appropriate doses, Mr. Puggleston made some gross overestimates of how much alcohol an average person might consume on a cruise. He purchased copious amounts of one hundred proof vodka, wanting only the best for his passengers, as he assumed that the higher the proof, the better the alcohol. Sometimes a little research goes a long way. This wealth of strong vodka had barely been touched.

So, of course, when a group of pirates happened across it, they knew they should put it to use because the pirate reputation includes drinking stuff like that. These ten pirates were feeling sick like everyone else, but were arguably more thoughtful than their compatriots, so they hoped to rekindle the crew's spirits by showing off a new vodka fountain. Perhaps only a pirate would desire strong libations to overcome an upset stomach. It's the thought that counts.

So after bailing all the water they could get out of the fountain, the pirates were currently dumping bottle after bottle after bottle back in. There was another pirate running back and forth with armfuls of more brightly labeled bottles.

Jamie found the whole operation rather interesting to spy on. Though high above the action, he could tell it was a certain type of hundred proof vodka, recognizing the bright red label as an old foe, whose aftereffects had once ruined a perfectly good weekend.

The helicopter-less helicopter pilot chuckled a little before sliding back off the glass that several signs told him not to climb on in the first place. He strode back over to the members of the resistance just as Benito finished his dramatic update. Jamie's absence was barely noticed.

44

In the throne room, Earnest was by and large ignoring the crummy-feeling persons in favor of the better-feeling moose. Despite the life-ring leash on his antler, Mickey became increasingly content with each grape he consumed. And despite a lack of change to his moose countenance, Earnest could tell. Though he was not incredibly interested by the groaning man in his funny hat, Earnest felt he was an okay guy. For the boy, few clues had surfaced during the grown-up conversation. He assumed Hans Heissel was an old friend of Shay-mee's or something.

Likewise, the pirate captain was not necessarily enraptured by Earnest. He kind of watched the little guy for a moment, but then returned to the business of rubbing his stomach.

"I will employ you as official moose wrangler," Hans said. "Until I feel you unnecessary."

Understanding he was being talked to, Earnest looked up and smiled. "I will keep petting the moose," Earnest stated.

Hans Heissel nodded, assuming that the child was a mumbler and had said, "Sounds great."

Ronaldinho, the young first mate, came bounding into the room. Shockingly, the youngest member of the pirate crew had not eaten any cake, lacking much in the way of a sweet tooth. Thus, he felt peachy. So while everyone else gorged themselves on wedding cake, he had explored the ship, playing with clean laundry, then hiding when the pirates called for a medic. Upon noticing a fellow boy and a moose, Ronaldinho forgot what he was going to tell his commanding officer.

"Hi," Ronaldinho said to Earnest, who was equally as interested in seeing someone his age.

"Hi," Earnest replied. And though neither boy spoke the same language, the simple greeting was much more decipherable for Earnest than all that grownup mumbo jumbo. He motioned Ronaldinho over to pet his prized possession (being unaware that Hans Heissel so recently claimed ownership). Ronaldinho beamed, and obliged Earnest, thrilled to run his fingers through the hair on the moose's rib cage. Thankfully for Mickey, Ronaldinho had made hand-washing a bigger priority since becoming a pirate.

"Captain," Ronaldinho said, continuing to pet. "Why is this here?"

Hans shifted and grimaced. "Young First Mate Ronaldinho, that is unknowable information. It cannot be known. It is one of life's great mysteries. Perhaps ask the boy that came with it."

Ronaldinho turned to Earnest and they shrugged. Now with four hands petting him, the great moose relaxed and decided to sit down. As large as he was, the sight was quite a production, and the boys nodded to each other, deeply impressed. Ronaldinho offered a small applause.

"Mickey," Earnest told Ronaldinho, pointing at the moose's backside. The first mate inspected the antlers and snout and agreed.

"I think the moose's name is Mickey," Ronaldinho told Hans Heissel.

"Perhaps," Hans said, "But I will keep thinking of names."

A number of peaceful minutes went by as the two boys enjoyed the moose's company. Then, abruptly, Mickey stood and started walking toward the banquet hall's open door. Who knows why. Animals just kind of do stuff sometimes. Mickey failed to brief them on his intentions. Earnest and Ronaldinho both felt compelled to follow.

"He does this sometimes," Earnest told his new friend.

"Don't lose him, First Mate Ronaldinho and the other guy," Hans called after them.

Out in the bright sunshine of the main deck, Mickey, still wearing the fashionable life ring on his antler and trailing the rope, made his way toward the ship's railing. The boys followed at a distance. A few pirates had to roll out of the moose's path, since Mickey was not looking where he stepped. The moose had become bored with life on a cruise ship and wanted to disembark. He walked along the ship's railing for a time, searching for an exit. Earnest and Ronaldinho followed him halfway around the ship as he scanned the railings. The boys grabbed the rope loosely and pretended to be walking a dog. The charade was funny to both of them, despite lacking any dialogue.

As the party of three came around the opposite side of the boat, Mickey finally stopped. It may have been simply moose fickleness, so maybe he didn't notice the scene unfolding in the distance, but Earnest certainly did. The boy squinted, then widened his eyes, then tugged on Ronaldinho's sleeve.

"Look, new friend!" he exclaimed, pointing to the mess that was approaching them from up the coast. Ronaldinho was surprised and impressed. But Earnest was elated.

Heading straight toward the *Queen Ivan* was a stampede, of sorts. From far away, the onlookers could make out a peacock hustling as fast as he could, making what sounded like calls for help. Just behind the flamboyant, whining bird bounded a large badger, which was followed by a snorting, heavy-set pig, whose path was less than straight. It was straighter than that of the porcupine, whose small limbs were set in overdrive. A gazelle, by far the fastest of these animals so which should have been leading the pack, bounced along near the porcupine. It was moving slowly because with every few hop-steps, it would pause to look back the way it came, which caused many a near-collision with the porcupine. A few steps back of the gazelle came the pitter-patter of an ocelot, which under normal circumstances may have tried to eat some of the tasty creatures in its sights, but at present seemed to be much more concerned with keeping pace. A cumbersome orangutan hobbled in the forerunners' tracks, like someone sneaking out of the hospital. Upon its back was a frightened koala.

Earnest could not shut his mouth for the life of him. At first he wondered if they were having a race. Of course, the youngster had never seen most of these species. But he recognized the last species, just coming into view, quite well. People. Two of them, to be exact. And though they were far away, they looked flustered. He assumed, correctly, they wanted to catch the animals. Earnest considered, *Who wouldn't want to catch up and look at these magnificent creatures?*

Koke and Kipchak were panting and stumbling, having a miserable time chasing the rogue animals along the hot African coast. They were not dressed for such activities. Their dark jumpsuits, heavy boots, and rattling weaponry kept them from hustling as fast as the animals, save the porcupine.

Though it would be a great deal of time before Earnest would learn this, the two poachers had been having a long day.

A few days prior, the crew of the shipwrecked crabbing vessel made an interesting discovery. While Kipchak and Koke were out hunting black rhinoceroses, Fred, the canceled show's whipping boy, had spotted a capsized dinghy. A bit of investigating by the crabbers led to the discovery of a number of nearly drowned environmentalists on the foggy beach. A coin flip resulted in the carrying of the unhealthy souls back to the crabbing boat. When Kipchak and Koke returned, they were informed of the new developments and saw firsthand just how out of sorts the rescued persons were. So after that strange morning, the craft had been shared by the original crew of crabbing folk, the Mongolian exotic medicine dealers, and the young and fiery troop of environmentalists. Space was limited.

Each of the rescued characters had ingested much too much seawater in their harrowing crash, so they were all quite ill for a while. The crabbers nursed them back to health, and were shown appreciation once the young men and women were more cognizant. Eventually one young man began rambling on about a lost moose. This was interpreted as delirium. Koke and Kipchak were intrigued, however, seeing as how a moose was an animal, and they loved selling ground-up animals.

When a fair amount of non-salty water and soup was ingested, the young environmentalists were well enough to wander about the boat. Of course, they did not take too well to finding the caged animals, even before they learned the poor critters were kidnapped from zoos. But the majority of them felt it was not their place to make a scene in front of their rescuers, and that action would have to wait until they rendezvoused with their fearless leader, ol' whatsherface.

Yet one member of the team, red-haired, fake-expensive-sunglasses-wearing Trevor, misread his colleagues' feelings. Deciding that someone needed to be a hero (in large part due to the presence of his pretty young female colleagues), he took it upon himself to set all the captive animals free. This was no easy task, as he needed to quietly rush a number of mildly dangerous creatures out of their holding cells without being noticed. Somehow he succeeded, though he failed to recognize the fact that now wild animals were running about on a beach all willy-nilly, far from their respective homes.

Nonetheless, Trevor was patting himself on the back when the Associates of Mr. Abominable Snowman Dragons recognized that the animals were not supposed to be on the beach. Koke and Kipchak sprang to action, though it took them precious minutes to disembark the boat as they fussed about what to bring. After departing, they decided to go back and grab some of their nets. Thus, the animals got a pretty good head start.

And here they were, a good distance from their starting point, panting, sweating, getting tangled in their own nets. The realization that the escaped animals would stay escaped was settling in. Koke looked at Kipchak, and Kipchak returned the look. They cursed the fleeing creatures and toppled to the ground in a heap of net and poachers. During that long explanation, though, the two men had gotten much closer to the *Queen Ivan*. They were in plain view of Earnest, though he was ignoring them in favor of the significantly more enthralling animals.

"Look!" Earnest was saying, essentially to Ronaldinho, but really to anyone within earshot. "Look at all those animals! That ... that's my zoo! Right there!"

The pirates paid the yelling boy little attention, but Koke and Kipchak looked up at Earnest. Being so focused on corralling the zoo animals, they had hardly noticed the cruise ship sitting there in the rocks and sand. Odd, they both thought, but their own boat had run aground, along with the environmentalists' dinghy, and any number of other boats. It was a popular pastime on the Skeleton Coast. So they both felt it wasn't that strange after all.

What was strange, Koke pointed out to Kipchak, was the big furry monstrosity beside the boy. Kipchak squinted and recognized a moose, one of their trade's prized commodities. Despite their disappointment at losing a number of hard-earned, stolen animals, both men were delighted at the idea of capturing the moose, for grinding-up purposes. They hugged.

Earnest stopped gazing at the fleeing animals and

decided he needed to retrieve them. It was what any good zookeeper would do.

"I have to go get those animals," Earnest told Ronaldinho, becoming serious. "I don't know how, but I have to help."

Ronaldinho took Mickey's leash from his friend. Then he watched as Earnest looked around for a means to lower the ship's remaining lifeboat once again. Ronaldinho puzzled at the sight of the other young man peering about with furrowed brow, checking in and around and under everything nearby. Feeling useless, Ronaldinho joined in the search, despite being unaware of the objective.

By now Kipchak and Koke were yelling up to the boys. "Hello there, boys!" called Koke.

"Can we please come up?" asked Kipchak.

And though the boys gave them the cold shoulder, it just so happened they were accidentally doing the poachers' bidding. Earnest finally resorted to hand communication and the first mate understood the goal of lowering the lone remaining lifeboat.

Below, the Mongolian smugglers kept trying to gain the boys' attention. That moose was going to make them rich! The men tossed a few rocks toward the boys. Their aim was poor and attention was still denied. Then the lifeboat came whirring down. Kipchak and Koke jumped out of the way. Ronaldinho had found the lever that lowered the lifeboat, but while inspecting it, Earnest flipped the switch before entering. The boys peered over the side to see that already the net-carrying men were clambering aboard. Once situated, they looked up and signaled to be hoisted. Earnest frowned.

Ronaldinho looked at Earnest semi-apologetically, shrugged, and switched the lever again. Earnest turned his attention to the horizon, which the fleeing animals were headed toward. Their pace had slowed a bit when some of the escapees noticed they were no longer being followed. Yet they continued hustling to be safe, making Earnest's chances of catching up very slim.

When Kipchak and Koke reached the deck and exited the lifeboat, they clapped their hands and patted the boys on the head. Ronaldinho did not take kindly to this gesture, but Earnest just entered the raft. He motioned for the boy pirate to follow him, and made faces and head nods indicating the need to retrieve those wondrous animals. But Ronaldinho was skeptically keeping an eye on the two mustachioed men as they approached Mickey. He didn't trust them.

"Um, young one," Kipchak began, "Who is in charge here?"

"I am," replied Ronaldinho, who then spit to show some authority.

Koke smiled. "Of course, little boy, I'm sure you are. But who is the grown-up who is in charge here?"

Earnest noticed Kipchak petting Mickey, while Koke leaned down to gather Mickey's leash. He was pleased to see that these grown men were also infatuated with his moose. Though, as he watched them, Earnest felt a strange sensation inside him that questioned their intentions. He pushed the thought aside and smiled at them. He liked their mustaches.

Ronaldinho coldly pointed to the banquet hall, and when asked if that was where the captain could be found, he continued pointing. Koke and Kipchak grinned and departed. Mickey, however, did not want to budge. Like Earnest, he felt there was something about these men he didn't trust. Maybe it was because they did not present him with food readily.

Earnest, looking back and forth between the faraway animals and the nearby animal, decided that the others could wait. After all, he was not friends with them yet, but was friends with Mickey. So he walked over, gently took the leash from Koke, and began walking to where all the pointing had been centered. Mickey obliged. The barefooted young man would stick with Mickey, he decided. Until he was sure his moose friend was safe, anyway.

45

Despite Melinda's insistence on checking the ship's radio booth, in case it was salvageable enough to contact the authorities about the *Queen Ivan's* fate, Benito insisted on taking his new allies to the kitchen.

"We need to stick together," he whispered loudly as he hustled below deck. "You need to meet the chef guy." He had forgotten Leonid's name.

Arriving in the kitchen, Leonid was surprised to see three new non-pirates accompanying Benito. Toby and Jamie immediately started looking for something to eat, which proved an easy task. Melinda reintroduced herself (they hadn't spoken since training) and shook Leonid's uncuffed hand. Through mouthfuls of cheese and crackers, Jamie and Toby did the same.

Though everyone save Toby had questions for each other, Benito spoke first. "So, now that we have allied ourselves, let's stage a takeover."

"Wait," replied Melinda. She pondered how the fake pirate and the cook thought their poisoned wedding cake plan would work. There seemed to be so many gaps. "Didn't you two think..."

Her query was meant to be *Didn't you two think there might be repercussions?* But before she could finish her sentence, the repercussions came down the stairs. In the form of five burly, indigestion-riddled pirates. Three had pouting faces, and all had accusatory glares.

"That's him!" the youngest hollered, pointing at Leonid, which caused two more fingers to needlessly emphasize the pointing. Leonid turned pale. Benito tried to make himself turn pale and started rolling on the ground, clutching his stomach. Melinda stared. Jamie and Toby stared but continued chewing.

The tallest pirate, Paul, spoke. "We've decided we think you might have had something to do with the bad cake. Or maybe not. But we are going to make you walk the plank either way."

"What?" Leonid said sheepishly, though he'd heard him quite well. Nonetheless, Paul repeated himself. Two of the pirates unlocked the handcuffs from Leonid's wrist. His new allies watched in horror as the poor chef was marched up the stairs.

"And you guys are supposed to hurry up and find something for the stomachs," Paul said as he followed his pals upstairs. "Or your pirate licenses will be revoked." He paused. "Which means that we'll make you walk the plank, too."

Benito popped up as soon as the real pirates had departed. "Good. They bought it," he said.

"But Leonid is going to die!" Melinda exclaimed.

"Who? Oh right," Benito said.

"He might make it out okay," offered Toby.

"Yeah, but we better go help him," Jamie said, spitting out his mouthful.

Before Melinda could advise everyone to make a plan first, the gents hurried out of the kitchen and toward the elevator. It took entirely too long to decipher which buttons would get them where, then the group waited on what seemed to be the slowest-closing elevator doors in the world.

Arriving on the deck, Leonid's rescue team blinked into the bright sun to see that the poor chef's demise would occur momentarily. The cranky pirates were densely amassed around the opposite railing, some still hobbling over, groaning and pale. Through the crowd, the pillagers pushed the accused. Jeers and accusations fell heavily on him, though thankfully very little spit, as most of the buccaneers' saliva had been discharged over the side of the boat.

Atop the railing the men had crudely fastened their second plank. It was the disconnected diving board from the deck's pool. Arguably a diving board is a nonessential on a cruise ship. But cruise line owner Fillmore R. Puggleston had insisted (even in the face of safety officials) that "a pool is not a pool without a diving board." Little did Fillmore R. Puggleston know that some day his precious diving board would be used as a means of execution.

So poor frightened Leonid was pushed onto the diving board, which wobbled due to its shoddy connection to the railing. Several pirates had to hang onto it to keep it from toppling over the edge. The unlucky chef looked to the pirate crew for sympathy, but, given how poorly everyone's stomachs felt, found none. Despite the pokes he was receiving, Leonid chose not to turn and face his terrible fate.

Jamie, Melinda, Benito, and Toby were shocked, to differing degrees, by the scene. Despite all the action at the railing, they noticed Hans Heissel emerge from his throne room, dragging a deck chair with him (his wish had been for his men to carry him on their shoulders, but they were too ill to comply). Trailing the pirate captain were Koke and Kipchak, strutting like bigwig diplomats. Jamie and Melinda rushed over to the newspaper hat-wearing leader. Toby followed, while Benito inconspicuously entered the crowd of pirates, now classified as "bloodthirsty."

"Captain," Melinda yelled as she came within talking distance of Hans.

Hans Heissel noticed them. "What are you people doing here?"

"You can't let your men make him walk the plank," Jamie said, arriving at Melinda's side.

"Why aren't you people finding upset-stomach medicine?" Hans whined, ignoring the plea.

"Stop them!" said Melinda.

"No. Why would I do that?"

"You don't know it's his fault about your stomachaches," Jamie said.

"Well ... I'm reasonably sure."

"Please, Captain," Melinda pleaded.

"No, thank you. I think a plank-walking is a grand idea. My tummy wants vengeance."

Jamie stepped forward. "Captain, the ship has run aground. There is no water over there. He'll die."

"You don't know that. Don't you believe in miracles? Besides, it was a very bad cake. You would agree with me if you had eaten it."

Toby's train of thought was once again elsewhere. He pointed to Kipchak and Koke.

"Who are they?" he asked.

Hans Heissel turned slightly and sized up the two

Mongolians. "I don't know."

In truth, Hans had a vague notion. The three men, accompanied by the two boys and the moose, had entered into bizarre negotiations in the banquet hall. The obsequious poachers had begun by lauding over Mickey, a practice that only served to confuse the pirate captain. When asked to get to their point, Kipchak and Koke explained their desire to kill the moose. And grind him up into paste. Hans found this idea less than desirable, and told them that the moose was his pet. And that he did not want any pet of his to be ground into paste, tooth or otherwise. The Mongolians smiled harder and said they only wished for Mickey's great antlers, but Hans pointed out that he liked the antlers very much and did not want an antler-less moose. Koke and Kipchak had pointed out that he would get to keep most of the moose, once they killed it and removed the antlers. Hans disliked the notion of having a big dead pet for a pet. He was about to cut off negotiations when the poachers brought out the big guns (figuratively) and pointed out that the pirate captain stood to gain a great deal of money, via their benefactor. Intrigued, Hans asked them to elaborate, which they could not do, as they had never met their benefactor, and just knew he had a fair amount of money invested in this poaching venture. Nonetheless, they were both positive the unnamed boss would be more than glad to compensate Hans Heissel for the loss of his pet. Though quite fond of the big moose, Hans felt it was his duty as a pirate to err on the side of money, so, after crunching some numbers, he permitted them to do with his pet as they pleased. So long as he still got all the parts that weren't antlers.

Still, when Toby inquired, Hans Heissel had little understanding of who the men actually were.

Leonid glanced up from the innumerable poking and prodding fingers to see the friends he'd made less than ten minutes beforehand.

"Hey! You guys! Help me, please!"

"We're trying!" Toby cupped his hands over his mouth to yell back. "The captain's being a pill."

"Hey," Hans said, meekly. Toby's words stung.

Leonid sat on the diving board. It felt safer than standing. Holding on with his hands, he shook his head when commanded to walk to the end and jump. The pirates grumbled and cawed while Jamie and Melinda tried unsuccessfully to sway Captain Hans Heissel. Losing patience, the ruffians pleaded with Leonid to just do as they asked. Eventually, as with many crowds, the pirates grew weary, and their rumblings quieted. It was strange, then, when they noticed that despite their best efforts to silence themselves, the rumbling noises continued. To a man, each pirate looked around quizzically, some shrugging. In fact, the noise was becoming louder, even as the pirates' decibel level dropped to zero.

Leonid found the courage to look down, as this was the direction from which the noise was emanating.

"Huh," was all the young chef breathed.

Far below him were a couple hundred stranded passengers from the *Queen Ivan* looking quite ready for battle, armed to the gills with kitchenware.

Though Hans Heissel had been progressive enough to have a 10-year-old for a first mate, he was still aloof enough to forget one important fact when discussing Mickey's fate with the poachers: children have the ability to listen to adult conversations. So, despite the Mongolians' assumption that the kids in the room would be oblivious, Ronaldinho heard Mickey's fate quite clearly. And although he was regularly loyal to his captain, the young man felt now was the time for insubordination. He did not want his new moose friend dead. Especially not before taking a ride on his back.

46

Kipchak and Koke cared little about the plight of the condemned cook. He looked friendly enough, but that was pirate business. They wished to appear impressed by the execution, but Hans Heissel was paying little attention to the two poachers. At the curious arrival of hollering people alongside the boat, they had found their moment to attend to personal affairs.

First on the agenda was licking their chops at the thought of moose antlers. For no good reason, moose antlers were the cream of the crop in the illegal medicine circles in which Koke and Kipchak ran. Those antlers would fetch more money than all the escaped animals combined. Besides, the zoo animals would likely tire, so they could retrieve them later in the day, when they were reconsidering their escape. Still, they commented on how their luck came a tad prematurely.

"It definitely would have been nice if we had found the *Treasure* by now," Kipchak pointed out.

"Yes," agreed Koke, as they strolled back toward the banquet hall. "But we'll have time to find it later. I'm sure we can find something on this ship to grind those antlers up with." For superstitious reasons, many in their trade felt it imperative to grind up animal parts while they were still fresh.

"You're right," said Kipchak, who then stopped short, putting a hand on Koke. "Hey. Where are those news-crew people?"

"Hmm..." realized Koke. "I thought they would be right behind us."

In their excitement, Koke and Kipchak had completely forgotten that the kidnapped news team was supposed to be right behind them. When Koke and Kipchak had urgently run out to apprehend the fugitive critters, they had called for Janet and Tom to come earn their keep, which was a strange thing to yell, seeing as how Janet and Tom were captives (though well-treated ones).

Though Kipchak and Koke's joint vision of the project suffered from their delusions of grandeur, the Mongolians' video was to be made up of impressive shots of the poachers poaching and then concocting their medicines. Few instructions had been relayed to Janet and Tom, as if Kipchak and Koke assumed they had previous experience making advertisements for shady poaching organizations. All that was clear was Tom should shoot the Mongolians busy at their work, while Janet would host the segment pointing out what Kipchak and Koke were doing. She had no clue about the intricacies of their vocation, and knew that when the time came she would be flying by the seat of her pants. At least it would not be the first time her job called for pants-seat-flying.

With the advent of their new target, Koke and Kipchak decided that filming was imperative. Potential buyers must see the Associates of Mr. Abominable Snowman Dragons hunting down a moose and witness its transformation into "medicine."

Reaching the banquet hall's entrance, Kipchak politely held the door for Koke, an uncommon gesture among these men which was indicative of their shared good mood. Thanking him as he stepped inside, Koke was the first to notice that their prey was missing. This development frazzled them, and the lethargic pirates splayed out on the banquet hall's floor were no help when asked.

Scratching their heads as they walked back into the sunlight, the Mongolian poachers did not take long to spot the two young boys leading the mighty beast in the opposite direction of all the hubbub, since, despite their best efforts, Ronaldinho and Earnest could not hide a moose very well. Koke and Kipchak smiled deviously at each other.

"Let's get it back," Koke said, starting his pursuit.

"Wait," Kipchak offered, an idea coming to mind. "An idea is coming to mind. Let's see what the boys are doing with it."

Koke nodded, understanding that "it" meant the moose and not Kipchak's idea. The two men began slinking along the ship's deck, keeping their distance from Mickey and his cohorts.

"I wish our camera crew was here for this," Koke whispered.

"Maybe they will be soon," Kipchak replied. "I hope they remembered to bring some guns."

Janet and Tom did not remember to bring any guns. So, gun-less, reporter and cameraman had hurried to keep up with Koke and Kipchak when the animals escaped, but what with Tom's heavy equipment and the bothersome terrain, the Channel 7 news team quickly fell behind the scurrying poachers.

"Hurry up, Tom!" Janet said, more than once. "They're getting away." The newscaster found herself back in her element at the thought of appearing on camera, even if her head was shaved. Tom was not so keen on being back in his element, getting bossed around by the "talent."

Starting out as far back from the pack as they had, it soon became apparent to Janet and Tom that catching up to the poachers was a fool's errand. *Those animals are really in shape!* thought Janet. Following the animals' tracks, however, their attention was diverted upon spotting another story taking place nearby. It began when Tom noticed a woman in a large puffy wedding gown hustling across the sand in the direction of the uninhabited beach. He pointed the woman out to his partner, who scratched her bald head. They both noticed she was carrying a large spatula in one hand and a blender in the other. Even from far away, they could tell there was vengeance in her eyes.

Seconds later, cresting the dune the bride just crested, came throngs of people, none wearing wedding dresses, but all wielding various pieces of kitchenware. Pots, pans, spatulas, large wooden spoons, whisks, egg beaters, ladles, a few cutting boards, rolling pins, garlic presses, ice trays, tea kettles, those things that kind of look like Popsicles that you use to stir batter: they were all there. These affluent-looking persons in khakis and polo shirts appeared ready for battle.

Tom had no idea what to make of the sight, though he hoped the people might help him become unkidnapped.

But it was too late for Janet.

"A story!" she yelled, pointing, as if Tom failed to notice what he just pointed out to her. And off she went, jogging across the sand. Tom sighed and followed. Though the group was well ahead of Janet and Tom, they were able to catch up to the tail end of the procession. Janet pointed and Tom got some good footage. Though the reporter called out politely in hopes of getting an interview, it seemed the hundreds of troops were of one mind.

A frowny-faced dark-haired woman carrying a nice bronze pot made up the caboose. She was yelling at the group. Seeing as how she was alone, Janet pounced.

"Excuse me, ma'am, but could I ask you what you are doing?" Then she thrust her microphone into Maria Martinez's displeased face.

"What am I doing? What am *I* doing? I'm trying to stop these morons from being as stupid as they're being."

"I see," Janet said. "Could you elaborate?"

Maria, having a supremely strange day, hardly noticed the added oddity of a news crew appearing beside her. "I found that stupid ship full of all of that kitchenware, and when I went to share my discovery, some idiot decided we should use it to attack the pirates and recapture our ship," she said into the microphone. "They just wanted to take action right away, and I thought I should try to keep some of them out of harm's way."

"You have a ship?" Janet asked.

"Of course we have a ship," Maria answered. "Do you think we all live here?"

Janet looked to Tom, who shrugged and indicated that he was capturing all of this enlightening conversation.

"I'm sorry, ma'am," Janet went on as she kept pace with Maria, "But I don't understand."

Maria sighed and looked at the microphone and camera. She hated television. Just hated it. "Listen, lady," she said, "My husband lied to me. For years and years. And he's on that ship, for all I know getting us into even more trouble."

"Your husband?"

"Yes. The allegedly famous Benito Martinez. Do you know him?" she asked snidely.

"*The* Benito Martinez? Like, the third baseman for the Orioles?" Janet asked, stopping short.

"I don't know what either of those things are, but if that means baseball player, then yes."

Janet could not believe her luck. "There you have it, ladies and gentlemen, a story of love, betrayal, fame, fortune, fighting, and a daring rescue attempt, here on the Gelatin Coast."

"I don't think that's what it's called," Tom told her.

"Who are you talking to?" Maria insisted. She really hated television.

"The viewers at home," Janet told her. "Do you mind if we trail you as you try to get your husband back?"

"I'm not trying to get him back," Maria told her. "I'm just trying to save his stupid life. As if he deserves it." She hesitated. "Fine. You can follow me."

Janet beamed, though she had planned to trail Maria regardless. Tom tried to ask some details about the outlandish situation for which he was still in the dark, but no one was listening as they hustled to catch the group. Janet had no idea what was going on either, but decided to focus on the part that sounded like it could win her a journalism award.

Onward marched the casual-wear militia to reclaim their cruise liner. Of course, their intention was to march to their lifeboats, board them, row out to the ship, and re-commandeer it. Numerous details of this plan were left out, such as the fact that launching a boat from the Skeleton Coast was nearly impossible, the ship may very well have traveled far from their location, and if they happened to catch up to it, the pirates may not let them on board. These were just some of the reasons that so many of the stranded passengers had stayed behind on the dunes, deeming the marchers ludicrous. But, of course, these concerns lost some validity when the army so luckily espied the newly shipwrecked *Queen Ivan*.

47

So anyway, here were all these people down below the plank Leonid Cupabascim was hugging. He peered down at them, but quickly regretted it.

The pirates who were healthy enough to lean over the railing had, by now, joined him in his peering. Some scratched their heads, some complained, and some turned and threw up (though probably not because of the passengers). Some new shouting began, as the pirates impolitely asked the militia to move so they could get on with the execution, and the militia yelled up some semi-courageous threats. Most of this was unintelligible.

Captain Hans Heissel Jr. rubbed his brow and sighed, then wordlessly pushed his way through the amassed pirates. *What is it now?* he thought, wishing these annoying developments would cease. Grumbling more than the other grumbling buccaneers, Hans straightened his headpiece upon reaching the *Queen Ivan's* railing and glared downward. The newspaper hat nearly fell off as the pirate captain threw his head back in frustration at the sight.

"Oh for the love of..." Hans groaned. "What are you people doing?"

Expecting a response with more vigor, the passengers were caught off guard, save for Delilah Johnson (oh, wait! Now it was Katsopolis!), who had appointed herself a four-star general in the kitchenware army.

"We're here to take our ship back!" she yelled, callously.

Hans Heissel groaned again. "No, you people. You can't have it."

"We'll take it by force if we have to!" the bride yelled, shaking her spatula. She was in quite an energetic mood, having gotten married just a couple hours ago.

Hans sighed again and his shoulders slunk. "Just ... just please go away, all of you." His limply waving hand indicated where he wished them to go. "It's been a very long day for all of us."

The non-pirate minority became curious about the strange conversation, so Benito, Melinda, and Toby followed Jamie to an unoccupied part of the railing, a couple Chrysler LeBaron lengths from where Hans stood. Toby was impressed by the resolve of the passengers, while Melinda was frustrated by their brash action. Benito was concerned. Jamie, on the other hand, did not know what to make of the spectacle, until he noticed two familiar faces and a familiar camera at the perimeter of the crowd.

The emotional subway ride started at shock, made a quick stop at disbelief, then arrived at joyfulness. The helicopter pilot nearly fell off the ship as he frantically waved at Janet and Tom.

"You guys!" Jamie yelled. "You guys! Up here!" Many of the passengers turned their attention to him, as he was louder than Hans's cranky voice. "Janet! Tom! Over here!"

It took a few more yells, but eventually Tom recognized the voice and instinctively turned the camera to Jamie.

Janet took another moment, then seethed as she looked to her former pilot. Happy to have gotten their attention, Jamie waved even harder.

"I found you!" he called proudly. "Janet! Tom! I can't believe it! I found you!"

Janet made slashing motions to stop Tom from filming. She composed herself as best a newswoman of her standing could before addressing Jamie.

"Yes, Jamie Brewster. It is us. But what, pray tell, are you doing here?"

"I came to find you! And I did!"

Janet smirked. "Mr. Brewster, I feel you take too much credit by saying that *you* found *us*."

Hans Heissel agitatedly peered over. Frowning, he turned back to the crowd. "We deny your request to come aboard," he shouted, raising his voice from moments before.

"Well, we aren't requesting!" Delilah the bride shouted back.

"What do you mean?" Jamie yelled.

"I mean from where I'm standing, we found *you*," Janet called.

"Oh," Jamie said, quieter, causing it to go unheard as Hans piped in.

"Well, whether or not you are requesting, you're still not allowed up here," Hans called.

"You stole our ship!" some guy yelled, waving a whisk.

"It is what we do," Hans replied.

"Then you ran it aground," some other guy yelled, causing some snickers among the militia.

"Who said that?" asked Hans Heissel, almost

embarrassed if not for the fact that he rarely became embarrassed.

"We could have died because of your stupid baseball cap," Janet yelled.

Jamie could see that his failed rescue attempt would continue to remain classified as "failed" for a little while longer. He decided to change the subject. "Why did you shave your head?"

Janet stamped her foot, but sand is not ideal for foot-stamping.

"Why did you wreck the ship?" called a woman.

"That is none of your concern," said Hans.

"It wasn't my idea to shave my head," called Janet.

"Did you mean to run the ship aground?" called another woman.

"Whose idea was it?" asked Jamie.

"No," called Hans. "Wait...yes."

"Remember those nice men, who kidnapped us?" Janet asked.

"Why would you run the ship aground?" yelled a man.

"Yes," said Jamie.

"Oh, just don't worry about it!" called Hans.

"Well, they decided they wanted my hair for some kind of medicine they were going to create," Janet said, all smarmy-like. (The Associates of Mr. Abominable Snowman Dragons said they needed blonde hair for a potion.)

"We are coming up," Delilah the bride called.

"It doesn't look that bad," Jamie called, trying to sound sincere.

"No you are not," Hans Heissel yelled, before he turned to Jamie. "All right, I'm sorry, but this is simply not working. Can you please move farther away or something? I can barely hear these people over the top of you two." Hans started to turn back toward the bride before rethinking his turn. "Actually, why are you not retrieving upset-stomach syrup?"

Jamie pretended to not hear the question.

Rubbing his brow, Captain Hans Heissel went on. "I will not send down our one lifeboat, so you will all starve down there or something."

"We don't need your stupid lifeboat," a guy said.

Hans Heissel chuckled. "Oh really?"

"Yeah," Delilah Katsopolis called. "We can just climb in through those windows."

As she pointed with her spatula, Captain Hans Heissel leaned further over the rail, to see that the woman in the wedding dress was indicating the first level of passengers' quarters, with their wide windows and luxurious interiors. Since the beach was especially soft and contained few rocks on this particular stretch of the Skeleton Coast, when the *Queen Ivan* ran aground, it had come in at such a speed as to really cut through the sand before coming to a complete stop. Therefore, without the pirate captain noticing, the *Queen Ivan* had lodged itself up to the first level of passengers' quarters. Or at least close enough that someone standing on someone else's shoulders should be able to climb in. This revelation concerned Hans Heissel, and he scrunched his face up in thought.

"Hmmmmm..." he ruminated.

The group of passengers shook their kitchenware and began moving closer to the *Queen Ivan*.

"Well, we're coming up," yelled Delilah.

The passengers noticed that they were going to become very wet getting to those windows.

"...As soon as the tide goes out a little bit more," the bride amended. And an unspoken agreement washed over the group of passengers. They could wait; the ship wasn't going anywhere.

Captain Hans Heissel bit his lip and turned away. "This is not ideal," he said to none of his pirates in particular. He went on thinking as he marched back through the crowd.

"Captain," said Christof the pirate, "We are too sick to fight them." The rest of the pirates nodded and clutched their midsections melodramatically.

"Then we cannot let them board us," replied the captain.

Amidst all of this, Toby had run off. Thankfully it wasn't for the nearest bathroom, since it had been reduced to smoldering rubble.

48

Earnest, Ronaldinho, and Mickey the moose were making a circuit of the ship's perimeter when they realized they were being tailed. As they got further from the fading sounds of the frustrated pirates, the trio heard footsteps, because the Mongolian poachers were overemphasizing their tiptoeing, which made more noise than simply walking. Also, Koke and Kipchak were unable to keep to the shadows, since it was such a bright, sunny day and much of the *Queen Ivan* was painted white. So when Ronaldinho turned, he noticed their reflection in a window.

The young first mate looked at Earnest and wordlessly confirmed that those mustachioed guys were in pursuit (his sign for mustache gave it all away). Nodding, Earnest knew his fears were becoming reality, that these men's motives might be in line with those of that portly fellow with the gun and the jeep. The group needed to find a way to shake them.

They proceeded as if nothing had changed, and rounded a corner near the back end (the stern?) of the boat. The boys looked around quickly in hopes of finding some sort of door or enclosure in which to hide a moose. There were doors, but none that fit their criteria. Earnest and Ronaldinho knew that at any moment two mustaches and the men attached to them would tiptoe loudly around the corner.

Incidentally, in their search they had stopped paying much attention to Mickey. So the great moose moved his large body over to the ship's pool for a drink. The pool was moderately sized, and had been the site of much merrymaking, before the passengers were jettisoned from the ship. And it was the same pool from which the diving board had been stripped only a handful of minutes prior. Mickey put his snout into the deep end and began lapping up the lukewarm pool water, which is another thing one should never do. But no one ever told Mickey that pool water was not for drinking.

Just as Koke and Kipchak popped their heads around the corner, there came a whizzing sound and a little splash in the water. Mickey raised his head. A moment later another whizzing sound peppered everyone's ears, followed by another splash, even closer to Mickey. Hugging the wall, Koke and Kipchak recognized this as gunfire.

Above them all appeared a helicopter, and precariously leaning out the open door of it, with a large rifle in hand, was the dastardly Clayton Stern. (Granted, all of them should have heard the sounds of the approaching aircraft, but they were all kind of busy and oblivious.)

Clayton Stern was of a single mind. His prize was finally in his sights (quite literally, because atop his big expensive gun were two big expensive sights to look through). This big, stupid animal that had caused him so much grief recently was about to be destroyed. All he needed was one good shot …

Thankfully, like many bad guys, Clayton Stern had

pretty lousy aim. He'd missed twice despite having a big, expensive gun designed to make a shooter's life easy. Of course, Stern blamed this on the helicopter that was jostling him around. His lawyer/maid, Isiah Burtlyre, was holding on tightly to prevent him from falling out. Also in the cramped but still luxurious cockpit was Clarence, Clayton Stern's personal driver, along with personal helicopter pilot of the eccentric rich man's personal helicopter. Behind his thick sunglasses, Clarence's interest in the project was minimal.

The last character in the cockpit was none other than Yancy Dunblatt, the portly trumpet-playing henchman of Clayton Stern's, who had orchestrated this helicopter flight. Since we last heard about him, the stranded Mr. Dunblatt had become unstranded, obviously. Though his jeep was still out of commission due to the dead battery, he had been able to contact his employer because in Earnest's village—the site of Yancy's harrowing bat adventure—there was one, and only one, telephone.

The telephone, which Dunblatt had been unaware of when he arrived, was a satellite phone donated to the village by a philanthropic organization and intended mainly for use during emergencies. Its intended use was not always respected, as some of the villagers used it to call distant radio stations and request fake songs. The solar-powered contraption was operated by the village's primary goat seller, an aging man with a distaste for technology. So using the phone always began with an argument and often ended with the purchase of goats. Dunblatt came away with two himself, just as a formality, after he used the phone to contact Clayton Stern with news of the moose's escape. This information was not taken well by the base billionaire. The following day, (after another phone call that left Dunblatt with two more goats) he was informed by the trumpet player that tracking the moose should be easy. Provided they had another jeep. Stern said he would do one better, and use his personal helicopter to track it down. Once Yancy was done being scolded, the helicopter left the villagers (and Yancy's newly traded goats). The small crew, with all the information they gleaned from villagers about Earnest, set off in the direction the moose/boy duo had traveled. And eventually they came across a ship, and realized there was a moose running around on deck, and the decision to shoot the moose soon followed.

Now, with the helicopter circling back over the pool, the shooter took aim again. But just as the diabolical Clayton Stern went to pull the trigger, he noticed that a boy had jumped in front of the large mammal. And beyond the boy was another confused boy, and hunched in a doorway near that boy were two grown men. And, while Clayton Stern was not really all that morally adept, he thought it may be unwise to shoot at people with a lawyer present. Even if it was *his* lawyer.

Stern pulled his gun and his self back in the helicopter and made an angry noise. If only he could get those stupid people out of the way! Seeing as he was rich and eccentric, the rich, eccentric man had been snacking on expensive shiitake mushrooms as if they were potato chips. In his frustration, he threw one at Earnest to get him to move.

Meanwhile, the amassed pirates and passengers and whonot at the front (bow?) of the boat, unlike the people being shot at, *had* noticed the approaching helicopter. Curiosity about the target led a few pirates to head over, though most groaned some more and stopped short of a full investigation.

Benito Martinez, however, of the healthy stomached minority, hustled toward the circling helicopter. He had been standing at the railing, paying little heed to the discussions, and scouring the crowd for his wife. But as he searched, the realization that she might be even angrier with him for joining a pirate crew settled in. The hoopla at the other end of the ship provided a welcome respite.

When he arrived at the ship's pool (where he had spent little time for fear of getting his disguise wet), he saw poor Earnest dodging raining mushrooms. Of course, being rare that you see mushrooms used as ammunition, Benito was confused and assumed the worst. If guns had been fired at young Earnest, then whatever was being thrown at him now must be really bad. And he was right; it was mushrooms, after all. But now Mickey was walking around the pool, hoping to find a quiet spot, and Earnest was in hot pursuit, emphatically waving for the helicopter to stop dropping its ghastly fungus bombs. Benito knew the boy needed saving, but had trouble thinking through the scene unfolding before his very eye (the unpatched one).

"Mr. Martinez!" a voice yelled. Benito spun to see Toby hustling toward him. Cradled in the young man's arms was the largest rolling pin Benito had ever seen. In fact, despite its sleek design and appealing veneer, it was so large that the handles were too far apart for use by anyone without an incredible wingspan. This contributed to the undoing of *Treasure* brand Kitchenware.

Though he was running, Toby cradled it like it was a particularly important baby. Until he fell. There wasn't any really good reason that he fell. He just tripped over his own feet. And the rolling pin earned its namesake and started rolling. Thank goodness it wasn't actually a baby.

The rolling pin sped right over to Benito Martinez's feet and he peered at it.

"Mr. Martinez!" yelled Toby from the ground. "Use it!"

Benito eyed it suspiciously.

"Like a bat!" yelled Toby, hoping things would sink in. "Because you're a professional baseball player." Sometimes Big Ben could be thick.

When the passengers had arrived below the ship and it appeared that a battle was forthcoming, an idea had struck Toby. Seeing as he still idolized Benito Martinez more than anyone else among these yahoos, Toby envisioned him as the white knight to lead the oppressed against the pirates. Benito did not see himself in this light. In fact it was quite dark under the eye patch. Toby thought that with a bat-like device, Benito could be the displaced shipmates' greatest warrior. So he sprinted to the window the passengers had threatened to enter and demanded the largest rolling pin they carried amongst them. Once the passengers were assured this was for a "hero," they obliged by standing on one another's shoulders to hand him the rolling pin. Thoughts of impressing Melinda also played a part, mind you.

Toby's idea finally sank in and Benito understood his destiny. The mushrooms mustn't hit anyone! He wasted precious seconds picking the rolling pin up and giving Toby a stoic head nod, but for the young man's psyche, it was beyond comparison. Then he lugged the enormous rolling pin to the pool, hefted it onto one shoulder, and stepped in front of Earnest. The boy knew not what his intentions were, until one of the terrible mushrooms whistled their way.

Benito Martinez, all-star third baseman, spit on the rolling pin and used both hands to rub it in, just as he did before every at-bat. He glared at the pitcher, the beady-eyed right-hander, peering at him from the helicopter and yelling obscenities that could not be heard over the sound of the blades. Benito cocked the pin above his head and hunkered down. Earnest, guessing what was about to occur, tugged gently at Mickey's leash to get him out of the way. They slowly backed around the pool.

And then came the pitch. The large mushroom hurled down from Clayton Stern's angry arm toward the deck. Benito gripped his weapon tightly, ready to knock the mushroom out of the park because of the danger it posed and because mushrooms are disgusting. Down it flew, right into his wheelhouse.

But despite it being an object thrown at a baseball player, the mushroom was dissimilar from a baseball, both in its being disgusting and also because it was not round. And therefore, as it fell, spinning, the mushroom caught a slight breeze and its trajectory changed. Its path bent away from Benito, making him lunge toward the fungi. And everyone who had ever watched Benito Martinez play baseball knew one thing. He couldn't hit the curve! Despite an ability to smack baseballs over fences, curve balls were his Kryptonite! Oh, the humanity! So as the mushroom tailed away from him, the hulking athlete swung, missed, and embarrassingly created a large gust of wind behind himself.

Consequently, the horrendous swing allowed the wretched mushroom to make contact with the moose walking behind Benito. Mickey was none too happy to take a mushroom to the face, because although a mushroom tossed across a dining room table might not hurt much, a mushroom falling from a helicopter and given time enough to generate momentum will hurt more. Or maybe Mickey just knew how disgusting mushrooms are. A great moose bellow rang out across the deck, and suddenly Mickey was off and running, or at least lumbering, away from the pool. Earnest pursued.

Benito Martinez fell to a knee, shamed, the way he did when he struck out on a curve to end a game. But there was usually no peril involved in striking out. Just booing. He glanced at Toby, still lying on the deck, wincing, and wishing he could unsee that terrible swing. Benito eyed the retreating moose, wondering if he would recover from being hit by the ... whatever it was. The object sat a few steps away and Benito picked it up. He saw that it was a mushroom, with seemingly nothing dangerous about it. Except that it was a mushroom, thought Benito, who recognized that, by default, it was gross.

With Mickey the moose running off behind the structures on the *Queen Ivan's* aft deck (does that sound right?), Clayton Stern threw a tantrum loud enough it *could* be heard over the sound of the helicopter's rotating blades.

He threw more mushrooms in frustration, all landing in the pool. After calming a smidge, he turned to Isiah Burtlyre and pointed to the large red-and-white target beyond the pool.

"Sugar Cheeks, tell Clarence to land this thing." He might have told the pilot to do so himself if not for the fact that Clayton Stern loved chains of command.

Seeing the helicopter landing pad behind the pool, his lawyer nodded and leaned forward to tell Clarence to land the aircraft, despite Clarence hearing his boss' wishes. So Clarence nodded his sunglasses-adorned face and began to take the helicopter down.

Then a funny thing happened. Well, a funny thing for those of us not in the helicopter, at least. And maybe it wasn't necessarily funny for the bystanders like Benito and the poachers, but when they looked back upon the incident they would come to see that it really should be classified as funny. Anyway, the funny thing that has really been built up way too much at this point, perhaps negating some of its humor, was that Clarence landed the helicopter in the pool. (Well, maybe it's not that funny after all, but that's what he did, either way.)

You see, he was shooting for the helicopter landing pad, a spot specifically placed atop the *Queen Ivan's* tower in case an emergency required a rescue helicopter. So far the landing pad had not been needed, so Clayton Stern and crew felt they would christen it. But Clarence dropped his lighter. So he used his knee to try to steer the helicopter toward the target as he leaned over to recover the lighter. Any other person might wait until landing to recover the lighter, but Clarence really wanted to light up that cigarette in his mouth. He reached toward the floor of the helicopter, much to the horror of the other people inside it. In fact, they were so horrified that none could speak. The pilot eventually grasped the lighter and sat back up, but it was too late already, as his knees had steered the helicopter dangerously close to the pool. He still took the time to light his cigarette.

At this point, fearing death, Stern, Burtlyre, and Dunblatt jumped out the open door of the aircraft and into the pool, now only feet below them. They frantically swam for safety, Stern pushing the other two out of his way. Only then did the pilot recognize that there was no hope for reaching the landing pad. Never one to lose his calm, even in potentially deadly situations created by his own negligence, Clarence decided a water landing would be just fine.

And it might have been, were it not for the properties of liquids, which caused the helicopter to immediately begin sinking. Thankfully, Clarence had stopped the helicopter, so the rotating blades were slowing down. But the rotation still created waves in the pool, which hampered the swimmers' escape. Rolling out of the way of the sinking helicopter, Stern watched Clarence go down with the ship, so to say, as the aircraft met its end in the water aboard a boat. The expected danger of the blades contacting the surface was mercifully avoided, though, when the helicopter's feet touched the pool's bottom (which should have been deeper, seeing as there had been a diving board until recently). In fact, the three men were all very, very lucky to have made it out of the incident alive.

And so the Skeleton Coast had claimed another victim. Sort of.

Now here they were, Clayton Stern, Isiah Burtlyre, and Yancy Dunblatt, three soggy men sitting on the deck of the *Queen Ivan*, all alone, since everyone else had run off when they saw the accident that was about to happen. Clayton could hardly believe what had just occurred, and it took him a moment to get his regular anger back. But just before his face turned scarlet and his mouth opened to yell, he was approached by two men who had seen the ordeal.

"Ah, hello, sir," said Kipchak.

"We were wondering why you were shooting at us," said Koke, smiling pleasantly.

Stern's anger was bubbling up further at their nerve, but the negotiator inside him said to make friends with these men. Well, that's not *exactly* what it said; it was more like *Now that all your stuff is underwater, these guys might come in handy*.

"I wasn't shooting at you fellows," Clayton began, noticing the surprise and relief that painted the men's faces. "I was shooting at that moose."

Koke and Kipchak looked impressed, then said something secretive to each other.

"We, too, are trying to shoot that moose," said Kipchak.

"We have this in common, then, sir," added Koke.

"I suppose we do," said Clayton, wary of their motives.

And then from the opposite end of the boat stomped Captain Hans Heissel, still frowny-faced and straightening his newspaper hat.

"What ridiculous thing is going on now aboard my

ship?" he inquired as he walked up to the poolside conversation. "Why is there a helicopter in the pool?"

Clayton Stern sized up this new character as Koke and Kipchak smiled at the pirate commander.

"Captain, this man is here for the moose, too," Koke relayed, as if it were the most important piece of information in the world.

"Of course he is. Just like everyone else," Hans said. Along with his upset stomach, he was beginning to get a headache.

"Captain, is it?" Clayton interrupted.

"Very much so," said Hans Heissel, looking down at the soggy man. "And who might you be?"

Clayton Stern gave him a deliciously evil grin. "I'm Clayton Stern, billionaire. And I think I am just the man who can help you."

Up bubbled Clarence at this point, who somehow made it to the poolside in one piece. He still looked pretty calm. After a silent few moments, Yancy pointed toward the big target.

"You were supposed to land the helicopter on the landing pad."

"Oh," Clarence said. "Nobody told me that." Then he asked if Koke or Kipchak had a lighter.

With all this hogwash going on nearby, Earnest had led Mickey (or perhaps Mickey had led Earnest) away from the pool, past the helicopter landing pad, around to the back end of the ship, and into an elevator. Mickey's antler had accidentally grazed the down button (there was no up button on the top deck) and both of them were startled as the doors opened. When his heartbeat slowed a touch, Earnest peered in and concluded that this would be a wonderful place to hide from the mushrooms. The small enclosure had lovely ruby carpeting and a framed painting of some heavily flowered countryside. And though not really designed to fit a moose, Mickey obliged, backing in.

Of course, being as large as they were, Mickey's antlers did not fully make it through the opening. So when the elevator doors automatically shut, they ran into the antlers and reopened. After a few moments, the doors tried again, but were still denied by the giant protrusions. This pattern continued while Earnest and Mickey hunkered down in their new hiding spot.

"So let me get this straight," the Great Captain Hans Heissel Jr. was saying. "If I let *you*"—he pointed to Clayton—"shoot my pet, then *you guys*"—he pointed to Koke and Kipchak—"will keep the antlers, and *I'll* get …"

"Your ship back to normal," said Stern, toweling himself off with the towel from the towel cart that Koke and Kipchak found.

Though he wasn't very good at it, Hans Heissel gave a smug chuckle. "Mr. Clayton, although there is a helicopter in the pool and a crazy woman in a wedding dress with a blender trying to attack us and a terrible stomach virus making the rounds and a moose hidden somewhere on board and also the ship has been crashed, I assure you that I am not that worried about getting things back to," (here Hans meant to make quote marks in the air but used the wrong gesture) "'normal.'"

"I can get your ship towed out of here," Stern told Hans.

Hans Heissel's eyes lit up, but he tried to be coy. "Oh, is that true?"

Stern liked to walk as he bluffed, so he got up and started strolling the ship's deck. The rest of the conspirators followed.

"Yes. No problem. I mean, like I told you, I am filthy rich. Just the filthiest. I can have this boat towed out of here and back on the high seas in a matter of hours." He was lying. No one could tow that boat out of that mire. But lying was what Clayton Stern did, and he did not care about Hans Heissel much, so long as he got his moose.

Of course, Hans Heissel was not aware that Clayton was lying, and his pace quickened as he became giddy at the idea of getting his ship back out to sea. This deal sounded great because all he would lose was his pet, and he had already agreed to give it up. A little more disarray on board would be worth the compensation.

"Yes, I see," the pirate captain said, trying to hide his joy. "I will consider." He turned in a circle. "Very well. I wish you luck."

"Well before you wish us any luck, and before I can get my tugboat fleet down here, I'll need something else from you," Stern told him.

Hans sighed melodramatically. "Now what?"

"You see, Captain," Clayton smirked as he reached the railing, "My gun seems to be at the bottom of that pool."

"And?"

"Well, I'll need something to kill the moose with."

"I suppose you will. But you could just use your hands, couldn't you?"

Stern was growing impatient, but tried not to let it

show. "Well, you are pirates, right?"

"Yes."

"Then you must have some guns."

Hans Heissel chuckled. "Oh, Mr. Clayton, you are so naïve. Who ever said pirates need guns?"

Stern seethed a little. "Do you have guns or not?"

"Yes."

"Good."

"But we have no bullets."

"What?" Clayton was angry again.

"But we have no bullets."

Clayton Stern did not believe this. He genuinely thought this odd pirate captain was joking. "Captain, is there a gun I could use on board this ship?"

Hans thought and thought. "Well, there might be one."

"With bullets?"

"I think so."

"Good."

"If you will be so kind as to excuse me for a few moments, I will have one of my lackeys go get it. You may be seated in those nice deck chairs." They certainly were nice chairs.

Each member of the consortium of badness nodded at the others to show support for the agreement. They all shook, and then Hans wiped his hand off on his shirt.

49

Having his conversation with Janet (and to a lesser extent, Tom) interrupted by the sound and sight of a helicopter, Jamie Brewster hustled toward the action. Like most people, he hoped that the helicopter was a step in the right direction. And his excitement eclipsed the others, because helicopters he knew! All this other garbage, what with shipwrecked cruise ships and kitchenware and little boys and moose was one thing, but he could deal with helicopters. It was his job.

That was before the gunfire, which changed his opinion a bit.

Then, like a curious little raccoon, he had poked his head around a corner of the banquet hall's outside wall and listened intently to the conversation among the obvious bad guys. It did not settle right with him, he realized upon his involuntary gasp. Jamie had grown attached to the moose, and none of these fellows discussing his fate seemed all that nice. And, more importantly, Jamie felt, he could not just let someone go about shooting in the vicinity of poor Earnest.

So as soon as the amassed villains took off to collect their weaponry, Jamie set off to track down Earnest. And Mickey. But where on earth did they run off to? He started his search by heading in the wrong direction.

The pirates were hustling downstairs. Well, hustling might be an overstatement. Tumbling, maybe. They were doing their best, though, to head below deck and stop the kitchenware militia from boarding the *Queen Ivan*. They continued to groan and roll around, and though you would think these burly to moderately burly men (and handful of women) might have finally given it a rest, even pirates suffer from hypochondria sometimes.

After some brief deliberating amongst the senior pirates, excluding Ronaldinho, wherever he might be, it was decided that a helicopter in the pool had no bearing on the fact that the passengers had to be stopped. So, tumbling down the stairs they went, hoping to reach the windows before the army had a chance to climb through. Despite a number of doors that led downstairs, they all decided to stick together and force their way through the big doors that led into the main hall.

Now, the main hall was just as fancy as you're imagining, and arguably fancier. Despite some of the *Queen Ivan's* shortcomings, Fillmore R. Puggleston was insistent on a big, fancy space in the middle of the ship. So when you walked into this room from the direction that the pirates were tumbling, you would be standing atop a fancy staircase with red carpeting that forked and wound down to the floor in two staircases, causing a major dilemma for indecisive people. It was a very large hall, so the staircase was very long, and you wouldn't want to tumble off it. If you did, you would rapidly descend into an ornate fountain surrounded by a pool that was better for tossing coins into than falling into, because it was about a foot and a half deep. Near the top of the staircase began a waterfall (which was not naturally occurring) that cascaded down into the fountain. A few streams shot upward from the base of the structure, and on either side of the waterfall were other ornate streams. Big chandeliers hung from the ceiling far above, along with hanging plants, which might lead you to wonder how anyone watered them. The assortment of hanging things added shadows to odd places on the hall's floor, since a portion of the ceiling was a big window, making it feel like you were in a greenhouse.

Anyway, it was fancy, and big, and there were plenty of the things you would expect in such a place, like tables and chairs and other similar luxuries. But there was something the pirates were not expecting to see: the passengers, slowly trickling into the hall on the bottom floor. With the tide receding enough for them to stand on each others' shoulders', the militia had been climbing through the bottom-floor windows for a number of minutes now, while the pirates putzed around on deck. So, as the buccaneers clambered over each other and slipped down the stairs, they beheld the reentry of the travelers to their seagoing hotel. One of the passengers yelled a pun about "check-in time," but it wasn't very funny, so it didn't take.

Adding to the pirates' confusion, however, was the general disregard they were paid. It seemed that as the passengers filed in, they were of one mind. That one mind was focused on a spot at the other end of the main hall. They were forming a disorderly queue back there.

Fingers the pirate, one of the more senior members of Hans Heissel's crew, leaned out over the staircase and squinted. Having not had much time to explore the ship before the cake incident, Fingers was momentarily confused about where the mob was going. Then he realized it was the bathroom.

Though the idea of taking back the ship was reasonably important to these armed members of the rebellion, the original group of castaways could easily be separated into two distinct factions: those who had no real problem substituting the far side of a dune for a lavatory, and those who found this idea appalling. The latter were, of course, the group that made up the kitchenware militia. The desire to once again use the cruise ship's restrooms was so important that their own safety was severely compromised.

The passengers' distraction bought the pirates a little time to act.

"There you are," Captain Hans Heissel was saying, "The finest gun aboard this ship probably." He handed the sleek, black firearm to Clayton Stern. Always an unwise move.

The gun was a big rifle, with a large scope on top and a long barrel. It was rather heavy, and a bit of an older model, apparently, but otherwise a very fancy gun. Stern did not care much about the gun's credentials so long as it could kill animals. He admired it only briefly before a wicked gleam came into his eye. Some would argue it was always there, but at this moment it got worse. Bad enough to see a doctor about.

Hans Heissel, Stern, Dunblatt, Burtlyre, and the two poachers stood in the original captain's quarters, where the pirates had stashed the guns they carried aboard. It was literally just a pile. Once Hans sent one of the younger pirates to retrieve what he believed would be the only weapon that met Stern's needs, they waited by the deck chairs, until the task occupied the pirate a little too long for Clayton's liking. Hans Heissel suggested the group wait by the other guns. When the pale and queasy young pirate walked into the room, he was polishing the weapon with a little rag. His captain confiscated it, then presented it to Clayton Stern ceremoniously. Koke and Kipchak clapped a little.

"What took you so long?" the captain asked the young pirate.

"I had to change clothes."

The comment went unnoticed by the group, because they all usually ignored what they considered people of lesser standing.

"And it's loaded?" Hans Heissel asked.

"Yes," the pirate replied. "I checked it twice."

"Very well," Hans said as he smugly turned back to Clayton. "You now have your gun. Commence shooting the moose and then perhaps leave the ship."

Clayton might have said something like, "Of course," or, "Yes," had been paying attention, but despite how much respect Captain Hans Heissel thought he should command, Stern just waltzed out the door of the captain's quarters to begin his pursuit of poor Mickey.

50

"What are you doing?" Melinda asked Toby, having found him in the executive bathroom, holding a pink bottle.

The mousy young man sighed. "Well, I figured I might as well finally find some Pepto-Bismol or Tums or something."

Melinda, stressed and exhausted, wished that a joke like this would be just the medicine for her. Too bad Toby wasn't joking. She gave a tired little chuckle, but accompanied it with a look that said "There's no time for joking."

"There's no time for joking," she told him, in case he failed to read her expression correctly. Again Toby wished his proactive thinking regarding the stomach remedy would impress the girl he wished to woo, but his wish turned to woe. Oh well.

"Okay," Toby obliged. He looked around, wondering what there was time for.

"We should try to help the passengers," Melinda told him.

"Of course we should."

Toby melodramatically dropped the pink bottle. Melinda hustled back into the hallway, and Toby tailed her. He was not astonished to find that, even under pressure and looking exhausted, Melinda was a vision of beauty. At least to him. He wondered briefly what the pirates thought of her, and that, if need be, he would perhaps fight them off for her hand. Perhaps.

Halfway down the hallway Toby noticed that his shoe had become untied, and the young man could not resist retying it. He tried to do it quickly, but by the time he finished Melinda had turned a corner and disappeared, making her successful search for him a waste of time. Once Toby got up and ran in the direction she disappeared, he was faced with the dilemma of choosing up the stairs or through one of two doors. Despite being informed that the plan revolved around helping the incoming passengers, Toby chose to go up the stairs.

Bursting onto the deck, he found no trace of Melinda, which was more disappointing for him than it would have been for anyone else. But before his pitter-pattering footsteps returned to the flight of stairs, Toby noticed someone who piqued his interest more than all the other non-Melindas.

Benito Martinez was propped up against a wall near the door, positioned much like a deflated balloon. It looked terribly uncomfortable. Toby approached cautiously.

"Um, hi Mr. Martinez," the mousy young man peeped. Benito, overacting, slowly turned to Toby, pretending as though he just noticed him standing there.

"Toby," Benito's newfound gravelly voice breathed. "I missed them. I missed them all."

Toby didn't know what he was talking about. "Right," he said, changing the subject, "but we should go downstairs now because all those passengers showed up and Melinda"—his heart fluttered saying her name—"thinks we should try to help them."

All of this sunk in, but Benito Martinez still wanted to

give the impression that he was suffering from some sort of post-traumatic stress. "I missed them all, man. Every last one." He, of course, was referring to the mushrooms, even though it had only been one mushroom he swung at. This version was more poetic, mind you.

Of course, swinging and missing at the foul little thing might have saved Mickey's life, seeing as the moose ran off after being pelted with it. But Benito did not see it that way.

"There'll be other chances to not miss," Toby told him, unsuccessfully attempting to lift Benito by his massive bicep. "Come on, we've got to go."

"I can't go down there," Benito said, looking up at Toby with his one unpatched eye.

Toby became uncharacteristically forceful as he stood. "But we have to." He offered Benito his hand.

The hand went unclasped. "I really can't go down there." Then, the hulking athlete put his head in his own hands. "My wife is down there."

When Delilah Katsopolis had entered the lavatory, her wedding dress was so large that it took up half the room. There was no way to keep an eye on the dress' entire train. So she failed to notice that part of it pushed right up against an air vent, which, because of the ship's structure, connected to the air vent in the restroom that was now smoldering rubble. A tiny chunk of rubble had fallen through the air vent and still smoldered just a touch. So, perhaps karmically, because of her "borrowing" the day before, Delilah Katsopolis' wedding dress just barely caught on fire.

The deck of a cruise ship is not the easiest place to look for footprints, but Clayton Stern had a keen eye, and nose, for tracking animals. At least he told himself that he did.

"Thankfully I have a nose for this, Ziploc," he told his lawyer, without turning to face him. Burtlyre nodded, but continued to stay back a number of steps, as he had been instructed.

Unlike Jamie, Stern headed toward the back end of the *Queen Ivan* upon exiting the captain's quarters. He crept around corners and then jumped out, ready to blast Mickey away if he was so unfortunate as to be standing there. Each corner offered the same disappointing result to Clayton. He slunk back past the pool, and around the still-vacant landing pad. He climbed up on the raised platform and looked down from where the helicopter was supposed to be to where the helicopter actually was. Still saw no sign of the moose. Stepping back down disgustedly, he continued around the perimeter toward the ship's back end.

As the billionaire gunman ran the gun against the rail, he peered over the side, momentarily considering that the moose jumped down to escape. *But that's impossible*, he thought. *Moose are stupid.* And before the thought occurred to him that it might make the moose stupider to jump off a cruise ship even if it were to escape gunfire, Clayton approached a waving flag that happened to be the midpoint of the stern (or bow ...). It flapped a bit in the growing breeze. Clayton raised his gun and considered shooting it for fun, then spotted an oblivious seagull and adjusted his aim. Before he could pull the trigger, however, he heard shushing.

Clayton looked through the gun's sight to investigate. Turning, he spotted what he had been searching for, cramped into an elevator. Stern smirked.

Earnest regretted shushing Mickey, who had not really been making that much noise in the first place. His precaution had given away their position. Earnest was frustrated with himself and put an apologetic hand on Mickey's neck as he stepped forward.

Isiah Burtlyre caught up to Stern at this point, and piped up to remind the rich hunter he was there. "Um, sir, I have to advise you don't try to take a shot with that kid in the way."

Stern noticed that the little boy was stepping in front of the moose, but did not lower the gun. He considered saying, *Why? You'd be the only witness, and you're not going to talk*, but considered that if Burtlyre suddenly had a conscience, he would have to shoot him, too, and who knew how many bullets were in that gun.

Earnest decided to try talking sense into Clayton Stern, hoping that maybe someone might finally understand him. "You cannot shoot this moose, sir. He is a friend of mine."

Clayton stepped closer, without taking his eye from the gun's sight. "Get out of the way, you stupid kid!" he snapped.

Earnest spread his arms wide to shield his friend. He was deadly serious about protecting Mickey. "Mr. Sir, put your gun down, please. This moose is not for shooting at."

"Get away! Get away from that moose!" Clayton hollered, sprinkling in some profanities that I will exclude in case my mother ever reads this.

There were about three Chrysler LeBaron lengths of

flooring between the rear railing and the elevator door, and Clayton was closing in. Mickey was standing mostly in, but partially out of, the elevator. Earnest had never been in an elevator and had no idea how to operate one, let alone, for that matter, what it did. So, as Clayton stepped closer, despite being a boy and a moose, the boy and the moose were sitting ducks.

"Um, Mr. Stern, please don't shoot that boy," Burtlyre chimed in again, seeing the determination on his employer's face.

Earnest recognized that this unruly adult was not swayed by his pleas. *If only he spoke my language*, thought Earnest, *maybe then he would adhere to my request.* He raised his voice, and at the same time tried to push Mickey all the way into the elevator. Perhaps then he could shut this stupid door. But pushing the moose did not seem to help. Mickey did not like being pushed. So he nudged Earnest back after each of the boy's fruitless attempts.

"I'm warning you!" Clayton Stern's face was turning red with white-hot anger. "Get away from there, you stupid, crappy kid!" He was now less than two Chrysler LeBaron lengths from the duo. Brackish sweat formulated on his brow. He was so close to his goal. Another step. And another.

Earnest was losing his cool. The thought of being shot stilled failed to register, but the thought that his best friend was going to be shot felt palpable. So Earnest gave Mickey a more forceful shove and nearly fell over. Mickey snorted, then leaned back to get some momentum behind the push he was about to deliver. Earnest's slip finally opened up a clear path for Clayton's bullet.

But Mickey's hindquarters rammed into the painting of a picturesque countryside on the back wall, and since his hindquarters had already brushed up against the painting a number of times, it was hanging loosely. The newest run-in was the final straw, and with an un-picturesque clatter the countryside fell to the floor. The sound caused Mickey to start. Earnest jumped back up. Like any normal warm-blooded creature, Mickey wanted to see what made the noise, so he strained to turn and investigate. In that moment Clayton's clear shot disappeared, as Earnest again stood in his way and Mickey's jiggling made aiming difficult. Stern finally decided to walk over to drag the boy out.

But just as Mickey started his laborious turn, his antler finally retracted into the elevator, allowing the automatic doors to finally close. Seeing this, Clayton broke into a run, even though he was wearing expensive non-running shoes. Earnest was delighted, or at least thought he should be delighted. And as the determined Mickey scraped his antlers along the interior to peek at the startling object at his feet, good luck befell the pair once more. One prong happened to graze the button adorned with the number 2. The button ecstatically lit up.

Had Clayton Stern been willing to leap, he may have been able to stop the elevator. But he did not leap, because when it came to his nice shoes he had to draw the line somewhere. So by the time he pressed the down button next to the closed door, the elevator was already dropping.

Neither Mickey nor Earnest was a veteran elevator rider. Both jumped a touch when it began moving, but without much room inside, they really had nowhere to jump to. Mickey found the new development disconcerting, but so many things had been disconcerting recently. Earnest, on the other hand, though at first spooked, quickly became enchanted. This room was moving! How fun! And despite the lack of space, he also quickly learned how fun it is to jump in an elevator.

"I have no idea what is going on," Earnest told his friend between jumps, "But it is best that we are away from that cranky man." Jump. "He wanted to shoot you!" Jump.

Of course, this elevator ride did not take long, and soon the door opened. This startled Earnest a bit, and he was disappointed that the effect of jumping had worn off. Then he glanced out.

"Oh neat," were the words he afforded the sight.

51

"What's in that case thingy?" asked a pirate. Said pirate was referring to the case that Yancy Dunblatt carried with him as he followed Captain Hans Heissel back into the throne room.

"It's a cooler." No it wasn't. It was his trumpet.

"No it isn't," said another pirate.

"It's my trumpet," the portly henchman replied, before wondering why he hadn't lied some more to this miscreant. (It was in his nature to do so.)

Yes, Yancy Dunblatt had saved his trumpet from the sinking helicopter. It was his nature to take his trumpet everywhere he went. Though the musical instrument seemed superfluous on the little hunting excursion, he always thought he might want to play it (which was interesting given his distaste for *practicing* with his trumpet). Of course, the trumpet was not in the best shape, having been submerged in pool water. But Yancy had been the only person aboard the helicopter to successfully rescue his property. Clayton Stern had scolded Isiah Burtlyre for not rescuing the rifle.

The trumpet case was still dripping water when Dunblatt walked into the converted banquet hall. News of what the wet box contained piqued the interest of the lazy pirates sprawled around. This gaggle should have been aiding its brethren below, but all decided they were far too sick to move. What they were healthy enough for, they realized, was a little music.

As Hans retreated to his makeshift throne, one of the pirates he stepped over spoke up. "Hey! Play something!"

Quickly a chorus of heads attached to inoperative bodies shouted their agreement. Yancy did not feel like playing his trumpet right now. His boss had dismissed him, saying that he would just get in the way during the hunt. So he looked forward to partaking in the feast Hans Heissel had bragged about, all spread out by his seat of power.

"Well, I can't..." said Dunblatt.

"No! Play!" Hans insisted, falling in love with his crew's suggestion.

"Well..."

"Play for us!" they yelled.

"It will make us feel better," someone added.

"Also, we'll make you walk the plank otherwise," advised a pirate propped against the wall.

"Oooh! Yes, that's it," Hans Heissel agreed. "Good point. And that will quite maybe kill you, I have been informed."

Groaning much like the pirates had been, Yancy Dunblatt unlocked the soggy case.

"Yay!" the pirates exclaimed, surprised he was following instructions.

The trumpet case was pretty damp inside, and when Yancy extracted the instrument, pool water leaked out of every valve. He sighed, knowing this trumpet may never be the same.

"What do I play?" he asked.

Like all pirates, the crew loved Sting, so the criminals requested something by The Police.

Swearing and jamming the elevator button, Clayton Stern was the stick-man-picture example of how not to act when riding the elevator. He was in the compartment with Isaiah Burtlyre, though he forgot the lawyer was present. There were only so many floors on the cruise ship, and they believed a moose could not have gotten far once it exited the elevator. And it must have exited, because when Stern entered on the top deck, the elevator was empty, causing another hissy fit. He had tried the first level, and he had tried the third level. No sign of any moose. With each level he unsuccessfully passed, his face became a deeper shade of red. It now resembled a newly polished fire engine.

Once more the elevator doors opened. This floor was a bit livelier than the previous stops.

Before them was the main hall, transformed into a war zone. On one side of the enormous hall were pirates, and on the other were returned passengers, waving their cookware. Both sides were ducking behind the tables and chairs they had claimed from the middle of the floor. The opposing forces were shouting at each other, but it all seemed like posturing. Clayton did not know who any of these people were, and did not care. Because he noticed that walking right through the neutral center of the battlefield, where the tables and chairs had been snatched from, were the moose and his boy.

Clayton picked a bad moment to show up, though, because it seemed the posturing was finally about to end, and the battle royale about to commence.

Exiting the elevator was for some reason considerably easier for Mickey than entering had been. But now that he was out, he recognized just how fortunate he was to have peace and quiet in that box.

Earnest was holding firmly to the leash and leading him across the main hall's floor at a brisk pace, making a beeline for the opposite end of the enormous room. At first the boy had been delighted to see the group of people who were yelling at someone other than him. As an added bonus, they were also not pointing guns at him. But these people obviously were not getting along with one another. He felt a touch of sympathy for all the sick gentlemen. The bullies on his right all had weapons, which seemed unfair. Earnest hoped they would solve their differences soon.

"Hello there," Earnest called with a smile. "Have any of you seen my friend Shay-mee?" No one responded, and many wondered what a moose could possibly be doing with a life ring around his antler. And how he got there. But mostly the two sides were preoccupied with the ensuing fight.

And all of a sudden it was no longer an ensuing fight, but a fight in earnest, with Earnest right in the middle of it. Whatever could be found was being thrown. Some food retrieved from the kitchen, some lightweight plastic chairs, some wine glasses, some romance novels, and much more all began to fly through the air. So Earnest decided to take leave of this odd group and continue searching for a place to hide.

With all the pulse-pounding action, neither Mickey nor Earnest noticed Clayton Stern exit the same elevator door. The fugitives had a decent lead on him, and the battle was clouding his path. Cursing, the scoundrel Stern trudged through the onslaught. The fighting intensified, and the neutral stretch down the center became less neutral. Here and there a woman would run over and paddle a pirate with a wooden spoon, or a pirate would crawl over with some cleaning solution to spray on unsuspecting passengers. Flying toilet-paper rolls and potted plants were added to the fracas, and the tables-turned-bunkers scooted inch by inch closer to their respective enemies.

Earnest, though alert, found the thrown objects more amusing than Mickey did. As it were, the tethered beast avoided being hit this time. It seemed to be an unwritten wartime agreement to avoid pelting the impartial moose.

"Stop them!" Clayton Stern yelled, to no avail. Half a second later a head of cabbage collided with his forehead. The ridges of his brow nearly caused the cabbage to explode.

Earnest tried to quicken their pace when he heard Stern yelling obscenities over the comparably mild hum of the battle. With the gap between overturned tables closing, the determined boy scanned the hall for an appropriate hiding spot. He was nearing the fountain that sat beneath the encircling staircase. Worrying that Mickey would get sidetracked for a drink, Earnest hoped for a break on one side of the battlefront. When suddenly a man with an empty pot and a woman with part of a blender started an attack by going through the fountain, Earnest hung a left between two large overturned tables. Six pirates were ducking behind the tables, and looked quizzically at Earnest and Mickey. The boy gave a polite wave to let these men know he felt bad for them.

In the growing melee Clayton lost sight of his target. Raising the gun to his shoulder, he began pointing it at everyone threateningly.

"Stop you idiots! I'll shoot you! I'll shoot you all!" Few of the soldiers listened, but those that did confusedly put their hands up in the air as if they were being arrested.

Beyond the troops, Earnest saw a door that appeared large enough to accommodate a moose. He headed toward it, with Mickey obliging, wishing to distance himself from the crossfire.

Clayton continued to threaten people on both sides of the conflict. Those paying attention were frightened, but he noticed that people closer to the fountain were instead taking their fight right into the foot and a half-deep liquid. Many a pirate was smacked by spatulas in the little pool. The braver ones were trying to repel the blows by wildly swinging their arms, though they turned away from their attackers to protect their pirate faces. Many were slipping and falling into the knee-deep pond as they yelled, "Stop it! Stop it!" at the spatula-wielders.

Clayton was about to shoot the gun straight up into the air to quell the insurgence, but decided not to because he suddenly realized that the ceiling was a gigantic window. Shooting it would be disastrous, while he was under it. But peering back down he caught sight of the moose entering a room along the wall to his left (it's difficult to lose sight of a moose for too long). Clayton followed.

The room Earnest led Mickey into was full of mirrors.

When Clayton Stern entered the Hall of Mirrors he saw a number of himselves sneering back at him. It's not nice to call people hideous, but a couple dozen dastardly Clayton Sterns would alarm anyone. Each waved its shiny black rifle in search of a target. A number of the Clayton Sterns pointed their guns at other Clayton Sterns, but not one of the Clayton Sterns fired. Each Clayton Stern was waiting for a good shot at Mickey. Or a Mickey. Of course, each Clayton Stern appeared jealous of all the other Clayton Sterns, hoping that he would be the one to shoot the real moose. But first to find the real moose. Or any moose...

The real Clayton Stern peered around the room, slowly. He stepped lightly (but did not tiptoe because he was not a tiptoer), hoping to use the element of surprise. There were these mirrors, sure, but there also were some chairs, the extensive bar, those low-hanging chandeliers (that's foreshadowing!), and a little stage, where he might have assumed a band or karaoke singers might stand had he not been so focused. But no sign of the moose.

Of course, the moose was right around the corner, because it is difficult for a moose to hide in a dance hall. Earnest had been wise enough to lead him around to the far side of the bar, which stood in the middle of the room, with seating on both sides and no wall to get in the way. Now, in many countries, children are not allowed to tend bar, but despite the fact that the ship had crashed, it had recently been in international waters, so the point was moot. There was a small amount of walking space behind the bar, so Earnest hoped to coax Mickey into walking back there and ducking down. The moose only half-obliged because some fruity liqueurs had crashed to the floor when the *Queen Ivan* struck land, and the aromatic scent enticed him.

The Clayton Sterns were straining their ears to listen, though only one of them was really hearing anything. Normally you should be able to hear a moose creaking about on wooden floorboards, but, unfortunately for Stern, the hubbub from the indoor battlefield was drowning out a bit of the noise within the Hall of Mirrors. Luckily for the boy and moose, the angle was just right, so that Clayton could not yet see them or their reflection. But the closer he got, the more those mirrors itched to give away their hiding spot. Earnest gently tugged at the leash to lead Mickey further into the bartender's quarters, while putting a finger to his lips to encourage the moose's continued silence. Earnest knew the man and the gun were in the room, and that this makeshift hiding spot might be their only chance. The hunter could sense the boy, and the boy could sense the hunter. They both held their breath. The tension in the room was palatable. No, wait, palpable. Yeah, palpable.

Then, *smash! Crash!* And something rhyming with *smash* and *crash!* Mickey's colossal antlers knocked into fancy bottles of alcohol adorning the shelves of the bar. And down they fell. Earnest jumped, but not half as high as Mickey. The powerful moose had had about enough of this sneaking around. Startled by the loud noises, he let out a moosey bellow and started kicking. Thankfully Earnest was out of the way before those dangerous hooves came down. The massive creature turned his muscular frame and kicked up on his back legs. More bottles toppled to the floor, answering the age-old question with a resounding no: A moose would not make a good bartender. The continued crashing caused Mickey to just want the heck out of there, so when his front legs landed on the bar, he tried to exit by hurdling it. All this noise made Clayton give up on the element of surprise, and he darted over. When he finally saw the moose's reflection, he witnessed a comical or heartbreaking sight rarely seen in the wild; that of a moose struggling to get over a counter top bar.

Though he backed away from the frustrated moose, Earnest continued his shushing. Mickey would have none of it. Being as large as he was, and despite getting high-centered on the bar for a moment, his mighty hind legs kicked and raised him toward the low ceiling. Another kick and he might be able to come out on the other side.

Clayton Stern broke around the end of the bar and raised his gun. He was within a few steps of Mickey, but stepped even closer, wanting to make sure there was no chance of missing. Earnest, facing the opposite direction, failed to see him, so he failed to jump in front of Mickey to shield the moose this time. Clayton smirked as he peered at the beleaguered mammal, and put his finger to the trigger.

He took a moment to think of a one-liner to deliver. In that moment, Mickey gave one last muscly kick, which dismantled a shelf behind him, and gave just enough oomph to carry him up and over the bar. In that mere second of going up, his gigantic antler, the one with the life-ring around it, struck one of those pesky, low-hanging chandeliers. Now, chandeliers are usually attached to ceilings quite well, and maybe this one had been until the ship struck Africa, but in any case, the antler and the life-ring got tied up in it for a split second, and as the moose came down, so did the stupid chandelier.

Earnest was lucky enough to be out of the way of the falling glass, as he was huddled on the opposite side of the bar from the blast sight. And, due to physics or something, the way Mickey came down and turned his great head away from the chandelier, he too was spared from the falling glass. Clayton Stern, however, was not so lucky. Though he was luckier than most people who have a chandelier fall on them. Because as Earnest stood up and drank in the situation, he noted that the sprawled-out man was losing no blood. Somehow, someway, (perhaps because of the intended audience for this story) the chandelier had struck him in such a manner as to simply render him unconscious. The large piece of glass had fallen sideways, and struck his head more like a frying pan than a knife. And besides, someone needs to get knocked unconscious in tales like this. It's just something that ends up happening somewhere along the line. Someone always gets knocked unconscious.

Earnest was taken aback, especially since he had not realized Stern was standing there. Strangely, the crashing chandelier stopped Mickey in his tracks. Perhaps he was just tired from the effort of leaping over a bar. Earnest did not care why. The young man hopped over and squatted next to Stern's body. He waved a hand in front of his face and poked him. Upon noticing that the man was still breathing, Earnest sighed. He did not want anyone dead, even if that person was shooting at him.

"He will be fine," the boy concluded as he popped up and addressed Mickey, perhaps thinking he saw a glimmer of guilt in the moose's eyes. "But we should leave here. I don't think he will be happy with you when he wakes up."

The tired animal again allowed himself to be led by the life ring's rope. The pair walked briskly toward the large silver door that the bright young Earnest had quickly recognized as an elevator. This one was a large freight elevator, so getting Mickey inside took less finagling.

52

Something was wrong with Yancy's trumpet. The noise emanating from it was what a humorless high school band teacher might call an abomination. Yancy was aware of the problem, but not the cause. When he attempted to investigate, the pirates again threatened his life. Although the pirates realized it sounded terrible, they just wanted to hear music. So on he played, despite the disgusting sound.

During his rendition of "Roxanne"(which had caused quite a stir, because some of the traditionalist pirates only wanted to hear songs from Sting's solo career and not songs by The Police), a new guest arrived. Perhaps it was another design flaw of the *Queen Ivan*, but the doors of the banquet hall were wide enough to fit an adult moose. So through the currently open doors strode Mickey, Earnest in tow. The lounging pirates were alarmed at the rapidity of his approach, as was Yancy Dunblatt, who stopped "Roxanne" mid-name. The pirates took offense to this and threatened his life, pointing out they could be surprised and listen to a broken trumpet at the same time.

Nonetheless, Yancy fled when the snorting moose hustled toward him. Stopping to bellow, Mickey peered around the banquet hall before galloping once more in the direction of where Yancy had been. He snorted a bit more, despite Earnest's protests and shushing. Once the great beast, now acting quite beast-like, reached the middle of the floor, he bellowed again and then turned a few circles.

By now the thrown objects and threats to Yancy's life had encouraged the hefty trumpet-player to play again. So from the safety of an overturned table, "Roxanne" continued. A number of sick pirates smiled contentedly. However, no one seemed more excited by the song's continuation than Mickey. Nobody was sure whether this was good excitement or bad excitement. Either way, it was entertaining for the audience as the moose tugged against the boy's leash and snorted his way toward the sound of the trumpet. Something about that song really seemed to get him going.

As it turned out, the mysteriously terrible-sounding trumpet just happened to mimic the call of a female moose during mating season. So his odd behavior sprung from the prospect of meeting an attractive young female moose.

When Yancy had had enough of being approached by what he viewed as an irate moose, he again stopped playing and made a break for it. This caused Mickey to halt once more and take a survey of the area. The survey results were mostly disappointing.

When Clayton Stern came to, Isiah Burtlyre was standing over him, waving a coaster in his face, hoping to revive his employer. The manservant had been trailing Clayton through the fracas in the main hall but became distracted by the curious weaponry in use by passenger and pirate alike. By the time he caught up, Clayton was lying unconscious in a circle of glass.

Stern snatched the coaster from his lackey and threw it at the bar. Isiah was pleased to see his boss was feeling like himself again.

"Where is that moose?" the mouth below Clayton's angry eyebrows demanded.

"I don't know," Burtlyre said.

Stern slapped him in the face for no good reason and stood up. His head ached, and it served him right. He looked about the room, picked up his gun, and in a huff, marched over to the nearest mirror-covered wall. Burtlyre silently observed.

Upon reaching the mirror, Clayton Stern did the unspeakable. He raised the rifle as his rage boiled over, and in a fluid motion the butt end of the gun came crashing down on the reflection. The mirror was shattered into a thousand pieces (well, probably not literally a thousand, but there wasn't time to count). Then he took two steps to his left and smashed that mirror, too. Oh dear, oh dear, it is hard to imagine a worse thing to do than break a mirror, except maybe to break two of them. Goodness gracious. And, as if he was unaware of the consequences, he showed no remorse for this atrocity. Unbelievable.

With glass once again encircling him (and two less Clayton Sterns), the ill-fated hunter opted to leave the room. He hardly noticed the continuing melee in the main hall as he ascended the stairs encircling the grand fountain. All it was to him was noise. Noise, noise, noise. And Clayton Stern was really coming to hate noise, more than he already did.

His plan was to return to the banquet hall to regroup and maybe get some pills to clear up his headache, then find the moose. After trekking from the main hall and across the deck through the inviting doors of Hans' throne room, he was met with the beginnings of a heated discussion. The amassed pirates appeared to be debating who should get up and find something.

When Captain Hans Heissel noticed Clayton's entrance, he shouted to him. "Hey, where is your trumpet player?"

"What?" Clayton snapped.

"That guy! That guy that plays that awful trumpet so awfully! He ran away!"

Stern huffed. "So?"

Hans Heissel straightened his newspaper hat. "So, we want to hear more music, no matter how terrible it sounds coming from that guy. And he ran off when the moose came in."

"What?" Clayton snapped again, more snappily.

"When the moose came in here, that guy left."

"Why did the moose come in?"

"I don't know! I guess he liked the trumpet playing, too. Probably more than the rest of us, because we only liked it because there was nothing else to listen to. It really sounded quite bad."

Clayton stared off into space. "The moose is attracted by the sound of the trumpet."

"That's what I just said," Hans told him. Because he missed most subtleties, the pirate captain missed the diabolical grin developing on Stern's face.

53

Sweating from calling out and running around and doing it all in a dark Old Navy sweater, Jamie Brewster was distressed. His search at the wrong end of the ship turned up no trace of Earnest nor Mickey. They weren't hiding around any corners. They weren't in the laundry closet. They weren't under any deck chairs. Jamie felt responsible for Earnest's safety, and after trekking through the Gelatin Coast with the disagreeable moose, Jamie wanted to do everything in his power to keep Mickey alive.

Doubling back around, Jamie picked up his pace. They couldn't have left the top deck, could they? Neither of them was experienced with elevator usage, were they? As Jamie came to the middle of the ship, he decided to give a quick peek into the main hall. He knew they couldn't be there, but the temptation to climb beyond multiple **DANGER!** signs onto the skylight again was too great.

Atop the glass, Jamie Brewster witnessed quite a mess. Pirates, passengers, food, paper towel rolls, potted plants, and kitchenware flew through the air. The glass was thick enough that he failed to hear much noise, but could tell from the gaping mouths that plenty of screaming accompanied it all. The melee looked not unlike a foosball game.

He searched through the action, past the swinging pots and pans, past the overturned tables and couches, past the pillows flying from who-knows-where, but saw no sign of

Mickey nor Earnest. The helicopter pilot's geography of the ship was rather poor, so he knew it would take some serious concentration to find any of the three taking part in the chase, and concentrating was difficult in all the hubbub. He hoped Earnest and Mickey would somehow find a way to elude the crazed gunman.

"Come on, Earnest," he whispered. "You're a bright kid. Get away from him."

Atop the skylight, the sight of all these little figures scurrying about trying to smack each other around and heave garbage at one another was almost surreal. Through his haze, Jamie noticed that the action seemed to be migrating toward the grand staircase. Some combatants were even ascending it as they sword-fought with such items as a cookie sheet and a loaf of French bread. He spotted the bellowing bride in her ornate wedding dress with a lengthy train that no one seemed to notice was on fire. She appeared to be leading her troops closer and closer to the base of the stairs.

And suddenly it hit Jamie. He might not be the strongest, smartest, or tallest person aboard the *Queen Ivan*, but he knew helicopters. Someone needed to save the day, and he just might be the only one who could do it. Sliding off the glass he was not supposed to be climbing on, he sprinted toward the pool as fast as a reasonably athletic adult in an Old Navy sweater could.

Passing plenty of exciting distractions that would have normally snagged his attention, Jamie's focus wouldn't be swayed. He had to save Earnest, had to save Mickey, had to save Janet and Tom (wherever they were now), and had to save all those other people he'd met, half of whose names he had managed to forget. He leaped over deck chairs and pushed a rolling laundry bin out of his way. The pool was in his sights. He went to remove his sweater (finally), but decided there simply was no time. His final approach to the chlorinated water was akin to a high jumper's (if the high jumper hadn't had much coaching). One step, two steps, three steps, and leap! Arms out in front of his head, Jamie Brewster dove majestically into the pool.

Of course, maybe Jamie Brewster should have stopped to catch his breath before diving into the water, but that thought failed to occur to his determined self as he kicked through the clear liquid. Cutting down through the chlorinated fluid like a knife, Jamie swam onward. To the helicopter. It was not hard to find, of course, since it took up most of the pool. The chlorine was already irritating Jamie's eyes, but some causes are worth opening your eyes in chlorinated water for. He reached out his hand and kicked all the harder. A couple more inches and ... his fist closed around edge of the helicopter door. He heaved and pulled himself inside. Though underwater, he was back in his element.

Now, it might seem apparent that Jamie Brewster decided his contribution to the welfare of the good guys was to get behind the joystick of that helicopter and fly it right out of that pool. And given some of his poor decisions that were touched on leading up to this, that assumption would seem in step with his character. But despite all the questionable ideas Jamie Brewster had recently acted upon, he was still no idiot. You just can't fly a helicopter out of a pool. Once a helicopter is submerged in a swimming pool, its flying days are over.

But Jamie Brewster still knew helicopters. So as his held breath trickled away, he frantically investigated the cockpit. There was a very specific object he was hunting down. And despite this helicopter's crazy former operator, every helicopter should have one.

The air in Jamie's lungs continued escaping. His cheeks ballooned out like a chipmunk storing food for winter. Every couple of seconds a meek bubble dribbled out of his mouth.

The design of this aircraft was slightly different from the familiar Channel 7 helicopter, because it was a fancy private thing. So what he was looking for wasn't where he was looking for it. This would have been annoying if the search was done without all this pool water, but now it was just scary. Jamie momentarily wished that he jogged more often.

Then, there it was! A small metallic cylinder, trapped beneath the back seat. It must have been kicked somehow when Clayton Stern and his cronies escaped the sinking aircraft. Jamie swam over the pilot's seat and reached out, then realized he would need to pull himself closer. Putting one hand on the back seat and gripping its luxurious leather covering, he tugged himself underneath. His hand extended its slender fingers outward. Almost there ... And ... He touched it and it rolled further away ... Stupid thing ... He adjusted his shoulder under the seat and reached again... Nearly got it ... But ... Then ...

And suddenly he had the small fire extinguisher. His fingers squeezed it, pretty much strangling it so it couldn't get away again.

Staring through the skylight he should not have

climbed on, Jamie had seen that the lengthy train of Delilah Katsopolis' wedding dress was on fire. It appeared to not hinder her fighting abilities. In fact, one of her bridesmaids had picked it up and tried to use it as a weapon.

Perhaps a wedding dress on fire is not a huge issue anywhere else, but Jamie Brewster noticed those pirates filling the large fountain with one-hundred-proof vodka. He knew just enough about fountain mechanics to be aware of the large amount of vaporized alcohol in the air near the structure. If that flaming dress got close enough to the fountain, it was going to ignite. Sure, if you're a pirate it's understandable to think an enormous vodka fountain is cool, but it's also a major fire hazard.

As the only person who recognized this threat, Jamie knew he alone could stop it. Knowing helicopters and knowing he needed a fire extinguisher, he rushed to the only place he knew he could find one (despite the fact that there were other fire extinguishers aboard the ship, though many of those were still hidden because of the fittingly aflame Delilah Katsopolis).

With the small extinguisher in hand, it was time to save the day. But, of course, first his sweater snagged on a sharp corner under the seat. He tugged but was in such a position that he failed to see just how he was caught. Jamie panicked, because in the heat of the moment he forgot that people's clothes always snag on something when they are underwater and on their way to save the day. He let out an underwater shout that was heard by no one, not even fish, because fish don't normally live in swimming pools. Then, with a burning sensation running through him because he had been holding his breath well past too long, he let go of his overpowering sense of fear and replaced it with a fierce determination to die somewhere else, preferably in the distant future. He heaved and pulled free, then pushed hard off the seat and kicked hard off the floor and swam like he'd never swum before. With his body furious at him, Jamie kicked once more and broke the surface. He took a deep breath and let out an embarrassingly odd scream that thankfully no one heard.

He was alive! But at a terrible price: his poor Old Navy sweater now sported a sizable tear.

Mickey and Earnest, moving in tandem, had retreated to the back of the boat. They hunkered down near the helicopter landing pad, where Earnest wanted to think things through. The young man considered the places they could hide and how to get to them. But Earnest was not gifted at planning.

He did, however, have an idea to make sure Mickey stayed by his side. Earnest made a loop with the leash and tied it around his own wrist. He was pretty proud of his great idea.

Surveying the goings-on aboard his flagship, The Great Captain Hans Heissel Jr. decided to excuse himself.

54

Sopping wet, Jamie sprinted from the pool, fire extinguisher in hand, making funny splish-splosh noises with each step. He was dead tired, as dead as he could remember being since seventh-grade P.E., but he couldn't slow down. Everyone in the main hall was depending on him. They just didn't know it yet.

The Old Navy sweater was finally getting to him. It had lasted through stowing away and trekking across the barren African coast, but soaking wet (and now sporting that catastrophic tear) the sweater had to go.

But there was no time to stop, so he tried to remove it as he ran. Some people are gifted at difficult things like removing a sweater as they run, but for most of us it's tricky. Jamie saw the door with the staircase to the main hall and took a wide turn as he began pulling the sweater over his head. He did not slow his pace, believing he generally knew the location of the deck chairs he'd hurdled a few minutes before. He also believed that he could remove the sweater in a couple of seconds. This was not the case. He struggled to get the soggy mess over his head, but it just wanted to keep clinging.

Then, smack—he ran right into a pair of large speakers. They toppled over with him. He did not realize they were speakers until he sat up and finally pulled the ruined garment halfway over his head (through that tear accidentally; his arms could not find the sleeves). While he was realizing stuff, he also saw that he wasn't alone. About a dozen pirates were standing around him, staring.

Out of the banquet hall stormed Clayton Stern, still toting that frightening gun and angry as all get-out, as per usual. The clatter of the speakers got him worked up again. He analyzed the situation briefly and glared accusingly at Jamie.

"What are you doing?" he hollered, mixing a few uncouth terms into his question.

"What are *you* doing?" Jamie replied, leaving out the uncouth terms. He genuinely wanted to know why there were speakers and wires and cables and boxes all over the deck.

The retort did not quell Stern's temper. "If you broke those speakers..."

Jamie stood, arms still stuck in the sweater. He was going to just ignore this guy until that wedding dress had been extinguished. But before he took a step, he realized that Clayton Stern was not letting him off that easy.

"Get him," Stern instructed the nearby pirates as he gave Jamie a textbook sneer.

The pirates put down the equipment and approached Jamie, who quickly comprehended that they were following orders from the gunman now. He looked to his feet and saw the extinguisher. His hands continued their search for the sleeves but the viscous properties of the sweater detained them. Jamie began kicking the extinguisher along as he hustled in the direction of the stairs. Growing up an average soccer player at best, he was hard-pressed to keep the little cylinder in front of him. Especially with the hands-free pirates bearing down on him. He knew in a second he would be apprehended.

Then, as luck would have it, Jamie spotted Benito Martinez standing outside a doorway up ahead, leaning dejectedly on the gigantic rolling pin. Knowing that the famed third baseman was still unrecognized as a non-pirate, Jamie hoped that Benito could succeed where he was about to fail. He gave the fire extinguisher a healthy kick. Mercifully it skidded along in just the right path to reach Benito. In the same moment, Jamie was tackled by three pirates.

"Benito!" Jamie yelled in a whisper.

The former All-Star had been in a state of total disarray until this moment, thinking he was at the onset of a mid-life crisis. Toby was standing there with him, trying to snap him out of this funk. Benito turned upon hearing his name, and saw the cylinder sliding rapidly toward his feet. Though surprised, he quickly understood this object was intended for him. With hands out, his large frame leaned forward to scoop this grounder up.

The fire extinguisher went right through his legs. With pirates on his back, Jamie closed his eyes and pressed his forehead to the floor.

The extinguisher bounced off the door behind Benito, and he stepped over to retrieve it. Befuddled, he looked to Jamie. Then he turned to Toby, who was facing in the opposite direction and rubbing his forehead. The mousy young man had barely been paying attention to the new turn of events, so frustrated was he with the conversation they'd been having.

"Listen, Mr. Martinez. I can't deal with this anymore." He reached up and put a hand on the baseball player's shoulder. "I hope you can work your new craziness out, but I've got a lot on my plate right now. I know you're no help at this point, but I've got to go try to save Melinda. Who knows where she could be right now."

Toby failed to realize that the appearance of the fire extinguisher brought Benito halfway back to reality. The young man took off hustling toward the ship's bow.

"Martinez!" Jamie yelled in a whisper again.

The disguised pirate turned to listen. Jamie was far away and insisted on this loud whisper, so what Benito was able to conclude was that there was an explosive wedding dress somewhere in the main hall. And that Jamie wanted a stiff drink or he was going to blow up. Or something.

From there he was able to glean that the fire extinguisher was meant for extinguishing the dress, and since there were multiple pirates restraining Jamie, Benito understood this job was being passed off to him. He gave a slow nod.

Jamie took a deep breath. It appeared his message sunk in. And since the pirates had not been given any instruction regarding the extinguisher, it appeared they could not care less about it. Now to be dragged off to learn what his fate would be.

Benito Martinez inspected the little cylinder. Then he, too, breathed deeply. A new obligation restored some more of his sanity. He turned to follow Toby.

"Wait, Toby!" he called. "We have to go extinguish this evil wedding dress!"

"What?"

"This wedding dress is going to explode in the main

hall!"

Toby, having no reason not to believe this new addition to the long list of stupid things going on, became invigorated. His next question, however, was drowned out by Maria Martinez's voice.

Benito's wife appeared suddenly from a doorway to his left and frightened the daylights out of him. He gave a meek scream.

"You!" Maria shouted. "I could be dead right now!"

And so began a rehashing of an earlier conversation, only this time Maria may have been angrier. Benito backed up further and further, and his frightened voice became higher and higher. He hoped she would not confiscate the huge rolling pin in his hand.

"You're a pirate now?" Maria inquired furiously.

"No!" Benito pleaded. "Of course not! I was left on the boat and they thought I was a pirate, so I thought I could help save everyone! I crashed this ship! For you!" The patchy truth failed to have the desired effect.

It did, however, have the effect of enticing the dozen or so pirates nearby to listen in. The more truth Benito was spitting, the deeper a hole he was digging with his wife, and the more the pirates heard secrets not meant for their ears. But Benito was focused solely on his wife, so failed to recognize this.

As Benito felt his back hit the railing, he saw three pirates approaching the heated disagreement. The pirate in front, Christof, who looked liked a viking, interrupted Maria.

"You're not a pirate?" he asked Benito, who barely heard the inquiry. Christof turned to Maria. "He is not a pirate?"

"Him? Of course not! He's apparently *Benito Martinez*, world-renowned baseball player."

The pirates turned to Benito. He shrugged and put a hand up to try to cover his wife's eyes as he made a face to tell the pirates that she was crazy, and then smiled at his wife when she pulled down his hand. This continuous motion, meant to fluidly appease both the pirates and Maria, did not have the desired effect, either.

Being mainly Europeans unfamiliar with most professional baseball players, the pirates stepped away to find someone to confirm his identity.

"Stay right here," Christof instructed as he left the scene.

Benito did not follow these instructions. Knowing full well that he was about to be captured and that the danger downstairs needed a heroic influence, the hulking athlete made a break for it. He would deal with his wife later. Toby, who had been entertained by the exchange for only a few moments, was in his sight. Unfortunately the mousy young man had stopped waiting for Benito and turned to go stop the wedding dress himself. Benito could just see his dirty blond hair bobbing along as he ran full speed toward the stairway.

"Toby! Wait!" he called.

Thankfully the boy heard him and turned, shrugging. Unthankfully, the pirates heard him, too, and concluded that he must be who his wife said he was, just as Zangley, the biggest baseball fan amongst the pirates, recognized Benito and yelled, "Hey! It's Benito Martinez! With an eyepatch!" So all the pirates on deck dropped what they were doing to chase Benito.

All pleaded-out from pleading with Maria, Benito had no desire to beg the buccaneers. It was too late for that, he knew, as he tucked the extinguisher under his arm and raised the rolling pin. Rapidly pirates came out of the woodwork, and though they were still sickly, there were considerably more of them than there were of Benito. The sound equipment they were carrying, which they picked back up after seeing Jamie's crash, was put back down for the new pursuit. Posing as a pirate was a crime considered unforgivable by the crew. And this was before they even found out about the cake. Benito would probably be put to death, they all thought. After giving autographs all around.

Toby saw the chase unfold and turned back toward the doorway.

"Hang on, Toby!" Benito yelled. He was now farther away then he had been because of the need to bob and weave through the attackers.

"What now?" Toby called back, more exasperated at his idol than he should have been, given the circumstances.

"This!" Benito screamed, jumping to his left as a would-be tackler leaped at him. "We need to put the fire out with this!"

Toby sighed. "Right. So hurry up!"

Then it became apparent even to Toby that there simply were too many men for Benito to get past. They were regrouping, and approaching the fake pirate from numerous angles. Using impressive teamwork, the men slowly coaxed the elusive athlete into a large circle, like prey. Then they began closing him in against the railing. Seeing he was trapped, Benito put the fire extinguisher on the floor and raised the rolling pin in defense. He had a healthy stomach on his side, but he was no superhero.

"Toby! That dress is going to set everything on fire!" Benito reminded the young man.

Toby yelled back. "Ummm ... throw it!"

Benito judged the distance. It was too great. Even for a major league baseball player with a cannon for an arm, such as Benito. In fact, it was a wonder they were hearing each other this well. Of course, this meant the pirates were hearing them, too, and were becoming increasingly interested in this little fire extinguisher.

"I can't!" Benito yelled back, knowing the closing pirates would intercept it.

Toby scooted forward, until he realized that two pirates were dropping out of the attack formation to come after him. His shoes skidded to a stop, leaving a mark he'd have to clean on the finished wooden floor, and he moved back toward the ship's railing. The mousy young man was out of ideas. He shrugged again at Benito.

Cautious of the large rolling pin but determined to bring this imposter to justice, the wide arc of buccaneers slowly closed in on Benito Martinez. He watched them in horror. And with regret. Regret at once again failing to be the hero. Rude little voices perforated his mind, reminding him of the mushroom he swung at and missed. It was his job to hit things, and he just missed them all. And his throwing arm was inadequate to heave the little cylinder to his compatriot. In a moment, he would be captured, and the wedding dress would light the whole ship on fire. And his wife would still be mad at him. This was turning out to be just the worst day.

Then, looking down at the little fire extinguisher, a light bulb exploded in Benito's brain. "Of course!" he thought. Every negative notion of his own incompetence dissipated. He smirked, then placed his feet beside the fire extinguisher and sized it up. He shook his hips. He drew the rolling pin from his shoulder and, gripping one end with both hands, methodically let the other end scoot right up beside the little cylinder. Then Benito grinned at Toby and gave him a dramatic nod.

Because what do professional athletes do with their spare time? Exactly. They play golf. Many of them become considerably better at golfing than they are at the sport they are paid to play. So, being a major league baseball player, Benito Martinez had naturally spent countless hours on the links. A moving object might be a challenge. A stationary object was dead meat.

Benito lifted the rolling pin and cocked it over his shoulder. His eyes locked on the extinguisher. Realizing his plan, the pirates tried to rush forward. But it was too late, as Benito's hips led the rest of his body in a beautifully fluid motion. His massive hands followed the hips' lead. The rolling pin swung musically and connected with the little tank. Even the pirates could appreciate the beauty of Benito's swing.

Then a loud *ping!* And the container was airborne. Up and over the outstretched hands of the pirates it flew, hurtling majestically end over end. Straight at Toby. The precision of its trajectory was impressive. Benito smiled and admired his shot. The pirates did not, however, and tackled him.

The two men approaching Toby watched the flightpath

as they bore down upon the recipient. Said recipient backed up a couple steps to try to get underneath the projectile. Without looking where his steps were taking him, Toby's back ran into the railing. Understanding the importance of this object, he knew there was no second chance. He needed to catch it at any cost. The pirates, who must have been two of the healthiest pirates on the ship (or perhaps the most immune to hypochondria) were getting all too close, and, unlike Benito, Toby had no rolling pin to shake at them. Despite the fire extinguisher's wonderfully straight path, the young man could see it was going to go a little long. Wishing there was another option, Toby winced as he stood up on the railing. He did not consider himself to be "afraid of heights" per se, but no one should really *like* standing up on a cruise ship's railing. Down the extinguisher fell, end over end, right to him. He did not need to step to his left or right, thankfully. If he could just balance for another second or two …

The two pirates, arms outstretched like the zombies in the "Thriller" video, were only a few paces away. Toby kept his eye on the hurtling talisman, however. Maybe if he could hook one of his feet around the railing, it would save him … In fact, why not just sit down …

Toby quickly took a seat on the rail, and no sooner had he done so than the fire extinguisher reached him, ending its seemingly endless flight. He used his hands to catch it instead of his body, which hurt his hands a bit. But he had it! Before that joyful realization settled in, though, Toby noticed that he was slipping backward. Sitting down had not been quite as helpful as hoped. The force of the falling cylinder drove him back and he was unable to balance on his seat. And now he was falling. The pirates rushed to the edge, but it was too late to recover the extinguisher. Or the boy.

Toby tumbled. Shock was all his system could muster as he lost contact with the railing. With the successfully recovered fire extinguisher in hand, he was going to fall to his doom. Instinctively, he held the canister with his right hand and hopelessly reached toward the deck with his left.

Then suddenly his left hand gripped something. Or rather, was gripped by something. In the split second of contact he had closed his eyes. When he opened them he stared up at an angel. Glowing brightly, shimmering hair streaming down, dressed all in spectacular white, he saw that an angel had saved his life. He stared dumbfounded with his mouth agape. What a confusing day.

With a wave of recognition, Toby saw, as he dangled there, that it was not an angel. It was better. To him. It was Melinda. Melinda had saved him. He had not thought it possible, but she was even more beautiful than he had realized.

She was straining as she tugged on his arm. Her face was turning red with the incredible pressure and there was sweat and fear in her eyes. Anyone else might not have been quite so convinced she looked too angelic in that moment.

Up Toby rose, slowly. Melinda pulled as hard as she could in an effort to bring Toby in through the window. Though he was dazed and useless, Melinda felt a burning determination that Toby would not die on her watch. With a forceful grimace, she put all her strength into one powerful tug, and the mousy young man was at the windowsill. She pulled him up onto the ledge, and then picked him up in an embrace like a brave firefighter carrying out a smoke-inhalation victim.

Confused and appreciative, Toby stared up into her eyes. He was trying to make sense of the situation, being cradled like a baby by the woman of his dreams. It was a lot to take in.

Melinda breathed heavily and stared back down into Toby's soft pupils. There the two young shipmates were, immobile for a moment. Then Melinda leaned down into the helpless form in her arms, and, closing her eyes, passionately kissed Toby.

Melinda, from as far back as she could remember, had a dream she kept secret. Always the mature, polite, responsible young lady, she longed for more. Deep down, she wanted to be the hero. Not the rational one. The one that saved someone's life in the crucial moment. After watching way too many movies growing up where a heroic man came to the rescue in the darkest hour, Melinda had wanted to be that man. Only in woman form. She held no desire to be swept off her feet by a charming prince or muscly action hero. Here and there a gentleman caller had attempted a feet-sweeping on her, but rarely with success. She once broke her ankle, and her high school's star basketball player had attempted to carry her to the nurse's office. She politely but ardently declined. Without admitting it, she wanted to be the person who stopped the runaway car, or runaway stroller, or battled the escaped zoo animal, or caught the victim from falling to their death. So catching Toby fell into the last category. And when she pulled him away from danger and realized she was the hero, Melinda could not help but want to kiss him. In that moment she suddenly thought he was kind of cute, too.

The mousy young man was so taken aback that he had no idea how to react. Never really expecting to actually get to kiss the object of his affection, something about the situation was slightly off-putting. While her lips pressed against his, he opened his eyes and looked about the room, half-expecting to see a camera crew or St. Peter or something. But she continued this whole kissing thing, so he relaxed and counted his lucky stars instead. There were about twelve of them.

When the lengthy smooch finally ended, Toby took a deep breath. Melinda smiled down at him, hoping that Toby liked her half as much as she liked him.

"Um ... thank you?" Toby said. It was not the poetic response he'd been meaning to come up with in the unlikely case this ever happened. She giggled. They looked at each other some more, and yeah, blah, blah, blah, wasted valuable time gazing into one another's eyes like characters seem to do when there is some pressing obligation elsewhere.

"But... how...?" Toby stammered after pinching himself thrice. He meant, how had she suddenly decided he was worthy of her hand.

"I didn't know where you went, so I tried to join the fight in the main hall," she responded, thinking Toby was referencing how she had come to save him. "The fighting started moving up here into the passengers' quarters, and I followed. I had been throwing heads of lettuce from the kitchen, but hoped to find something more substantial in here."

Toby finally looked about his surroundings and realized he was in one of the top level passengers' rooms, so he hadn't fallen all that far. He was not completely following Melinda's story, but did not really care. She had kissed him!

"I was looking around when I heard a really strange *ping* noise," she continued. "So I stuck my head out the window for some reason. That's when you fell, and I caught you."

"Oh."

"I guess the sound was that fire extinguisher," she told him, indicating the little canister without releasing him from her grip. "Did somebody hit it?"

"Oh goodness," Toby said, suddenly remembering important things other than getting all kissy-face.

"What?" Melinda asked him, alert in case there were more heroic things to do.

"There's a maniac wedding dress that is going to make the whole ship catch on fire!"

"What?" Melinda said again, appropriately.

"I don't really know," Toby said frantically. "But we're the only ones left. We *have* to use this to put out the fire on the wedding dress."

Melinda thought back to the bride's train all ablaze that she beheld a few minutes prior, being wielded by a ferocious bridesmaid in the main hall. She coaxed herself back to reality and away from the dreamboat in her arms. Unfortunately, reality also made her realize how much pain she was in.

"Let's go," she said, becoming the leader again. "And I

think you broke my arm."

Still holding Toby, the heroic young lady turned to the door. Their departure was halted, however, by the appearance of a large gun. Accompanying the gun was the dastardly Clayton Stern. Toby gasped and clutched at Melinda, who glared at the intruder.

Stern smirked back at them. Then he removed one hand from the gun and displayed his palm. "I'm going to want that fire extinguisher now."

55

By now, almost the whole skeleton was visible.

Susie Ebbert and her crack-team of immigrant dinosaur excavators were all wiping their brows, almost in unison, as they stood over the bones of the Tyrannosaurus Rex which Mickey Moose had begun digging up for them, when they were approached by someone none of them knew.

He smiled and pulled out a badge that none of them recognized. Susie had to put on her glasses to read it.

56

Leonid Cupabascim was glad to have company. It would have been nice to be allowed to leave the gangplank instead, but the second best option had just been realized. He had been joined by pleasant company. His new friends were here. Melinda, Toby, Jamie, the allegedly famous Benito Martinez, and even his wife, Maria, who had been strung up for good measure, came to join the young chef. Or rather, had the poachers' net thrown over them and were forcibly pushed onto the plank.

Of course, the transformed diving board was under no small amount of duress. Diving boards are usually meant for one. Simply placing Leonid on the poorly connected plank was stressful enough, but now with no less than six people on it, the board creaked and groaned in protest. Some more rope was dug up from around the ship, but the main element keeping the plank in place was manpower. The pirates who had been lounging around the throne room feeling sorry for themselves, then been put to work moving speakers and electrical equipment around, had now been tasked with providing leverage so the diving board did not fall. Though it was a delicate balance which might give way at any moment, the people on the gangplank were not meant to die just yet.

They were not meant to be comfortable, either. There they sat, all crammed together under the thick net and trying not to fall off. No one looked down, because, just like the knowledge of how bad it is to break a mirror, it is common knowledge that you don't look down when dangling from considerable heights.

The scene before the crowded heroes was peculiar, again. Clayton Stern, rifle in hand, oversaw the final stages in the construction of a trap. With many pirates having been put to work by the scheming gunman, said trap consisted of the sound system from the banquet hall being moved out onto the deck. Every last piece was transported out into the sunlight, along with a considerable length of extension cord.

The idea behind the relocation of the sound system was reasonably simple: the moose had come running when he heard the trumpet. With these big fancy speakers and the microphone (which was intended for toasts at the wedding reception), Clayton would be able to blast the sound of the trumpet out across the whole ship. So, theoretically, the moose would come running from wherever his hiding spot was. Because Stern was a brash, cocky person, he left out the word "theoretically."

Our heroes on the diving board were paying attention to this in varying degrees. Surprisingly Melinda, up until now the most likely to scrutinize the situation, was paying the least amount of attention, so enamored was she with Toby (and also distracted by her probably-broken arm). The thought that she might die in the near future was apparent, sure, but at least she would die beside the boy of her dreams. She squeezed his hand. Toby kept showing her a polite half-smile, but was a little more concerned about their plight. Melinda was getting weird, he thought. Benito was trying to think of a way to get out of the situation, but in the back of his head he was still proud of that magnificent tee shot. Maria had calmed down a bit. It wasn't worth dying in a huff, she told herself. Leonid was just really happy to have someone to talk to. At least he would no longer die alone.

Jamie Brewster was probably the most upset. Channel 7's daring helicopter pilot was kicking himself (though not literally for fear of falling) for thinking there was some meager amount of goodwill in Clayton Stern. After Jamie knocked the speakers over and was being dragged away at the villain's behest, he frantically spat out the importance of extinguishing the flames on the wedding dress. The pirates did not listen (some paid him no heed, some were stuck on the idea of a vodka fountain, and some did not speak English), but Clayton Stern just smirked. A fiery end to the wrecked ship might be just the cover he needed for his getaway. Though it had not been his intention to kill anyone but the moose, he felt he could hardly be blamed for what sounded like nature's plan. The mess unfolding downstairs was at first no concern to him, but soon he worried that if those noisy, noisy mongrels got on deck, his best-laid plans would again be stalled. And Clayton Stern was sick of stalling. This moose was going to die. Pronto.

"Please, sir," Jamie called out again. "The whole main hall is going to go up in flames any second!" He struggled against the netting.

Stern cackled. He did not even turn to acknowledge Jamie's plea. Some of the other prisoners made the same plea, and Clayton quickly grew tired of cackling. The squawking downstairs, the whiny henchmen, the people on the plank. The noise was really getting to him. He needed some ear plugs.

The pleas also went unanswered from the nearby pirates, who should have been more concerned about their coworkers downstairs. Unfortunately, none of the pirates within earshot spoke English. They did understand a waving gun, however, so they were more or less loyal minions of Clayton Stern at this point. Wherever their captain was, his authority was diminishing.

The Associates of Mr. Abominable Snowman Dragons were also becoming more and more loyal to the villainous hunter. Eager for their prize, Koke and Kipchak were coming down with what is known as "antler fever," an ailment common among poachers such as themselves. The symptom was an insatiable lust for moose antlers, and the only cure was getting one's hands on moose antlers. Given their current predicament, both men felt their best bet was to treat Clayton Stern like a deity. So when he sent them to lock all the doors leading up to the deck, Kipchak and Koke had followed the order without question. There were numerous doors leading up, so the task took them across the whole deck. Finding some rope attached to life-rings, they reinforced the locks, making sure no one would come through. Clayton Stern was so sick of noise and commotion; he just wanted some peace and quiet to shoot Mickey. Of course, it did not occur to him that the moose might be downstairs.

It did, however, occur to Clayton that the elevators were still operational, and if he really wanted to keep all those human noisemakers off the deck, that problem needed to be addressed. So he sent Koke and Kipchak off to destroy all the elevator controls with a couple of wine bottles from the banquet hall. Thinking that was the last step in his master plan, Clayton smirked again.

"You'll never get away with this!" shouted Jamie Brewster, not knowing what else to shout.

"Oh, I already have," said Clayton, without putting much thought into the response. "You see, when this ship catches on fire, I will be long gone. I met up with a hapless group of stupid environmentalists who were searching for their friends." (This was true; hadn't mentioned it yet. Between picking up Yancy and reaching the ship, Clayton randomly met with the heads of ABABAHAB.) "I tricked them into thinking I was a contributor to their cause and they believe I am trying to save the moose. And then there's some weird scientists in a village who also think I'm a real humanitarian. The point is that there are no less than two jeeps on their way, which I will meet about a mile from here as my henchmen carry the carcass of my moose, while you all catch on fire or fall off planks or whatever else you choose to do. So I will be luxuriously transported out of here with a dead moose that I will explain I tried to save. My plan is foolproof."

Of course, he did not say all this out loud, because that would have been silly.

So there it all was: half a dozen good guy-types sitting on a gangplank, waiting for their execution; about double that number of pirates, now loyal to Clayton, who had promised them stomach medicine and a new fleet; the speakers of the banquet hall's sound system standing dangerously close to the skylight with numerous wires and extension cords running every which way; and Yancy Dunblatt, who had been found cowering in a broom closet after being charged by the moose, now standing at the ready next to the microphone stand, prepared to play his trumpet once more.

Clayton Stern surveyed it all. After the many ways people had been disappointing him lately, he was about to finally kill the elusive moose.

Before anyone really noticed, a thick fog rolled in and enveloped the *Queen Ivan* and the surrounding coastline. Fog was common on the Skeleton Coast, but since those present were unfamiliar with the area, it came unexpectedly. Nonetheless, it provided no comfort nor disruption to the situation. It was thick, but the deck remained visible. So despite the fact that no one could see beyond the boundaries of the railing, the fog did little to change the state of affairs.

Clayton Stern sucked some of the fog in through his nostrils. He liked this foreboding weather. He was kind of a foreboding guy. Then the billionaire turned to Yancy and nodded.

"Well, don't you think I should clean out my trumpet first to make it sound better?" Dunblatt inquired.

This ruined Clayton's calmly confident mood. "No, Yancy! The stupid moose obviously likes it that way! Don't touch it!" He sprinkled in a few choice words again.

Dunblatt followed the directions. Wetting his lips, the portly trumpet-player brought the instrument to his mouth. He breathed deeply and began a bad rendition of Prince's "Raspberry Beret."

The music, if this botched version could be called that, hauntingly stretched out through the fog. Everyone on deck listened intently. The people you are hopefully rooting for on the plank prayed that Mickey would not respond.

The anticipatory lull was broken as Koke and Kipchak opened the aft freight elevator. When, quite unexpectedly, Mickey was standing there, Koke screamed a little in surprise, which made Kipchak scream a little in surprise. Earnest screamed, too.

And so the chase began. Again. So it kind of just continued. Mickey rushed out of the elevator when the door opened. Earnest, being bright and curious, had become enamored with elevators, so after leaving the banquet hall, the boy had led his friend into the big freight elevator to explore it and hide at the same time. His plan had been working until the poachers had to go and ruin it. So Earnest was pulled in the direction of more terrible-sounding trumpet music by the life-ring rope. When Kipchak and Koke recovered from almost being trampled, they took off after the pair.

Clayton Stern could hardly believe his luck. The moose was coming right his way. He smiled and waited. Yancy wanted to stop playing but Stern told him, in no polite terms, that it was out of the question. So on went the song, despite no one caring for this rendition besides Mickey. Clayton saw that meddlesome boy was still with the moose, so he waited for a clear shot.

"This time, I've got you," he whispered along the gun's barrel to Mickey, who wasn't listening.

The great moose clopped right across the deck, searching for the female moose that was not there. He bellowed a bit. Earnest again tugged the leash, wanting to calm his pal and lead him from danger. Kipchak and Koke followed, shaking their wine bottles.

The crowd on the plank could hardly watch.

"Earnest, get out of there!" Jamie yelped. Toby turned away. Melinda squeezed his hand harder.

Mickey came closer to Clayton, who dropped to a knee and took aim. He hoped the moose would quit moving before he wasted any bullets. To one side of him were the fretting captives on the diving board. To the other side were the large speakers, the microphone, and Dunblatt's inflated cheeks. Somewhere behind Clayton was Isiah Burtlyre, trying to turn a blind eye. In front of him came the clip-clopping moose. All about was the ghostly fog. Clayton's finger went to release the rifle's safety, but he realized he never had the safety on in the first place.

And then, as should have been expected at this point, something new interrupted the foggy scene. A deafening honk shook everyone. Clayton nearly dropped the gun. Startled, the crowd on the plank screamed in unison, once at the sound, and again when the diving board wobbled as half the pirates holding it tried to cover their ears. Perhaps the most startled, though, was Mickey. The male moose, so fed up with trying to find this enigmatic female moose, began kicking wildly and snorting. His chaotic path wound away from the gunman. Mickey hated that stupid sound.

The moose did not really care where the sound was coming from, but Clayton Stern did. His first guess was correct. That sneering, impatient, devilish face of his turned toward the *Queen Ivan's* tower. There in the window he saw a newspaper hat, atop a head with a wide, goofy grin. The Great Captain Hans Heissel, Jr. took a bite from a sandwich and gave Clayton a nod. Though he could not see it, Stern knew that his other hand was firmly placed on the ship's horn.

The horn continued as Clayton sprinted off to stop it. He yelled for the pirates to wrangle the berserk moose, but they were too busy holding on to the diving board and/or their ears to comply. Of course, they couldn't hear the order anyway.

Mickey had gone bonkers, kicking and hopping about. It might have been an amusing sight if you weren't on the deck with him, fearing for your life. An angry moose does not make good company. Kipchak and Koke witnessed his hysteria and opted to keep their distance. They backed up toward the ship's rail to wait for Mickey to mellow out. But with the horn still wailing, the great beast had no intention of mellowing out. Yancy Dunblatt cowered near the pirates while Earnest, against his better judgment, tried to quell this tantrum. The boy tugged on the leash, hoping to guide Mickey back toward safety. Mickey wouldn't give him an inch.

"Earnest, stop!" Jamie yelled helplessly.

"Leave him alone! Run away!" called Benito.

"Please, listen to them!" Maria added, worried for this odd young man.

Mickey the moose then angrily surveyed the people in his path. Instead of charging Koke and Kipchak or trying to run down the escaping Clayton Stern, Mickey turned on poor Earnest. Which came as a reminder that wild animals are called wild for a reason. As delightful as it might sound to ride a bear or play cards with a gorilla, wild animals remain quite unpredictable. So even after all the tender loving care Earnest had provided, his dear friend spurned it all during this fit. The moose charged little Earnest. The young man was astonished.

"Aaaagghhh!" he yelled, going wide-eyed. He took off in the opposite direction. So surprised was Earnest that he forgot that Mickey's leash was tied around his wrist.

"Mickey! What are you doing?" he pleaded, looking back over his shoulder. "It's me! Your friend, Earnest!"

Mickey was not listening. His annoyance at being tugged by the rope was coupled with the blasting horn. The antlered giant chased Earnest forward, and then followed the boy as he veered toward the skylight.

"Please, Mickey! Chase someone else!" yelled Earnest, perplexed and heartbroken. He saw the beams between the windowpanes of the domed skylight and figured he could climb them and likely would not be followed. Perhaps from atop the skylight he could reason with his dangerous, backstabbing friend. He hustled past the microphone and ducked under the sound equipment. Up the glass Earnest scrambled, twice as easily as Jamie had. Jamie noticed. The domed shape was not much of a challenge to Earnest, who soon found himself sitting and looking back at Mickey.

"What did I do?" Earnest wailed. "I can change!"

The moose slowed, then picked up his pace again and strode toward the glass. For some reason, possibly because he hoped for a change of heart, Earnest still had the rope tied around his wrist. This was really getting Mickey's goat. He recognized it as the symbol of his prolonged irritation.

"Untie the rope, Earnest!" Jamie screamed, praying this would appease the moose. With hands netted together,

Toby tried to mime dropping the rope using only his head. Earnest was too busy to pay them any heed. He was looking into Mickey's eyes, searching for some sign of goodness. However, Earnest followed the advice of his own accord, loosening the loop around his wrist and dropping it.

But Mickey charged again. Earnest knew he was safe from his friend up there on the glass so he stayed put. What he did not consider was what stood between Mickey and himself. As the moose snorted and galloped forward he ran straight into the sound system. Like the winner breaking through the tape at the end of a race, his massive antlers forced through the line of cables and extension cords connecting the big speakers. Unlike a race, however, the cables did not break, but continued with him. Mickey hardly noticed. Tugged along, the huge speakers fell, right back into the glass of the skylight. Thump thump. They fell one after the other.

From the gangplank, it appeared, for a moment, like maybe all would be forgiven. But then the glass started cracking and the netted captives cried out in unison. Earnest did not need them pointing out the danger he was in. He saw the cracks work their way up the glass in streaks, as if chasing him. When they reached him, Earnest's expression froze in dismay. Then he fell through.

57

The Great Captain Hans Heissel Jr. was unruffled when Clayton Stern burst into the control room with gun aimed to kill. Hans did not even look over at first. When the livid huntsman shouted, the pirate captain shifted his elbow off the large green button that was sounding the horn, but he still did not look at him. He kept his eyes on the table adjacent to the control panel, where the original captain of the *Queen Ivan* probably had his lunch. Atop it were a stack of completed Sudoku puzzles, but Hans Heissel's gaze was stuck to a crossword puzzle. He had yet to fill in any boxes.

"What's a six-letter word that means 'buccaneer'?" he asked, furrowing his brow. When Clayton, stunned at Hans's lack of concern for having a gun trained on his chest, failed to answer, the buccaneer continued. "This is really tough." Hans Heissel Jr. was not born for crossword puzzles.

Clayton peered around the room briefly. The sandwich was gone, which proved that Hans was feeling much better. The truth was that Hans Heissel had never felt quite as ill as most of his crew. Acting sick just seemed like the popular thing to do at the time. Of course, Hans *thought* he was just as ill, but Hans Heissel was a bit of a hypochondriac, he just wouldn't admit it. Because he didn't know that word (it happened to be 22 Down on the crossword puzzle). On the back wall, Hans Heissel had used a permanent marker to map out some enormous and elaborate math problem. There were a bunch of letters along with numbers, and Clayton was not sure where it even began.

"What's that?" Clayton insisted.

Taking his time, Captain Hans Heissel turned to look at the math problem, then gave a flippant wave at it as he sighed. "That's just for fun."

Hans turned back to his crossword and sighed at it, too. Clayton was just about to threaten him when Hans Heissel stood and turned to the control room's big wraparound window. This, too, garnered a sigh from the pirate captain.

"This is the end of it, then, isn't it?" he asked.

"That's right it is…" Clayton started angrily.

Hans did not actually pay attention. "My crew has mutinied to you, haven't they?" His usage of the verb was questionable. Somehow Hans was still unaware of the danger posed to his crew below decks, and assumed they, too, were under Stern's control.

"Your men are listening to me now, and…"

Clayton tried to get his two cents into the conversation but kept being ignored. It was an unfamiliar feeling. Hans Heissel was too focused on his poetic end to pay any attention to the lunatic gunman or his gun.

"And you won't actually be towing us, will you?"

"No, you idiot." Now Clayton laughed a little, through his anger. "No one could tow this boat. It's stuck here for good."

Hans stared out the window and sighed again. "Well, it was a good ride."

"I don't care! Now shut up, we're going downstairs!"

Hans Heissel removed his newspaper hat and stared out through the thick fog. His eyes gave the impression that he was staring off for miles and miles. Hans then put his newspaper hat back on.

Clayton was about to hit him with the butt of the rifle when he noticed a pair of headphones on the floor. They, like a number of objects on board, had fallen when the *Queen Ivan* knocked into Africa. He picked them up. While on the floor, he saw that under the seat was a little packet containing some earplugs. This was turning out to be his lucky day. With those noisy people downstairs, and the noisy whining pirates, and the noisy people out on the plank, and the awful noise from that trumpet, and every other noise, Clayton Stern had really come to hate noise, much like the Grinch. So he was going to give himself some peace and quiet when he finally got his clear shot at the moose.

He put the rifle down on the floor when he reached underneath the seat to grab the earplugs. It was the perfect time for Captain Hans Heissel to steal the gun and take back control. If he had been paying attention.

When Clayton stood back up, he poked his newest prisoner with the barrel of the rifle. Hans breathed deeply and turned.

"Well ... shall we?" he asked, as if he had proposed the idea.

Captain Hans Heissel Jr. bravely exited the room, leaving the crossword puzzle untouched.

58

Mickey was not necessarily apologetic for attacking his best friend in the world, but he did seem to show some sign of remorse. Once Earnest had dropped out of sight, the giant moose calmed. But only for a moment. There was more rampaging to do. Turning, he shot toward the ship's railing, a stone's throw from where the diving board creaked and buckled. The poachers made a good target.

While the netted denizens of the gangplank tried to overcome their shock and sorrow at seeing Earnest fall through the skylight, Koke and Kipchak realized that the moose had singled them out. Maybe they should not have chased him so much, or have been so conveniently close by.

But Mickey did not make it very far before he stopped short. The rope connected to the life-ring went taut, and like a twig, Mickey's antler popped right off his head.

Everyone seemed to have forgotten, or simply not considered, the fact that antlers fall off each year. Unlike horns, antlers are temporary. Usually they don't have a life-ring around them and fall off naturally. This particular one had kind of been on its last legs, so the tugging just made the separation occur a little sooner. Now, apparently it does not hurt much to have your antler fall off, so it was just the suddenness of its parting that halted the moose. It was only for a moment, however, because even with one antler, Mickey still felt like charging Koke and Kipchak.

The poachers, however, changed their objective. Suffering from undiagnosed "antler fever," their attention turned to recovering the antler rather than staying alive. There it was, lying on the hardwood floor, spinning slightly after its fall. Behind it, the life-ring skidded off, back toward the skylight.

As Koke and Kipchak moved from the railing, ignoring the furious beast, a new character entered the scene. Ronaldinho had pretty much checked out when the helicopter landed in the pool. While everyone scattered, the young first mate decided things had just gotten too weird, and he felt like a snack or a nap. A sound sleeper, he'd been just fine snoozing in the dark, quiet broom closet. Until the horn sounded. That horn could wake the dead. So, waltzing out onto the deck in the hopes things had calmed down, Ronaldinho was disappointed to see the opposite.

Groggily, he spotted a problem that he wished to remedy. His pal Mickey had dropped his antler. Now, Ronaldinho was a sharp enough kid, but lacked much experience with moose aside from his adventure earlier in the day. Thus, he felt the antler should not be on the floor but on Mickey's head.

Ronaldinho hustled over and picked up the great antler in the moose's wake. Goodness, it was heavy. He heaved and followed Mickey, struggling to carry the cumbersome appendage. Kipchak and Koke gasped in shock that this boy had their prize. Mickey snorted and bellowed at the poachers, but they paid no attention to him. Nonetheless, when the pair moved to intercept Ronaldinho, Mickey blocked their way and gave them a dirty look. Koke and

Kipchak slunk back along the railing. Mickey (again, a fickle and unpredictable animal) charged to where they had been standing instead of pursuing them. He stared them down again for a moment. Then he turned and sniffed the railing. As he leaned his head down, his other antler fell off.

It tumbled overboard into the fog. Koke and Kipchak were horrified, but Mickey couldn't seem to care less. The poachers stood with mouths agape, panting. Ronaldinho approached the rail. Seeing that Mickey had just dropped his other one over the side of the ship, the young first mate sighed at the wasted effort in recovering the hefty antler. So he tossed it overboard, too.

The Associates of Mr. Abominable Snowman Dragons were doubly horrified. Of one mind, they wasted no time scolding Ronaldinho, but rushed over to that last remaining lifeboat. Koke hopped in while Kipchak released it. He then ran over and leaped the railing to join his partner in the rapidly descending inflatable boat. It all happened in a matter of seconds. Those moose antlers were their livelihood, and at present the only thing that mattered in either of their minds. Into the fog they went.

From the diving board, the netted would-be heroes watched the whole scene unfold in a general state of shock. Toby rationalized that, if nothing else, at least he was being entertained.

At this point, the horn stopped. A new loud noise took its place.

59

Despite being one of the most inhospitable places on Earth, a handful of animals frequent the Skeleton Coast. Whether they mean to or get lost on their way to somewhere nicer is unclear. Among these gluttons for punishment are transient seals. Big ones. They pop up on the Skeleton Coast in vast numbers to mate. In short order, a relatively serene beach can become a happening party spot for an immense population of seals, all barking like crazy. Very few will be in a good mood. The large males are sometimes referred to as Beach Masters, and rightfully so. Woe to he who crosses the path of a Beach Master.

It just so happened that a large grouping of seals always returned to a certain spot along the Skeleton Coast, and when they came back to it this time there was a cruise ship on it. This did little to improve the seals' already short tempers. They would have barked and barked just because they were seals, but this time they barked even more because they did not want this giant obstacle on *their* beach. Some inspected it with displeasure, some butted into it, but the majority just barked at it as they continued to go about their normal seal business.

The fog was beginning to clear so the unhappy pinnipeds could see a bit more of the stupid ship, and some of them noticed a bright orange thingy falling toward them. They barked at it, of course. The bright orange thingy landed, and out stepped Koke and Kipchak. The antlers were only about two and a half Chrysler LeBaron lengths from where they stood. But there were so many, many seals surrounding them. And that, too, should have been a welcome sight.

Kipchak and Koke marveled at the creatures before them. This was the reason the Associates of Mr. Abominable Snowman Dragons had trekked to the Skeleton Coast in the first place. Seals. Massive, beefy, glorious seals. Their blubber, like moose antlers, was a precious commodity in the exotic medicine racket. Kipchak and Koke had dreamt of them long before succumbing to "antler fever."

Of course, if their original plans had been executed correctly, they would not be staring these seals in the face. They would be aboard the crabbing boat, netting seals left and right, with the help of the crabbers. They would be laughing gaily at the haul, ready to chop up the seals to obtain that beautiful blubber. Then, as the plan went, they would use the free *Treasure* brand kitchenware to prepare the newly extracted blubber to make placebos, right there aboard the crabbing vessel. (Word of the *Treasure* brand shipwreck reached their organization long ago, and since the *Treasure* company went under, the kitchenware was abandoned. Thus, free.) The boat was going to be filled to the gills with extract of seal blubber medicine. This was supposed to make the Associates of Mr. Abominable Snowman Dragons rich beyond their wildest dreams, and the fact that it was all going to be filmed by the American news team was going to help advertise, putting them at the top of their field. Aside from the cost-cutting step of acquiring free kitchenware, it was a well-funded operation.

Instead, they stood here amongst the seals, unarmed and without an obvious way back up to the ship. Politely, the poachers stepped forward. They reached the antlers unimpeded. But the seals seemed to sense the intentions of Kipchak and Koke (or just didn't like anyone else on *their* beach). As a touch of fog lifted to show that it was actually a bright and sunny day, the path back to the lifeboat closed up. About a baker's dozen Beach Masters waddled over to address what to do with the intruders.

Though not long ago things looked to be so promising, it appeared now that it was not going to be a good day for Koke and Kipchak.

60

Mickey the moose had had enough. It seemed like he had had enough previously, but now he had really had so much enough that it was really enough this time. The great beast was tuckered out from charging everybody, and his antlers were gone, and he still was in this boiling climate, and he still hadn't eaten enough. It was time for Mickey to retire. No more walking around, no more hiding, no more chasing, no more searching for that elusive female moose. So there, by the ship's railing, just a handful of moose paces from the heavily populated plank, Mickey sat down.

This development was less exciting than other recent events on the deck, so the people balanced precariously on the diving board paid little heed. Each hoped and prayed that Earnest was still alive. Especially Jamie Brewster. They also puzzled over the strange new sound. The fog so far lent no clues.

Then Melinda heard a noise amidst the other noise, and soon everyone else heard it.

"Shay-mee! Shay-mee!"

All eyes shot over toward the skylight, where it was observed that the life-ring was snagged on the leg of a toppled speaker.

Earnest was dangling through the broken glass of the skylight. Usually composed, Earnest quickly concluded he felt uncomfortable dangling halfway between the top deck and the main hall's floor. Through an almost unreasonable turn of good luck, the loop of rope that Earnest had had around his wrist had somehow caught his foot. So as the broken glass fell, Earnest followed it, then lurched to a stop as the life-ring caught on a leg of one of the speakers. The abrupt halt did not do much for Earnest's nerves. He saw the glass shatter on the floor directly below him. Thankfully no one was underneath, because the battle had moved down the main hall toward the fountain. The combatants paused for a moment. In spite of his terror, the upside-down Earnest politely waved.

Jamie's heart jumped, as did the rest of the hearts on the diving board, which jostled the board some more. Although the little African boy was alive at the moment, all eyes could see the tension on the rope was slowly inching the speaker closer to the broken skylight. Few people would survive having a speaker fall on them from that height.

Toby was the first to let his mind waft back to the other, noisier noise. It wasn't the creaking plank that was just itching to break; that noise was mostly drowned out by this new one. The fog was lifting, and he knew the hubbub was coming from underneath him. Toby gulped and then broke the cardinal rule of heights: he looked down.

"Huh," he managed to say. He would have scratched his head if he could reach it.

Everyone else also broke that same cardinal rule. They witnessed a sprawling landscape of seals, all angry or at least looking like it. Seals and seals and seals, pretty much climbing on top of one another. It was an army in disarray, with all their rotund bodies bandying about to show off whose beach it was.

It finally made sense to Jamie: all these seals, the true rulers of this area, must be the place's namesake. Jamie admitted to himself that he did not actually know the proper definition of gelatin, but deduced it must be made out of seal blubber. Toby, too, felt a light bulb pop in his brain when he saw that the area's gelatin must come from these seals.

"The Gelatin Coast," both of them whispered in unison.

About the same time, the six captives saw Koke and Kipchak amongst the seals. The Beach Masters were bullying them like professional wrestlers. The mammoth pinnipeds were unforgiving. The poachers' screams were barely audible amongst all the barking.

Mercifully, the fog rolled back in to cover up the savagery.

As it washed back across the ship, Clayton Stern reemerged on deck. Jamie et al saw that he now sported a pair of heavy-duty headphones, the type worn around noisy things like helicopters. What they could not see were the earplugs underneath the headphones. Clayton Stern did not want to hear a thing.

In front of him, being prodded along at gunpoint, was Captain Hans Heissel. The displaced pirate leader wanted to be (and thought he was) the quintessential picture of stoicism, but he could not stop smiling. Every few steps he giggled. This puzzled the plank-sitters. It was not as worrisome as the young boy about to plummet to his doom, but it added to the growing list of curiosities.

Stern led Hans Heissel over to the plank, where the newspaper hat-wearing former mathematician tried to stop giggling so he could scowl at his mutinous crew, now hanging on to the plank in funny, uncomfortable positions with what little strength they had left. As much as their betrayal should have bothered him, it still took a great effort to remedy his case of the giggles.

Clayton gave him one last shove with the gun and out he stepped onto the diving board. It buckled and creaked more, and his foot slipped. Somehow, seemingly unafraid, Hans Heissel transitioned the misstep into a cross-legged sitting position. The board bounced twice and moved two inches further out. Unlike the rest of the gangplank occupants, Hans did not fret. In fact, he turned to them and chuckled, despite a failed attempt to conceal it.

Jamie again pleaded with Stern. "Please! That boy fell through the skylight! You've got to help him!"

Clayton gave a mocking smile and pointed to his muffled ears. "I'm sorry. I can't hear you!" With a maniacal laugh, he turned around.

Hans Heissel had another giggle fit. Despite their worries about Earnest, and their concerns about the coming explosion, and their own approaching doom, the six turned their heads to him and his newspaper hat. Glad to have their attention, Hans let his mouth run.

"You guys! You guys!" he said, seemingly unaware of their laundry list of problems. "You know what?" The stunned looks on their faces relayed their astonishment at being addressed by the same man who had exiled three of them, sentenced at least one of them to death, and ruined the vacation for all of them. Hans was oblivious to this. He smiled and went on. "Guess what?"

Suddenly, Hans looked at Benito and changed his expression. "Oh," he said in a different tone. "I will need that."

Hans proceeded to reach over, quite dangerously, to Benito's face. Everyone's weight shifted, which made the diving board slip out of the hands of one more pirate, so that it had a decidedly downward angle. It now took quite an effort from Leonid to keep from sliding off. They all shouted at Hans Heissel, but couldn't do anything beyond that. The displaced pirate captain leaned back to his original spot and placed Benito's fake mustache on his face. Wiggling his upper lip to show it off, he giggled once more, checked his watch, then looked up and grinned at them all.

"This is going to be good."

61

Clayton Stern could not hear a thing. Without any noise, he felt as if he were swimming. Except he hated swimming. It felt like some sort of surrealist painting, then. Everything was at peace. It was wonderful. His surroundings seemed to move at a much slower pace than before. He felt that he might never take the headphones off again.

The fog was helping to slow things down, too. It was drifting back in thicker, and he loved it. Peering through it at the pleading mouths of the people on the plank made him smile. Looking at the sweating pirates whose muscles were not going be able to hold the plank for much longer made him feel powerful. He saw Isiah Burtlyre, fretting about whether things had gone too far, and it reminded him how rich he was. He glanced a little further and saw Yancy Dunblatt trying to figure out what was wrong with his trumpet. But Stern didn't care about the stupid trumpet anymore, because the thing that improved his mood the most was sitting down on the hardwood floor near the railing. Mickey the moose was a sitting duck (figuratively speaking, because he was actually a moose). Antler-less and uneducated about gun safety, the tired beast stared blankly at Clayton Stern.

Stern had not expected his prey to become so submissive. He could walk right up to the moose and shoot him from point blank. It would be the easiest shot he'd ever made.

"I guess it's my lucky day," Clayton said as he slowly advanced. He could not hear himself.

The chaos around the hunter was forgotten. The highly anticipated moment was finally upon him. He strode closer, until he was about one Chrysler LeBaron-length away, then took a knee. *This will do*, Clayton thought. *Don't want to get too close*. He sniggered at the doomed moose, and gleefully imagined Mickey's head on his wall. He might have fake antlers fashioned, but otherwise this cold dead mug would look magnificent. Lowering the gun, he looked through the scope at Mickey's face.

"This might hurt a little," he laughed. Then Clayton Stern, dastardly billionaire, squeezed the trigger.

And it went *click*. This is the type of noise you expect to hear from clothespins, not a high-powered rifle. When the trigger was depressed again, it said *click* again. And then *click*, followed by *click*. Clayton tried to imagine he wasn't seething and then tried again. Thrice. *Click click click*.

The peacefulness was quickly abandoned. He scowled at the moose, who didn't care. The infuriated huntsman bellowed and stood. After waving his arms around wildly in dismay his beady eyes searched out Hans Heissel. Hans was preoccupied by his own giggles and not paying attention to Stern.

"What is wrong with this gun?" Clayton screamed.

Hans was taken aback. "What do you mean?"

Clayton did not take off the headphones because he felt he had a decent understanding of the stupid response he would get. "This gun doesn't work! What did you do?"

"Huh?" Hans had stopped the giggling and seemed genuinely surprised. "It should work." He shrugged and readjusted his newspaper hat. "You brought it with you."

Clayton did not want to remove his ear coverings because he knew once he left his noiseless world he may never return. When he furiously shook the gun around and a bit of water trickled out, he realized what Hans had said. And it was almost unbelievable.

The pirate captain had been completely honest when he told Clayton Stern that there was one gun on board with bullets in it. Hans felt the fact that it happened to be the gun Clayton brought with him was inconsequential. Obviously Clayton was not going to go in the water and retrieve it, so Captain Hans Heissel was nice enough to send a pirate to do so. Now he was a bit offended that Stern was so unappreciative. How was Hans supposed to know that a gun could be ruined if it fell in a pool?

Clayton closed his eyes and screamed again. When his eyelids opened he turned to warn Hans of his imminent death, but Hans, along with the rest of the diving board occupants, was looking elsewhere. Clayton didn't care. He would have their attention when he personally kicked the diving board off the side of the ship.

Not far away, Yancy Dunblatt suddenly stopped puzzling over what was making his trumpet sound so horrible. His archenemy, that pesky bat from his glove compartment, had somehow burrowed itself deep into the dark coils of the trumpet left in the backseat of the jeep and laid dormant for quite some time, hidden and safe. But now the bat was ready to let loose. Right in Yancy's face. So out it flew, disoriented as ever, and scared the dickens out of Yancy (who had assumed the trumpet's problem stemmed from pool water).

Yancy quickly tripped over his own feet and found himself on the floor of the deck. The spasmodic flying mammal was not done terrorizing, however, and flew straight into Clayton Stern's face. The bat was arguably more surprised than Clayton.

This was the final straw for the billionaire. He screeched again and lifted the gun into the air. So blinded with anger was he that he didn't care whether his gun was functional. He aimed it at the bat and fired. *Click*. Again and again. *Click click*.

"Aaaaaaagggghhhhh!" exclaimed Clayton's wide-open mouth. His eyes closed.

Again he fired. *Click*. And again. This time the gun fired. Clayton was shocked. As was the blond gentleman he saw above him when he opened his eyes.

"What?" Clayton's quiet world had gotten confusing again.

Another gentleman, this one with darker hair, was wafting down nearby. The blond gentleman looked up. Right over his shoulder, there was a bullet hole in his parachute.

So the military had arrived. Someone's military, anyway. Just as the fog was conveniently lifting once again. And not a moment too soon. There was plenty of work to be done.

Before the parachutists had even landed, Jamie was screaming at them to save Earnest. They couldn't figure out who Earnest was, but it sounded like he was important. At least to Jamie. When two of the men hustled over to the broken skylight, they saw that the speaker had inched so close to the edge that Earnest was nearly touching the floor of the main hall. The first man who ran to the skylight failed to see the danger Earnest was in, but heard the boy yelling "Help!" Interestingly, the word *help* in Earnest's language sounded a lot like *extinguisher* in English. Seeing the helicopter's little fire extinguisher near the skylight, the man tossed it down to Earnest, then anchored the speaker. Earnest caught the cylinder, not realizing how talented he was to be able to catch things while hanging upside-down. Earnest did not know a thing about fire extinguishers, but could tell from the pictures on the side that it might do some good on that wedding dress that was nearly at the fountain. He swung himself over to the flames and fired away (poor choice of words). With this the battle was effectively over.

62

It was turning into a lovely, sunny day topside. In the aftermath of things, Jamie realized how nice the weather had suddenly decided to be. Toby, on the other hand, realized something else.

"Why did they keep waiting to kill us?" he asked as the military officials removed the gangplank occupants. They were being seated along the railing for questioning, and handed standard-issue blankets. "I mean, it was quite an effort to stop us from falling to our deaths, so why didn't they just get it over with?"

Melinda may have found this thought distasteful before, but now she laughed at Toby's adorable quirkiness. Toby didn't see what was so funny.

Clayton Stern, too, was set aside for questioning, but his hands were cuffed. Despite how much trouble he was in, he remained smug.

The military investigator sighed and looked at his notepad. "Mr. Stern, we have a lot to talk about."

"We have nothing to talk about," Clayton spat. "You can talk to my lawyer."

"Actually," said Isiah Burtlyre, "I'd rather you didn't. I don't think I want this headache." Stern could barely believe what he was hearing. "Besides," the former lawyer-maid continued as handcuffs were placed upon his wrists, "I feel at this point I've got enough problems of my own." It appeared he was an accomplice to some major crimes.

"You're going to need a good lawyer," the military investigator told him.

Clayton recovered and smirked again. "So what? You don't have anything on me." He was bluffing, but it seemed like the proper thing to say under the circumstances.

"Actually," the investigator said, "We've got quite a lot of dirt on you. Starting with your illegal importation of some pretty exotic animals. Coupled with the fact that you're funding a major exotic medicine cartel." (Clayton was not even aware that he happened to be the benefactor behind the Associates of Mr. Abominable Snowman Dragons). "And amongst a number of other things, you just attempted to murder a high-ranking military officer."

Clayton sneered again. "I'll get another high-priced lawyer. You can't prove anything."

That was when Janet and Tom finally stepped forward. They had done an excellent job of staying out of sight while they recorded *everything*.

And for the first time it occurred to Clayton Stern that he never should have broken those mirrors. You just *don't break mirrors*! Everybody knows that! He was now cursed with bad luck for the foreseeable future. For everyone else, this was a wonderful development.

Janet and Tom—especially Janet—had planned to have it out with Jamie Brewster, but after recording what was most likely footage that would earn multiple journalism awards, they let their nutty helicopter pilot off easy.

Janet inquired with the military men whether they would be able to recover her hair, but when the obvious answer came she realized that she liked the 'do, anyway.

Through all this, Captain Hans Heissel Jr. was laughing hysterically. He had seen this coming. The elaborate math formula on the wall had accurately predicted that the authorities were on their way. With his fleet, the pirate captain could keep moving. On a grounded cruise ship, it was only a matter of time before they were intercepted. It just depended on a few variables, which Hans had plugged in correctly. So it was a matter of getting away once the military arrived. His plan seemed foolproof. He would pretend to be a poor, hapless passenger.

"I couldn't be the Great Captain Hans Heissel. He does not have a mustache, such as mine," Hans was telling one of the officials.

The grizzled man smiled at him. "Mr. Heissel, we know who you are. And we've been after you for quite a while."

"I'm sure I don't know what you're talking about," Hans replied. He didn't know when he was beat.

"The thing is, Mr. Heissel, you might be able to get out of this if you want to listen to our offer."

Hans Heissel removed the fake mustache and furrowed his brow.

Leonid Cupabascim never wanted to go to sea again. He was glad to have both his hands back, and wondered if he should use them to work on cars again instead of food. Cars usually stick to land, and Leonid Cupabascim never wanted to go to sea again.

Ronaldinho, when he woke up from another nap, decided he was done with pirating.

Eventually, what was left of Koke and Kipchak was recovered from the clutches of the Beach Masters. They were in rough shape. And an awful lot of trouble.

"Hang on," Toby said, stepping away from Melinda's patting hand on his back. The military officials sighed at the now impertinent young man. Toby did not mean to be ungrateful for the rescue, but it was starting to sound that way to his rescuers. "How...?"

From the deck of the nearby battleship, no longer hidden by fog, Riggins peered at the *Queen Ivan* through binoculars. "Well done, boys."

The salty, crotchety, ancient, semi-mangled sailor had, of course, been the old man with frosting on his face, spotted by Benito and Leonid upon exiting the cruise ship's refrigerator. Riggins had shared the same fate as Benito: When the ship was overtaken by Hans Heissel's crew, the pirates mistook the grizzled mariner for one of their own. Unlike Benito, however, Riggins rolled with the punches. (It wasn't the first time this had happened.) So, once the passengers were exiled, Riggins enjoyed the confines of the *Queen Ivan* for a while, taking in some rays from the deck, rifling through the passengers' clothes, and sampling the wedding cake before Benito and Leonid got their hands on it. Feeling this mini-holiday was sufficient, Riggins briefly debated his obligation to help versus his new life as a pirate. The coin he flipped came up heads, so the old man commandeered the second-to-last life raft, answering the few pirates who asked by saying he was paddling over to one of the other boats in the fleet. It was true. He fought the brazen waves and after considerable effort was able to reach the *Helga II*. The old sailor's intuition told him this was the fleet's flagship, at least until the takeover of the *Queen Ivan*. So, unlike the other vessels, its radio was still intact (Hans did not want to ruin his parents' boat). He excused himself and used it to radio for help.

Without Riggins' information, finding the *Queen Ivan* may have been impossible. Of course, by the time the authorities got word from Riggins, they were already on their way. While the stranded crowd from the ship were cut off from the rest of the world, the rest of the world was trying to figure out what had happened to them. Strange connections came to light when Candy the flight attendant went to Clayton Stern's fortress. Finding out about the location of Clayton's secret excavation struck a chord. Candy happened to be one-sixteenth Native American, or First Nation in Canada, and she traced her heritage to a tribe that was located partially in Alberta. Already displeased with her employer, she quickly informed tribal police about the illegal excavation happening on their land. Then she left a polite note about her resignation and used Clayton's computer to research law schools.

The man who mysteriously approached Susie Ebbert's dinosaur dig was a tribal police officer. Informing Susie and her men that they were digging on tribal land resulted in full confessions from Enrique and Carlos, Susie's workers. The confessions were not asked for, but Enrique and Carlos were still upset about the plight of that poor moose, so they wanted to purge all their guilt. Soon more agencies were brought into the growing mess and Clayton Stern was a wanted man.

Found on tribal land, the resplendent Tyrannosaurus Rex skeleton belonged to the tribe.

Soon word of a kidnapped news team in Savannah, Georgia was tied into the plot by some brilliant investigators, who had been tracking the kidnapping of several zoo animals, which was traced to the Associates of Mr. Abominable Snowman Dragons, a group that in-depth investigation revealed was funded by none other than Clayton Stern. The investigation really picked up when one of the detectives happened to catch a rerun of the crabbers' reality television program. She recognized the boat from pictures taken after the kidnapping of the Channel 7 news team. From there, many conclusions were drawn, some incorrectly, and these barely-mentioned investigators set about informing authorities. It was all quite hazy at best, but it worked out, apparently.

The story of the investigators might also have been an interesting tale to tell, but it involved way too much paperwork.

It would be some time before our heroes aboard the *Queen Ivan* got all the details. But for everyone besides Toby, that was just fine.

Guided back to the deck by the friendly military officials, Earnest was flabbergasted when he spotted Mickey with no antlers, still sitting in the same spot where Clayton Stern tried to shoot him. He approached the moose cautiously, ignoring the people who had shown so much concern about his well-being. The boy inspected Mickey hesitantly.

"This is not my moose," he told the nearest military man. The man, unfortunately, did not speak Earnest's language and just shrugged. Earnest turned back to his massive friend. Searching deeply into the beast's eyes, he felt a brimming joy well up inside him.

"Mickey! What has happened to you?" he exclaimed.

The moose did not respond, but had a calm look upon his lengthy face.

"Those things on top of your head, they are missing," Earnest informed him, making antlers with his hands. Taking a seat right next to the moose, they stared at each other for a prolonged moment. Mickey, though a moose and not a human being, was happy to see Earnest again.

Earnest spoke. "I forgive you."

And though he was still a wild animal, and unpredictable, and it wasn't a safe thing to do, and his friends noticed and tried to stop him, Earnest leaned over and hugged Mickey. The great moose put his tired head on the little African boy's shoulder.

63

Later on, there was a beautiful sunset in the west (where it normally is), and the departing sun stretched out its pink and orange fingers across the surprisingly calm waters of the Skeleton Coast. With the tranquil waves rolling in, the fingers seemed to wiggle to say good-bye and "What a day!" At least, if you looked at the sunset a certain way. No one on board the *Queen Ivan* did.

The information garnered from eyewitnesses led to the recovery of the runaway zoo animals, who had all gotten pooped less than a mile away. The environmentalists and the TV crabbers were recovered, too. There were plenty of military guys to go around.

The pirates were arrested and being led away while the passengers were being aided, in a rather one-sided verdict of who was right in the battle for the cruise ship. The pirates whined about their stomachs and how mean the passengers had been, swatting them with kitchenware, leaving bruises and whatnot. The military personnel did not care much. They were, however, interested in the idea behind the vodka fountain and praised Earnest for stopping the threat with his quick thinking. With all that vaporized alcohol in the air, that could have been quite a fireball, they deduced.

The one pirate spared an arrest was Hans Heissel, who was led to the deck of the battleship, where he met Riggins.

"Ah! You're the variable!" he said in delight.

Then, behind closed doors, Captain Hans Heissel was offered a lucrative position employing his prestigious mathematical skills to crack codes for the Central Intelligence Agency.

The Great Captain Hans Heissel Jr. pondered for many minutes before replying, "I will accept on one condition: that I can continue to wear this hat."

Learning about her husband's recreational golf habits worsened Maria's mood. Benito and Maria Martinez would be needing years of marriage counseling. But they were recommended some very good counselors, which in itself was a bonding experience. Thankfully he could afford the very best.

Benito Martinez signed hundreds of autographs for the military personnel. Maria only signed four.

Melinda and Toby sat on the deck and discussed the possibility of trying to go to college in the same town. Though Melinda might be planning on becoming a senator or a founder of some philanthropic organization, Toby considered for the first time that he might find a nice little community college where he could finally learn to throw a Frisbee correctly.

In awkward, embarrassing terms that would have been excruciating for anyone else to listen to, Melinda and Toby said they liked each other while they stared at their feet. Melinda tucked her hair behind her ear as she spoke. Toby mimicked the motion with his mousy hair. Then the young couple watched the sunset, holding hands. Toby got bored with it pretty quickly.

Kissing again could wait for some day down the road.

Jamie Brewster wished he could call his mother to tell her that he was okay. He sighed deeply and tried to relax, happy that it was all over. He knew he would get to call her soon enough. Thinking of his little friend Earnest, he wondered if his mother would like to have a pen pal. He also thought about how he would probably end up on the news for this ordeal. That might be fun, he acknowledged, but he would rather just fly over the news when it happened.

The helicopter pilot looked over at Earnest. Exhausted, the boy had fallen asleep on the moose, who had also fallen asleep. That sounded like a good idea to him. He thought he might just go look for a comfortable place to lie down, perhaps in his old hiding spot, perhaps in the honeymoon suite.

Jamie smiled as he watched the sleeping pair, and hoped that he would stay friends with both of them.

Earnest was dreaming about his zoo. He'd get one. Someday. He knew it.

Mickey was dreaming of the new antlers he would grow someday. And about Earnest riding on his back. During this dream, he didn't shake him off.

In the morning, the harsh, unforgiving, inhospitable Gelatin Coast was glad to be rid of them all.

THE END

ACKNOWLEDGMENTS

Well, I should probably start by thanking my parents, who seemed to be supportive about all this. My sincere thanks to Gregg Olsen, who gave me an internship once upon a time, and always provided me with unflinching encouragement. And who then went ahead and said he'd publish this, right about the time I felt this would never see the light of day. Thanks to Jim Thomsen, who edited it, but who also helped me feel for the first time that it might actually be a real book when he gave me genuine compliments; thanks to Maria, who made it all look nice; and thanks to Raquel Segal for making a cover that I think is really great. There are probably some other people behind the scenes on Gregg's end who I haven't met but thanks to them as well.

As far as I can figure, I possess very little practical knowledge of how the world works, so thank you to all the people who answered my questions to help make this story at least vaguely believable. Thanks especially to Alex Larson, Kyle Drevniak, and my dad, who all, over the course of multiple years, answered countless inane questions, from how helicopters work to the subtleties of moose culture, all without being given any context. Any mistakes still present are my own fault.

Thanks to my sister, Kate, for actually reading and editing an early draft, and not just saying she would, as well as for her resolute support from the beginning. And to my dear mother, who has always given heartfelt encouragement, in book writing and all other matters. Thanks as well to anyone who gave me a pat on the back and said I could finish this, whether you were being sincere or not. Since I was able to write it, I should also thank the teachers I've had along the way, especially those I really liked. There's probably a lot of other people I should thank, so if you think you deserve it, give yourself a pat on the back from me.

And lastly, thanks to Elvis Costello for writing a song called *"Everyday I Write the Book,"* which, when taken quite literally, is great motivation for writing a book.

Oh, and to you, if you actually read this book. I sincerely appreciate it.

CPSIA information can be obtained
at www.ICGtesting.com
Printed in the USA
FSOW01n0702130516
20422FS